Lantern for Lord Rhys

To Dilys
with love & best wishes,
Margot

A Lantern For Lord Rhys

By
Margot James

To G. and N.

GOMER

Also by Margot James
The Cardi Comes Home (Jonathan Cape, 1956)

ISBN 0 86383 380 2

Distribution: The Welsh Books Centre, Glanrafon Estate,
Aberystwyth (Tel: 0970 4455)

Cover Illustration by Terry Higgins

Text-Preparation by Milestone Systems Limited,
2 Hillhead Cottages, Avonbridge, Falkirk, Scotland FK1 2NL.

CONTENTS

Foreword	vii
Sketch Map of Deheubarth	viii
I The Forebears	1
II The Brothers Deheubarth	45
III The Lord Rhys ap Gruffydd	103
IV The Lord Justiciar	153
V The Lion Rampant	229
Bibliography	291
Glossary	292

Endpaper—The Line of Power in Deheubarth
In the Twelfth Century

FOREWORD

The Cistercian monastery of Strata Florida in Cardiganshire, which was dissolved by Henry VIII, suffered great destruction during the seventeenth century Civil War. Presumably these manuscripts, which were kept in the monks' library, were burnt then, for they have not survived. That they did exist is clear to anyone who listens to the objective witness of the wind above Tregaron Bog. You may call this hearsay evidence and therefore inadmissible, but it does appear to corroborate portions of the monastic chronicle called 'Brut y Tywysogion', as well as the writings of Gerallt Cymro (Giraldus Cambrensis), and all these you may read for yourself.

And if you complain that the picture conjured by these pages picks out other details than those discovered by Gerallt's vivid torch, I can only say, he held it so high that these other matters were, I suppose, lost in his own considerable shadow.

M.J.

THE OLD KINGDOMS OF CYMRU

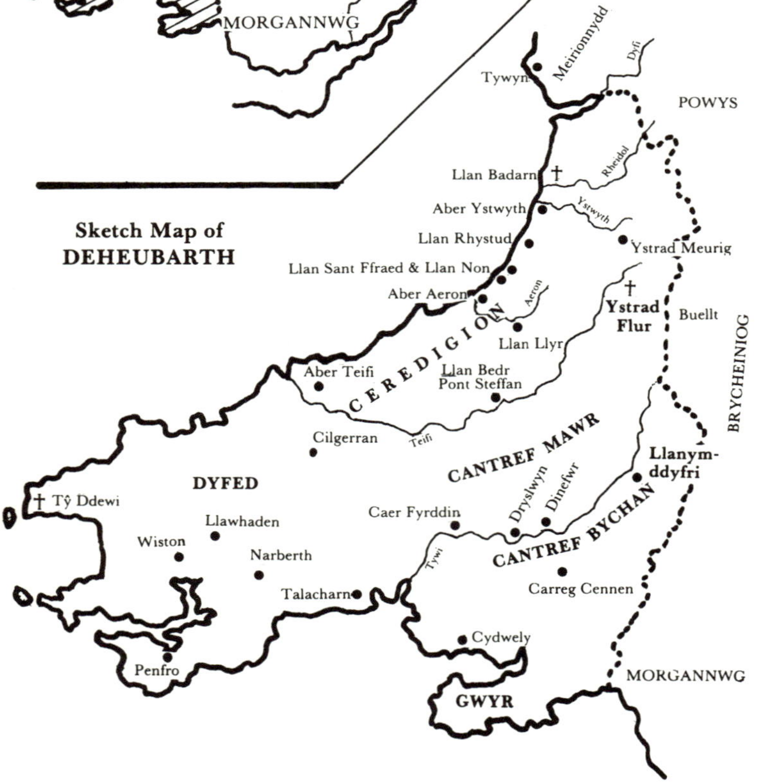

Sketch Map of DEHEUBARTH

I

The Forebears

(1079—1137)

1

'I am Rhys ap Tewdr!' said the red-haired young man. 'I could, if I chose, recite you my lineage six hundred years back to the sixth century after Our Lord's birth. I am twenty-first in the direct line of Cunedda himself, who came out of the North into Cymru. But I leave these recitations to the bards. It is enough for you to know that I am Tewdr's son, of the line of King Hywel Dda, who caused all the laws of Cymru to be collected, agreed, and written down. Is this an examination? Do you require me also to recite the laws, and the events of Hywel's reign, to tell you that he and Saxon Athelstan were on friendly terms? That he went on pilgrimage to Rome? That he made so great a name for himself that your chronicling monks of Llan Badarn called him the head and glory of all Britons? Either you believe me,' ended the young man rudely, 'or you don't. I have no further time to waste.'

The old man regarded him with amusement, compassion, and growing excitement. It was long since any man had dared to address him with such careless authority, and he was inclined to believe the fellow, but he had to be certain. When a man with a remnant of men bangs on the door of a cathedral, calls himself a king, and demands, not so much sanctuary, as immediate subventions of food, arms, clothing, and troops, a mere bishop may be forgiven for indulging in a delicate initial probe.

'What is the name of your kingdom?' asked the Bishop quietly.

The young man blazed.

'I am King of all Deheubarth from Dyfi to Tawe, as well you know!' he roared. 'I claim all the kingdom that my ancestor Seisyll carved out for himself four hundred years ago from the lands of Ceredigion, Dyfed, and Ystrad Tywi! My father was killed by his enemies, and since I was twelve years old, I have had to lurk in Llydaw and bide my time. Now in my manhood I come to Cymru, and I claim my own! I thought that in Ty Ddewi, I would surely find support. If you are indeed Bishop Sulien, then acknowledge me, you who knew and valued my father!'

The canons of Ty Ddewi, who witnessed this encounter with bated, shocked breath, were alarmed by the curious twitch that raised and lowered the young man's right eyebrow as he shouted in his rage. But Bishop Sulien smiled, and to everyone's surprise, he advanced on the stranger with outstretched arms.

'Of course you are Tewdr's son!' he said. 'Any pretender could learn a pedigree! But no one else would have his father's furious countenance and twitching eyebrows! Now that you have lost your temper, it is easy to recognize you as King Rhys of Deheubarth. Come, let us consider how you may recover your kingdom!'

Then Sulien took Rhys aside, and talked. He was an old scholar from Penweddig in North Ceredigion, who had with reluctance abandoned his quiet academy of Llan Badarn to undertake the perils of the episcopate. He noticed that Rhys was staring at the comparative ruin of his cathedral.

'Norse raiders,' said Sulien. 'It has been ravaged and burned and pillaged so often that it is not now worth repairing. It is time to pull down and build anew, but someone else shall do it, not I. I welcome and bless you, Rhys ap Tewdr, and I look to you to rebuild Deheubarth, and bring the line of old kings back again.'

He paused. Rhys, like a lion appeased, listened with approval. This old grey oyster was slow to open, but perhaps there was a pearl inside.

'I have lived long,' said Sulien. 'I remember the vigour of Gruffydd ap Llewellyn of Gwynedd, a great-great-grandson of Hywel Dda, and how, forty years ago, he united North and South and Central Cymru against the infiltrating Saeson. After his success came the short and sharp invasions of Earl Harold of Wessex, the betrayal of Gruffydd, his murder, and the resulting chaos throughout the gwledydd when your father, too, suffered, and when men fell away from religion. But Harold, too, fell at Hastings,' said the gentle voice with satisfaction. 'How we rejoiced!'

Rhys nodded impatiently. All this he knew. News was slow to reach Llydaw, the land of Brittany on the far north-west of Europe, but this was an old tale now.

'But this Bastard, William, and his men, are worse,' said Sulien sourly. 'They have plunged in to conquer and stay. But you have come, strong and fresh, to invigorate the gwlad! With you beside me, my lord Rhys, to keep the French in their place, to make peace true for the Cymry, the Church may rise once more to take her ancient place in men's hearts. Now the position is this. The land is divided between little men. Cymru is plagued by a clutch of claimants, of whom we are sickened and tired. For you, of the line of Cunedda, Rhodri, Hywel, and Tewdr Mawr, the boneddigion will rise like the seventh wave of a spring high tide, and overwhelm the lesser claimants. You have come at the right moment, my lord. And by the mercy of God, your kinsman is at hand to help you.'

'Which one?' asked Rhys quickly. 'I told no man in Cymru of my plans, for I wished to take my enemies by surprise.'

Bishop Sulien opened the door of the dilapidated house with pretensions to dignity that he called his plâs.

'He has come from Iwerddon,' he said. 'His name is Gruffydd ap Cynan of Gwynedd, and he has come for the blessing of God and Dewi Sant upon his quest. He has an army of Norse and Irish mercenaries. He too has a kingdom to recover.'

A tall, grim-faced man stood before them, grasping a sword that he made no offer to sheathe, even in the Bishop's presence.

'A kinsman? Of what degree?'

'Of the eighth degree,' said Sulien, who, like the bards, kept royal and other notable pedigrees in his head. 'It is within the statutory limits of mutual responsibility. You are sixth cousins.'

He allowed them time to exchange the frozen and suspicious stares of men more accustomed to watch for enemies than to hail friends. Slowly, Gruffydd sheathed his sword. Then the Bishop clapped his hands, and a servant brought a frugal dish of meat, with wine, bread, apples, cheese, and honey.

'Eat and drink at my table,' said Sulien. 'God has arranged this meeting, that you may make an alliance against your foes, vanquish them, and win your separate thrones.'

They shared the meal with deliberation. Between long silences, each elicited necessary facts from the other. The son of Cynan, King of Gwynedd, had been born during an Irish exile. His mother was Ragnillt, grand-daughter of Sihtric Silver-beard, the Norse King of Dublin, and Gruffydd, who was fair, had a Viking look that Rhys mistrusted, but his own red hair and choleric eyes did not recommend him to his kinsman, either. The meal, however, under Sulien's guidance, and the mass in Ty Ddewi next morning, laid the basis of the mutual, if distant, respect required between two generals in the field. Sulien heaved a sigh of relief. That they should contrive to work together, in a reliable alliance, was the first essential. They were both hard-eyed soldiers; it was enough for the moment that they accepted each other, with trust enough in God and Sulien to make plans. North and South, prayed Sulien the Wise from Mid-Cymru, who understood and loved them both, let them make friends.

With the blessing of Sulien to lift their hearts, and his eloquence to rouse the fervour of their friends, the two kings bestirred themselves, and soon the young boneddigion rushed to their standards. Gruffydd's enemies, alarmed, sent their armies south under Trahaearn, a prince of Powys. Gruffydd and Rhys, and a great company, went out to do battle at the south-west gate of Cymru, at Mynydd Carn among the Preselau hills. They shook off their rivals like dogs that scatter rats, and went each to his gwlad. But despite Sulien's prayer, they fell out soon after victory; they could not like each other enough to overcome the disagreements incidental to every campaign; and Gruffydd, to mark his scorn, burnt up a township or two on his ride up north through Ceredigion. It was as well that they had the flats and marshes of the Dyfi between their realms, and the bleak array of Pen Pumlumon's heights. It was not easy to maintain a state of war between Gwynedd and Deheubarth, but with Powys it was different. Powys was lodged like a wedge between, for either side to sharpen claws upon.

As for Rhys, he had gained his kingdom, and he spat in the dust raised by the heels of Gruffydd's horse. The anger died out of his face; he went to Powys to find a wife, chose a lady of the royal line who took his fancy, Gwladus, daughter of Rhiwallon ap Cynfyn, married her, wrapped her in furs, and brought her in triumph all the way home to the rough fort that awaited them in Ystrad Tywi. They climbed the hill as night fell, and entered the gate of Dinefwr.

'This is my Queen, my cariad, the wife I love!' he told his teulu, amid their wild acclamations. 'On her body I shall beget strong sons to inherit the kingdom of the South!'

The news that two fresh kings in Cymru, North and South, had arisen like the sturdy building timbers of a vast new hall, reached William, the king in Lloegr. He was violently uneasy. The resounding nature of the victory at Mynydd Carn was too much the counterpart of his own triumph at Hastings, fifteen years before, to permit complacency. His thick peasant fingers unrolled a map of the Marches of Wales.

'Bah!' he muttered at last. 'Chester, Shrewsbury, Hereford —three Marcher earls, with Gloucester, should suffice to hold them.'

He had chosen the toughest trouble-makers in his train to undertake these remote dominions, as much to get rid of them as in the hope of making some impression on Wales in its more accessible parts. To attempt a total conquest was a waste of time. England, loosely united, had been comparatively easy for him to master after that one battle. Largely a flat land, it had passed through the stage of quarrelling kingdoms more swiftly than a mountain country could. Also the Anglo-Saxon temperament, stolid, beef-eating, and given to arable agriculture, was more amenable to the effective lash of a Norman French monarch than he suspected the Welsh could ever be, with their more independent, hardy ways, and more mobile, pastoral habits.

William swore. Homage he would extort, at least, from whatever king rose up in this island; but owing to the nature of the terrain, a full campaign in South Wales would be even more inconvenient and difficult than the invasion whereby nine years ago, King Malcom of Scotland had become his vassal.

Aloud he told his councillors, 'I am going on a pilgrimage to the shrine of St. David.'

'A pilgrimage?' said Rhys ap Tewdr, when he heard the news. 'He has come to spy out the land! His sons are unruly, his vassals turbulent. He wants to know how much rein he can give the barons in Cymru.'

Lifting his chin, he put the Queen and the fort of Dinefwr in charge of the teulu, and summoned his wisest uchelwyr; then he, too, journeyed west.

'You must make up your mind,' Sulien told him. 'It's homage he's after. Cymru, harrassed by Norsemen all round the coast two hundred years ago, harrassed by Angles on the East, turned to King Alfred for help. In line with the other kings of Lloegr, King Anarawd of Gwynedd acknowledged him as overlord. It was no shame to admit his greater power, and it was from Cymru that Alfred received the spiritual and intellectual blessings that gave him greatness, through the teaching of Bishop Asser. Friendship and homage between Deheubarth and Wessex became established during the reigns of several kings. Now Wessex has swallowed the rest of Lloegr, and a Norseman from France has seized the throne, claiming to inherit from his predecessors every precedent for homage. This man is a tiger, not a tame domestic tabby like the Confessor. You must draw his teeth. His teeth are the barons of the Border. Purchase, if not his protection from their depredations, at least immunity from his punishment when you repel their attacks. Pay homage, establish your power firmly, and recover all your realm as far as you are able.'

'Must I be bound by the actions of my forebears?' demanded Rhys angrily.

The Bishop regarded him with sternness.

'You must be bound by wisdom, as they were,' he said. 'Order, with justice, there must be within this island, and actual degrees of strength between kings are facts to be acknowledged before God's work can be pursued with success in any kingdom.'

He contrived to reduce Rhys to a state of resentful resignation.

After hearing a mass for pilgrims, the two kings met on comparatively neutral ground at Sulien's house, for supper. William, disdainful already of the cathedral's poverty, stood regarding the young King of Deheubarth with arrogance. Rhys was not tall, so he lifted his head until he too was looking down his nose through half-closed eyes at William's enormous person. Then he sat down.

'I beg you will not stand, my lord William,' he said politely. 'It is a pleasure to welcome you as pilgrim to the shrine of Dewi Sant in my kingdom of Deheubarth.'

William glared at the young pup.

'I will not beat about the bush, Lord Rhys,' he said roughly. 'I demand your homage to me, in accordance with precedent.'

'I have examined the precedents,' said Rhys, putting his fingers together precisely. 'And I am inclined to agree with my advisers that homage may indeed be paid, on condition, of course, that you guarantee to me and my heirs male, permanent security of tenure and quiet possession at all times of my inheritance.' He spoke as to a prospective business partner, and William's ready choler rose.

'Conditions do not enter into the affair!' he barked, conveniently ignoring a lord's own feudal obligations to his vassal. His inheritance! Where did it lie? What exactly was the square mileage, the amount of forest land, pasture, arable? He checked his surveyor's instincts. At this stage it would be imprudent to inquire. His barons would adventure more freely in official ignorance of whose toes they trod on.

'Come, come!' he said, with an attempt at affability. 'The lawyers shall take care of all these little problems, and I shall be quite satisfied with an annual payment from you of one hundred pounds.'

'Ten,' said Rhys. 'And my condition must be met.'

'I do not bargain with vassals!' said William, with a roar of rage.

'I am not yet your vassal,' said Rhys, with a quelling look. So they bargained. An undisguised quarrel developed, during which each man was able to gauge the pugnacity of the other. Finally William, descending grandly by tens, and Rhys, rising grudgingly by fives, arrived at an agreed figure, with Rhys's condition thrown in.

William turned to the clerk at his elbow.

'Put him down for forty pounds,' he growled.

Homage was paid, perfunctorily, and William returned to Lloegr in much irritation, trying to convince himself that he had not been bested. On one point, however, he was satisfied. King Rhys ap Tewdr would provide trouble enough to keep the

Border barons' hands too full to allow them opportunity for rebellion against himself.

When he had gone, six years of relative peace gave Rhys ap Tewdr time to pull his realm together, establish an authority that was rough but true, punish the attacks of border kings by two pitched battles bloody enough to discourage further encroachments, and raise a family of three sons, Gruffydd, Hywel, and Cadwgan, and one daughter, Nest. She was the eldest, a tomboy, the beauty and the pride of all. For the most part the French, disconcerted by his trenchant action and imperious tongue, held off, until William's death in 1087, and the advent of a bully, William Rufus, to the throne of Lloegr, and the rise to manhood of their own pushing youngsters, gave them the spirit and impulse to plunge further into Cymru. They acted, in their more pretentious way, like the pirate Northmen they had ever shown themselves to be, though they were more careful to organize than those sea-happy Vikings who used to descend in capricious forays on the shores of Gwynedd and Deheubarth. They galloped and slew in the valleys, the French, in their invincible armour, heavy on horseback, irresistibly strong on the plains; Rhys, studying their methods with care, learned a trick or two from them. But in the hills they were nowhere. Like a poisonous vapour too heavy to rise, they covered only the lower lands of Morgannwg and Brycheiniog and filtered into Dyfed, wherever the fields were greenest beside the river banks. Gwent had already been snatched by William FitzOsbern in 1086; one Philip de Breos fought his way into Radnor in 1090, and later into Buellt, while in the South Robert FitzHamon was devastating the Glamorgan plain. They swarmed like bees, drunk with power and the honey of the spoils of war; then, eager to settle, and running short, in a hostile country, of women of their own kind, they seized every slender chance to marry the daughter of a Cymric prince. Sometimes a Cymro, too, took a French wife. These marriages were moved by one belief on either side; each party thought the alliance would keep the other one under its thumb.

'Who is this Bernard of Neufmarché, who has his claws stretched out towards Brycheiniog ?' demanded Rhys.

'A man clever enough to have married Agnes, or Nest, the daughter of Osbern FitzRichard,' came the answer from his spies. 'She is a grand-daughter of Gruffydd ap Llewellyn, so she is a great-great-great-great-grandchild of King Hywel Dda. Her mother therefore is your fourth cousin.'

'It is all folly!' said Rhys hotly. 'We breed a mongrel race to inherit the kingdoms!'

His Powys wife reproached him. On the Borders, intermarriage, in between battles, had been accepted for generations by both sides as a necessary modus vivendi.

'You are sometimes narrow and sinful in your pride, Rhys,' she said. 'It stands between your God and you.'

He stared at her fiercely.

'How can I strip myself of that which is my essence? Let God have mercy if He will!'

Three weeks later, Rhys ap Tewdr, with his whole teulu, and the uchelwyr of Deheubarth, broke over the border that separated Cantref Bychan from Brycheiniog. Together with the harrassed king of that gwlad, they met the armies of Bernard arrayed on the flat meadows of the valley's bowl. At the moment when the hills on each side rang with the clash and clang of iron swords and armour, the horse on which Rhys was riding tripped on a stone. Rhys was thrown, dragging in the stirrups. Some Frenchman stuck a long sword into his vitals, and with a gasp, the King of Deheubarth died.

Cadwgan, the delicate youngest child, was being fostered on his own estate on the coast of Ceredigion, but Hywel was lost, and the eleven-year-old Princess Nest was captured and taken to William Rufus as hostage. The Queen, fleeing from a crumbling kingdom, took ship to Iwerddon with Gruffydd, the one child left, to rear him there until he was of age to restore the fortunes of his house.

Twenty harsh years followed, with Ceredigion bandied to and fro, from French baron to Cymric prince, to King again, and King's man. The Cymry seized Montgomery Castle, and invaded all the Border lordships. There was a struggle like the meeting of two tides, and the heavier sea from Lloegr rose the higher. The bards of Cymru remembered, and the household teulu of Deheubarth were later to tell the heir how, after the massive Cymric uprisings were at long last put down, the barons rode into Ceredigion through the eastern passes; Roger Montgomery the Earl of Shrewsbury summoned his men and his horse and his stoutest armour, licked his lips, and came. They entered by lines of least resistance, like knives cutting butter; summer was high, and even in the mountains of Pumlumon they prevailed by their superior might in clear and favourable weather. Most of the leaders of Cymru had been slain; any left were thwarted by lack of their natural advantages, the rain and storm and mist that they contrived to wind like chains round their enemies before they picked them off at leisure in the slippery, treacherous, ever-faithful mud.

The French rode hard through the wilder parts of Ceredigion, rejecting all they saw until they came to Teifi's side. There they drew rein, for at last they began to breathe the rich pastoral airs that always aroused their desire to establish fat manors. A castle first; the site was ready made at Aber Teifi, at the river's mouth. They had but to seize Din Geraint, where the ancient people built their fortress-refuge once, centuries before the Romans came to plant their eagles at the four corners of Cymru. The rest of Ceredigion the Frenchmen did not care much for; dislike was mutual. To them it was but a stepping-stone to richer Dyfed in the green South-West, where Arnulf of Montgomery, a younger son, pitched a rude fort at Penfro between two rivers. There they built themselves, in the fulness of time, a more mighty castle, such as to reach the peak of their heart's pride.

Bishop Sulien, broken and disappointed, had but one hope, and his son Rhigyfarch feared that it was vain. He stood on the cliffs and stared over the churning sea towards Iwerddon.

'Gruffydd ap Rhys is over there,' muttered Sulien with longing. 'The French will not have it all their own way. They edge themselves now into the best places, but they will have to fight hard to retain them, and sometimes they will slip from their grasp. He is only a child now, but Gruffydd will come back. I must live to do him the same service that I did his father.'

But he died with the hope unfulfilled. Rhigyfarch, who had expected to succeed his father as Bishop, became involved in disputes with the other canons, and saw the office he regarded as his rightful inheritance diverted to a quiet but obstinate man named Wilfrid, with whom he was on bad terms. He clung, however to the title of Bishop, and retired in dudgeon to the family's Llan Badarn academy, certain that the world was ending. He wrote a long Latin poem that gave the last groan of a grievous century, then also died.

But his pessimism was not altogether justified. On the whole the French found Mid-Cymru a land too hard, poor, and expensive in blood and supplies to be worth the holding, and the successive Earls of Shrewsbury, Hugh, and Robert of Bellême, were glad to settle for alliance in 1099 with Cadwgan ap Bleddyn of Powys, the heir whose claim at last they recognized; and they threw in Ceredigion as a make-weight, because it was too indigestible a morsel for them to manage. So, a respite came for Ceredigion with Cadwgan, father of a son whose scandals were to furnish gossip for every court in Cymru. After the forays of the French, the burnings, and the violations, peace of a bitter kind came creeping back to the kingdom on rheumatic autumn knees, allowing the loud moan of the sea, and hunger's pinch, and the long wind's thunder, to seize the monarchy of winter days. The rocking world at last stood still.

2

Prince Henry was a clever fellow. All the world said so. Handsome, too. 'Beau Clerk', they called him. He read books, and talked to scholars, and could write, and speak Latin, besides his elegant native Norman French. 'And English,' said the English, rather pleased that he took the trouble to polish his knowledge of their rough tongue. But why not? Wasn't he English born, the only son of the Conqueror who could make this claim?

Quietly, he made the most of this asset, for he had few. His father had left him five thousand pounds, but no land to lord it in. Normandy and Maine had gone to the eldest son, Robert, England and its appanages to William Rufus. Robert, who got through a lot of money fighting against his brother William, heard about the five thousand, and called on his young brother for immediate aid. After some bickering, he sold to Henry Mont St. Michel, which dominated the Normandy coast, and a bit of land thrown in, for three thousand pounds.

Robert wanted the crown of England. William wanted Normandy, or at least, security from his brother's continual intrigues. William was a strong king, so the barons wanted Robert, a more amenable man. Henry, at Mont St Michel, held a fort of considerable influence, and the balance of power; so he was, thought William, worth winning as a friend. Henry was willing to be pleased by his brother the King of England, and to spend much time with him, and to appease the English as against the barons, and make sure of his place in the sun. He had his eye on the crown after William's day. William was unmarried, and his way of life was evil.

Meanwhile, there was this ward, the child Nest. William expected Henry to keep an eye on her, but she was difficult. In public she maintained a fierce silence; her storms of grief she kept for her pillow. But instinct told her to face each new day with decision, inspecting all that it might bring, sucking some virtue, learning some new thing, and keeping her dignity intact as became a Princess of Deheubarth.

But Henry found her one day sobbing with rage. He lifted her chin, astonished.

'What is troubling you, my dear?' he asked gently. 'Are they unkind?'

She shook her head impatiently.

'Unkind? No! But I am a waiting-maid!' she stormed. 'I fetch and carry, mend old linen, take messages—I, a Princess of Cymru!'

'My dear, every young lady has to learn the arts of housewifery—'

'Housewifery, yes, but do I learn those? Who teaches me the use of herbs and spices, the art of spinning and weaving, of embroidery? Other ladies sing and play the lute, and it is said that there are some—' She paused, for this was indeed to dare.

'Well?'

'There are some who even read!'

He laughed outright.

'They are rare indeed!' he said.

But he was interested. It was true, the Court ladies had not much time for her. She was in his care, the King of England's ward, an asset that must not be allowed to depreciate. His conscience accused him of neglect of a rather tiresome duty. He considered her vivid little face with its impatient cheek-bones and imperious nose. The great eyes stared back, demanding. She was twelve, coming up to an age when they must guard her with greater care. He must see to her more regularly than hitherto.

'Shall I teach you to read?'

Nest caught her breath at this prospect of a marvel.

'Yes please,' she said, and added grudgingly, 'Your Grace!' It was the first time she had deigned to acknowledge the rank of any of her captors, and Prince Henry felt inordinately pleased.

So, he gave her lessons, as often as he could find the time to spare. She was intelligent and quick, and made a satisfying pupil. He taught her French, and a smattering of Latin. They talked, she asked questions, but never about Cymru. She concealed from everyone the memory, and the painful hope, of home. She listened, learned, and wondered. She began to appreciate the value of this companionship, such as was given to few. She was grateful; at last she had a friend, a focus for her starved affections, and she loved him.

The change in her was remarked. The angry tension disappeared, bloom and grace appeared as she grew, giving calm to her dignity.

'The Prince goes about with a bright gleam in his eyes these days,' men said. 'The young Welsh lady keeps him well entertained.'

It was a friendship that deepened and changed as the years passed. Henry valued her devotion to himself. She would make a queen, he thought. For his own marriage, he had in mind Matilda of Scotland, niece to Edgar Atheling, and heiress to the old English line of kings. A marriage with her would conciliate the English, when he became king. He had no doubt that he would one day be king, though not for long years hence, for William Rufus had a constitution like an ox. He sighed. It would have to be Matilda. He ought, he supposed, to begin negotiations now, but there was no immediate hurry, for she was much younger than Nest. She might never live to reach womanhood. He toyed with the idea, in that event, of marrying Nest. It would ease relations with Wales, bring some authority to bear upon Deheubarth.

He looked at Nest, growing daily in beauty and in love for him, and groaned. He did not share his thoughts with her; her eyes, like two stars, seemed to shed light in darkness, and they dazzled him, bent though he was on his cool calculations. As for Nest, she loved him with strength, with arrogant simplicity, and truth, and pride for once took second place. Life was uncertain, and might be very short. Love was bond enough for her, and they clutched it while they could, lest it eluded them. They were very happy, and before she was eighteen, Nest had borne one son, Robert, and conceived another.

But Matilda lived, and grew, and flourished.

A poor woodman in the New Forest was picking up deadwood late one afternoon, in the wake of a royal hunting party; many old trees had been disturbed, and he followed a trail of broken branches, greatly to his profit. His avid but short-sighted gaze remarked a particularly good log, awkwardly disposed upon the ground. As he trundled his cart forward, the log became clearer, and he noticed an arrow lodged fast in its side.

'Too drunk to aim properly at the quarry,' he grumbled.

But it was not a log. It was a man lying there, with an arrow in his back; the white face was ghastly against the red hair. The woodman dropped to his knees, fainting with terror. The dead hunter was William Rufus, the Red King.

'King William dead? My brother shot?'

Henry was thunderstruck. By whom? How? Why? Never mind! He turned to immediate essentials. He galloped to Winchester to seize the Treasury; gold and central control were the first imperative. He got them. He summoned the witenagemot to meet with all haste, to elect him King. He was going to have to stand up to Robert in a struggle for the crown, but Robert was away east, flambuoyant on the First Crusade, having pledged Normandy to William for a necessary ten thousand marks; and Henry's fort of Mont St. Michel stood watch-dog there. Now, he must please the barons; so he imprisoned Ranulf Flambard, William's clever, unscrupulous Domesday surveyor and extorter of exorbitant feudal dues from them, and he issued a Charter of Liberties redressing the worst grievances of both barons and clergy, so far as a prudent monarch might. Now for the English; yes, he said, he would marry Edgar Atheling's niece, Matilda of Scotland.

'Our children will be descended from both William the Conqueror and Alfred the Great,' he said, and they hailed him King.

Henry, crowned, with eyes still watchful, but breathing less hard, turned his thoughts for a short painful moment to his domestic state, and did necessary violence to his feelings. He summoned Nest, and he called for Sir Gerald of Windsor, who held Penfro Castle for his lord, Arnulf of Montgomery. He was a strong, silent man, a faithful dog of a knight, with a hard hand for offenders. Henry had seen him often, tearing a fascinated gaze away from the Lady Nest.

Nest came into the King's presence with her head held high, determined to suppress love as strongly as once she had suppressed grief. Shock had frozen the outraged pride and anger in her heart, and only her mind was alive. There was a pattern to be followed; Henry, with a royal touch, strong, authoritative, remorseless, and true, must do his part. It was hers to go, with dignity, into some desert.

'Lady,' said Henry at last, huskily. 'I marry for reasons of state. You are my ward. Your hand is mine to give to whom I choose. I think of your welfare, and I wish to make peace with the people of Deheubarth. So I give you in marriage to this good man. He is Sir Gerald de Windsor, Constable of Pembroke Castle for his lord, Arnulf de Montgomery.'

As he spoke, a surge of rage in Nest drove out love. He has found another use for me, she thought. She scarcely looked at Gerald, but a blind instinct to punish Henry led her to accept at once.

'I felicitate Your Grace,' she said coldly. 'I wish you happy and fruitful in your marriage. As for my own, the world speaks well of Sir Gerald, and I agree, for I desire to be well established in my own domain.'

Henry winced, but proceeded to the bitter end.

'We shall divide our sons,' he said stiffly. 'Robert I keep.

Henry—' Henry had only recently been born. 'Guard him well.'

'Guard well Robert!' she retorted in an anguished whisper. She turned to look at Gerald, who gazed at her in rapture.

'I shall have other sons, by you,' said Nest, half to herself. 'And they will be kings!' She gave her hand to him, turned her back on King Henry, and they left the presence chamber. At the threshold she turned, a stranger already, to look at him for the last time.

'As for the peace of Deheubarth,' she said clearly, 'it will always flourish when it is in the hands of its own true princes, Your Grace. Otherwise, I fear, it will always trouble England's king.'

Gruffydd ap Rhys, in his middle age, was inclined to look back on his time in Iwerddon through the rosy cloud that casts a glow over the adventures of past youth and softens all asperities.

'When I was young and in Ireland, with the Norsemen and the leprechauns and the horses and the weird women—' His children loved that tale. To be on a green island, they thought, with violet mountains round the edges, with mist and rain and a silver sun shooting beams into the middle of all the shouting, fighting kings! That was a place where one might indeed dig for gold!

But the truth was rough in contrast to the tales he told; short fierce raids in revenge for stored resentments were the best that came his way, as he roamed through Iwerddon. The quality of life in the courts was cruder than in that of Deheubarth; grimly he compared its people with his father's own uchelwyr, his teulu, and his bards. Ulster and Munster, Leinster and Connaught, he went round them all, boasting his parentage at palace and abbey, paying his way with the growing strength of his arm, and a quick way he had with his sword and his dagger. He could master a horse, and master his company, grew into a handsome strong young fellow, and left a trail of not a few broken hearts in his passage. Restless, hard, and discontented, he passed the time in impatient preparation until his day should come, taking, using, and rejecting what Iwerddon offered him.

For Nest, wife to Gerald, and mistress of Pembroke castle, life in the early years of the twelfth century was often peaceful and free in between battles. Arnulf, her husband's lord, fell in the struggle between his rebellious brother Robert de Bellême and Henry, the king who would allow no overmighty barons to shackle his power. Henry kept Pembroke, and kept Gerald as Constable, responsible directly to himself, and continued the work that Arnulf had begun, of transforming the stout wooden fort into a great stone castle.

Nest built also, a good life for her husband and her children. Besides Henry FitzHenry, she had three FitzGerald sons, William, Maurice, and David, and a daughter, Angharad. She put aside the painful memory of King Henry, and of Robert growing up a stranger; and Gerald grew dear to her. All who sought shelter in her hall received a royal welcome, whether they were French, Cymry, or one of these Flemings to whom Henry had granted a refuge in Dyfed after the sea had overwhelmed their lands in the Low Countries. She kept a good table, and attracted some of the best bards and story-tellers in Cymru, especially Bleddyn, a young cyfarwydd from Meirionnydd, who was beginning to make a name for himself.

Always, in Bleddyn's audience, there was one person who served as the vessel into which he poured the wine of his tales—perhaps an old man, thin and warped; or a young girl serving with a sullen face, starved of all but dreams; or a laughing soldier in a thoughtful hour between the necessary boasts. But when Nest was present, her beauty, kindness, and eagerness inspired Bleddyn's art as no other yet had done. He had found his best listener.

He went with Nest and Gerald and the children to Cenarth at Teifiside to that winter feast which Cadwgan gave to celebrate his tenth Christmas as lord of Ceredigion, and so was witness of Nest's undignified misadventure at the hands of Cadwgan's son Owain, her second cousin. She, with her children, had gone unwillingly, for her brother Gruffydd was the rightful lord of Ceredigion; but Gerald, as Royal Constable of Pembroke, had felt obliged to attend the feast of a neighbouring lord, with his family. They had been nobly entertained, with much respect, but that Owain had annoyed his cousin with undesired attentions that roused Gerald's temper to so dangerous a degree that Bleddyn hastily averted open trouble by embarking on the absorbing tale of Pwyll, Prince of Dyfed.

But in the winter night's silence, when all lay sleeping, Owain with his troop of men burned some buildings about the castle, set up a roar as they fought with Gerald's men, and burst into Gerald's chamber to capture Nest, whose beauty had inflamed him to a mad jealousy.

Everything happened swiftly. Bleddyn, who had rushed to the rescue, was kicked aside with a broken ankle, and watched helplessly as Nest and her children, screaming with fright and anger, were bundled up in carthenni and taken away to some fastness in Powys. Gerald, in his nightgown, with sword in hand, fighting furiously with his back to the wall, felt a door handle behind him. He opened it, found himself in the privy, and dropped through the hole in the floor into Teifi, swirling darkly deep below the castle walls.

Gerald emerged from Teifi with an injured arm. By the time the remnant of his men found him, Owain and his captives were well on their way to Powys. The men of Penfro scoured the countryside in vain, and weeks passed without news.

Gossip flared and argued about Nest and Owain.

'They looked too long into each other's eyes, and a flame of love leapt between them!' claimed the bards, seizing the juicy titbit. Bleddyn, blaming their eager zest for detail, quarrelled with them for singing the story too often, and magnifying it beyond its due importance.

'But let a scandal last long enough,' he said scathingly, 'and you are bound to accord it the honours proper to romance!' But they laughed at him; the rivalry between the cyfarwydd and the bards was long established.

Swearing, he limped north to Llan Badarn, to his old academy, to put matters right. The monks kept the Chronicle; he told them the true story, and they set the facts down plainly, that Owain took Nest by force from Cenarth, and that Gerald escaped by the privy. Wisely they refrained from any reflections on Nest's virtue.

'Poor thing,' they said. 'She has ever been the victim of violent men, and whatever she does, Heaven will judge her, not we.'

Nest and her children made an uncomfortable houseful. The children plagued Owain, biting, kicking, and screaming, with her hearty encouragement. He packed the youngsters off home to Pembroke, and then came to court and flatter her each night with tenderness and song. At least, such was his intention. But she received him with so biting a tongue, so many weary yawns, such a dirty face, unkempt attire, and shrill complaints, that his ardour gave way to disgust, and he failed to find her even moderately pretty. Angrily he went off hunting with his cronies one morning, leaving her rather carelessly guarded, and when he returned, she was missing. Owain was furious. He did not really want her any more, but it had been for him, not her, to choose the moment of their parting.

It was an uncomfortable homecoming. Nest, thankful to be back, resumed her life as though no adventure had occurred. But Gerald was jealous, and it took a long time for his suspicions of her fidelity to be dispelled, until at last a sharp quarrel cleared the air, and domestic peace returned. But the quarrel marked a change in the marriage. It had warped, like a door of unseasoned wood exposed to the rain, and was thereafter full of minor irritations which increased in number with the shorter temper and hardened arteries of age. Together, however, they watched for their chance to restore Gruffydd to Ceredigion, and to be revenged on Owain.

They kept their ears cocked for any news of him. After Nest escaped, Owain consoled himself with a new career as pirate and slave trader. He would make periodic raids into Dyfed in revenge for her loss, round up some of the local Flemings to whom the French had granted lands, and ship them across to Iwerddon for a handsome profit, to his own unbounded glee, and Gerald's fury. Cadwgan, already stricken by King Henry's displeasure and the temporary loss of Ceredigion on account of his son's wildness, shuddered within his castle walls in Powys, and trembled at the approach of every messenger.

At last, Owain overreached himself, as usual. In his careless way, he held up a Flemish bishop on the Whitland road, and slew him in the scuffle that ensued.

'He was one William of Brabant,' said Gerald. 'This murder will enrage the King.'

He was right; King Henry's patience snapped, and Cadwgan, of course, not Owain, was the immediate loser. He finally lost Ceredigion, and the King sent his baron Gilbert FitzRichard of Clare, and his son, and his petty vassals, to dig themselves into the land. Nest, bewailing Gruffydd's failure to be on hand when such a splendid chance occurred, sent frantic messages across the water by way of Bleddyn, who had contacts amongst the Irish bards. It was time that he recovered his own without delay at least in Ystrad Tywi.

Three years passed before Gruffydd ap Rhys returned to Cymru. When Bleddyn first saw him one autumn morning newly disembarked on a remote Pembroke shore, he was disappointed. He saw a young man of middle height, swinging across the sands with a careless stride, looking about him with haggard, unsmiling eyes, a king's son rather than a king, one who had been obliged to use his wits hitherto to win his bread rather than his crown.

Gruffydd was in fact still suffering from a bad sea crossing. He stood there bewildered by an emotional greeting from the beautiful woman whose black hair and dark cloak were streaming wildly in the south-west wind, who clutched him with urgent, possessive hands, and, sobbing, said she was his sister Nest. Gruffydd, who had lived since he was a child with memories that he could share with no one, looked at her dully, and wondered how far he could trust her. She had loved Henry, and married Gerald. She was with the French.

She sensed his stiffness.

'You are Gruffydd ap Rhys? You have my father's nose and my mother's mouth, but your eyes—they are those of a stranger!'

Something in her own eyes, wide open like a child's, and her drooping, disappointed lips, touched him with pity and truth, and his face became alive again.

'Gruffydd I am indeed, and you are Nest fach, my sister still—'

He hugged her; long buried hiraeth welled up in each, and they wept openly, standing on the shore.

'Why didn't you come long ago, to be on the spot when your chance came?' demanded Nest the next morning, her eyes sparkling impatiently. 'I thought when Owain blundered, and his father Cadwgan was dismissed from Ceredigion, if you pushed your claims, and won a battle or two, I might get round Henry to help you recover Deheubarth! But you were too slow, Gruffydd, three years too slow! Henry's a prompt man. He handed your kingdom to Gilbert FitzRichard, so once again Ceredigion endures the grinding French heel!'

'You talk like a Cymraes,' said Gruffydd slowly. 'What does your husband say to my presence here?'

'He grants you shelter, as he does to every traveller,' said Nest at once. 'He will not openly support your claims for fear of offending Henry, but your success would strengthen his own status in Cymru, and make the King look twice at his Constable of Pembroke!'

Her tone changed.

'Why don't you answer me?' she demanded. 'What kept you there so long? Have you a wife? And have you sons?'

'I had a wife,' said Gruffydd quietly. 'She died. Many people died that winter. The harvest was poor. I have left behind me two sons, Anarawd and Cadell, in the care of my wife's sister.'

There was silence. Nest looked at him with sorrow, sympathy, and some irritation. Was this a reed broken before the wind began to blow?

'You shall find another wife,' said Nest robustly, 'who shall make you strong sons, and you shall be happy again and King of Deheubarth.'

He gave her an ironic smile.

'The delay was caused by other matters,' he said. 'Not all the Irish were my friends. Owain found a refuge there, and a warm welcome. His career was reckless enough to please their readiness to dare, and they have enjoyed watching him twisting the tails of the French. He made a pile out of the Flemish slave trade, and had gold enough to fan their praise. Oh, I've been in some tight places in the last few years,' he told his sister. 'I had to fight my way out of Iwerddon.' He yawned. 'Now, it seems, I have to fight my way into Deheubarth.' He still looked too tired to relish the prospect, and Nest looked at him earnestly.

'You're too thin,' she said at last. 'It's not a wife you need just yet, it's a mother. Fattening up, that's the best gift I can make you, Gruffydd. You shall have the best cream and eggs, beef and mutton, wine and cwrw, in all Penfro.'

Gruffydd's health was in fact more seriously undermined by famine than anyone realized. He remained at Penfro throughout the winter, enduring with patience his sister's determined efforts to build him up. Slowly, however, vigour returned to his frame; spring brought back to his eyes the eager look that Nest remembered, and when at Easter he donned her gift of a green hunting cap and mantle, her court at last admired the rather drab young man she had lavished so much care upon. Even Gerald, out of all patience with her preoccupation, admitted that he looked well enough, and would certainly take with the Cymry.

It pleased Nest that in his quiet way Gerald had become firm friends with Gruffydd. First drawn together by a common hostility to the resilient Owain, lately reinstated as ruler of Powys, a continuing sympathy between them was revealed by their long, monotonous conversations in corners.

One day he turned to Gruffydd, and asked him curiously, 'Did you never think to find a crown out there in Ireland, where the world lies wide open to a strong man's lash?'

Gruffydd looked at him in scorn.

'It's his own crown that a man must win,' he said flatly. 'My father was King of Deheubarth. What other would be good enough for me?'

'The prospect of any crown, anywhere, would be enough to lure away a Norman overseas,' said Nest drily. 'Here we are cooped up on the edge of Cymru, and Gerald sees Iwerddon in his dreams.'

'Opportunities out there for the right man,' said Gerald wistfully. 'Arnulf took his chance over the water. Married the daughter of King Murkertagh—'

'Druan a ch'i, you had to put up with King Rhys ap Tewdr's daughter!' said Nest, with a flash of temper. 'Let's leave adventure to our sons! Each one is King already in his own imagination!'

'I am quite willing,' retorted Gerald. 'It was you yourself who promised me they would be kings!'

3

Gruffydd stayed some months in Penfro, marking time, marking the lie of the land, and holding his tongue when he was not discussing tactics with Gerald, who was not above offering his quite unofficial counsel. He learned to distinguish friend from foe, perfected his French, and recovered his command of Cymraeg in conference with Bleddyn, who had remained spellbound in his corner, to stir events with his spoon and taste at secondhand the sweets of power. Bleddyn knew the uchelwyr everywhere, their ins and outs, and where their interests lay.

'Ceredigion is fortified from north to south by Gilbert and his gang,' he told Gruffydd. 'At Llan Fihangel, at the mouth of Ystwyth, at Ystrad Meurig, at Blaen Porth, and Llan Bedr, the castles rise like a row of bared teeth. You should go north-east into Ystrad Tywi, where the French are more careless, and the Cymry, in the uplands, are keen and hungry, waiting like dry tinder for a leader's spark. I'll go before you,' said Bleddyn, 'dropping hints as I pass by.'

So he began quietly to cultivate the uchelwyr of Deheubarth in Gruffydd's favour, to prepare them for a rising there. Presently Gruffydd followed, in the guise of a bard. The French in their strength suffered such men to wander across Cymru, purveying an evening's entertainment and the latest news. They were often spies, employed by this side and by that. Gruffydd by-passed the manors beyond Caer Fyrddin, keeping to the hill paths, straining his eyes for Drysllwyn and Dinefwr; then he saw them, through the yellow mists of spring, the outlines of the cliffs and violated castles of his house. His imperious looks attracted the attention of some elderly caethion out gathering brushwood for the fire of some gwrbonheddig.

They murmured, 'It is Rhys ap Tewdr!' Then they said 'Na! Rhys was slain in Brycheiniog many years ago.'

They drew near like dogs, eager for forbidden meat.

'Whose men are you?' asked Gruffydd.

They said softly, 'Geraint's men,' and waited for him to declare himself.

'Geraint!' said Gruffydd. 'There was a Geraint once who was penteulu to King Rhys ap Tewdr, the captain of his men-at-arms.'

'It is he,' said the men, staring.

'Then your master is rich and I am hungry,' said Gruffydd. 'Go and tell him that I have a strange song to sing to him, the sequel to many another that his bards have sung.'

Geraint was old, but still vigorous. His sons, with eyes like those of chained hounds, watched Gruffydd, resentful of his height and size, which exceeded theirs. But the old uchelwr's welcome was generous.

'Croeso, gwrbonheddig,' he said. 'Geraint bids every stranger welcome in Our Lord's name.'

He bade Gruffydd sit on his right hand, and eat the venison plucked out of the wood from under French noses. They spoke of the mildness of the previous winter, of the sharp frost that had come late to shrink the ground, and of summer prospects. The household bard, jealous and inquisitive, tried to discuss the weather's suitability for war, the French advance in south and west, King Henry's invasion of the North, and 'Had the stranger bard any firm rumour to retail? Owain of Powys, now, people said he was hustling his cattle and women and goods into the mountain fastnesses—' But Geraint checked him; Gruffydd had not yet stayed his hunger.

At last, when the meat and the cawl and the milk and the oat cakes and honey and cheese and apples were removed, and the mead was passed round, Gruffydd took out his harp. Half talking, half chanting, he opened his mind in freedom, for these, his father's own people, were men he must trust. The household bard leaned back in his chair of honour, and allowed his thoughts to wander, satisfied that in this young man he need fear no rival; the rhymes were too rough, although the voice was true. But presently his eyes opened. Geraint and his sons, the women of the house, the porter, and the caethion crowding at the door, had fallen captive to the tale this travelling bard was telling, corroborated by idle runs and chords upon his harp.

He told them of the noble king that Geraint had served, the king slain in battle. He told them of the son Gruffydd, snatched as a child from peril, growing in safety to manhood beyond the Irish Sea, yearning for home and his kin and lands, struggling to keep the native tongue that bound him to his country and held his own heart true. He spoke of petty kings and monks in Iwerddon, who allowed him refuge and a noble education in return for a squire's service, of his strong purpose to restore the fortunes of his house, of news of home that came upon the tide into Irish harbours that curved like listening ears towards the coast of Cymru.

When the strange bard spoke of Gruffydd's farewell to Iwerddon, the company trembled and clenched their fists on the table. When he spoke of the landing in Penfro, they rose and gripped their swords. After he chanted, in a hush, of Gruffydd's decision to roam Ystrad Tywi in search of his friends, they cheered and roared; and Geraint stood before him with tears rolling down his cheeks.

'Who are you?' asked Geraint hoarsely. 'What token do you bring?'

Gruffydd looked at him and smiled, with Rhys ap Tewdr's smile, and Geraint knelt to kiss hands.

'I have no token,' said Gruffydd. 'Yet I am Gruffydd ap Rhys, your rightful lord.'

Then the triumph in the hall broke out and spread like fire through dry grass over all the hills on either side of Tywi.

Next day it was raining, and the men had to go about their farm work as usual, but nothing would do for the women but that they must bustle to prepare a feast. Gruffydd spent the time with Geraint discussing tactics and strategy. There was coming and going; Gruffydd went openly visiting the old vassals of Rhys ap Tewdr, who ran to swear fealty to his son. They were lean-faced, light-footed uchelwyr, who welcomed him without hesitation, and talked with glee of how they would storm the twin castles above Tywi, smoke out the French from their manors, surge down the valley in flood, and capture Caer

Fyrddin. It sounded well, but the rumour grew too loud, and reached the ears of King Henry.

Forced by expediency, Henry had come to a pact with Owain of Powys. Now came Nest's brother Gruffydd out of Ireland, expecting to don his father's crown. Let him fight for it! Henry had his own bastards to consider and provide for, first. Ystrad Tywi might well suit Robert, when he was older, together with Glamorgan and Gloucester through marriage with the heiress Mabel, now growing up, and a very proper match for him. If any of Rhys ap Tewdr's kin were ever to inherit Deheubarth, or part of it, they should be his own sons by Nest.

King Henry ordered the arrest of Gruffydd ap Rhys, and put a flattering price on his head.

At the same time he made a grant of lands to his second son by Nest, young Henry. He was to be Lord of Narberth and Pebidiog within Penfro.

Nest was furious at the first order, and puzzled by the second.

'Has his regard for me become so low that he tries to kick my brother out of Deheubarth?' she stormed. 'And young Henry fobbed off with a petty lordship! What of my eldest son, Robert? Why does he not provide for him?'

It was Gerald, wincing at this reference to a past in which he had no share, who drew the desired conclusion.

'Perhaps he is reserving Ystrad Tywi for Robert,' he said.

Nest was shocked, and rebellious.

'I will not suffer my father's eldest son to be disinherited by any bastard child of mine!' she declared.

Gruffydd heard in silence the news of his ordered arrest, and considered. Had it occurred later, it would have been a trifle to ignore, but he was still insecure. His friends and vassals were still too widely scattered on the upland edges of the gwlad for him to muster strength with any ease. The French, massed in the valley, had been alerted and would grasp more tightly their interior lines of communication, and strengthen the garrisons of the Tywi castles and of Caer Fyrddin. To attack now would be certain disaster.

He pondered the possibilities of a counter-stroke in Ceredigion. That meant he must seek an ally amongst the kings of Cymru. Not Powys; Cadwgan was dead, and Owain was now

Henry's man, trying to live down a disreputable past in the shining armour of a French knight. He had lately returned with Henry from Normandy. Gruffydd stood up suddenly.

'I will go north,' he told Geraint. 'I will ask Gruffydd ap Cynan of Gwynedd to remember the alliance with my father Rhys whereby they both won their kingdoms.'

'Gruffydd ap Cynan?' repeated Geraint anxiously. 'But he has only just made peace with Henry!'

But Gruffydd ap Rhys was an optimist, and brushed aside this information. In Gwynedd, however, the hard facts of politics were made clear to him. The welcome he got was cool. Men watched their king, who sat back and listened with narrowed lips and eyes, and they interpreted these signs. Gruffydd ap Cynan had spent the years of Rhys ap Tewdr's reign and of his son's exile in consolidating his position in Gwynedd. Now, he was formidable, active, and wary of every peril to his state. After the usual jostle and thrust with the French he had reached equilibrium, and terms of uneasy goodwill with their king in Lloegr. This young man, an outlaw come out from the South, armed with his sword and his boldness only, angered and embarrassed him. For years Gruffydd had planted the feet of his fortresses down against Powys, Deheubarth, and Cheshire; he had turned his back on the stir of the South; he was fenced in and trim with no pity to spare for men beyond Gwynedd. If Rhys ap Tewdr had failed to hold his kingdom for his son, so much the worse for them; let the heir struggle to prove his quality. Gruffydd ap Cynan would not spoil Henry's good mood to prop the fortunes of an untried pup.

He frowned at his young daughter, Gwenllian, who was listening eagerly; he bade her withdraw to the women's quarters. She did so, still looking at Gruffydd ap Rhys, and there was laughter. Gruffydd ap Cynan's frown increased. He bowed in reply to the young man's appeal, said he would consider, rose from the table, and bade his son, Cadwaladr, to see to the entertainment of this unwanted guest.

It was the usual meagre accommodation, in a draughty alcove off the main hall, with a pile of dusty twigs and a few well-worn deerskins for bedding. Gruffydd ap Cynan's men-at-arms slept nearby; they were grumbling because the mead was short.

Cadwaladr wasted little politeness on this handsome fellow who called himself a king.

'A king, are you? As long as you're here, you shall live like one. In Gwynedd, a king lives rough.'

Gruffydd waited for a night and a day for the King of Gwynedd to make up his mind. He suffered Cadwaladr's snubs with the indifference he accorded the malice of strange dogs. Then at evening an old man clutched his arm in the shadows outside the hall, with a warning from Gwenllian.

'You are Prince Gruffydd ap Rhys?' he whispered. 'My wife was nurse to the Lady Gwenllian. I am a bondman, sir, from the banks of Dyfi, but my mother was a free woman, a boneddiges from Ceredigion across the water. Don't you stay in the court of Gruffydd ap Cynan, my lord. He can't afford to offend the Frenchman. A message has come from Henry, and you're not safe. Shun you King Gruffydd's presence until you know how the world may turn. Get you to the monks of Aberdaron in Lleyn, and take sanctuary with them.'

Gwenllian! Suddenly Gruffydd's path became clear to him, and he knew what he must do. He smiled.

'Tell your mistress,' he said impressively, 'that she is as a rose in winter for me, a river in a desert place. Tell her that, if I can but win her love, my kingdom is already won. I will not leave her father's court until she swears to come with me to Aberdaron, and to wed me there.'

As the man departed, Gruffydd lifted his head in triumph.

'If the King of Gwynedd will give me no man to fight for my kingdom,' he muttered, 'I'll take his daughter to make me an heir.' He chuckled. He needed a wife, and a link with Gwynedd pleased him best. 'God brought me here!' he said.

The messenger repeated Gruffydd's words to Gwenllian, who blushed with excitement, but she knew exactly how to reply. She ignored his pretty phrases; they were only a bouquet picked in a hurry to garnish a bald offer.

'Tell him,' she said in the high quick voice of one burning her boats behind her, 'I'll go with him gladly. I trust his honour as a prince and king, and I'll be his true wife.' She was beckoned less by love than by the fine spring weather, the thought of living free and far from her prison court of the North, where winter lingered, bleak and long. She liked the look of Gruffydd ap

Rhys, cared not for the little lords of Nantconwy who sought her hand, and longed to help him win his kingdom and to be queen herself.

When she saw him waiting, his face aglow with ardour, a pang of fright assailed her, but she quelled her nerves sharply.

'I am by the laws of Hywel Dda of age to choose my husband!' she declared, more to herself than to Gruffydd, in justification of her boldness. 'It is my right, and my father cannot vent his spite on you!'

Right or not, and whether moved by spite or guile, to delude Henry, the King of Gwynedd sent a small force after them, and in the hot flight south-west there was little time for making love. Yet love did spring between them, of course, young and strong. It brooked no opposition from the hesitating monks of Aberdaron, who feared their prince's firm and heavy hand, and shrank from uniting this determined couple.

'Oh, peace to your bones!' said Caradoc, the youngest priest, at last, exasperated. 'Can you not see they are of a mind to have each other, with God's blessing, or without? It were sin to refuse them!' He turned to Gruffydd and Gwenllian. 'I'll marry you, and I'll come south with you as chaplain to your court!' he said, and they welcomed him.

Caradoc muttered enough Latin prayers to marry them beyond a doubt, and they cast off on the tide in a fishing ship before the Gwynedd men arrived in force at the llan gate, swarmed in, and spent their King's fury on the stout church door. The soldiers went unpunished. Gruffydd ap Cynan learned of the marriage with public wrath redeemed by secret satisfaction. It would be no bad thing for Gwynedd if one day a grandchild of his were to inherit the Kingdom of the South.

Three years saw the swift rise and fall of Gruffydd's first war, before his long, disgruntled ease and peace in Caeo. When they landed in Deheubarth at the mouth of Aeron in Mid-Ceredigion, one morning in June in 1115, it was like a god returning. The word had spread from mouth to mouth, from harp to harp, along the line of hills, that Gruffydd ap Rhys had gone to Gwynedd to seek an ally, and found a wife instead. Reckless and insecure, yet safe from the French as a bird is free of earth-bound foes, Gruffydd fell among friends, and darted uphill and south-east into Ystrad Tywi, accompanied by a swelling retinue of fighting men, the cheerful prayers of Caradoc, and the bright glances of Gwenllian.

King Henry was alarmed at the dangerous stir that ensued in the South; Gruffydd eluded every baron sent to crush him. Then down in Ty Ddewi in the far south-west, Bishop Wilfrid died. Quietly, he had been applauding the struggle of Lady Nest's brother, and the clustering canons made another eager push to secure another Cymro as the new bishop.

'Daniel!' they cried to each other. 'Old Bishop Sulien's son, prudent, wise, and learned, Archdeacon of Powys! The very man!'

But Henry thought otherwise.

'Oh, no!' he said. 'Time for the intervention of a French bishop between the Cymry and their God. That should establish a more reliable local control, and frighten them.'

He forced the canons to elect Bernard, a bland man, but firm, one of the chaplains of his wife Matilda. But the Cymry resisted his authority. Bernard, holding his head proudly as he rode into his diocese, encountered difficulties; he found it necessary to lower the angle of his jaw. Matters improved, but the canons remained implacable. He had authority, but power stayed somehow out of reach. Bernard, an agreeable man, accustomed to popularity, was piqued. How could he win these thorny people? They were angry because he was not one of themselves.

'I'll be a Cymro,' he decided. 'Gruffydd's rebellion? Lady Nest's brother? I'll not interfere. I'll speak her fair. I'll cultivate the canons, ask them to advise me, admire Sulien, discover the history of the diocese—'

So quietness returned to Ty Dewi, Gruffydd and Gwenllian laughed, Henry was baffled, and from the Church at least there was peace for the army of the Cymry to grow. The autumn was spent in exercises and the discipline of harrassing raids into the river plain; in winter, the blacksmiths forged new swords for youngsters eager to flesh them before the iron cooled and the snow melted; the tanners cured the toughest skins for battle jackets, the women provisioned the army with salted meat and cheese, and conceived children to be born when the men were in distant places, and Caeo was quiet in the veils of summer.

One of these was Gwenllian. A born organizer, she had set herself the task of supervising the kitchen in their camp at Caeo. In the summer she had taken one look at the flimsy buildings on the upland slopes.

'But this is a hafod!' she exclaimed in disgust. 'Well, if we have to live here all the winter through, we'll have to build a stronger house to hold the stores!'

Gruffydd, amused by her energy, and proud of it, set his men hacking substantial timbers from the more accessible oaks in the forest; and a stout building, worthy of a hendref, arose to Gwenllian's design, with a place for cheese, and beams for bacon to hang from, a great stone hearth for cooking, and a vast table, where her own army of cooks and scullions bustled to do her bidding. She was everywhere, exhorting, encouraging, reminding, and scolding, an undoubted queen determined to establish her husband's authority at root level, in men's stomachs.

'Keeps a good table, Gwenllian!' the hungry young boneddigion told each other, as they hastened to enrol under her husband, and they smacked their lips. Gwenllian, on her feet all day, heedlessly used her strength, until unaccustomed languor and weakness took her by surprise, with some alarm, until it dawned on her that she was with child.

She said nothing, and she went with Gruffydd, and with the army, when spring beckoned, on a flying gallop west. She did not speak until they were camped outside Narberth Castle in April, when she turned in triumph to her husband, and beamed encouragement at him.

'Go now and win a castle for our son!' she said.

Ecstatically, Gruffydd and his men attacked the castle with aplomb and the strength of joy. They destroyed it, for they would not waste their strength in manning it; they levelled the site, and rode away to Llanymddyfri. It was a mad, successful summer. They laid the French by the heels in unexpected places, burning and plundering and destroying at Sweyn's Ey, Caer Fyrddin, and Gwyr, each fresh success bringing hot young heads to flock into Gruffydd's army. The peak of his first war saw the fighting spirit of Deheubarth fully roused, and all the lukewarm fired by his cause. Even his cautious uncle, Rhydderch ap Tewdr, shook off his bondage to the French, and rallied to Gruffydd with his sons Maredudd and Owain. Gruffydd greeted him well. All the malice he allowed himself was to say that he had taken care to assault Caer Fyrddin castle when he knew his uncle was not there. The French, short-handed and desperate, had press-ganged some of the local Cymry into supplying the reserves they lacked.

Now all was changed. Gruffydd's kindred in Ceredigion urged him to invade their gwlad.

'You are certainly King of Deheubarth if Ceredigion claims you!' said Gwenllian proudly. She knew the rest of Cymru kept a wary eye on the men of Ceredigion; they could be troublesome; they scorned to fear Henry, the mighty King who had seized all Britain in his grip, and who was, fair play to him, at least restoring a considerable degree of order to the land, with local justice, largely baron-free. The magnates had been tamed; and after ding-dong wars with his brother Robert, Duke of Normandy, the latter had been caught, hauled down to Cardiff Castle, and dumped in a stout dungeon in the basement. Ceredigion was unimpressed; it called loudly for Gruffydd.

'They are subjects worth having!' he replied, and he plunged cheerfully across country into Iscoed in South Ceredigion to a place where the Flemings of Gilbert FitzRichard were dwelling. Gruffydd's army besieged the tower and slew the men and burned the wooden town and gained a large following as they wheeled about into the countryside and harried the Saxons imported by Gilbert to plough up the empty land. They plundered, despoiled, and burned their way up to the northern cwmmwd of Penweddig, where Gruffydd had never been before. With the chaotic roar of the army in his ears, he looked through bloodshot eyes at a bright clear hilly country by the sea. All was shining and still; he thought of Gwenllian, long since sent home to Caeo, and he yearned for her company and common sense; his army, he feared, was too large for cohesion; the men were accustomed to fighting in small, fierce, independent units; and vigorous leader though he was, Gruffydd lacked his father's ultimate power to weld them into one.

He sighed, and rallied his men for an attack on the castle of Gilbert's officer Ralf at Ystrad Peithyll, which they burned before going off to camp for the night at Glasgrug within a mile of Llan Badarn.

The French monks who had replaced the banished Cymry were much displeased because Gruffydd's men, being hungry, carried off cattle from the sanctuary fields for their supper. Angry cries, cordially ignored, were exchanged over the river for the smell of roast beef as the company, replete, planned the next day's attack on the castle of Aber Ystwyth. They were strong, but the French were stronger, for a message had gone to Gilbert's other castle at Ystrad Meurig in the high north-east of Ceredigion, and by night a great force of men came down to strengthen the garrison at Aber Ystwyth. Next morning when the Cymry advanced over Antaron in the somewhat loose array of easy confidence, Gilbert's men bided their time before they fell upon them and slew without mercy. Gruffydd's force was decimated; he himself by hidden ways groped down to Ystrad Tywi and Caeo. There he found comfort; Gwenllian had borne him a son.

The scribes of Cymru scrawled one minor footnote to this campaign. There was a roar through the South when Gruffydd disappeared, and all the King's men combed all the forests to find him. Some were Flemings of Gerald's, and some were a company under their enemy Owain ap Cadwgan. So the Flemings turned aside from the King's business to do their own, and Gerald's, to hunt down Owain. They found in a clearing by the river, and cornered and slew him straight. Thus was Gerald avenged, just where Cothi meets Tywi at Ystrad Rwnws.

4

Apart from one other abortive rebellion, Gruffydd lived quietly at home in Caeo for several years. Having rocked the might of the French, and picked himself up from the rebound, he faced the fact that he was powerless while the first Henry stayed King.

'I am young still, and must wait,' he said.

So he went to the King of Lloegr's court to make submission for the Lordship of Caeo, and made friends on the way home with Miles son of the Sheriff of Gloucester who had just married Sibyl, the heiress of Bernard of Neufmarché; he was proud to inspect his new lands on the way. They had a curious contest on the shores of Llyn Llangors; Miles wished to try his power over the birds. Local legend had it that these would answer the call of none but the true Lord of Brycheiniog. Unfortunately, he was not much of a fowler, but Gruffydd, who had learned to charm the birds of all Iwerddon since his boyhood days, grinned, and agreed to a contest in which Miles had by far the worst of it, and Gruffydd went away much cheered. A certain amount of bickering interrupted their friendship as a result, until both sides tired of belligerence, and Gruffydd settled down in earnest to possess his soul in a degree of patience, establish his local fame, and rear a brood of sons who should dislodge some day the foreigners from his inheritance.

They were all born at Caeo, the sons of Gruffydd by Gwenllian; Morgan and Maelgwyn were separated by two sisters, Gwladus and Nest, from their brothers Maredudd and Rhys. In this nursery there were also the two older brothers Anarawd and Cadell, who were adored by the youngsters, and reared with such kindness by Gwenllian that they all forgot she was not their true mother, and regarded her kin as their own. These sons knew but a short childhood before battle; it was a vigorous, intensive training for a soldier's life, learning as they did from the cradle to handle real swords. From Caeo they watched the ebb and flow of the invader, and clung together under their father's hand, for unity was the one great lesson he taught them that they all remembered.

'Serve the head of the house of Deheubarth, whoever he be, and do not divide the kingdom!' he said, looking over to Powys, where the remaining sons of Cadwgan wrangled like dogs over the pickings of a dead fox. Cadwgan's wives had been several and his concubines many, and his sons were separated by indifference and hatred.

'Choose one woman and have your children all by her,' said Gruffydd, with his arm around Gwenllian's ample waist. 'Keep her in health and joy to bear you sons, each to pride himself in all. Scorn to complicate your lives with bastards to compete with your legitimate heirs!'

They listened to him; Rhys alone was too young to understand.

As for Nest, she was widowed early, and for a while was plunged in grief for the loss of Gerald's steady discipline and devotion, and even of his jealousy. At last she lifted herself out of sorrow to rebuild her family's fortunes. She persuaded King Henry to allow William to succeed his father as Constable of Pembroke Castle, with his brother Maurice as lieutenant. She turned her charm on Bishop Bernard, pushed her youngest son David into minor Church orders, and she married off Angharad to William de Barri, son of Odo, of Manorbier.

Then she pondered her own position. She was only thirty-eight, and beautiful still. It was a man's world; wife to someone she must be, she supposed. William FitzGerald was struggling gallantly to support the sudden weight of power's harness, and if she remained at the castle, full authority would elude her son's grasp, for every man looked up to her for orders. She sighed, looked over the several offers of marriage she received daily, considering them well. She fixed on Stephen, Constable at Aber Teifi for the Clares. He was an old friend of Gerald's, honest and faithful to his lord, and she liked a plain man best.

Gruffydd would doubtless be displeased, but she had lost all hope now that he would ever recover Ceredigion.

King Henry raised no objection to the marriage. He had learned of the Lady Nest's choice in a silence that concealed relief as well as sadness. His own Queen Matilda had recently died, his only son William had been drowned at sea in the White Ship, and he needed a male heir. For a brief moment he had toyed with the idea of marrying his old mistress, who was young enough to bear him another son. But she had matured, men told him, into a most wilful beauty. Much as he valued the memory of her love, he was not a young man now; he was a strong and busy monarch without desire or time for an argumentative marriage. It was true, he had a daughter, seventeen-year-old Matilda, married to the Emperor Henry V since she was eight years of age; but she had as yet no child, and besides, how could a woman govern England? Henry groaned, and married the Lady Adela of Louvain.

His marriage to the Lady Adela proved childless, but Nest, at the age of forty, bore a son, Robert Fitzstephen. All the Cymry laughed.

'It serves Henry right!' they said. 'He should have married Nest in the first place.'

Henry bit his nails as he tried to thrust aside the mocking vision of Nest's domestic prosperity. All he could do now was to pin his hopes on his daughter. The Empress Matilda, recently widowed, was married off hastily to young Count Geoffrey of Anjou, who was only fifteen, eleven years younger than his bride. Henry had five years to wait, getting thinner, greyer, and shorter-tempered, before the longed-for grandson, another Henry, came.

Then the King, in great relief, looked round. There was no brother Robert now to trouble him, and Robert's son William Clito was dead. But Henry did fear the popularity of his sister Adela's rather pushing son, Stephen of Blois. He had been shrewdly married off by his mother to Queen Matilda's niece, thus pleasing the English, and the Londoners loved him, a handsome, florid man in his prime. Tensely Henry hurried to tighten all his ropes before the storm broke, and made his councillors swear loyalty to the ex-Empress and to little Henry too. Then, exhausted, he went to Normandy on business and to breathe a freer air; and died.

While England crumbled into factious war in 1135 as Stephen tilted against Matilda's throne, the Cymry grasped their swords, crouched in a lion's pause, and sprang. The first to jump was Hywel ap Maredudd in the hills of Brycheiniog, who made a circuit about the anxious lowland foe, and fell upon Penllergaer and Gwyr in the old traditional and slaughtering forays. In Caeo, Gwenllian was all for a similar attack and commotion down into Ystrad Tywi, the easy, accessible land.

'No!' said Gruffydd acutely. 'I shall make for Ceredigion. That's the hard core of Deheubarth! I shall invade it from the North with your father's help, march south, and take Caer Fyrddin by surprise from the rear.'

He had long since made peace with his father-in-law, and now he rode to Gwynedd with a more certain judgement of success than eighteen years before. King Gruffydd, keen-eyed and mellowed not at all, agreed that times were ripe for readjustment in Cymru, and put in hand a mighty preparation with little care for the reactions of Powys.

Caeo waited, but not for long. Gwenllian, provoked and inflamed by her own impatience and the angry grumbles of the remaining uchelwyr, burst out of Caeo with the four eldest boys, roused the men of Ystrad Tywi, and marched on Cydweli with a great company, as a queen on her kingdom.

The youngsters Maredudd and Rhys had been left behind. They had followed the march as far as they dared, watching their elder brothers riding down the valley. Then the women pounced on them, and they were jailed with high cries behind a fence of apron strings. Two days passed in trembling suspense before three riders returned, three men distraught with disaster. Gwenllian's army was beaten, north of Cydwely. The army was overwhelmed, and all the followers put to death. Gwenllian was slain. Maes Gwenllian they call that bloody meadow still. Morgan was slain, and Maelgwn had vanished.

A roar of pain arose such as never before nor since was heard in Caeo, but the boys were dazed, and heard nothing, for they were convulsed with horror. Anarawd opened his arms, and the others crept inside the circle of safety that he provided. All night they huddled together, staring and shivering, under the carthenni that their people brought to cover them. Rhys cried himself to sleep, and the women took him away. In the morning they shuddered, took a little hot mead and bread, and then they wept, not like children, but like men, in silence. While they were yet sore with grief, Anarawd arranged matters. The men in amazement observed the dignity and self-control of his demeanour. It was not possible to recover the bodies, so it had to suffice that the prayers for the dead were uttered in Caeo. The priest Caradoc tried to comfort them, but Anarawd stopped him.

'Let us alone,' he said. 'We know where our duty lies, when we are stronger.'

The special bitterness of a Cymric fury seethed in the South to avenge Gwenllian in countless acts of violence against the French. Amongst those who suffered was Richard FitzGilbert, heir to Gruffydd's old enemy at the castle of Aber Ystwyth.

Richard, returning from Stephen's court in Lloegr by way of the vales of the South, rode through the forests in easy disdain of the escort suggested by Brian FitzCount; with a minstrel and fiddler before him to rouse the echoes and a few attendants beside him to flatter his pride, he rode into ambush, and died.

It had been a bitter thing for the men of Deheubarth to watch the establishment in Cymru of a second generation of strangers.

'Mark these people well,' Gruffydd used to say. 'Watch their ways, and learn from their strength and from their weakness.'

They obeyed him. They discovered how the French built their strong forts, and how these could be undermined or overcome; the Cymry adapted their armour to withstand the heavy lances of their foes. Gruffydd ap Rhys and his teulu were well equipped when they rode north to Gwynedd to a welcome very different from his first reception. They found King Gruffydd ap Cynan too old for campaigning, but his sons Owain and Cadwaladr with an army came down with Gruffydd to take Ceredigion from the Dyfi shore. When they had crossed the river, news from the South reached them, and they halted awhile, perforce arrested by Gruffydd's grief.

In the morning, when speech returned to him, he reappeared, and the men of Gwynedd stared to see his grey beard and hair so streaked with white, and his strong face crumpled like an apple stored too long.

'I shall kill them and burn them throughout Ceredigion and Dyfed and Ystrad Tywi and beyond,' he said in quiet tones. 'And their women we shall make our slaves.' He looked round him at King Gruffydd's array of sons, proud in their numbers and their strength and length of limbs, and jealousy increased his grief. A wife cut down in her power and beauty, two fine sons crushed! He fought down the sobs that came rising, and turned to his penteulu.

'Send for my son Anarawd!' he commanded. 'He shall partake of my revenge and conquest. He shall earn his right to be my heir.'

Anarawd heard the summons with a light so fierce blazing in his eyes that his youngest brothers, watching, moved away from his side. But Cadell darted forward.

'Let me come with you, Anarawd!' he begged. But Anarawd shook his head.

'You must stay at home to guard the women and children. It is different for me.' His chin rose. He was the heir. 'It is not seemly for our father to be without a son to fight by his side.'

'Next year!' said Cadell enviously. 'I swear to be with you next year. Anarawd, beg my father to summon me!'

But Anarawd, with a magisterial wave, was gone.

He was present throughout that campaign of 1136 as squire to his father. They took every French fort in their path, inflicting dreadful losses. Llan Fihangel fell, and the castle of Aber Ystwyth itself. At Llan Badarn, the celibate French monks were sent packing, and the married monks of Cymru returned to their old routine of hunting and poetry, prayers, and a quiet life. Their sons crowded into Gruffydd's army; and the monks' Chronicle, like a stream hushed by frost, melted and thundered into the garrulous roar of spring, and glorified Gruffydd ap Rhys and his brothers-in-law. The castles of mid-Ceredigion fell to them one by one—De La Mare, Dineirth, and Caerwedros. All were destroyed; the victors' hands were so full of spoil that they could hold no more.

'Well, cousin, what about it?' said Prince Owain in a satisfied voice. 'It's been a good campaign—'

'Been?' echoed Gruffydd, with the wild stare that now never left his eyes. 'We have scarcely begun!'

Owain laughed indulgently, and patted his back.

'Summer grows high, Gruffydd! The men are tired of ravaging other men's crops. They want to go home to get their own harvests in! Winter will stride towards us before we can cheat its grabbing claws! No, I think we'll carry our plunder home now, and your men can do with a change as well. We'll come back for more in October, fresh for another campaign!'

Reluctantly, Gruffydd agreed, and the armies parted with goodwill. Cadwaladr, in particular, had been pleased by the expedition, and showed an eagerness to return. It had struck him that Ceredigion was desirable cattle country. Anarawd, riding behind the brooding figure of his father, watched Cadwaladr darting glances of appraisal about the countryside, and conceived a mistrust of this uncle.

Gruffydd, deaf to every shout of victory, came home to Caeo, gathered together the remnant of his family, and summoned Cadell. 'You're old enough,' he told him. 'Time for you to be your brother's lieutenant now,' and Cadell, in transports of delight, flew to his armour.

The respite that summer's end was short. The day soon came when Maredudd and Rhys tugged at the new sword that their father had bestowed on Cadell, took away his favourite knife to have it sharpened, curried his horse themselves, and watched the blacksmith forge the shoes. The smell of sun-warmed heather was on the hills as the army rode north-west at Michaelmas. Cadell followed Anarawd with his spine held stiffly, and he did not once look back at Caeo. They had a rendez-vous with their uncles at Teifi's side. The sun, the fine weather, the massive array, the loitering, snorting horses, and the savage looks of the men of Gwynedd, mingled and blurred in glancing lights above the river. Confusion thudded through Cadell's breast, and he kept close to Anarawd. There was to be a great advance down the valley to the river mouth where Constable Stephen held the castle still in great strength; this was now the last Clare stronghold in Ceredigion. The Cymry possessed substantial equipment for battle, but when Cadell asked how they proposed to take the castle, Anarawd said he supposed they would depend upon the traditional engines of war. He pointed to the primitive battering-rams in the form of hewn oaks from Ystrad Tywi, piled on the military carts. Cadell snorted contemptuously.

'Feeble!' he declared. 'Who can expect them to push down a fort as stout as this?'

'Who are you to criticize my father's dispositions?' retorted Anarawd, and Cadell subsided. His head ached as he looked around him. It had been a long, noisy day, and autumn's reverberant air carried and magnified the clamour of their preparations over the river and down to the castle, causing alarm to seize the alien garrison. Cadell had never ridden so hard nor so far across Cymru as on the previous day, but he was to say long afterwards that he remembered the ride not so much for the discomfort of his saddle sores as for the smell of excitement, the sweat of men and horses, and the drifting smoke of Saxon hovels that the soldiers fired as they moved forward. The bodies of the occupiers, put to sword by the outriders, lay where they fell. Cadell turned green; Anarawd was pale enough when he saw their condition, but he had campaigned longer. He steered Cadell aside when his younger brother's stomach turned, and shielded him from view. It was worse than Cydwely.

The battle itself was a brisk bloody business with little time for thought. Strong as the French and Saxons were, arrayed on Crug Mawr outside the castle, the Cymry were the greater force, greater by impetus as well as by numbers, greater in the energy of their cruelty. His second battle frustrated Cadell. Though tall, he was thin, and not a good mark, so he had the advantage over the massive French knights and solid Saxons, and he was quicker than all his brothers in the practice of arms. But he had no chance at Crug Mawr. He was caught in a press of Ystrad Tywi men, and they guarded him like their last gold coin; push and thrust as he might, they would not divide to let him get at the enemy, and cut his own comrades with his sword he could not. Anarawd had a better chance and fought a desperate battle. Cadell saw him kill a blond young fellow with a shrewd delivery of his blade, and at last, when a Cymro fell in front of Cadell, even he contrived to wound at least a horse. The armoured rider fell like a tree, to be despatched at once by the Cymric swordsmen.

They gained the day. The uncles, Owain and Cadwaladr, fought with a display of fierce and smiling panache that went down well with the men of Gwynedd, but did not endear them to those of the South. Gruffydd ap Rhys fought like an avenging angel, and so did all the men of Ystrad Tywi.

They failed to take the castle.

'Those battering-rams were as useless as I told you they would be,' said Cadell afterwards furiously. 'Why didn't my father use fireballs? Why didn't—'

'We did use fireballs,' growled Anarawd. 'Our uncles started using them—didn't you see? But my father stopped them. He thought his sister Nest might be inside, and his heart failed him. Damage enough was done to send the defenders and the towns-folk fleeing, anyway. Did you see them swarming on the bridge?

Many drowned in the river, pushed off by the haste of others seeking to escape.'

'What happened to the wounded?'

'There weren't many on our side, and none on theirs, that lived. I think they were taken away on some of the carts on which the men carried off all that great plunder of arms, apparel, and armour.'

The Cymry took, in addition, a vast number of slaves, mostly women, and all was divided between the men of Deheubarth and those of Gwynedd in unequal proportions. The sons of Gruffydd took this ill, and the victory celebrations were marred by disputes between Cadwaladr and Anarawd; but Gruffydd's intervention forced a compromise, and the appearance of goodwill. The uncles retired north with considerable satisfaction and the bulk of the plunder, and Gruffydd's sons were glad to see them go.

Nest, haggard and dirty, emerged from the keep of Aber Teifi castle. She surveyed the smoking town with fury, and the torn and battered courtyard with dismay. She would never forgive her brother Gruffydd! Stephen, her husband, silently counted his losses as her torrent of complaints burst forth, against Gruffydd, against himself, against King Stephen, against the Clares, and against the trembling and indignant widow of Robert FitzGilbert, to whom they had been obliged to give shelter when she fled south from Aber Ystwyth, in terror at the Cymric advance from the North. Nest had shown every kindness to the countess and little Alice, and the two small sons Gilbert and Roger. But the countess, as Stephen's late lord's widow, had taken all Nest's kindness as her due, and complained with freedom. Dislike between the Cymraes and the Frenchwoman was by now flourishing, and Nest had had enough.

'Why don't those brothers-in-law of hers come and fetch her, that Baldwin and Gilbert, who spend their time in hanging on King Stephen's sleeve?'

But Stephen shook his head, frowning.

'She would never get through without capture,' he said. 'We're beleaguered still.'

The Cymry were indeed swarming in the lower cantrefydd of Ceredigion, inspecting these regions, and helping themselves. Gruffydd gathered his army together, and spent the rest of the autumn and winter in a more regular progress throughout the gwlad, before turning south into Dyfed. They passed from one gwestfa to another, receiving sincere if rather nervous welcomes, but they did not linger long in any, partly because Gruffydd was anxious to seize and survey as much of his conquest as he could, and partly in mercy for his subjects, with whose herds of cattle the men of Gwynedd had already made too free during their passage north.

On Lady Day, the balm of spring came to Dyfed. Gruffydd, approaching the regions round Ty Ddewi, paused, pitched camp, and lay down to fight in silence his last battle. In the past months, his grief had fed his fury and the force of war; now, in the low season, a sudden illness and self-pity pounced and discovered him disarmoured, between campaigns. Anarawd and Cadell, weak with fear, watched him in misery as the fever rose, and longed for a wisewoman. Their anxious officers crowded in with remedies. Each carried a pocket full of herbs against sickness, and balm to cure wounds. Anarawd and Cadell tried them all. As the night wore on, the fever gained the victory over the body of the dying King. Once, Gruffydd sighed, and spoke.

'Pity,' he whispered. 'Pity you're not a little more experienced, Anarawd. Time for you to take the reins now. Cadell—help him.' He glanced anxiously at his eldest son. 'Be careful,' he gasped. 'And now and then—be bold!'

He lay for a full minute striving for breath, heaved one great sigh at last, and lay still. Anarawd and Cadell went on sitting there for a long time, staring at him in silence.

II

The Brothers Deheubarth

(1137—1153)

1

Anarawd was proclaimed king at once. He put on his father's crown, and went immediately into action, making at first a series of vigorous blunders by leading his men into further unnecessary attacks against the Flemings when Gruffydd, more likely, would have wisely stayed his hand. The local clergy were not displeased when Anarawd killed Letard, the Flemish little king, a man they called the enemy of God and of St. David, but the Flemings were stung to reprisals of unusual fury throughout Dyfed, and all things considered, Anarawd thought it best to lead the army back to Ystrad Tywi.

News of their father's death had sped on wings before them to Caeo, and they came home to a hush of sorrow broken only by their sisters's sobs. Anarawd greeted Gwladus and Nest with a grave dignity which they recognized at once as setting him apart and above them. Never again, thought Anarawd with secret satisfaction, could Gwladus, the commander of the household since their mother's death, subject her older brother to her rather overbearing ways.

Amid all the crowd in the hall, one silent figure stood apart, and the brothers stared at him, then brightened, and the court looked up in the hope of leaving grief at last behind.

'Bleddyn!' cried the brothers simultaneously, and Anarawd said, 'Where have you been all these years? What lord has stayed you in his court?'

Bleddyn smiled. All trace of youth had left his face, which was lined and pallid now; the bright hair was dull, the gay clothes replaced by mud-coloured garments. Could such a one tell any merry tales again? Only the authority and deliberate grace of movement, that had always compelled attention, were the same.

'Life stayed me,' he said simply, 'And then Death. I loved, I married, I begot a son, and first my wife died, then my father.'

The boys were silent, and a pang went through Anarawd.

'Tell us your story this time, Bleddyn, instead of other tales,' he said.

So for a time the court of Caeo forgot their own troubles in listening to those of the cyfarwydd from the north. For once, when he lay down at night on his couch of deerskins on a pile of pliant twigs, Anarawd's mind was filled with thoughts of another man's affairs. Sleepily he imagined the six older brothers of Bleddyn, and the married sister who had mothered her little brother and loved him well.

'As youngest son, I have had much to do,' Bleddyn had told them. 'The task of dividing the gwely fell to me.' His smile reappeared; evidently, for a time, calculation had elbowed out sorrow. 'I took the usual precaution of allotting good land with bad in every portion, lest my older brothers, choosing first, left the dregs to me.'

Nobody had been pleased with his divisions. Each brother complained that his fractions of moorland and forest and meadow were too far apart for convenience.

'But at least no one could say that his portion was too small! I was glad to take to the road again. I left them,' said Bleddyn loftily, 'Arguing and making bargains amongst themselves.'

What of his child, his son?

'He, and his interests, are safe with my sister,' said Bleddyn with complete assurance, and Anarawd marvelled at such dependence on a mere woman, until Bleddyn described her. It seemed that this lady's voice was louder, and her figure broader, than those of many another; she had enemies, but they dared not declare themselves, and the friends on whom she bestowed her hospitality, remembered its majesty. Her husband and her sons were the keenest hunters in the tref. None but they ranged so far nor so successfully; hers was the richest pot on the coast of Meirionnydd, and while she watched and declared, they sat spent and silent, taking nourishment from the sound of her voice, as dry ground from rain.

Anarawd frowned, and turned over in bed, pricked by a stray twig and uneasy thoughts. Bleddyn's story had made him consider critically the ancient Cymric customs of inheritance that he had always taken for granted. Cutting the land up into little bits, he saw, meant dividing and diluting power. The French took care to hand down their broad acres undiminished to their eldest sons. But that again bred envy amongst the youngest sons, who must struggle or sink; no wonder the Norman French went swarming abroad in such numbers over continents in search of distant realms to rule. They took their pugnacity elsewhere. In Cymru it remained between sons like a fence of swords; but men are more equal here, thought Anarawd sleepily. Except for kings, of course; it's different for us. I shall not allow my gwlad to be parcelled out between my brothers like the gwely of a gwr bonheddig; I'll make them my friends, my colleagues, and we'll win back Deheubarth together, as my father told us to, in spite of my Aunt Nest and her French husband.

Something that Bleddyn had said confirmed and fired his purpose. Someone had asked him why it was his custom to spend so much time travelling in the South, when all the northern princes would have welcomed him. His answer had lifted up the boy's heart.

'Because I love to watch greatness growing and to trump its way,' he had replied, and as he spoke, he had turned on Anarawd a clear, expectant regard, that was like the summons of a seer. It was as if a wind had arisen, blowing away discouragement and grief. The glowing embers of his hopes and his ambitions were rekindled to a steady flame. Quite suddenly, he knew that he could and would achieve them; and that was when Anarawd became a man.

Grief apart, those were times that stirred the hearts of Gruffydd's sons. The barons were divided. They looked in fear on the victors of Crug Mawr. The little company of French who still held out in the castle of Aber Teifi under Constable Stephen with the widow of Richard FitzGilbert were hedged about by Cymry, whose strength, fed by Bleddyn's power to fan rumour, daily increased to such a pitch that public opinion in Lloegr obliged King Stephen to pity the lady, and command Miles of Gloucester to effect her rescue. So he plunged across Cymru into Ceredigion, and thought himself right bold to meet no army. Indeed, the Cymry divided before him to speed his passage; they let him come, and they let him take her away, for they cared nothing for the widow, nor for Miles. It was her brother-in-law, Baldwin FitzGilbert, they were concerned to baffle, him and his light-armed knights and the five hundred archers supplied at the royal expense. The sons of Gruffydd were not, this time, going to lose their grip on the gwlad that they had bled to seize, and

Baldwin quailed in the face of the stories that met him in Brecon, of how all passes into Ceredigion and Cantref Bychan were blocked by felled trees. He blustered, and dared not go further, and waited all winter at Brecon, outstaying both the patience of Miles of Gloucester and the depth of his own purse. When both were exhausted, and his army was well soured by waiting, he beat an ignoble retreat, leaving the men of Deheubarth stronger and more formidable than they had ever been before.

Early in 1137, events in Gwynedd sent ripples into Deheubarth. It was still Lent when a lean tall man from the North arrived at Caeo with the famished look of a man who had travelled hard across mountains. He was a herald sent to announce the death of Gruffydd ap Cynan; his son Owain was now king, and there was a private message for Anarawd.

Cadell waited in jealous suspense for the outcome. He feared that Anarawd, as he waded deeper into power's stream, would become distant from him, and he had no intention of being left with dry feet on the shore. Would Anarawd turn to others for counsel? He trembled, ready to resent a snub. But when at last the conference ended, Anarawd never hesitated. He ignored the older members of the teulu, turned to Cadell, and did him the honour and justice of saying to him aloud in public, 'I want your counsel, brother.' With a light heart and with important feet, Cadell joined his King.

It seemed that Owain, who suggested another campaign in the West, wanted too a marriage alliance with Deheubarth, and offered one of his daughters to Anarawd, who was disposed to agree.

'My father and my uncle Owain used to talk of this,' said Anarawd with some elation. 'We are not really first cousins which would be odious to the Church, but we need a strong link with the North. I cannot trust Cadwaladr, but Owain has goodwill towards the house of Deheubarth, and it's he who has power. What do you say? Gwenllian came from Gwynedd too. I think I shall indeed marry this girl at once, and secure my ally in the North and beget a son as soon as God allows,' said Anarawd, speaking fast in natural haste to perpetuate his line before his enemy should strike him down, and Cadell nodded, seriously. 'I know Cadwaladr will twist a knife into my belly if he can, lest my issue should ever unite the two kingdoms,' continued Anarawd. 'Listen, Cadell. If I should die and leave a son a child, Deheubarth must pass to you, with Maredudd and Rhys to help you. My son shall wait for his inheritance.'

So the pact was made, and Cadell walked back to the hall in a glow, his claims and dignity and worth acknowledged, for Anarawd had turned to him first, before any other counsellor; Cadell was bound to him now for ever by the strongest bond of confidence received.

The uncles came south again in summer, careless and blunt. They announced their advent but the week before, by the mouth of an uncouth messenger who passed also for a herald, but looked better fitted, this time, to round up sheep. It was May. Gwynedd came south in a swarm, strong and secure, free at last of the late King Henry's hand hard upon their eastern flank. They were bringing the girl with them, Anarawd's bride. What was she like? The rumours conflicted. She is old, said one, and plain. No, no! said another; she is beautiful, but a shrew. Anarawd grew sick with apprehension, and his sisters, already resenting in advance the intrusion of a queen who would reduce their own importance, grew sulky and careless; the housekeeping suffered, the bread was sour, the floor dirty. When he scolded them, they flew into a rage.

'We have ourselves to think of!' cried Gwladus. 'We have our own dresses to make fine, our own hair to curl, our own husbands to look for! We are daughters of a king, not Anarawd's household drudges!'

Anarawd retired into his dignity, much perplexed. It was high time they were married. There was no lack of local offers for their hands, but their pride, and his shrewdness, required more important and distant alliances, and so far, he had lacked the time and opportunity to negotiate for them. Next year, he swore, after the harvest, after his next successful campaign; after his son was born—

'Oh, come on, never mind them!' said Cadell. 'It's your wedding, not theirs. Look, try this surcoat on for size.'

When they reached the meeting-place at Teifi's side, the men of the North were in high good humour, having wreaked their will upon the residue of the Ceredigion French. They had cut off the coast and ridden down from Ystrad Meurig after razing the castle there; Llan Bedr too they had destroyed and Humphrey's castle, and now they meant to oust the enemy from Caer Fyrddin. But they wanted the marriage first, to bring them luck, and to cast a respectable air over their interference in another man's domain. Owain could decently claim to order matters during his son-in-law's youth, but the excuse was thin to cover the sneers of Cadwaladr and the arrogant ease of his men-at-arms. Several times the men of the South were nearly provoked into quarrels, but Anarawd had warned them that peace must, if only for his bride's sake, at all costs be preserved. Many times, their hands itched to use their daggers, but their king's cold eye dared them do anything other than grind their teeth down to the bone.

A trumpet announced the formal meeting of the kings, and Owain greeted Anarawd with frank pleasure. He had made a good choice for his girl, he decided. He liked the arrow glance that bored a hole in his own, and the firm, no-nonsense mouth. In imagination, he saw this tall thin youth filled out with royal strength into a majestic presence. He would be more handsome than his father Gruffydd in a few years' time.

'It is my delight, Anarawd, to give to you my dear child,' he said. 'Guard her and cherish her for my sake. You will, I trust, be worthy of my gift and of this alliance.'

'You honour me, my lord,' returned Anarawd more stiffly than had been his intention; but then Cadwaladr had been twitching his tail. 'I trust I shall know how to value my wife for her sake and for my own, and as a pledge of truth and peace between us.'

He's a king all right, thought Owain grudgingly. Not, perhaps, quite so easy to mould as he had supposed. They exchanged thoughtful and measuring glances not entirely free from belligerence; and the princess of Gwynedd appeared just in time, to the sound of loud cheering from both armies, who for the first time roared as one.

She delighted the Deheubarth men. She stood before them, blushing, fair, and timid. She was too shy to meet her bridegroom's frequent glances, but there was promise of liking between them. She was about Anarawd's age, slight and delicate. Their hands met under Owain's eye, they kissed, and smiled uncertainly at each other.

'She's more sturdy than she looks, Anarawd,' said Owain, loudly and proudly, with a wink at the company. 'Fit to bear you the many strong sons that you no doubt will give her.'

Immediately they both stared at the ground, their cheeks flaming, and the two armies rocked with laughter. After that, the night proceeded better than it had begun. Peace was no longer in danger of being broken by the armies' rivalry; not even Cadwaladr could lessen men's enjoyment of the feast that followed the ceremony, and after the married pair withdrew, trembling, amid coarse and riotous laughter, geniality reigned triumphant, thanks to the bards' impartial and alternate mutual praise of Gwynedd and of Deheubarth.

Both Owain and Anarawd had set their hearts first on the capture of Caer Fyrddin, and each in his way was wise. Owain wished to plunge as far south as possible, to safeguard his gains in Ceredigion; Anarawd knew that as Lord of Ystrad Tywi he must first eliminate the French on his doorstep before he could push the men of Gwynedd out of Ceredigion. It was curious how goodwill twisted with suspicion bound each to the other at a constant but reliable tension; and how the mistrust of each grew deeper towards Cadwaladr, who grew loud and shrill in his desire for land and independent power. For a season, the three agreed; the marriage had made a mood of harmony; Anarawd and his bride rode down the valleys with shining faces in the midst of the large company; Prince Hywel, Owain's natural son, kept up the gaiety with his nimble wit; and the armies arrived at Caer Fyrddin, cheerful and confident.

Cadell was the first to set eyes on it. Impatience sent him galloping far beyond the outriders; the sun was setting; as he rode in from the north-west, gleams of gold came shining through the trees, where the sun's rays fell full tilt against the walls.

'Castell aur!' muttered Cadell, who had never seen stone walls like these before. How could such a place be taken? It loomed aloft like a tooth too deeply rooted to be drawn. Challenged and fascinated, he drew nearer to observe this strong and splendid creation of the French builders' craft. He examined the walls as closely as he dared, and marvelled at their power. He measured them with his eyes and by his pacing, and made a crude likeness on slate of how the solid building lay. He returned to the camp, and listened in horror to the engineers, who were full of plans to use their battering-rams.

'Don't let us spend our strength and effort on a useless battery against those walls!' he begged the kings. 'Let's capture it whole and unharmed!'

Loud argument followed as Cadwaladr hastened to pour scorn on this suggestion; but Anarawd thought his brother wise, and Owain, to please his daughter, agreed.

So Cadell got his wish. They starved out the French; the garrison, tired of the irritating though futile assaults, and down to their last stale fish barrel, lacked the strength and the inspiration to continue their efforts to hold the castle for a usurping king who could not pay their wages with regularity. A few weeks sufficed, for the onset of the siege had coincided with the arrival by sea and by river of their belated stores, which the Cymry immediately diverted to the use of their own commissariat. The garrison, mixed French and Flemish with a few locally imprest Cymry under a French commander, yielded themselves prisoners, so were not put to the sword. In the sultry heat of late summer, it was weather for fever in a crowded and unwholesome camp, and tempers were inclined to be short on every side.

King Owain and Cadwaladr, having gained their point, were not disposed to argue overlong when Anarawd stood foursquare against his uncles and announced, that Caer Fyrddin castle was to be under the command of Cadell.

'What, a lad of sixteen?' said Cadwaladr sarcastically. Prince Hywel ab Owain laughed. It was hard for Cadell to keep silence, and the easy blushes stained his face and neck for several minutes before giving way to the pallor of rage.

'My brother is shrewd for his years!' retorted Anarawd. 'He is stouter-hearted than many a seasoned soldier, and his will is stubborn. Within my domain I trust no one better than him with what is mine!'

Cadell was too angry to accept the meaning of these glorious words. It was later, in tranquillity, that they brought him joy. Hywel laughed again, and this time he patted his young cousin's shoulder with a condescension more deeply insulting than words. Clearly he meant no harm to Cadell, but his light touch at the time sent a violent spasm through the boy's whole body; slender though he was, his fist sent Hywel sprawling to the ground. The ensuring uproar between their followers was quelled by the victim, who picked himself up, shaking with laughter.

Cadell stared at him. This man could laugh not only at others, but at himself as well! This fact surprised him so much that he forgot his own feelings, and tried to understand Hywel's. His first instinct was to despise his cousin's refusal to continue the argument, but when he found the two armies beginning to laugh with Hywel, and against himself, another blush rose up within him, but this time it was a flag of shame.

'Uncle Cadwaladr, let him guard Caer Fyrddin castle!' begged Hywel. 'Here is the most ferocious custodian we could find!'

There was affection in his chuckle; Cadell found it irresistible; and he could not resent it when Hywel gave him a comrade's grasp on his arm. Despite himself, Cadell warmed to him, and he thought obscurely, as he was to think in later years, that if it were not for the conflict of interest between them, they could have been true friends. A bard was Hywel, and a great lover, in the estimation of the courts of Cymru, less perhaps by reason of his conquests than by the measure of the passion of his verse. The lords of Meirionnydd did take care, however, to lock up their daughters when Hywel came to stay. He was a tall, thin fellow, with ardent eyes that seemed to absorb rather than to penetrate. It was disconcerting to find that they could also sharpen to a powerful amusement.

So Cadell was left, with the eldest son of Geraint, to guard Caer Fyrddin. Anarawd and the northern princes once more turned their strength against Aber Teifi.

Nest, in a lull when the Cymry's backs were turned, had left Aber Teifi. Her husband Stephen had feared for her safety as she travelled south towards Ty Ddewi, but he could not dissuade her from her purpose. Had he ever had that power? he reflected wryly. They were happily, though not equally, matched. Henry alone, himself mastered by the greater passion for power, had ever been able truly to dominate this woman to whom Stephen was enslaved.

'Oh, I shall take no harm!' she had told him lightly. 'I am free to come and go in Cymru. My nephews, for love of their father, will never offend my person!'

She waited until she saw Aber Teifi castle well stocked for winter by the sister ship of the one seized at Caer Fyrddin; she saw to the disposal of the stores, instructed her women and the cooks, scolded Robert in advance against inevitable mischief in her absence, donned her most sombre yet most costly gown, and rode away, well furred, with a modest escort and a sense of freedom.

Her moments alone were rare and precious; even these were clouded by the warring emotions that so often assailed her. I am facing both ways, she thought wearily. I am like the old god, like the first month of the year. Not only do I stand staring between past and future, life and death, but also I have roots in two races, and they pull me apart. I want my own people, from whom I came, to prevail; yet I long for my sons to surge forward, at any cost to Cymru.

Only one hope of peace remained to her, and she might find it, she thought, on pilgrimage to Ty Ddewi. She would not be able to rest until she had had masses said there to her brother Gruffydd's memory. Then, she felt her heart could open undisturbed to the glory of God the Father, who had made her, God the Son, who had saved and pitied her; and God the Holy Ghost, who would show her what to do.

Her practical mind noted that this would also be an opportunity to make useful contacts with the clergy on behalf of her son David, that cheerful and sociable young canon, who had few cares in life other than to provide for his own comfort. He was a greater anxiety to Nest than any of her other children; and it infuriated her that he had recently contracted what he blandly described as a marriage 'in the tradition of the Celtic Church'. His disgusted brothers gave it a more vulgar appellation. They had counted on getting him ensconced in the Church, in a way to be Bishop one day; there was no land to spare for his support, and episcopal authority within the family would increase their own power.

Bishop Bernard was ageing; his innumerable journeys to Rheims, Westminster, Winchester, Canterbury, and Rome, were exhausting him; his endless activity as courtier, ecclesiastic, and protagonist of the primacy of St. David's were telling on his health, and he could not last much longer. Already people were beginning to look around them for his successor; in these days when the English crown's influence on the farthest edge of Cymru was slight, the canons were intent on regaining much of their old importance, and Nest, setting her mouth into determined lines, spurred her horse forward. She intended to bring her son to reason, and the canons to a sense of what was due to a grandson of Rhys ap Tewdr.

The Cymry failed to wrest Aber Teifi from Stephen. It was well-provisioned, and held by a stout garrison. Also the auxiliary castle at Cemais on the opposite shore of the estuary was in the enemy hands of FitzMartin, and both were well placed to get undisturbed aid from the sea. Autumn was dark and stormy, and the armies retired. Anarawd took his bride home to Caeo; she was with child, and joy made him careless of his uncles. Behind his back, Owain and Cadwaladr divided Ceredigion between them, deriving their rights from their planted swords. As the nephew was young, so the uncles were careless of law. Cadwaladr's portion ranged from Aeron to Dyfi; it marched with his lands in Meirionnydd, and at last his nostrils curled in contentment above the flattering bouquet of achievement. Owain gave southern Ceredigion to Hywel, who promptly rebuilt a burnt-out castle put up by one Humphrey, one of Gilbert's men, upon the south-east frontier, and renamed it Castell Hywel.

Cadell erupted when he heard this, but when he dared to speak his mind in front of his sister-in-law, Anarawd took him aside.

'Now, brother Cadell,' he said, so coldly that Cadell blinked. 'Let us understand each other. I forbid you to discuss this matter in my wife's presence. You shall not add to her fears. Childbirth is ordeal enough for a woman to face, but as it is, she lives also in dread for the day that we give battle to her father. We will suffer these discourtesies until we are older and stronger. It is better for Ceredigion to be governed by Cymry, though they be for a season men of Gwynedd, than to be ground by the French. Now, we have a duty to our younger brothers. I shall govern Maredudd. See you to Rhys. When we are mighty, we shall recover our own. Meanwhile, we have all to do here. Let us consolidate ourselves in Ystrad Tywi, and act with our uncles and cousin as we may in Ceredigion. They think they use us; let us rather use them, until our moment comes.'

So, they disposed their minds to learn patience, like Gruffydd their father before them, and like him, they found it hard. For a time they turned their attention inwards to their neglected domestic affairs. There were flocks to rear and mouths to feed and royal dues awaiting collection by the treasurer of the king of Deheubarth, and within Anarawd's shrunken and split-across domain, the penteulu did his best. The mayors of every maerdref throughout the cwmmwdau exercised their authority in brisk review amongst the uchelwyr and the boneddigion, the free gentlemen of Ystrad Tywi, and in so far as they could organize control free from the bleeding lance of French power, with gradual haste they erected Anarawd's fragile yet articulate dominion, light but living, as tender yet strong as the child in his young bride's womb.

2

Because the men of Ceredigion were restless under their alien hands, Hywel and Cadwaladr were loud in their public claims to friendship with the sons of Gruffydd, of whose Ceredigion lands they now pretended to be the guardians. They agreed with Anarawd that sea power was the key to Aber Teifi, and when the next campaigning season opened in the early summer of 1138, another pact was made. They chose their moment well, when Lloegr was rent afresh by the quarrels of the partisans of Matilda and Stephen.

'The south-west gales have passed,' said Anarawd. 'The heavy seas have abated in Ceredigion Bay, and the wind has changed to the right quarter. The French are in turmoil. We shall accept my uncle's invitation. We shall go on a joint foraging expedition to Iwerddon in search of naval aid.'

There was a new light in his eyes. He was in exalted mood; his son Einion had been born but the week before. Owain greeted the news with pleasure, and all went smoothly. Anarawd had warned Cadell to keep his temper, and he contrived, though with difficulty, to obey. He began to feel that in all but a few contacts with other people he seemed destined either to give offence, or to take it. He excelled at the chase; when their Irish hosts invited the Cymry to join them in their favourite sport, Cadell gave no joy to the men of Gwynedd, for he was the fleetest hunter of any in the field, and every time outstripped his cousins. Cadwaladr's looks were black, and even Hywel's geniality diminished, but Anarawd's tact prevented quarrels.

They stayed some weeks at the court of the Norse king of Dublin while the ships and crews were bargained for and prepared. The Norsemen had a kindly regard for Gruffydd's memory as well as for the sons and grandsons of Cynan, and a general desire to help their kin across the water without too close an enquiry as to where authority lay between them within the several kingdoms. Also they liked the colour of their gold. In the harbours of Dublin, Wexford, and Waterford, the old Norse appetite for plunder grew strong. Cadell could not help thinking that it was like leading a foreign invasion into their own country.

'The French are the foe, true enough,' he said. 'But I find these Norsemen more savage and unfamiliar! With the French we seem to be more closely linked in death and love and hate and marriage, than with these others. Why, at home we spit in their eyes daily!' But Anarawd only laughed.

It was the first time that they had been overseas, in a foreign land, and it was strange to hear all men around them speak another tongue. Cadell picked up some words referring to their business, just as he used to collect mincing foreign words at home from stray French prisoners, wandering bards, and Flemish merchants. They all sank steadily into his mind, and stuck. When he repeated them, Anarawd laughed. He loved laughing. His personality was expanding; since his son's birth, he leaned on life with confidence. Cadell looked at him with surprise.

'Does it not still seize you?' he asked him. 'The savage purpose that possessed us when our father died?'

Anarawd gave him an indulgent smile that seemed to part his manhood from his brother's youth with a cool hand.

'It is always with me,' he said. 'But a cheerful spirit sheds a light on problems too. Look around you and take your ease now in this interval of peace. Wipe off that scowl, and give Our Lord the courtesy of laughter!'

But Cadell could not emulate Anarawd's easy enjoyment of the society of all men and women, young and old, of both high degree and low. Perhaps, he thought dourly, it is a kingly quality with which I am not endowed. It is just as well. No doubt I shall serve my brother better without it.

Fifteen ships and a fine company of men set Anarawd's hopes high as they sailed to Aber Teifi after midsummer, but Cadell was anxious. These men from Iwerddon were after all mere hireling wolves, out for quick victory and loot at least expense of blood. Desperation lit a flame in the Cymry as they attacked, with the Norsemen shouting and hurling their savage brands upon the keep. Nobody wondered, this time, whether Nest was in residence or not; by this time, they did not care.

The castle resisted the first assault by burning and battery, for the French had built well of earth and stone and timber intermixed, and their arrows came stabbing down between the buckets of boiling oil with such steadiness and accuracy that the Norsemen, all fighting show and yells, gave ground with speed. The human tide retreated steadily from the base of the castle walls, muttering angrily amongst themselves, ignoring encouragement, reproaches, and flattery alike. Even Hywel's honeyed promises failed to stir their rapacity, and they swore that they would not waste their energy and time and blood on a fortress impregnable without these modern mangonels and catapults. Deaf to the curses of the Cymry, the Norsemen took to their boats, and made off down the silver estuary, as the mists of a wet day drying rose to speed the setting sun. As Anarawd and Cadell watched them go, their powerless disgust grew loud, for the Dublin men were making straight for Robert FitzMartin's abbey of St. Dogmael's on the other side of Teifi, where consecrated gold and silver gave them hope of more painless plunder to take home for their greed and glory.

They parted from the men of Gwynedd with the looks and words of discontent and recrimination that follow every unsuccessful joint enterprise, but proceeded to no open breach with them.

'After all, your wife links us with them, whether we like it or not, I suppose,' said Cadell sulkily as they turned to go. 'She is my sister now as well as cousin, and I like her very well, but—'

Anarawd glared at him, and Cadell did not finish his sentence. He wished this marriage did not bind them so closely to the North. He was silent as he rode home beside his brother. He was trying to remember the names of some of the Powys girls he had lately been listening for. He wondered whether, by his marriage to one of these, they might acquire some counterpoise against their Uncle Owain's unacknowledged dominion over them. There was a Lady Gwenllian, and this was the name that pleased him best, as it also had his father. But she was still a little girl, and much too young for him. They rode home to Caeo in silence and sullen spirits, with clouds of unshed rain casting their shadows across the length and breadth of Ystrad Tywi.

In the following years, Anarawd carried out his purpose of establishing firmer control over his borders east and south of Tywi. Opportunities arose on every side as the mighty internecine conflict in Lloegr diverted the attention of one after another of his French neighbours. Anarawd kept Cadell and the teulu busy with assault and capture of strong points, manors and castles. They grew watchful and shrewd and swift to wring the neck of weak authority, and mile by mile his dominion was in large part delivered; the sons of Gruffydd were lords again of Drysllwyn, and at Dinefwr, Anarawd kept his court as king.

Anarawd allowed all his brothers, however young, to sit in his council's deliberations. In his alert and easy style, he set about the government of his lands with the flexibility and opportunism that had to shape his every project in such swiftly changing times. Maredudd watched and listened with undivided attention and such shrewd asides that Anarawd determined to train this brother up for civil government. It was on Cadell that he relied for first advice on matters of policy beyond the boundaries, and in war, he did nothing until he knew that Cadell and he were of one mind. Cadell held all military matters in his grasp under Anarawd. It was he who ordered the repair of every stronghold in Ystrad Tywi by the several castellans; the old motte and bailey erections of stout but perishable timber were falling out of fashion in favour of stone buildings, and Caer Fyrddin was his special care. His squire was Rhys, whose mischief often maddened him, but Cadell asked no better pupil in archery and swordsmanship. Maredudd strove with less success in military accomplishments, although he squeezed his strength until Cadell pitied him. He grew too tall too soon, and was languid; like Cadell he longed for Caeo's freshness, and he welcomed every spring's campaigns as much for the pleasure of ranging abroad as for the keen joy of pushing the frontiers ever eastward, or westward nearer Ceredigion. Maredudd and Rhys had never been there. Teifi was Jordan to them, and Ceredigion their promised land. They went about their business with the discontented hearts of the half-successful whose minds were elsewhere.

Over in Lloegr, as war screamed more loudly still, Stephen's fortunes began to crack and those of imperial Matilda to flourish; the Deheubarth brothers watched with care for the effect on Cymru. One day in early March, when they were on cylch in Caeo, on the judicial circuit, a visit from Bleddyn brought them news of their uncle Cadwaladr.

They loved going to Caeo. Anarawd's visit there was overdue, and an early spring beckoned men and women out to explore a world renewed by winter. The court set out on horseback, with a minimum of men-at-arms. The day was clear and crisp, with the dragon-snap of twigs loud on the track. Dull winter rolled back behind them, and they rode up Ystrad Tywi with almost the careless joy of a holy day pilgrimage.

They were away from Dinefwr for three untroubled, windless days. A blue sky imposed its peace upon the earth; hunting, not war, beckoned them through the aromatic woods; and they broke their fast each morning on the hillside grasses under a warm sun. As they passed through the trefydd, the people came running to see them with every expression of pleasure, and complaints were few, for their barns were still reasonably full. Idly Cadell witnessed Anarawd dispensing justice in the courthouses, with Maredudd registering his decrees, and the maer or rhingyll introducing every suppliant for his king's intervention. The halls were crowded, for each party tried to bring with him kin of every degree to the ninth as his supporters; and for Cadell the memory of each bright morning was plunged below the litigation of a stuffy afternoon. For a time he contrived to keep awake, but he was dismayed by the petty quarrels of the common folk. The disputed ownership of two feet of land was enough to disrupt a whole teulu and set an entire cantref in a roar. Revenge and envy, he decided sleepily, are ignoble emotions, except on the grandest scale, permissible only in kings. He listened with perfunctory attention, for he had little patience with the details of the administration of justice. They trip up the knees of princes, he thought with exasperation. A ruler lulled by quietness into a false security can easily allow the arts of peace and government to ramify and occupy his mind beyond a strict regard for basic needs.

Bleddyn's news, he felt, came as an abrupt corrective.

'Cadwaladr?' said Anarawd, with a curling lip. They had begun to forget about him. Indeed, their suspicion of him had sagged into something like contempt. 'From what court do you come, and what is this news?'

'King Madog of Powys was my amiable host over Christmas,' said Bleddyn. 'But the court was up and away in mid-January. Madog led his troops to meet those of Cadwaladr and of Earl Ranulf of Chester, tyrant of the North, the man who seized Lincoln castle not so long ago. Ranulf came hot-foot from Lincoln to secure their help against the citizens, who have begged King Stephen to drive out the Earl.'

'Earl Ranulf?' said Anarawd, frowning. 'What's the link there, then? And why?'

Bleddyn smiled drily.

'Oh, they are all in each other's pockets, now,' he said. 'As you know, your aunt Susannah, daughter of Gruffydd ap Cynan, is not only Cadwaladr's sister, but also King Madog's wife. And Cadwaladr is not only King Madog's brother-in-law, but also husband to Earl Ranulf's niece.'

'His niece's husband!' exclaimed Anarawd with a snort of contempt. 'What niece is this?'

Bleddyn replied, significantly, 'Alice of Clare.'

Maredudd gasped with sudden fury.

'That is the daughter of Richard FitzGilbert who once held Ceredigion! Her uncle Gilbert is the one who wheedled the earldom of Pembroke out of Stephen but who dares not come into Cymru to claim it amongst all the loyal supporters of Matilda!'

Anarawd said acidly, 'Cadwaladr tries to act the ruling prince, it seems, and by this alliance seeks to strengthen his claim to Ceredigion! Two wrongs righted, presumably, by matching usurper with foe!'

'Treacherous dog!' uttered Cadell, trembling with rage. He spat furiously into the fire.

Anarawd said coldly, 'By how many acres do these gestures enlarge his lands in north Ceredigion? That is what matters to us.'

None could declare to him, and he, too, spat into the fire, but ceremonially.

'Cadwaladr is still beyond Aeron,' he said. 'Let's keep our heads clear. It is Hywel's entrenched position as our neighbour that we should first resent.'

So he banked down their fire with the ash of contempt, but underneath, it continued to smoulder, and to feed on the news from the East. At the battle of Lincoln, King Stephen was imprisoned after a victory in which men praised the prowess of Cadwaladr, and of Nest's son Robert, Earl of Gloucester; at Dinefwr, the court heard of this in jealous silence. Matilda had it all her own way now, they learned; Oxford yielded to her armies, Bishop Henry of Winchester, Stephen's own brother, came over to the winning side, London submitted, and with the South and West behind her, Matilda was formally hailed as Lady of the English.

Anarawd reconsidered his position, as her French supporters in Cymru rejoiced. These had been reconciled to Gilbert, the new Earl of Pembroke, who prudently abandoned Stephen's cause in time to cut a dash at the battle of Lincoln for Matilda.

Too many cheerful foes lay round about Deheubarth; the brothers had not finished rebuilding their castles, vast numbers of new weapons were needed, and they brooded on the difficulty of dividing the costs of attack and defence.

At last Anarawd decided on a policy requiring less outlay of gold. He decided to marry off his sister Gwladus to Caradog ab Iestyn, lord of Morgannwg. He was the son of Iestyn ap Gwrgant, who lost his broad Glamorgan lands to a bastard of the first Henry. Iestyn, wounded and exhausted, found shelter for his old age in the secluded priory of Llangennydd down in Gwyr, but his son Caradoc had fought back hard to win again all the little hills and valleys that ran between the Nedd and Afan, a useful rampart to Deheubarth to the south and east.

But would she have him?

'How can I tell before I have set eyes on him?' she demanded, determined to exact her last ounce of authority. 'And here is Lent already upon us! What bride clothes can be prepared in six weeks? I'll have to summon all the sewing-women of Ystrad Tywi! No one shall say that a Princess of Deheubarth goes forth from Dinefwr a shabby bride!'

Anarawd sighed as she pattered upstairs to her chamber.

'Talk of bride clothes is a good omen, I suppose.' he muttered anxiously. 'But will she have him? That's the point!'

Cadell was in no doubt.

'She'll take the first honest lord who comes asking,' he declared. 'And she has chests full of bride clothes spun already against the day. So has our sister Nest!'

Weeks of ordered confusion followed while Gwladus and her concerns took precedence over far more weighty matters. But would she take the bridegroom? She kept Anarawd on tenter-hooks to the end. She was, after all, a careful student, like her mother before her, of women's rights under the laws of Hywel Dda, and made the most of her knowledge.

Easter brought Caradog ab Iestyn to Dinefwr, bathed, brushed, and eager, in his finest apparel. True, he was no longer young, but he had a blunt straight stare announcing honesty and purpose if not a mighty understanding. Anxiously the brothers watched Gwladus inspecting him between the carthenni that guarded the privacy of the ladies' quarters.

'I am willing,' she said at last, and they sighed. She added, with her customary candour, 'I have been young a long time now, and have waited enough for an alliance to suit your pride.'

It was true. Every fresh campaigning season lessened her hopes of a husband from amongst the Ystrad Tywi nobles, for the summer killings were heavy, and Anarawd would entertain no Frenchman's offer for her hand.

'We shall do well enough,' she said, and twitched the skirt of her gown, smoothed her banded hair, and advancing with grace into the hall, she smiled at the bridegroom. She reminded herself, no doubt, that her husband could not beat her unless she betrayed him, and that if the worst came to the worst, she would, like any free boneddiges of the hills, at least be mistress of half the household goods and bedclothes, an axe, a hedge-bill, a ploughshare, all her own clothes, and all the cats but one. At the betrothal, she offered a jewel to Anarawd in payment of the bride's customary marriage fee to her lord; he took it from her with a confusion from which she was entirely free, and returned it to her.

They celebrated the nuptials at Dinefwr with all the pomp of peace. Anarawd played the king right well, and sent the bridal pair away up the valley with an escort of armed men. They watched with satisfaction their sister's cheerful progress on her horse as long as they could see the kerchief waving in her hand.

Cadell thought that Anarawd's wife, with whom she had occasionally bickered, would not be sorry to see the last of her. But to his surprise, when he looked at her, she was crying. Strangely enough, the brothers felt a certain bleakness, too. Only their sister Nest looked pleased, and preened herself.

'She's the only princess left at home,' said Cadell. 'I suppose it will have to be her turn next. What about a Powys bridegroom?'

But Anarawd was not so sure.

'Madog is hand in glove with Cadwaladr at the moment,' he said. 'Wait for the wind to blow from another direction.'

In the end, a little man with blazing eyes and a deep voice came riding in from the East to claim her, and her brothers were satisfied. Ifor ap Meurig was a thorn in the side of the French, firmly planted just beyond their reach. On sufferance, therefore, he stayed lord of the hills of Senghennydd between

Rhymney and Taff. He was well placed to dole out occasional retribution. The brothers found him a good fellow with many a tall tale to tell. Dinefwr rang with gales of laughter.

'Ifor Bach?' said Nest with a snort, when she was summoned into the hall, and her sister-in-law was silly enough to titter. But when Nest, who was well-grown, sailed into his presence, and cast her rather scornful gaze at him, and received the full impact of his admiration, she blushed vividly, curtsied lower than was her custom, and for the rest of the evening took care not to stand in his presence more than was necessary. The wedding, which took place a few days later, went off well, though all deplored the bride's determined stoop.

These alliances, and the strength of their castle at Carreg Cennen, gave them such security to the East that Anarawd felt better inclined to allow Cadell to spend a bit more on stonemasons' wages for further work on Caer Fyrddin. These men were hard to find, but Cadell ferreted them out; he had found some who worked on the castle with King Henry, and certain others amongst the mountain people who displayed an age-old, inbred talent for working in stone.

As for Anarawd, his first concern was for his people, for the men he led in battle, and for their families. In summer he moved his armies about the hills with care for the crops and the herds of cattle; in autumn he caused a tally to be made of the places where the harvest had failed, diverted a portion of his own to their use, and pardoned their taxes, for the weather in these years was poor, with deep frost in winter, long days of rain in summer, and but a few fine days of sunshine in autumn and spring, when men hastened to sow, without much hope, a few acres of poor oats and barley. But the forests flourished in such weather, and Anarawd's heart rejoiced as he cantered through the heart of Cantref Mawr and Ystrad Tywi, with only his sword and a scanty retinue; he was intent upon government, and he loved the views of his great woods and his fertile pasture land.

But his habits were too well known, and treachery leapt without sound. Anarawd, abroad one day riding near to Ceredigion's border, met a large company of men-at-arms, hunting. When challenged, they were Cadwaladr's men, they said, boldly. Their master was visiting Hywel, and they meanwhile were enjoying good sport, and had pricked off several deer. It was a clear case of trespass, for they were across the border on Ystrad Tywi soil, and Anarawd told them so in round terms to which they were not slow to take exception, and they called him various unkingly names. Fighting began, provoked by deliberate ugly words out of the mouth of a Gwynedd man, and he and his companions were seen of set design to plunge their knives into Anarawd's body. His small train was slain, but one wounded man escaped, and was at last brought back to Cadell.

As thunder is slow to follow a flash of lightning that strikes far away, the brothers were slow to feel anguish. They stood in a circle about the messenger to stare into his eyes, but he had been blinded, and there was no further message in them.

3

Cadell was twenty-one on that dark day in 1143 when they called him king. Sorrow so stultified him that he sat all night beside his brother's body, scarcely knowing where he was. Only Maredudd, thinking clearly and coldly, at last roused him when he urged him to moderate his thoughts of vengeance.

'I speak from no coward's heart, you know that, Cadell,' he said. 'Now listen. Owain Gwynedd has been greatly injured too. His daughter has been widowed by his own brother's crime. Hold your revenge while the North turns in its own turmoil. Anarawd always counselled us to wait while our enemies confounded themselves, and this murder becomes a sacrifice to our own enlargement if you hold your hand now. It welds the whole of Deheubarth, north and south of Teifi, into one people, outraged by the slaughter of their king. Besides, the French are still weak, still torn between Matilda and Stephen. Why should we start our own civil war in Cymru to give them yet another chance to strut into our lands?'

Bitterly Cadell swallowed this advice, hearing Maredudd out as though he were old and venerable. There was a long silence. At last,

'Esteem for you comes from one of my years on a grudging shuffle,' he remarked stiffly. 'But it is your due.'

So Cadell held his hand and nothing more was said about revenge. The men of Deheubarth made great mourning for their king, and gave him stately burial. Then Cadell very firmly placed the golden circle on his head amid the roars of every man's approval, and turned his mind to the task of making Anarawd's kingdom more suspicious, more secure, and kept the gwlad clear of French from the uplands in the east of Cantref Mawr to west across Dyfed.

Then another grief beset them. Anarawd's widow died of grief and weakness, leaving Einion to be mothered by every woman in the court, until Cadell put his foot down; he was not going to have Anarawd's boy brought up soft.

'I'll foster him with one of Geraint's sons to harden him—and us,' said Cadell, but his lips quivered. The court of Dinefwr enquired after Einion's welfare anxiously and often, for the first month of his absence; then other matters engaged their attention. The brothers Deheubarth, all three, paid him regular visits for six months. Then, Cadell had no time; and winter struck, when Maredudd was, as usual, laid low; but Rhys went to see him, all through the rough weather. Rhys became his friend.

Maredudd betrayed no more than modest satisfaction when events proved him a true prophet. King Owain sent his son Hywel to avenge the crime. Hywel marched across Aeron with half his men, burned Cadwaladr's castle at Aber Ystwyth, and beat down his uncle's company to their knees with massive slaughter, so that the river's stench poisoned all the valley's air. Cadwaladr fled by sea, and for months there was silence. But Hywel was still too strong for the men of Deheubarth to master, so must pass for their friend. They were poised between enemies on a double front, for the French were moving once more. Next year, they were almost indifferent when news came sounding down from Gwynedd that Cadwaladr, having found a fleet in Dublin, had landed in might at Aber Menai to compel his brother to reinstate him in his lands. Owain, whose anger had died into grief, was in no mood to continue the quarrel, and gave in. This sudden peace deprived the Dublin Norsemen of their promised plunder of war, and since there was no gold to be got in lieu out of Cadwaladr, the shore hamlets suffered a savage battery of blood and fire before the fleet retired empty-handed save for a few screaming women of Môn.

Throughout the South, the reins of power were changing hands. Hugh Mortimer's recovery in 1144 of the valley lands of Elfael and Maeliennydd in Central Cymru disturbed Cadell. So did the arrival of a new lord in Brycheiniog; young Roger succeeded his father Miles of Gloucester when the latter was slain by a stray arrow during a New Forest hunt. As Mortimer kept hand-in-glove, when it suited him, with the new lord of Brycheiniog, the French had indeed thrust a fresh pair of fists between Deheubarth and Powys. Then, two years later, another man came west to try a throw against the Cymry. This was Gilbert FitzGilbert, bold enough at last to venture amongst the supporters of Matilda in Dyfed. But Matilda was losing both popularity and strength in Lloegr. After provoking the Londoners into rising against her, and enduring an uncomfortable and hungry midwinter siege at Oxford at Stephen's hands, from which she did at last escape by stealth in white garments over the snow-covered ground, she was now pushed hard to the West, pent up in Bristol, or Gloucester, or Cardiff, as her faithful brother Robert or her own humour directed. Her councils were now but thinly attended, as one after another of her barons was forced on the defensive against Stephen. Gilbert, reading the signs aright, had prudently withdrawn his presence.

'Where has the fellow gone?' demanded Robert irritably of his brother Henry FitzHenry.

'He's frightened of Stephen's advance!' said Henry. 'He told me he was going west to the earldom he winkled out of Stephen himself. He said he was going to raise more troops, and give cheer to Matilda's supporters in Dyfed!'

'Double-faced, impudent coward!' said Robert hotly. 'May the Cymry give him what he deserves!'

'You wait, he'll be a bully on his own ground,' said Henry. 'Mother Nest can't stand the sound of his name. The Constable will have to do as Gilbert tells him, like it or lump it, but Mother is a free agent, as ever. I wouldn't put it past her to drop a few hints to our Deheubarth cousins, bidding them stir up against him!' He had dropped into Cymric, as was his habit when roused. Robert understood, but did not speak, his mother's tongue.

'I hope she does!' he answered shortly, in French. 'If they steer clear of Glamorgan, I don't care how much damage they do to Gilbert's lands!'

He sat down, exhausted, tired suddenly of this interminable war in which the enemy was more reliable than the allies.

'You need rest,' said Henry. 'If you collapse, it will be all up with poor Matilda. You're the lynch-pin of her camp.'

Robert said nothing. He was not well. He prayed to live long enough for young Henry of Anjou to take over in full strength as his mother's champion, or his own.

The Lady Nest did indeed send warning messages to her nephew Cadell, which he received at first with amazed distrust, though they came by Bleddyn, and were therefore genuine.

'She has a heart for you still, Lord Cadell!' said Bleddyn, doing his utmost to make peace between the courts that he loved best. Cadell, sour and rather hardened after two bitter years of kingship, considered that his aunt's heart was too divided to be of much esteem. But it was no trap. Even as Bleddyn delivered the message at Dinefwr, Earl Gilbert was silently seizing Caer Fyrddin by surprise, scattering the stone-masons that Cadell had so patiently assembled. Before Cadell could give full vent to his particular shame and fury, Gilbert had roughly strengthened it yet further, and cut across country to Dinwileir near Pencader in Mabudryd cwmmwd, and thrown up a castle there as well; but that was all the rope that Cadell allowed him.

Maredudd now at sixteen was putting on muscle at last; his lean frame acquired greater resistance. As for Rhys, he was going to be a big man of short stature, broad but difficult to push over in the heat of battle. They knew how to put heart into their men; they were captains that Cadell could use, and here was a chance to try their mettle.

They attacked the new castle, took it by storm, and slew the garrison. Well did the younger brothers play their part; fame of the action flew swiftly afar, and brought Cadell an unexpected proposal from Hywel ab Owain. Hywel was worried by Gilbert's activities and alarmed at his pretensions to Ceredigion, and offered his assistance free of all conditions to help Cadell to win back Caer Fyrddin.

'Cousin Hywel!' said Cadell, stared at the messenger, and laughed. 'It's a long time since I pushed him over!' He considered, smiling, for a moment, then clapped his hands. 'Done!' he said, and the man retired north, satisfied.

It was a merry campaign, with Hywel's wit to spur them on. They showed Gilbert the value of his building work at Caer Fyrddin. They laid siege to the castle, and gave the impression that they meant to starve the defenders out. But Cadell was in a hurry, and saw no call to exercise his patience beyond a week of cat and mouse. He and Hywel tackled the walls on a Wednesday with hooked ropes in the last hour of dark when sleep was most profound in the weary and drew a wing across the watcher too; they and their men swarmed up in force before the French had time to loose their second round of arrows. Cymric losses were few; Gilbert was wounded but was smuggled away somehow out of sight into darkness; and the rest of the defenders were put to the sword, as the harvest was bad and the rations too short that year for a show of mercy. Then they left Maredudd in charge with a few seasoned campaigners, and continued downriver swiftly to Llan Stephan, eager to make the most of their strength and the enemy's dismay.

'What happened to Gilbert, though?' wondered Rhys, as they wiped their swords for the second time in a week.

'Gone screaming to his fellows,' said Cadell contemptuously. 'Watch out for punishment!'

It came. The anxious French rallied about in Dyfed under the sons of Nest, William and Maurice FitzGerald, with their friend William FitzHay. They stirred up the Flemish burghers, and made a mass attack on Caer Fyrddin before Cadell and Hywel could reach it to succour Maredudd. But they need not have worried. Maredudd and his men, prowling about inside Caer

Fyrddin castle, had pounced gleefully on a good supply of building timber; when the French attacked, Maredudd and his men took quiet delight in watching their tall opponents climb half-way up their wooden ladders. Then, with the longest timbers they could find, they gently pushed the ladders over, and counted the bodies as they fell off into the fosse below.

'I think we've mastered eastern Dyfed, cousin,' said Hywel heartily, and Cadell, with some complacency, agreed.

He allowed his men one short season for celebration over the Twelve Days of Christmas, 1146. They were merry, as befitted the birthday of Our Lord, but it was the short, loud mirth of marching men, and their New Year readiness to spring to arms pleased him. He and Hywel had made so good a showing in the last campaign that William FitzGerald, at least, was at pains to cultivate a more gentle acquaintance with them. Prodded by his mother, he called Cadell cousin, and when the spring days lengthened, even begged his aid in some trifling quarrel that he had with one Walter FitzWizo, Lord of Aberdaugleddau.

Maredudd laughed.

'Here's a sign of the times!' he said. 'He can see your star rising, Cadell. He thinks it wise to claim his kinship!'

William was not alone in these ideas, and the fall of Walter's Castell Gwis, the work of the brothers Deheubarth, with a hand from Hywel, who was enjoying himself, was further guarantee of their predominance in Dyfed. Gilbert, they heard, was on his deathbed, leaving a young sprig behind him, Richard Strongbow, heir to lower Gwent as well as Penfro and Ceredigion, for his uncle Walter had died without sons. It's all one to me who has lower Gwent, thought Cadell, his mind on Ceredigion.

But no one mentioned Ceredigion. Cadell gave Hywel a proper share of the season's spoils, and they parted at Easter in cheerful mood. The cousins shook hands strongly, then each with a shrewd smile turned away, supposing that he understood the other better than he himself was known.

Cadell went home to Dinefwr, after necessary business at Caer Fyrddin. Hywel, with energy still unexpended, turned north, and before Whitsun was driving his uncle Cadwaladr hard in the mountains. He attacked Meirionnydd from the south while his half-brother Cynan ab Owain marched down from Gwynedd. They cornered their quarry and drove him out;

Cadwaladr, a dwindling candle, fled with his agitated family by sea to his remnant, the northern half of Ceredigion. Cadell, once so hot for revenge on his uncle, heard the news without emotion. He was King of Deheubarth; power had returned to him at last; and he had other cares.

Robert FitzHenry, Earl of Gloucester, was dying. Outside his castle, the world of Lloegr still turned in its cawdel. He was dying unsatisfied, angry with his own failure to restore the kingdom to Matilda, his father's daughter. Matilda, awake at last to the fidelity that she had so long taken for granted, alone found the right words in her heart to comfort him.

'A man is more than his apparent achievements!' declared his sister, with sudden inspiration. 'So is a woman greater than her clumsy movements in the affairs of men! We are part of the struggle, of which another will gather the fruit. My son shall prevail because we struggled to keep my cause alive, and through him England shall regain her glory! You were the wisest of my counsellors! Your failure is only a strong thread left hanging because the needle slipped out of your hand! My son shall pick it up again and finish the pattern!'

'It will never finish,' said Robert, strangely filled with joy. 'God's will be done!'

News of his death was sombrely received throughout Glamorgan, where he had been esteemed for the wisdom and generosity of his justice, worthy of Rhys ap Tewdr's grandson. The men of Deheubarth kept a sharp eye on Matilda's movements. She was going back to the Continent. Young Henry was nearly fifteen, and she had to be present when he was formally invested as Duke of Normandy.

'That's the last that Lloegr will see of her!' decided Gwladus. She and her husband had arrived at Dinefwr to advise her brother. 'It will be only a matter of time before this youngster Henry comes storming in to fan the blaze afresh. But never mind Lloegr. What about Deheubarth? Why don't you claim Ceredigion, Cadell? Why don't you take a wife? Gwenllian of Powys would be the very bride for you!'

The uchelwyr of Deheubarth heard her with pleasure. They

had been urging marriage on Cadell since the day he became king. But Cadell was obstinate and furious.

'I'll marry when my kingdom is complete and not before!' he roared. 'I'll have my pick of brides then, with interference from nobody!'

'But she ought to be a Powys bride, you have always said so yourself,' pursued Gwladus imperturbably. 'There are only the two girls, and Marared is already promised to Iorwerth ab Owain Gwynedd, the one they call Drwyndynn because he gets so many colds and is always talking through his nose, poor thing. And if I don't stir in the matter, no one else will, it seems to me. Gwenllian is the only one left, and someone else will soon snap her up if you don't.'

In spite of his anger, Cadell knew that his sister was right. But he was not a man who could concentrate on more than one thing at a time, and his mind and heart alike were filled with desire for Ceredigion. He never moved too far from his uneasy borders, where he and his brothers and the teulu, happiest in action, had every excuse to ride in cohorts, watching the still unconquered gwlad, and rattling their now much heavier armour at every fancied glint of metal glancing through the trees. They were half army, half court, eager to strike the enemy if he declared himself, yet ready to govern and repair the ravaged land. He was undoubted king in time of war; all the men and boys of Ystrad Tywi rushed to follow his banner; but peace embarrassed him by the claims of civil life, for which he felt himself unfitted.

So Cadell allowed an unspoken division of the royal functions, and turned Maredudd's learning to good account. He judged for Cadell in his absence in minor matters, and on great occasions sat on his right hand, for Cadell knew that, young though his brother was, he was wise not only in the law, but also in the hearts of men.

His chance in Ceredigion did not come until the late spring of 1149. Cadell was standing on the reinforced battlements of his castle at Caer Fyrddin, watching Tywi flowing slowly out to sea, flat as a gold plate as the sun went down, and hearing the town's murmur rising through the silence. He felt strangely happy; it was rare in him, and he took it for a portent of change. He opened his heart to his priest Caradoc, as they watched the rooks busy with their nests in the treetops across the river.

'What is happiness? Why do I feel it now?' he demanded. 'There's no reason for it, with Ceredigion yet to be won! But when I stand here sometimes, and look over there—' He waved his hand vaguely, and was silent.

Caradoc smiled.

'He who obeys God is often, though not always, happy,' he replied. 'You are following the path marked out for you by God, Lord Cadell, and so from time to time His grace approaches you.'

Caradoc pondered this.

'But I am not devout,' he said, puzzled. 'To tell the truth, the talk of priests, all but yours, Caradoc, wearies me! And a paternoster is enough to content me in my prayers, as it seems to me it should all Christian men! What else can we require of Our Father but what His Son Himself has taught us we should ask? That's all the piety that I can claim, and I must many times have shocked you!'

Caradoc, the old campaigner-priest, laughed.

'You do not shock me, Lord Cadell. Neither will God be shocked by any good man's honest thoughts.'

'I good?' said Cadell, disbelieving. 'All I do is follow a straight line towards my goal, and shun all inessentials on the way! No women—they're too distracting. Not too much wine—I like to keep in training. If you call that good! I call it convenient.'

'I call it discipline,' said Caradoc. 'It gives power to the virtue that you exercise, as high and narrow walls make a river's flood run harder. You use it well. That I call good.'

Cadell had, in fact, worked himself and his brothers and all his men, hard. Dinefwr had proved inadequate as the centre of a domain that now spread over much of Dyfed and as far as the Brycheiniog border, so he had caused his central administration to be transferred to Caer Fyrddin, which had power to control each major route throughout his gwlad; it was a brisk place full of working-men and soldiers, and not gay enough, grumbled the uchelwyr, for a young king's hall, and indeed the ladies stayed away, discouraged, for Gwladus had been dropping secret hints to Powys, and all the world had heard about Gwenllian.

The sound of galloping hoof beats on the river bank below rose through the air.

'A messenger!' said Cadell, as the hoof beats of an exhausted horse clattered into the courtyard. He leaned over the battlements. 'Send him up to me at once!' he roared. Then he summoned Maredudd and Rhys and the teulu, for the messenger had come from Bleddyn, who, at the king's desire, had been telling stories on the other side of Teifi. Cadell had quite a good spy system. He had always, of course, relied loosely upon the natural speed of gossip's wings, and this so far had served him tolerably well. But now that his kingdom was coming together, he had arranged for a more efficient and regular service whereby hard news as distinct from uncertain rumour could be passed to him without delay from every cantref in the gwlad. It was largely a matter of choosing reliable messengers and organizing posting stations with fresh horses at the ready; but in Ceredigion, he had to rely on the travelling story-tellers. It was as good a way as any, for the cyfarwydd was a welcome arrival at every court, whether French or Cymric.

Bleddyn had sent word that Cadwaladr's hand, unsteadier than ever after his loss of Meirionnydd, had now lost its grip on Ceredigion. True, he had built himself a well-placed castle at Llan Rhystyd, just where access to and from the north could be barred with ease at the entrance to a narrow cwm; and he managed to hold off Hywel; but he could not, within the castle walls, withstand the eagerness of Cadfan, his hothead son. Overborne, he yielded him his bit of kingdom, and went up north to Môn, to seek shelter in Cymru's bosom.

'Gone north?' exclaimed Cadell. 'Left his lands to the son's inexperienced care? Cadwaladr is a spent force, and Cadfan will crumble under Hywel's weight!'

When that happened, he thought, at last his chance would come. But the cautious Hywel, with an eye on Caer Fyrddin, gave his cousin no opportunity to invade Ceredigion, and months of impatient waiting followed.

'What a laggard the fellow is!' grumbled Cadell to his brothers. 'Why doesn't he push north now?'

'He fears your intentions' said Rhys promptly. 'Knows your plans!'

'Then delude him!' said Maredudd. 'Turn your face elsewhere! Let's advance to the south-east, Cadell, and push back the borders. Hywel's attention will relax. Cadell is busy, he will say. Lulled into safety, he will then creep north to drive out Cadfan with too large an army.'

Cadell seized on this, mustered his companies, and spent the autumn, winter and spring in a series of profitable sallies that made noise and stir enough to reach Hywel's ears. It was Bleddyn himself who told Cadell at last what he wished to know, one March evening when the brothers and a company of the teulu returned to Caer Fyrddin after a successful raid on Cydweli.

They had savaged this region with especial zest on account of their dead mother Gwenllian and their two brothers. They left no crops unburnt, nor any wooden houses; the men and boys they killed, the old also they struck down, and the likely girls they brought home to share out between the bondmen. Not enough girls had been born in the kingdom to meet the demand for wives. Cadell was tired of judging the cases of murder and mutilation to which such a situation gave rise, and provision had to be made somehow. He did not much care where the caethion got their women—Saxon or French or Fleming was all one to him—but he had charged his uchelwyr to pick their wives from amongst none but the daughters of Cymru. Unfortunately some had grown tired of waiting and had begotten children by the Flemish women around Caer Fyrddin. Now Bleddyn's news opened up to them the prospect of a campaign in Ceredigion, where there were many fine women, noble in their ways.

'Prince Hywel is at Llan Rhystyd,' announced Bleddyn. 'His army surrounded Cadfan, starved him out, and took him prisoner. Hywel has the whole gwlad of Ceredigion and is riding freely through the mountains, surveying his new lands between Ystwyth and Dyfi. He has his seven foster-brothers with him, the sons of Cadifor, and all their great force.'

There was a roar of delight, for the sons of Cadifor and their companies were the choice flowers of Hywel's army.

'Hywel has taken my quietness on the Ceredigion front for slumber,' said Cadell, chuckling. 'And has dared to leave underlings in charge of his back door!'

It occurred to Cadell that he owed this happy state of affairs to his brother Maredudd, and he turned impulsively to him.

'Your advice was good, Maredudd, and I am grateful for it. Ask me any favour, and I shall grant it!'

Maredudd smiled with pleasure, but considered his reply, for he was prudent. The court waited in much curiosity, which was disappointed when at last he merely thanked his brother, and said cautiously that he would think the matter over, and let Cadell know at his later convenience, if he did not mind.

4

Bleddyn rode north with the army, for the recovery of Ceredigion by the King of Deheubarth would be a tale to tell the generations; but he found there was not much roar of battle to relate. The men of Deheubarth went up quietly, halting only to take Castell Hywel at the border, with little opposition from the astonished defenders. Then they spread quickly, filling southern Ceredigion up to Aeron's bank, and quietly, like water rising to find its own level. The uchelwyr rode rejoicing though the lower cantrefydd of the gwlad, each eager to be the first to charm the daughters of the local boneddigion. But they were disappointed. The people recoiled from the soldiers with suspicion, and kept their young women out of sight.

'All I can see is a lot of old crones!' grunted Rhys in disgust. 'Bleddyn and his beauties!'

'Hywel has been here before us,' said Maredudd. 'He's had his pick. It looks as if he has governed here with a bandit's hand, rough and insecure.'

'Don't judge by this hamlet. These are Saeson,' said Cadell quickly. 'It's only natural these men should look at us with fear.' He drew rein, and shouted to the sullen faces that peeped from behind sheds and trees. 'I have not come to ravage nor to kill,' he called to them. 'I am the rightful king, and this is my kingdom, and you are my people, and I shall govern well, as did all my forefathers!'

Most of his hearers understood Cadell, for since the Clares had abandoned them, they had been forced to mingle with the Cymry, and to speak the tongue of those they married. But still men stood glowering, even in the trefydd of the Cymry; they would judge by results, not by the king's fair words spoken in a harsh voice, and Cadell had his work cut out to win them. After smiling for a whole morning in one tref, he found that scowls, in another, came more naturally to his facial muscles in the afternoon, so that his reputation for geniality varied within even short distances.

He worked hard. He caused every maer and rhingyll to be brought to him, and where he found none, appointed them, and on the pattern that Anarawd had long ago laid down, he built authority. Some exactions he was bound to make, for an army must be fed, but these he kept low, in pity for the poverty he saw. Maredudd feared the soldiers would grow dissatisfied, but Rhys reassured him.

'Nonsense!' he said roundly. 'Our men knew it was going to be a lean campaign. They took care to fatten up at the outset on the stores and spoils of Hywel's forts, and there are plenty of those still left in sight—just look how he has scattered them about the countryside!'

'He's a careless general,' said Cadell drily. 'He has pleased both his soldier's eye and his poet's heart as well, for I notice that no fair prospect goes without its slapdash fort to serve as vantage point.'

After midsummer, Cadell and his army made swifter progress. The hay harvest was in, and his firm imposition of order, if not his charm, had won the people's favour. Also, the sudden illness of Constable Stephen dispelled any lingering fear of a French attack from the South. The dismay that reigned amongst the French at Aber Teifi and Penfro grew as the sweep of Cymric power increased in strength. Respect grew also, and from now on, in every cwmmwd and cantref, men ran to call Cadell king. He was even embarrassed by the number of boneddigion who wished to join his army.

'Someone will have to stay behind to get in the corn, do the autumn ploughing, and carry on the life of the trefydd through the winter!' he objected. 'From now on, I shall confine recruits to horsemen and bowmen with the best mounts and equipment, though their best is poor enough.'

But this test caused such resentment amongst the rejected, that he was forced to adopt a better plan. Christmas-tide found him well dug in at Llan Bedr, where Stephen's bridge conveniently facilitated the passage across Teifi, and there Cadell put the Twelve Days' respite to good use by holding the traditional trials of skill at arms to eliminate youngsters whose enthusiasm outran their competence. He was willing to be pleased, but he meant to keep his army's standards high. The Ceredigion men looked wilder than most, with the daring of those who had nothing to lose and all to gain by a reckless venture. Secretly, he was delighted by the swift movements and sharp glances of his new subjects, their blunt remarks, goodwill, and readiness for mirth on what was little more than a starvation diet.

'These are certainly the men for us!' said Rhys frankly. 'Our other Cymry are more expensive to feed up to a gleam in the eye. I like them!'

'Nevertheless we are strangers amongst them,' said Maredudd. 'We must not presume too much upon our power.'

So they did their best to make themselves agreeable, and Cadell and his army kept the feast with devout mirth, in company as mixed as may be found in Heaven itself. All comers were welcomed in his hall; every singer, every cyfarwydd, every travelling juggler knew the kindness that awaited him. The common people of the valley crowded in unrestrained and eager to see their new lord. Even the local fortune-teller appeared, to cause a sudden stir.

'She is the Woman of Ystrad Teifi, and she tells the true secrets of men's hearts!' said the awe-stricken soldiers, snatching their palms from her grasping hand. 'She knows Prince Hywel's every movement, though he be thirty leagues away!'

Only Cadell remained unimpressed. Superstition repelled him, and he shot hostile glances when the woman stood before him, tall, old, and bony, and carelessly majestic in her cloak of shabby grey.

'Why, what's he doing now, then?' he demanded with disdain.

'On a feast day? What a question!' retorted the woman impudently. 'It is as my lord supposes!'

The company roared, but were hushed when she snatched up the king's own hand to bend over the palm with avidity.

'Well, hurry up!' said Cadell, mannerless and impatient. 'When shall I complete my conquest of Ceredigion?'

Bleddyn nudged him urgently as the woman looked up in anger.

'Do not displease her!' he breathed. 'She has magic powers!'

But Cadell felt obliged to sneer as she threw his hand back, with an implacable expression.

'You will have successes in Ceredigion, and you will live and die there, after many years,' she said, remotely. Then her sudden hiss made a wider space between herself and her audience. 'But oh, the pride in you! Pride will have its fall!' she said. Then she turned to Maredudd and Rhys. 'Here are two more kings!' she intoned, and a thrill ran through the assembly. She kissed their hands, but did not trouble to read their palms. Her voice was kind as she addressed Maredudd.

'Here's true love and steady wisdom,' she said. 'A pure flame, but without fuel enough to sustain it.'

She passed to Rhys, who waited for her, standing still as a tree on a hot day waiting for a wind, strangely anticipating her words. But her slow curtsy, of an astonishing grace, amazed him. Her voice was charged with satisfaction, with triumph even.

'This green tree is young and strong,' she said loudly. 'Wholesome enough to overcome the outer blemishes. Large enough when it is fully grown to give shade and shelter to a whole gwlad. Strong enough to stand or bend against the storm from the East that will come! And the acorns!' She lifted her great hands in ironic wonder. 'I see them everywhere, sprouting new life!'

Then she departed, in a deep hush, between two lines of secretly crossed fingers, and the three brothers, impelled by a common impulse, drew closer together, and called rather loudly for wine. Gaiety was resumed, but a drop of the witch's poison remained, to envenom their ideas.

Cadell slept ill that night. He did not distrust his brothers, but for once felt out of charity with them, though he felt his anger was directed at the witch. Her words to Maredudd did not bother him, but he resented what she had said to Rhys.

'Acorns, indeed!' he said. 'We'll see about that! I am the one who shall provide the heirs!' And next morning he astonished Bleddyn by his abrupt request to act as his ambassador to Powys, to open formal negotiations for the Lady Gwenllian's hand. He knew by this time what she looked like; Bleddyn was a faithful reporter; she was a fair plump girl of fourteen, squarely built, with honest eyes, an exquisite complexion, and a scowl.

'I like the sound of her, except for the scowl,' said Cadell.

'She is shy, you see,' said Bleddyn, 'Still a child in a woman's body. She is kind, but with the sullen look of a fat girl who will not be flattered into beauty except by the look in her lover's eyes. She is proud, but I think you will like her.'

Cadell grunted, and turned to the cyfarwydd a face as vulnerable as Gwenllian's.

'Will she like me? That's the point!' he mumbled, but Bleddyn put a hand on his arm and spoke with authority.

'In marriage, do not seek to receive love. Seek to give it,' he said. 'Here is a human soul that God made, with hopes and fears much like your own. Let pity and your wisdom guide you in your dealings with a wife, my lord.'

Cadell said nothing. Here was a new thought, and he turned it over with interest and caution. Possibly it was a good one, but he hoped that someone would give similar advice to his bride.

This decision, and a mass, helped to clear his mind, and with a better temper he directed his army to divide. Maredudd with a considerable force took the direct route up Aeron and beyond, to attack the new Llan Rhystyd castle in Hywel's absence at Llan Fihangel Geneu'r Glyn. Cadell himself, with Rhys, rode north by another route to inspect Ystrad Meurig and the eastern approaches to Ceredigion. They seemed to him too easy of access in a fine summer, though in winter and spring men told him that snow and morasses made adventure then too expensive for an enemy. And he wanted to know how strong that ruined Clare castle could be made.

He led his troops away from the green vale of Teifi which was choked with virgin woods as they rode upstream. The little oak trees spread their hoods above and linked their gnarled old roots below, forming a thicket impenetrable to any company of horse, a powerful obstacle to a party of bowmen, and a friend to every little group of Cymry who crept about it unencumbered with only their knives in their hands.

They rode up towards the crest of hills that swelled about them broad and high, north and east, towards a far, intimidating range. They rode on the roof of Cymru, across the forum of the winds, and they rode hard, until in the afternoon they descended into Llan Ddewi Brefi, dipped within its cwm. The clas of canons at this holy place were at vespers, and the sound of their chant rang across the valley. But at the thunder of the soldiers' approach, they came running out of church, their thin, startled faces gaping with the dismay of half-starved men who believed that at best their small harvest was going to be sacrificed to yet another army's needs. Pity smote the two brothers, and Cadell begged them not to be disturbed.

'I am Cadell ap Gruffydd, your king! I respect every man of God, and I have come to guard, not rob you!'

Then the men of Ceredigion round him chorused praise of their new king, until at last the watchful canons relaxed their anxiety, and all their reverend looks returned.

'How can we serve you, my lord?' asked the eldest, in quavering, reluctant tones. 'There have been soldiers of a kind in the district plaguing us for many weary years. That Hywel, prince of thieves, has shorn us without mercy. Those men of Gwynedd, devils from the North—'

Hastily, Cadell reassured him, begged to enter the church built on the miraculous tumulus that rose beneath Dewi Sant's short legs when he preached against the Pelagian heresy to pressing crowds so many centuries ago, and made a liberal donation to the llan after hearing yet another mass.

'We'll go now,' said Cadell. 'Up the river, past St. Caron's llan, and beyond the great red bog that men tell me hangs between the mountains and the hills. I am bound for Ystrad Meurig, which I wish to reach before sunset.'

'You will find it held now by Cymry from the hills,' said the now delighted canon. 'They dominate the Saxons who remain, for not all of these were scattered with the Clares. These lords are strange people, of an ancient race. Evil things are whispered of them, ancient beliefs persist, and it is said that spells are cast.' He crossed himself, and his hearers did the same with irritated apprehension, for they had had enough of superstition.

'Already the sun is low. Will you not stay? I fear we may have a storm,' said the canon anxiously. 'Well, if go you must, have a care for the bog, and keep to the path, well beaten, that runs below the eastern hills. Go, and God keep you, my lord.'

They were thankful to see the castle of Ystrad Meurig looming ahead of them in the growing darkness and heavy rain that delivered them, chilled, wet through, and grumbling, before the castle gates. A small man with sharp, suspicious eyes hailed them, running forward to guide them with a lantern.

'I heard you coming this morning, my lord!' he cried in a high, imperious voice. 'I put my ear to the ground and I heard the thunder of your approach from sixteen miles away. Enter, and be welcome, warm, and dry. All has been prepared since noon for your arrival. You delayed some time at Llan Ddewi Brefi, but the women have kept your supper hot for you!'

Perturbed by this strange welcome, they entered, and looked about them. By the lantern's thin illumination, Cadell saw what was essentially a timber fort, easy to destroy and to re-erect. It was not in bad condition; these people had repaired it extensively, effected a considerable settlement about the castle's base, and enclosed the whole within a defensive wooden stockade, of not much use against a determined enemy attack, but doubtless able to repel the attentions of smaller bands and hungry winter wolves.

In a rough timber hall, warmth, comfort, food and drink, and smiling, excited faces awaited them. Presently, filled with food and mead, they swayed and nodded on their benches. An evil place? thought Rhys sleepily. Nonsense. The canons of Llan Ddewi Brefi had been listening to jealous gossip. Here were kindness and good company, a plump, admiring hostess, two or three very pretty daughters, and a quiverful of short but sturdy sons. His gaze followed one of the daughters. She had black hair and bright eyes like her father's, and she giggled whenever Rhys caught her eye.

Cadell found that Iestyn Fychan was a man to value. He claimed large tracts in the mountains for his gwely, and ruled not only his wife and his sons and daughters, but also his brothers and their families. He had dominated two or three dozen Saeson whom he had turned into useful caethion, and caused them to clear a considerable area of encroaching trees round about the castle. Cadell condescended to praise his efforts.

'But I intend to strengthen the fort in stone by the masons I have brought. You shall yoke the Saeson to their needs. Prince Rhys shall stay to direct the work, but I must hasten to join Prince Maredudd before Hywel's castle at Llan Rhystyd.'

'As you wish, but there is no haste for your departure,' said Iestyn quietly. 'Your brother has taken Llan Rhystyd. Like you, he broke his march at a holy place, at Llan Non. In the same storm that drenched you, Llan Rhystyd keep was struck by lightning, and fell, killing half the defenders. The rest ran the gauntlet of your brother's troops. I heard their anguished cries as they perished.'

Cadell drew back in amazement. What was this strange assumption of knowledge hid from other men? In the morning, when a sweating messenger arrived from Maredudd to confirm this news, a cold wave of fear crept down his spine.

'This man is a seer!' he muttered, but Rhys, with a nervous laugh, dismissed it as good guess-work and better local knowledge.

'He's a man who loves to impress by making mysteries!' he said. 'Well, now you can stay to see the work well started.'

So Cadell stayed, to prospect the neighbouring hills for suitable stone, and to initiate the building work. The weather improved, the sun shone, and the air was filled with the wild thin summons of the uplands. Cadell rode out each day, buoyed by delight, and when he cantered back each evening along the bog's edge, the light was still and clear as honey from the comb, and far across the waste of reeds and birds and cotton-flowers the low western rim of its bowl lay tilted up as though to stay the sun from setting. Riding back towards a good supper, he told himself that all this wilderness of game and air and gleaming ponds, inland and high, belonged to him. For the first time since Anarawd's death, he rejoiced that he was king.

'I will visit this region as often as the cares of Deheubarth will let me come!' he decided.

Iestyn proved to be the ideal foreman. Never loth to exercise his importance, he went to work with a will, drumming up his Saeson caethion with his high voice and sharp gestures. The men of Ystrad Tywi listened with amusement to their exchanges. The Saeson could speak a kind of debased Cymraeg, with the vowels bent quaintly into narrow shapes, and the consonants lisped out with a fumbling tongue. It was sport to hear them, and the soldiers stood round them in a roar.

'If Hywel and his men surprised us now, we could be slain laughing,' said Cadell drily, as they entered the hall on their last evening, to enjoy once more the eager hospitality of an isolated community, and to listen idly to their host's interminable conversation, the talk of a quick mind starved of equal company.

Iestyn knew all about the weather, the lore of horses, the use of herbs, how to cure battle wounds, and how to set broken bones. He was too talkative to please Cadell, but Rhys, who had taken a fancy to him as well as to his daughter, picked up some useful tips, for Iestyn was as generous with his knowledge as he was with his food. Now, after taking too much of his own mead, he became tipsy and confidential, making open claim to a magician's powers. He could see the future in a star's fall, in a chicken's entrails, and in the bubbles that formed on the surface of a boiling cauldron. And he could control the weather.

'By the storm I summoned, Llan Rhystyd castle fell to Maredudd!' he declared in triumph, but Cadell, who had been listening with growing horror, leapt to his feet and held the crossed hilt of his sword between himself and Iestyn.

'This is blasphemy!' he cried. 'Do you not fear the eternal fires of hell that await all conjurers?' And suddenly, 'Can it be that you have never been baptized?'

'Baptized?' Iestyn drew back, frowning, then laughed with bitterness. 'What would your clergy want with our wilderness?' he demanded with a force equal to his king's. 'What do they care for the men of the cefn gwlad? When do the canons of Llan Ddewi Brefi care or dare to go out of their way? They choose the fattest places for their habitations. What do they care for lost souls? There are no more saints and hermits in Ceredigion, my lord, who forgot themselves in their concern for others! No, for years since they died out, we have had to do the best we could without them, like our ancestors before us, and struggle to keep alive out of the way of you warring kings and lords of Cymru and Lloegr! We follow the ancient ways still, though we have dared to encroach on the valleys since we helped to drive out the Clares—yes, my lord, my magic powers, that you so despise, played their part in this! As even for my ancestors, the gods of earth and water, fire and air, these are the lords of life for me!'

'No more!' cried Cadell furiously, pointing his sword directly at Iestyn's breast. 'I'll have no pagans in my kingdom! Forswear your magic and accept the Christian faith, or else—'

'Or else?' echoed Iestyn ironically. 'You will not frighten me, Lord Cadell. Is this how your own Lord gained His following?'

Angry and helpless, Cadell fell to his knees, and in a loud, desperate voice, repeated the Pater Noster, his only prayer. Rhys, sobered by the sudden struggle between good and evil, murmured the words while he crossed himself, and Iestyn, with a bitter smile, waited, as the unfamiliar Latin rang through the air like a peal of bells.

Even as he prayed, God answered Cadell, not by winning Iestyn's soul, but by touching his own. Iestyn's last words echoed in his mind. It was true, Our Lord gained His followers through love. Swords and force had not come into it. This mountain wizard was a brother, God's other child, though he was ignorant of this. If Cadell were to win Iestyn for the true religion, he must first give his own love, God's love, to Iestyn. A warmth crept into the King's heart. Who was Iestyn? He had not even troubled to discover his origins. If God loved Iestyn, there must be something in him for him, Cadell, to appreciate. He understood at last that Iestyn was a lonely, clever man, longing for the friendship of his king, possessing considerable powers of intellect that in ignorance he misused.

When Cadell opened his eyes again, he returned Iestyn's disappointed and defiant gaze with a look of shame.

'I have abused the grace of your hospitality,' muttered Cadell with difficulty. 'It is not your fault that the Gospel has not been preached in these parts for many years. I will arrange for priests to talk to you, Iestyn. You are wise enough to receive the truth of the good news they will give you. I am a soldier, and use my sword with greater readiness than I use my tongue, as my brothers will tell you.'

Iestyn responded with friendship to this apology, and for the rest of the evening, Rhys rejoiced to see Cadell, who always scolded him for enjoying gossip, at last unbending to discover the value of simple and kindly human curiosity in the affairs of other men. His touch was heavy, but it was true.

'I belong to the old people,' said Iestyn, with a flash of contempt for the new. 'We were here long before your ancestor Ceredig came storming in with a wooden cross in one hand and an iron sword in the other. My father was king of all the lakes and rivers in Cymru, and of the mountain tops, lord of all the stags of the forest, no hunter was greater than he, no fisherman better than he could discern the dark fish lurking in the blackest pools. He had the power, as his forefathers had the power, and as I have the power now—'

As he listened, Cadell was sorely troubled to think that the vile practice of witchcraft had such a strong and ancient hold on the gwlad. A few priests would hardly be enough to root it out, though if Iestyn could be gained for Christ, his influence would draw many to follow. The canons of Llan Ddewi Brefi, though virtuous, were old and useless, anxious only to promote the welfare of their families in between their prayers. A young company of men was wanted, who would go out to preach and teach, unencumbered by wordly cares and ties, and live amongst the mountain people. Where could he find them? He felt curiously challenged, and his back stiffened. It occurred to him for the first time that he must conquer Ceredigion, not for the glory of his house, but for the honour of God, and now the whole campaign achieved for him a deeper meaning.

By Michaelmas, Ceredigion was largely won, except for Aber Teifi, where Robert FitzStephen, having buried his father and packed off his now ailing mother Lady Nest to her daughter Angharad at Maenor Pyrr, clung like a wasp to the dregs of a honey pot. Also at Llan Fihangel, Hywel was still entrenched, but thought to be short of supplies. The marriage proposals to

Powys prospered, and Cadell decided it was safe to leave the cares of Ceredigion to his brothers. He himself returned to Caer Fyrddin to clear up matters awaiting his attention, to prepare for his wedding, to make a short progress through Dyfed, and to enjoy a little hunting on the way.

That was how he came to be passing through Coed Rhath on the fringe of the Bay of Tenby one October morning when the sea and the woods sparkled coldly under the sun. The land lay crisp and mellow once the morning mist was thinned out and up towards the sun's heat; he and his teulu cantered endlessly between fine trees, and up and over banks that stood between them and the surprising turmoil of the sea. They were in pursuit of a deer whose splendid antlers lured Cadell into a thunderous gallop that as usual left his teulu far behind.

The hoof-beats of his horse were regular and light and strong; so swift and steady was their course that almost Cadell thought they had left contact with the ground; his nimble horse was like a bow-sped arrow, rushing through the air. I am king! thought Cadell, I am glorious! Branches and trees parted before them, wings seemed to lift them over stumps and streams, sunlight flashed and faded above his head, and brought him visions of himself as founder, with Gwenllian, of a line of kings of unending power throughout the broad and broken heights of Cymru.

Then something felled him. He was on the ground, with feet by his face, and faces and armour above him. A knife drove into his body, and all was agony until the blackness came.

5

A party of French knights and archers went shouting back to Tenby, unable to contain their glee.

'Killed!' they cried to the applauding burghers. 'Cadell ap Gruffydd is dead! The land is well rid of a murdering foe!'

'Killed!' echoed the Cymry in the hills, distraught. 'King Cadell is killed! His brothers are in the far north of Ceredigion! Where is our defence?'

From hill to hill the woeful message ran, from south to north of Cymru. In Powys, King Madog grieved for his lost alliance, while in her chamber Gwenllian wept unheeded. Torn with grief, Maredudd and Rhys fell back from Llan Fihangel as Hywel surged south, and they retired to Llan Rhystyd and Ystrad Meurig before the truth reached them.

Cadell was alive, although the French had set their traps for him in several places at the wood's edge. He fell a victim to the old vile trick of a rope across the path, and was left for dead with stabs and cries of spite and malice. His men had found him; they managed somehow to stop the bleeding, and conveyed him to Ty Gwyn ar Daf, to Whitland, where a few Cistercian monks had come to live. These succoured him, and saved him from immediate death.

Maredudd rode south like a whirlwind to stare down at his brother and rain tears of relief and grief to see him lying there. Cadell struggled to collect his thoughts, to bring into focus the blurred and painful consequence of his wild ride. He remembered pain and feebleness, rage and fevered sweats. He had blasphemed. He left the Cistercians to be within Caer Fyrddin's heart, to hold the reins of power—

'Had to let the Augustinians nurse me,' he muttered. 'French to a man, and how we hated each other! How I cursed them!'

Cadell chuckled feebly.

'They held services of exorcism at my bedside because they thought me possessed of a devil, but when my penteulu heard the words I used, he took heart. He cried out that this was no dying man's language! He thrust out the Augustinians and found me some woman from Llyn y Fan Fawr in the mountains beyond Carreg Cennen. She has skill in the cure of even heavier wounds than mine. So, I lived.'

'Thank God!' muttered Maredudd, but Cadell broke into a sudden sob. His left leg was badly broken. He had a wound in his left side, and the tendons of his right arm had been severed. He whispered, 'They say that I can never lift my sword again.'

Maredudd, speechless and trembling, remembered the Woman of Ystrad Teifi who had prophesied his brother's fall. A king who could not wield a sword was no longer king. In his distress he broke into one of his prolonged fits of coughing.

'I am too short of heirs!' said Cadell irritably. 'Two brothers and a nephew, all unwed! I should have listened to advice. I should have married earlier, as Anarawd did, before I could be struck down. Get you to the wisewoman, Maredudd, before your coughing bursts your lungs, and let her herbs and simples give you health. After you win Ceredigion, you shall be king. You, and not I, must prepare to marry Gwenllian at Christmas.'

'No!' exclaimed Maredudd. Cadell glared at him.

'I command you!' he cried. But Maredudd shook his head.

'I must remind you,' he said quietly, 'That I never claimed that favour you promised me, after Cydwely. I claim it now.'

'What is it you want, then?' grumbled Cadell sulkily.

'Freedom in my choice of bride.'

'Ah!' said Cadell sourly. 'I thought as much. Got some one else in mind, have you? You were mooning about all last winter. Well, marry you must. Any gentlewoman who pleases you, then. Who is she?' But already he knew his brother's choice. It was not high, nor low, but it would pass. It would serve to get heirs, thought Cadell wearily, and the girl was strong. Maredudd's eyes were always lingering on the young woman who teased him with her glances; it was Elen, the penteulu's daughter.

'It is the Lady Elen,' said Maredudd, with a look that dared any man to disparage his choice of bride.

'Very well,' said Cadell bleakly. 'But I had meant to marry you more splendidly, for kings should marry for alliances.'

As Maredudd left him to look for Elen and to collect fresh troops, Cadell sighed. He doubted if the wisewoman could do much to restore his brother's health. He feared that Maredudd's life would be short, and he thought, it might as well be merry.

He sighed again. He was still left with the problem of Powys. One of them must marry Gwenllian. He couldn't. Maredudd wouldn't. It would have to be Rhys. The Woman of Ystrad Teifi would have the last laugh, after all.

As his wounds healed and strength returned slowly, Cadell could do nothing but worry about Ceredigion, where Hywel recaptured Llan Rhystyd from Maredudd and Rhys. He feared

Hywel's residual influence in north Ceredigion. After Cadwaladr's heavy hand, and Cadfan's rashness, the poet-warrior had come to the people as a deliverer. His handsome looks, his verse, and his rough justice, had appealed to them; they took pleasure in the treasure of his name; and even the spring where he paused to water his horses was remembered as Ffynnon Hywel.

Cadell groaned, and struggled to rise, but the effort distorted his body into ungainly shapes, for no one could join the severed tendons of his right arm, and his left leg from thigh to ankle grew stiff as an old tree, nor could he breathe with ease, and sat panting for minutes when he tried to rise. His ambitions shrank. His kingdom might crumble could he but get his strength! He prayed. His prayers were fierce, desperate, and poor. He made a grant of land to the Cistercians of Ty Gwyn ar Daf that they might enlarge their monastery on the banks of the Taf where Hywel Dda and his lawyers had met to confer. Even the Augustinians derived some minor benefit. And at last Cadell remembered to send Caradoc up to Ystrad Meurig to explain the Gospel to Iestyn Fychan. Masses were sung on the King's behalf in Caer Fyrddin, Llan Deilo, Llan Badarn, Llan Ddewi Brefi, and the lesser churches of the realm. Bells rang everywhere, doleful and slow, until 'It's too soon to ring them for my funeral!' snapped Cadell. So they stopped, and because he could only walk five steps at a time, leaning on his penteulu's arm, Cadell cursed him and the priests together for their inadequate prayers.

But at Christmas, 1150, Maredudd married Elen amid pent-up rejoicing, for the teulu were weary of mourning their King's disaster, and hope at last returned to the court of Deheubarth.

'Cadell is getting better. He'll be stirring next,' said the optimists. 'Maredudd will have but a short honeymoon, for Rhys needs him up north. Aber Teifi wants watching, too, now that Constable Stephen is dead. That son of his, Robert, will break out now that his mother, the Lady Nest, has left. She put a curb on him, with her soft spot for her own brother's sons. Poor thing, where has she gone?'

'To her daughter Angharad,' Bleddyn told them. He always knew Nest's movements. 'She is a favourite with the grand-children, Philip and Robert, and little Gerallt.'

'Has she any beauty left?' queried the gossips coarsely. 'Abandoned by her lover and widowed twice, druan! Let me see, how old would she be now?'

Bleddyn arose in dudgeon.

'She is ageless!' he declared angrily. 'And her beauty endures all her vicissitudes!'

The gossips chuckled, and turned to the other matter that preoccupied them that winter. Rumour had come from Iwerddon that Devorgil, wife of O'Ruarc of Connaught, had been carried off by Diarmaid, King of Leinster. Adultery on so grand a scale of course invoked comparison with Nest again, and Helen of Troy. Cadell, when he heard the story, dismissed it with a caustic tongue.

'I expect passion and policy are equally involved!' he observed. 'This latest scandal will only make bad worse. Ireland and its tangled politics! They lie over the water from us!' he told Maredudd, who had tried to entertain him with the tale. 'If you want to look outside our borders, why don't you watch young Henry of Anjou? His father Geoffrey is dead, and he himself is Duke of Normandy, and Count of Anjou, Maine, and Touraine!'

'What's that to us?' returned Maredudd sulkily. 'It's Ceredigion that concerns us now, and it's time you sent me up north on another campaign. We cannot leave it all to Rhys! When can I go?'

'When your wife is with child!' said Cadell promptly. 'As for young Henry, he's going to make a strong push to inherit Stephen's shaky throne, and one day he will try to edge his way into Cymru, unless we establish our strength now. And your son by Elen will increase that strength!' He stumped away, leaving Maredudd to simmer. Henry, indeed! Who cared about him? Let him win the throne of Lloegr if he could! His vigour might at last pull that sad land out of her miseries. Almost he pitied the Saeson, not only ravaged by robbers, but also pillaged by barons roaring unrestrained and devising ever more intricate instruments of torture. The land lay wasted, many died, and those that lived said bitterly that God and His saints were sleeping.

The next day, his face alight with triumph, Maredudd announced that his wife was expecting a child. Then he drummed up his soldiers and rode away north.

Somehow, Cadell struggled through the dark months. When at last spring came, and he dragged himself on to the battlements, and observed the shabby marks of winter, he made his presence felt with vigour. He gave orders for this and that to be repaired and strengthened, and criticized the poor condition of the equipment of his men-at-arms.

'Wonderful campaigning weather!' he muttered, clutching his sword with his left hand. He would certainly hear soon of a great push north in Ceredigion, and sudden misery engulfed him. He was a soldier who could not wage war. How could he go on living? But a bitter moment must alway have its interruption, and presently someone nudged him gently on his elbow. Snarling, Cadell turned with a curse on his tongue's end. But it was his priest, old Caradoc, back from Ceredigion, and they embraced with joy.

'I bring good news from your brothers,' said Caradoc. 'They have pushed Prince Hywel back to Llan Fihangel, which is now at its last gasp. And Iestyn Fychan has accepted baptism at my hands. He has promised me to lay aside his magic powers, though with such reluctance with regard to his control of weather that I agreed to let him retain one small spell, provided he used it only at harvest time in the name of Our Lord and to His glory. It is innocent enough. But you, my lord, how do you fare?' and the old man broke into tears as he regarded the broken warrior. Cadell, exasperated, was the one who had to administer comfort.

'Do not make me angry,' said Cadell. 'My griefs are doubled if I see them shared. At least I live, though at first I wished to die. Now, I no longer wish this, but my heart is empty, and my mind is full of riddles. Why did God let me live? What can His purposes be?'

Caradoc wiped his eyes.

'God tells you that you have worked for your own kingdom long enough,' he said at last. 'Perhaps now He wants you to work for His. He comes like a plough to us sometimes, Cadell, upturning the deeper soil of souls as yet unstirred. You have raised up Deheubarth and put together the broken pieces. Maredudd will bind the whole together, if God wills, with the help of Rhys. For you, a new world opens, that you must explore.'

Nothing quenches misery so surely as a new idea. 'Explore,' said Caradoc, and left him. What could a broken king explore? Cadell looked down at Tywi, flowing with ease through the kingdom that he must put aside. It moved with such peace that an answering peace rose within him, and into this God put two replies.

'Yourself.'

'The world around you.'

Cadell looked first within. He saw pride, driving ambition, and impatience. He saw excellence in war and lack of interest in the arts of peace. Why did he lack this interest? Cadell burrowed further in his mind, like a mole struggling up to the light of day. Perhaps it was because he did not know much about those arts. His education in the wilds of Caeo had been stern and military under his father and Geraint. The pencerdd had taught the boys the old traditions of Cymru, and Caradoc had told them of Christ and His apostles. Poetry and song had indeed been his daily companions; but Cadell was not like his fellows. He had no ear for music, so it was a hardship to listen to the bards. I am ignorant, thought Cadell, but faithful. I lack popularity, for pride has separated me so far from other men that they have always been slow to speak well of me; but since I am just and hard, they respect me. I am, I suppose, narrow. A last sly thought taunted him with lack of intelligence, but he could laugh at that. He knew it was false.

His explorations disclosed to Cadell that his ideas were few, fixed, and beginning to be rather parched.

'I must find others!' he exclaimed eagerly. 'I must open my mind, listen, ask, and learn!'

Curiosity invaded him slowly about those Augustinians to whom he had taken such a strong dislike. They seemed to think they were the repository of all knowledge. Was it possible? Cadell summoned the youngest monk, whose countenance least repelled him, and ordered him to teach him the French tongue. He found it not difficult, for he had a smattering already, and in many words he saw a likeness to Latin and Cymraeg. He was pleased to find in himself an aptitude that surprised his teacher, who praised his pupil's progress without flattery; and after that, their conversations grew more friendly. Cadell questioned him closely, and the replies extended his knowledge. They discussed the great matters that impassioned Christendom—the long struggle between Emperors and Popes for supremacy, the Church reforms of the late Pope Hildebrand, the progress of the Crusades, the marvels of the new cathedral architecture, and the great new centres of learning that were taking root all over Europe. Cadell felt his dim perceptions clarify. He grew ashamed to think that he had been content to know so little for so long.

'I must tell Maredudd,' murmured Cadell. 'I wish he could hear this man. I must tell Rhys.' He began to have a better respect for these cold Augustinians, with their keen resentment of the Cymric capture of Caer Fyrddin, which they regarded as the creation of their own King Henry. Cadell began to envy the French invaders because they had the loyalty of these lean, harsh pillars of religion and learning. The monk took fire at his eagerness, and spoke with zeal of the grammar, logic, rhetoric, and theology that he had learned.

'Why, you must have spent your life in study!' observed Cadell with some pity. The monk's eyes blazed.

'Oh, but I love learning!' he cried. 'Next to Our Lord and the Virgin, I love learning, and all true knowledge comes from Him!' The number of scholars was increasing apace, he said. In Lloegr, under the heirs of the Conqueror, they would flourish, he declared; already they were beginning to gather in two river towns especially favourable for commerce at their highest navigable points, and for the exchange of ideas, in Oxenford and Cantebruge.

'Where can these places be?' demanded Cadell afterwards of Bleddyn, whose knowledge of topography was unrivalled. 'I have never heard of them!'

'They are modern Saeson towns that have arisen on the sites of two older British strong points of which no doubt you will have heard, my lord,' replied Bleddyn blandly. 'Rhydychen and Caergrawnt.'

'Of course!' said Cadell irritably. 'Why in the world couldn't he say so in the first place, then?'

These conversations began to fill the empty places in his mind, and kept despair at bay. His instinct was to hide the body that had once served him well, but matters of state were stronger. Duty dragged Cadell from his chamber into the great hall, to summon councils and conduct affairs. He had himself carried on a war cart along the banks of Tywi to Dinefwr, Drysllwyn, Carreg Cennen, and to all the minor forts and castles in Ystrad Tywi. The sweet and thrilling scents and sounds of spring mocked the young blood that surged in answer through him, and he avoided every woman's eye. He heard whispers as he passed.

'How he is changed, King Cadell! Yet his pride is as high as before!'

The words brought a bitter comfort, and when he heard 'Druan a Cadell!' less often, he was cast into less disorder than when he first heard it. In May he could look back on a useful survey, boundaries firmly held, proper measures taken for the repair of all forts, and an exact counting of their military strength. Power must be handed over intact when the time came.

Cadell also did his best, in Maredudd's absence, to end the disputes that were brought to him to settle; somehow they seemed to him less petty than they did before. Perhaps it was because he himself had been brought low. At any rate, these anxious faces, these greedy eyes, these indignant looks, seemed to him at last to hold the significance of separate and differing souls, all personally troubled, as he was, in their own degrees. Above all else, his journey brought one great surprise. It seemed that now Cadell had not only the respect of his people. That was something he had always received and scarcely valued more than breath. But now they gave him, quite spontaneously, their love as well, though God knew Cadell never sought to please them. Had it only been pity, he would have quickly shown his teeth; but it was something deeper, a kind of recognition of quality that they now wordlessly exchanged.

Summer's first rumour to come down from Ceredigion roused Cadell to fury at a moment when he was in danger of lapsing again into melancholy, and the whole court brightened up. Young Rhys had got with child the black-haired eldest daughter of Iestyn Fychan.

'To saddle himself with a bastard at his age!' roared Cadell in contempt. He foresaw endless trouble from this undesired connection, and groaned impatiently as he thought of the projected alliance with Powys, that had been so long so near his heart. This adventure might be tolerated by King Madog, but it would hardly recommend Rhys to Gwenllian.

The next news, however, raised his heart to genuine and lasting joy. 'Ceredigion is clear of Hywel!' came the longed-for shout at last. He had acknowledged defeat and withdrawn into Meirionnydd. From Dyfi to Teifi, the whole gwlad rejoiced in the rule of the Brothers Deheubarth; Maredudd and Rhys were repairing the damaged castles with stone defences, and were organizing the necessary garrisons. As for Cadwaladr, he had fallen out again with Owain, and fled from Môn into an exile that was to prove permanent.

'His French wife has taken him to the Clares, her own people, and there amongst that foreign kin no doubt he'll stay,' said Bleddyn, 'Biting their charity to his dying day.'

Cadell sat on his throne, beaming.

'Excellent!' he said. 'Now I can call my brothers home for my own purposes.'

One fine morning, Maredudd and Rhys with their army re-entered Caer Fyrddin to the sound of wild cheering from the populace. Flushed and smiling, the conquerors of Ceredigion tasted to the full the delights of triumph and the prospect of further action. With Ceredigion well and truly won, it was time for a show of force in the South.

'East into Gwyr,' said Rhys.

'And west into Tenby,' said Maredudd. 'Lest our enemies there say that we fear to take our revenge!'

'Yes,' said Cadell, looking at his useless right arm. Maredudd and Rhys were moved to kiss it, and Cadell to embrace them roughly with his one sound arm.

So they left Cadell again for a late autumn campaign that took them with seasoned impetus first in a sweep to the East. The castle at Llwchr fell and gave them Gwyr, where they rode unchecked from end to end of that peninsula, destroying every Flemish settlement they found. They reached even Aberafan on the further side of Swein's Ey, as the people there called the hamlet at Aber Tawe, and they rattled their arms within sound of their brother-in-law Caradog ab Iestyn. They reckoned they had gone far enough to display their power to strike if not to hold, then recrossed Llwchr into a south-west wind that blew the smoke of their burnings deep into Morgannwg and told the French and Cymry both, that Maredudd and Rhys had nearly passed over their land.

They came back in the wake of a swelling shout about their exploit, and reached Caer Fyrddin on the day that Elen gave birth to a daughter, and news arrived that the girl in Ceredigion had produced a son. How the court laughed! Cadell scowled as his brothers struggled to conceal, Maredudd his disappointment, and Rhys his primitive glee. But he made no comment. He cleared his throat instead, and made public his plans.

'Matters go well,' said Cadell, 'My kingdom has come together. But now, when I value it most, it seems I must let it go, for the King of Deheubarth must always be active and strong. I commit the kingdom into your care, Maredudd, during my absence, with Rhys for your general under your command. I go on a pilgrimage in search of a miracle. I go to Rome.'

His brothers gazed at him, silent with shock, and dismayed by the prospect of instant power. But they did not dissuade him.

'If go you must,' said Maredudd, 'You shall go in all a king's majesty,' and he began to calculate the needs of a considerable train. But Cadell waved his hands impatiently.

'No!' he said. 'A pilgrim goes humbly. I want Caradoc and one servant. I can see the world more closely if I have no pretensions to uphold.'

With reluctance he removed the circle of wrought gold that he wore on his head, that his father had worn, and Anarawd.

'Perhaps I had better leave this behind,' he said. 'When I come home again, if I am no better, I shall be ready to give it to Maredudd.'

Only one matter then remained to be settled before he left. Maredudd and Rhys made quiet but thorough arrangements of their troops and arms, fell upon Tenby, took it, and took their revenge. When they came back to Cadell, the rage of battle marred their faces still, and he had never seen so much blood upon their clothes before.

But it was May before good sailing weather brought the first of the next season's trading ships to Caer Fyrddin. Cadell chose one that came up part laden from Bristol and was in haste to make a speedy passage back to Bordeaux. The crowds always rushed down to the quayside as soon as word came up from Llan Stephan that sails were spied on the horizon, and horses and wagons began to converge on Caer Fyrddin from every castle, fort, and monastery within a radius of twenty miles. Flemish, French, and Cymry struck a truce those days, though undeclared. Trade from over the water often cut across the dry land's quarrels, and the people made the most of what they could get by purchase or barter every time the ships cast anchor under the castle walls. The burgesses stood sharp and stolid, ready to jump for their turn after the garrison's wants were satisfied, after the local lords and monks had had their pick of wine, after close bargaining.

Cadell waited until the roar of business had died down, and embarked in the evening quiet when the crowds were thinning out. The ship lifted anchor on the ebb, and the land slipped away. The master was a Gascon, broad and blunt and regular in his rages. His cataract of oaths was better than a whip across the sailors' backs as the oars dug into the irresistible current that carried the vessel out beyond Llan Stephan, into the rocking sea. Then they hoisted sail in a favourable wind, and Cadell turned his back on his kingdom.

After they landed in Bordeaux, Cadell and his companions advanced through the sun-baked land of Acquitaine south-east into the gwlad of the King of France, into deeper layers of summer heat. His hwyl was good as he explored a land and people strange to him; food and wine with unfamiliar smells and savours put strength into him, and he had never felt better since the day he had been struck down at Tenby. They met many pilgrims, of both sexes, of every age and degree, some bound for Rome, others for north-west Spain, where the shrine of St. Iago da Compostela drew the devout from many lands. At each encounter, Cadell took fresh bearings on the affairs of France.

'King Louis? Two years ago it was since he came home from the Holy Land. The trouble with that Queen he's had! Couldn't get an heir from her, just the two little princesses. He divorced her, though by what juggling with the canon law it's hard to say. Ah, people in high places can do things that Holy Church wouldn't tolerate in the likes of us!'

'And the Queen? What happened to her?'

'She came back here to her Duchy of Acquitaine, and is known once more as the Duchess Eleanor. A fine land she has. Louis lost all that, just as she lost the title of Queen. But she's not the woman to be kept under. Amusing herself now with what she calls a Court of Love, if you please! No one could fail to notice her. Stay on the shelf? Not she! She and the young Duke of Normandy, young Henry, are to make a match of it, though he's her junior by a good few years. She doesn't care. She's going to be Queen again, Queen of England this time. King Stephen's son is dying, people say, the long wars are coming to an end at last, and it looks as if Henry will be acknowledged to be the heir.'

The Duchy was indeed a prize. Cadell envied the look of order, wealth, and security in this immense wine country of Acquitaine, and he ground his teeth to think that it had fallen into the lap of Henry of Anjou, who might soon become Deheubarth's next adversary.

'A failure that Second Crusade was!' people grumbled, but it was obvious to Cadell that the adventure had brought opportunity to the people of Bordeaux. With half the nobility gone overseas with Louis, the townspeople had seized their chance with both hands to establish their liberties; fine houses were a-building in the best positions, financed by the wealth that came pouring in from a great Crusading wave of increased Mediterranean commerce and trade. Cadell was jealous of all this prosperity; it sharpened his critical tongue.

'The monks, too, seem to know what's good for them in Acquitaine!' he observed caustically. 'Big strong fellows, all of them, living in buildings fit for kings' palaces! But it is the multitude of all these religious orders that amazes me, Caradoc! Who can tell in what kind of house we shall lie tonight? Will it be Cluniac or Carthusian? Cistercian or Augustinian? I marvel that Christians can disagree so heartily on the way to reach God! Such a divided mind, and the late scandal of a Papal Schism, makes but a poor display for Christendom before the Turk!'

Caradoc knew better than to contradict his king directly.

'You know, Lord Cadell,' he murmured gently, 'I applaud the wisdom of one Bernard, a monk of Clairvaux, and a Cistercian, like our brethren of Ty Gwyn ar Daf. He it was who used his authority with kings to end the Great Schism. He also set on foot the Second Crusade, as much, I dare say, to drain off evil humours in the minds of men, as to deliver Jerusalem!'

'Did he, now?' replied Cadell, impressed. 'Well, at least it served in part the former purpose, but in view of all that went before, I do not wonder that they failed to dislodge the infidel from the Holy Places.'

Caradoc shook his head in silence.

'Perhaps they never will,' he said, 'until Our Lord comes again.'

They proceeded slowly along old Roman ways, halted occasionally by a fair view that held them open-mouthed in wonder. They crossed themselves when strangers came towards them, for Caradoc had heard at the monasteries that heretics lived in this land, men who had brought a strange teaching home from the Orient, back from the Crusade. But no one troubled them; they came safely to Marseilles, sold their horses, and then took ship for Rome.

It was as they lifted anchor that at last Cadell felt himself to be fully freed from care. Thoughts of his brothers never left him on land, for he compared every castle that he saw with his own in Deheubarth. He wondered how Maredudd was getting on, whether the French were giving trouble, and whether Rhys was behaving himself. But now, as the sun beat down with violence as if to crack their very skulls, and as they stood on deck afloat upon the sea of St. Paul that lapped the ancient world from Palestine to the shores of Spain, his old life slipped away. Caradoc's face was turned with rapture towards the east; the servant's apprehensive gaze was on the blue clear water and on all the sturdy boats and ships that lay upon it like a flock of gulls. As for Cadell, he ailed not, save in leg and arm, and a weakness in his side, and perhaps God would restore him; perhaps He would work a miracle if his faith was great, and he could return to be king again. If so, he would build a peace in the land as firmly as did Hywel Dda, where virtue and all the arts might flourish in a kingdom full of towns. If not, he must learn to be humble; to some upland part of Ceredigion he would go, like the Saints of Cymru, to seek wisdom and a knowledge of God; there, he would oversee his brothers' government

III

The Lord Rhys ap Gruffydd

(1153—1171)

1

In the absence of Cadell, his brothers were not slow to grasp authority. While Maredudd dealt careful justice with his quills and parchments in the South, Rhys and his army were left to strut and flaunt in a military progress on the north-eastern passes in the style traditional and necessary to those newly fledged in power.

Then the scene changed swiftly. A year later, Cadell returned, Maredudd died, and Rhys, now King of Deheubarth, at last married Gwenllian, after making noise enough on the Powys border to convince Madog that this youngster was no lightweight, and that in Deheubarth he would have to deal with either a good friend, or a bad enemy. There was, to be sure, a little difficulty with Gwenllian, who was resentful of the existence of Rhys's Ystrad Meurig son, Maelgwn. Rhys heard of her attitude, and was angry in his turn. What was a man's past to do with a woman's future? But that was before they were persuaded at last to meet, when a curious thing happened. All their indignation died, to be replaced slowly by kindness and warmth, as each, in the other, recognized the counterpart subconsciously desired; and pride subsided.

As for Cadell, he retired to his Cistercians at Ty Gwyn ar Daf, where he could watch events in Cymru. The miracle that he had sought in Rome had been denied him; nothing could flex his sword arm, nor bend his stiff left leg. It was not that his faith was too weak, presumably, but that God's design did not include his cure. 'But he performed a greater miracle instead,' thought Cadell. 'He granted me tranquillity, for which somehow I had never thought of asking Him.' He decided to devote his remaining energy to promoting God's will, instead of wasting it on self-pity. There was a younger brother to direct, if not to rule.

'But he doesn't listen to me!' he blurted out to Bleddyn, who was his frequent visitor. 'Maredudd was more amenable, but kingship has gone to Rhys's head! Not that he governs ill, but his hold on Ceredigion is but shaky after all, under this new French thrust, and he will not hear advice! And I find it hard to curb the more caustic comments that come to my lips when I survey another's government!'

A soaring chant from the chapel rose victoriously through the air to cheer them.

'Ah, there's peace at the heart of all the woes that beset us, Lord Cadell!' exclaimed Bleddyn. 'The heart of life is joy—just listen to that! Although this new King in Lloegr, the second Henry, has been roaring through Gwynedd and Powys, when you think of it, Our Lord Himself lived and died for us, loving all men, in a conquered land!'

Cadell answered slowly, 'I learned something in Rome, Bleddyn. Nothing that the monks and clergy said—their sermons were too deep and difficult for me. But I had leisure to think, and I begin to understand it better now, our great salvation. The Son's obedience it was that redeemed our value. It was so perfect, tested to the death, that He made the rest of mankind worth God's trouble in creating us. Perhaps that's heresy, but who cares? The thought pleases me.'

'Shall you join the Order?'

'Not yet. I am of the world still, though not in it. I am full of curiosity as to what is to come, here, as well as hereafter. I cock my ears at the sound of a horse, and wait for a message from Rhys. I lift up my heart at the sound of a bell, and wait for a revelation at the altar. This delays, but is surely coming, for I learn better now how to make my prayers. It is not for nothing I have been to Rome! I come to terms with my condition, and slowly I learn to forgive. True, these are the vindictive wounds made by our foes the French who set upon me as I hunted in my pride in the woods near Tenby, but we can well match them for crudeness and woe, with our feuds and our killings and mutual mutilations, against their own internecine villainies.'

Bleddyn dared to ask him if he suffered much.

'What suffering I cannot avoid, I endure well enough so long as it goes unremarked. But when a fool comes to tell me I bear my infirmities well, that is when I rise and spit! I once had the satisfaction of provoking a blow on the cheek, which allowed me to gauge the success of a dagger thrust I have taught my left hand. It was not ill done. The fellow fell groaning on the floor, and dyed the rushes red with the blood from the hole in his thigh. I have not since been troubled, but the difference in my estate is plain to see! To think, Bleddyn, that in old times, an insult to the King of Deheubarth could be wiped out but by a fine of as many white cows, with a bull between every twenty, as would stretch between Argoed and the court of Dinefwr! I struggled to master a kingdom, once! Now, I struggle to master myself. Enough!' His voice changed as he turned to politics. 'What is this new King of Lloegr doing now? This second Henry has brought a blast of power to the English throne, and showed a fine, filibustering, burly zeal when he laid those Border barons low, Earl Roger of Hereford, and Hugh Mortimer of Wigmore!'

'You know that Owain Gwynedd decided to catch what he could between kings,' said Bleddyn. 'He pushed his borders nearly to Chester, and dug down into Iâl, which was for centuries a part of Powys. Henry had every excuse to invade the North, with the indignant King Madog's connivance, if not his active support. But before he did so, he was absent in France on urgent business, dealing his windmill blows elsewhere. Then he came home to receive the King of Scotland's submission, and to turn the belligerence of the Marcher lords into a more traditional direction, against Cymru. Well, he has been battering his head against the natural ramparts of Gwynedd, and has found out, now, which is the harder. His naval adventure against Môn came to grief on landing, and his uncle, your cousin Henry FitzHenry, the Lady Nest's second son, was slain. Owain seized Basingwerk, but on the other hand, King Henry came out best in a clash with some mountain troops.'

'Each has taken the rough measure of his opponent,' said Cadell intently. 'But neither is strong enough to overcome the other.'

'Now Henry is moving south with a great army to deal with your brother Rhys,' said Bleddyn urgently, leaning forward as he approached the purpose of his visit. 'The Lady Nest says the fate of Cymru is in your brother's hands. "Come to terms with Henry," she begs, "before they kill any more of my sons! Cymro or Norman," she says, "all men are the same, all are God's children! Tell Rhys that power is worth more than false pride," she says, "if he cannot have both, and that acknowledgement of Henry's might is no dishonesty." What do you think should be done? And the French are besieging Caer Fyrddin, and it's likely to fall, I'm told,' added Bleddyn, not fearing to provoke an explosion. It came; Cadell came out of the dumps at once, and looked all the better for the blaze of temper that scorched his visitor.

'It cannot fall!' he cried. 'I made it too strong! But they can starve us out, for Henry has the power of the sea, and we have not. He has half France, all Lloegr, the ocean between, and the allegiance of the Scottish King. We have no mountain fastnesses equal to those of Gwynedd where we may defy him with impunity, so we can never hope to win, in fine weather, any short strong war he makes against us! My aunt Nest is right, and Maredudd would have agreed with her. Go to Dinefwr, Bleddyn, and tell Rhys to stop moving his women and children and cattle into the hills, and sharpening his knife for a desperate war! I know the way his mind works! It's time to make bargains with Henry, and test the value of his word. Otherwise the men of Deheubarth will choke in their own blood before they can beget enough sons to take their place. We must be quiet and recover strength. Our chance will come another spring.'

As Bleddyn left, Cadell put his head down like a bull before charging and shouted after him, 'Tell him to remember Hywel Dda!'

Hywel Dda? Bleddyn pondered, all the way to Dinefwr. There, Rhys heard the messages with anger, and said that his aunt's heart was with the French, and as for Cadell, he had listened too long to the bells, heard too many Roman prayers, and was half a monk already. Both were lost to Cymru!

'I think they look to a new Cymru,' said Bleddyn, who began at last to understand Cadell. He was still hot for Deheubarth's glory, but less now for pride's sake than for the sake of his vision of God's peace untroubled in the hills, and to achieve this, he would condescend to an understanding with Lloegr.

'Cadell of all men!' groaned Rhys, twisting his golden beard, and marching from end to end of his massive hall. Bleddyn became aware that Queen Gwenllian was listening, and resenting this conference. The cyfarwydd knew that he was too friendly with Nest to please her, for Gwenllian did not trust her husband's aunt and her French connections. She herself was a true princess of Cymru, and her back was as stiff as the Lady

Nest's once used to be. She was well formed, with firm, judicious eyes in a pleasant, but not a very pretty face; but her complexion was famed, and her ruddy hair glorious. The marriage had secured the border with Powys, and Rhys was fond of his wife. But his kindness was too tepid to please her, for she adored him, and he spoiled their children to a degree that angered her. Their married quarters were sometimes rocked by storms, and it appeared that one had recently occurred, for the waiting-women were turning up their eyes, and the teulu were making exasperated loud noises with their weapons.

Gwenllian is royal, young, and rather spoiled herself, thought Bleddyn, bowing deeply to the Queen. She will grow more gay when she grows wiser. Rhys has an eye for gaiety.

'What is the matter with Cadell? When have we ever failed to give battle?' shouted the King, thumping the table. 'Already the cattle move into the hills! Tomorrow the Queen and the children go to Caeo until I have cleared the French from the valleys and secured the gwlad!' He turned his massive displeasure totally on his brother's messenger. Power rose in him uncontrolled like water in some unfailing well, but this splendid quality now seemed to Bleddyn to be misused, in too wild a fashion for the times.

He withstood him, and said gently, 'Listen, Lord Rhys. It is not for a cyfarwydd to presume to advise the King of Deheubarth, but a friend may speak his mind to a friend.'

'I do not deny it,' said Rhys. 'Sit down.' His anger diminished, and he looked at Bleddyn with hostile curiosity.

Bleddyn said, 'It is easy, and it is natural, to fight. It is difficult to look for peace. Great is the prince who can swallow his pride and face the facts of power. Hywel Dda—Prince Cadell desires you to remember Hywel Dda.'

'Yes, yes, he went to Rome!' said Rhys. 'I know that. That would appeal to my brother. What else did he do, besides establish the Laws?'

'He made a friend of the Saxon king,' said Bleddyn, 'to their mutual benefit.' Then he begged leave to withdraw. It was not the moment to offer to entertain the company. Besides, he was very tired.

Not many rulers learn to rule themselves. Those who do, succeed, and are blessed by those who follow. But the struggle is bitter enough, and King Rhys spent the night alone in the great hall. He sent his men-at-arms away to their houses at the bottom of the hill where their anxious wives were packing in haste for their flight to the mountains. Gwenllian in her bedchamber waited in vain for her husband. Rhys stormed through the hall, kicking the log fire aside, leaving the embers to take their chance of death or life. Anarawd, his brother, had lit that fire when he recovered Dinefwr from the French, and it had never been allowed to go out since.

The porter, not daring to enter, was watching Rhys through the great keyhole when, sleepless, long after midnight, Bleddyn approached him.

'What is he doing?' he murmured.

'His rage, like an ocean, is heaving into calmer seas,' said the porter. 'He is standing by the dying fire, taking omens. He is on his knees, now. He is blowing sparks! Why doesn't he use the bellows?'

He opened the door, and darted forward with the bellows. Rhys took them from him with a rough pull, and began to puff life into the hesitating embers. Soon the old blaze roared again. Rhys stretched his burly frame, and laughed, and the caethion, at a signal, surged into the hall with a new day's supply of logs. The King snapped his fingers, and called out his commands, and when last Bleddyn saw him, he was sitting on his wooden throne, tilting it well back, with his legs on the table. He was chewing apples from a dish piled high with the fruit, and his free, strong gaze was focused on some distant object far beyond Deheubarth.

'He'll be quiet enough for some hours.' said the porter, reappearing at the cyfarwydd's side. 'There's a good few pounds of apples in that dish. You can go back to bed now, Master Bleddyn.'

In Deheubarth, as elsewhere in Cymru, it was the monarch's custom to sound out opinion on important policies. The canghellor, the penteulu, and the senior lords were generally consulted, lest their loyal pride be offended, and even the bards and cyfarwyddwyr had to be allowed to drop hints.

But Rhys was his own chief counsellor, and men were becoming accustomed to his vigorous and overriding decisions. They were, however, astounded when the word went round that Lord Rhys had changed his mind. The Queen and the children were to stay at Dinefwr; no more cattle were to travel north until their usual journey into the mountains at the calends of May.

'He is going to make terms,' said Einion ab Anarawd, the young penteulu, 'while we are still strong.' Rhys would take none but a few attendants, his indignant army he disposed at various key points with instructions to defend but not to attack; and away he rode, imperious and with gleaming eyes, and trooped off down the hill. The Queen was left in the castle, with her ladies, her children, the caethion, and a garrison of older soldiers. A pale spring silence like the peace of death ensued.

Bleddyn had never known so tense a fortnight, nor a valley of such perilous quiet. He did not think of leaving. He endured with patience the Queen's anxious temper, laughed, and told his gayest stories. She pretended not to listen, but sat within earshot. Each night passed in this fashion fourteen times; each night Bleddyn watched Gwenllian draw nearer until at last her gaze was locked in his, and he was able, by his art, to make her courage strong.

On the fifteenth day Lord Rhys returned with the grim looks of a fighter who had used his strength for speech. He had measured Henry. They had eaten and drunk together, spoken and shouted and eyed each other with contempt and curiosity, for they understood each other but imperfectly in bad Latin. Rhys had pledged himself as Henry's man and put the kingdom in his hands, to be received of him again with a Frenchman's honour for guarantee of quiet possession, for what that was worth. One province he got, Ystrad Tywi, and another to come at Henry's later pleasure. Nobody liked it, but it might have been worse.

'One province to come,' muttered the uchelwyr. 'That can only mean Ceredigion! Dyfed is too much the Frenchman's, and Cantref Bychan is already raked by him. We have the heart, if we have Ystrad Tywi and Ceredigion. We have the great core of the gwlad.'

Bleddyn watched the King slaking his hunger and thirst and recovering the rough aplomb that usually accompanied his health; and suddenly Rhys smiled at him.

'I'll be as true to Henry as he to me, no more, no less,' he said. 'One province to come. We shall see, Bleddyn. I've put him in debt to his own honour, so I'm stronger than he.'

Then he told the cyfarwydd what sort of people they were beyond Clawdd Offa. He had been learning, as Cadell did in Rome. They were savage but luxurious men, prizing the cold and valuable learning of their clerics. They were avaricious and orderly, and had many scribes to keep their careful accounts. They had a passion for building great churches for their pride and piety, and they built them in stone to last for ever and strike posterity with awe. By contrast, he knew Cymru better now; it was rich there, over the Clawdd, but flat! There was no surprising anyone in such a land.

He did not tell Bleddyn that his own bold eloquence had been heard at Henry's court in the silence of astonishment; this enemy was greater than his size had been in their imaginations.

In May, Henry's decision was announced. Rhys got Cantref Mawr, the central land from which he could only with difficulty and at great cost be dislodged, and which it was no sacrifice to bestow on him. He also got, instead of the promised additional cantref, a few scattered lordships between the main French holdings in Cantref Bychan and Dyfed. Between them, they did not even equal the size of a cantref, and the power they offered was diluted by their separation.

'So, that's his honour's worth!' cried Rhys, in a high rage above his court's anger, as men for the first time turned to blame their lord, in an uproar that he failed for once to quell. It took the clear incisive tones of Queen Gwenllian to restore order with her cool douche of common sense and loyalty.

'Men of Deheubarth, be thankful for the wisdom and courage of your King, whose actions have spared you disaster!' she told them stoutly, clinging to her husband's arm. They stared at each other as the angry sounds died down, and Rhys, greatly comforted, embraced her publicly. She who had so often shewn her qualities as shrew now revealed her worth as friend; and he was never to forget her constancy and her rather bitter sweetness. Her intervention succeeded; she swayed all to her opinion, and restored a better temper to the court. The marriage between them became at last a deep and true devotion, for all that the King's eyes might on occasion stray elsewhere.

The summer was full of abrupt and angry battles. Ceredigion had been tossed back to Earl Roger of Hertford, son of its old French lord Richard FitzGilbert of Clare, and he began to build his forts straight away on June the First at Ystrad Meurig, Castell Hywel, Aber Dyfi, Dineirth, and Llan Rhystyd. Rhys watched for a chance to unleash his army; it came from the north-east, where the Cliffords, restored to Cantref Bychan, made a taunting raid across the river into Cantref Mawr.

Rhys bared his teeth.

'They sit on both my shoulders, do they?' he said. 'I'm King Henry's man, so if he revenges me, well. If not, why, he's too busy, and I must shake them off myself. As for Ceredigion, it is not neighbourly for one king's man to threaten the border of another with an array of castles!'

So, when Rhys paraded his indignation by messenger before Henry and got a negligent or no reply, he spat into Tywi and spurred his horse up the valley with an army behind him. The attack on a wet night in June on Walter Clifford's castle at Llanymddyfri was swift and successful. They slew the garrison and put their own men there instead.

'That's one shoulder free,' said Rhys heartily. 'Now for the other.' And off they went towards Ceredigion, where Einion ab Anarawd had already gone to tackle Castell Wmffre across Teifi. It was not a long campaign, but Rhys and Einion made such trenchant and successful raids into so many strong places in Ceredigion that King Henry himself was obliged to bring an army to reduce Rhys to order. He was in a hurry to get back to his problems in France, and first he turned to crush the eruption in Ceredigion as a man will pause to squash a fly on the back of his horse before going into battle. He cornered Rhys at last.

'I'll take hostages from you as earnest of your good behaviour!' barked Henry. 'One of your sons included!'

One of his sons! Well, at least Gwenllian should not suffer. Sourly, Rhys yielded Hywel, his natural son by Ysteder, the daughter of his chief huntsman. A hostage was safe enough, he told himself anxiously, or should be.

'Harm him, and I'll harm you!' growled Rhys.

In fact Hywel was treated fairly in Lloegr, and educated with some French lord's sons. Not until the final peace years later was he sent home to Cymru, not until he had lost all comfort in his mother tongue, and was obliged to stand about in his father's court, silent, rather than stumble in Cymric in front of his sneering and suspicious brothers. Hywel Sais, they called him ever afterwards. Henry had grown quite fond of him, and was sorry, men said, to let him go.

Gloomily, Rhys went home with his army to reap what was left of the harvest. There was not much; the French had stamped on most of what they could not make their own. The loss of Hywel rankled, but it was a chance for the lad to see the world. There should be at least one traveller in every family to leaven the rest; he himself must be content with Cymru; but there was Cadell, he had been to Rome.

'What is Rome like?' demanded Rhys, suddenly. The autumn was poor, a rainy season; there was time on his hands before the weather turned the ground firm enough for hunting. He allowed his curiosity to curl up the corners of his military mind, and rode over to the Cistercians at Ty Gwyn ar Daf.

It was true that the brothers were mostly French, with here and there a Cymro to swell their numbers, including Abbot Cynan himself, but they had not the same close links with the invader as had the imported Benedictine brethren. These men of Ty Gwyn ar Daf were of a different breed, Burgundians from Citeaux Abbey, the mother of many foundations that had recently arisen in the wilder parts of Cymru and of Lloegr too. They had come less by the invitation of the French as by their permission, though the Bishop of St. David's had given them his hearty encouragement. The Cymry liked them; they found them firm and friendly, calm and kind.

It was four years since Cadell and Rhys had met, and they embraced with delight.

'How old are you now?' demanded Cadell.

'Twenty-six. I'm at the end of youth, brother!' cried Rhys ruefully. 'I've lived hard!'

He had indeed. As warrior, governor of his realm, and judge of his people, he had played each rôle with zest. Now he felt the need of another source of strength to support him when his own should fail. It was a natural need for reflection that had brought him to Ty Gwyn ar Daf. To reflect was not his habit, but the need to do so comes to all men, and when it comes to men of action, it comes, like all else, with force. Vigour was the mark of all this king undertook, in war, peace, love, hate, virtue and sin, wisdom and folly. Round was his character, as rather round about the middle now he began to be.

'What news from Dinefwr, my lord?' begged the Abbot eagerly at the supper table. But Rhys did not want to talk about his own affairs. He dismissed his own unlucky year with the grin of a man who knew how to cut his losses, and mentioned Ifor Bach instead, his sister Nest's husband.

'You haven't heard? Well, then—' And he began to tell the tale with relish, for Rhys was great enough to glory in every triumph of the lesser lords who were beginning to look to him for leadership. His spirit was nourished by their vigour, too, just as his status magnified their own.

'Dangerous little man, Ifor,' said Rhys. 'Slew his enemy Morgan ab Owain the other day, lord of Gwynllwg and Caerleon. Slew Morgan's chief bard, too, Gwrgant ap Rhys, because he had been singing evil songs about Ifor. Well, Ifor has been quarrelling for some time with his overlord Earl William, lord of Morgannwg. You know, my poor cousin Robert of Gloucester's son. They disagreed about Ifor's boundaries—as though a Cymro wouldn't know every square inch that came to him from his fathers! He went to Caerdydd to plead his case solemnly, according to him, before William, but more likely to shout and swear and threaten, if I know Ifor. He knows no other method of persuasion, short of arms. He failed, of course. But he carried gold, and he made friends in Caerdydd. Then he went home until the fuss died down. Presently, he returned. You know Caerdydd castle, what strong walls it has, how many score of men-at-arms are set to guard it? Ifor and his friends passed in disguise through the town below full of burghers and soldiers, and in the darkness climbed the castle walls by rope ladders let down by his friends within, and so gained entry.'

His audience gasped.

'They seized the Earl, the Countess Hawys, and the little Robert, slung them down over the wall in neatly trussed up bundles, and carted them away to Senghennydd in warmth if not in comfort, wrapped in carthenni that the Countess later complained were over full of fleas. She endured her vicissitudes with spirit, my sister told me. Oh, Ifor treated them with all the hospitality due to his own dignity, of course, but for all that, he kept them his prisoners until Earl William had yielded every point that Ifor had been demanding. Caerdydd is quiet enough towards Senghennydd now,' ended Rhys with satisfaction, 'But the hills are ringing.'

The Cymry who heard him did not withold their enjoyment, and even the French monks all but applauded.

Rhys stayed a week at Ty Gwyn ar Daf, talking to Cadell and the monks about Rome and France and Lloegr, asking practical questions and listening with care to the replies. Finding himself in an Abbey amongst holy men, his thoughts took a holier turn. He joined the brethren in their devotions with enthusiasm, and a joy it was to Cadell to hear his brother's burly baritone ascending in the choir. The Abbot and the monks approved Lord Rhys himself as well as his large gift of cattle, and took trouble to please him; Father Cynan was anxious, by honouring Cadell also, to give Rhys grounds for gratitude when his days of glory should come perhaps one day. Inspired by Cadell, he had begun to yearn to send a daughter house into the eastern wilds of Ceredigion, and he in turn questioned Rhys about that remote, enormous, and scarcely populated region.

'In winter, you can travel there for three days without meeting a man,' said Rhys. 'The hills are blue-black with shadows before the rain is loosed, and when the sun shines, the yellow patches move swiftly upon the mountains just where they catch its grace between the clouds. Oh, it's a harsh place, and the wind has it,' he said. 'Fit only for campaigning, and wolves, and bards, and holy men, are the high empty spaces of the roof of Cymru. I divide it roughly, you see, like the rest of the world, between God and the Devil.'

In his coarse Latin, his light words sounded singularly shocking. He added, 'Indeed, we need the men of God out there, to fill the silence with their prayers and bells. Yes, by all means send a daughter house into the wilds, and may God bless it, though I fear it can't have my protection—yet!' He grinned, and rode home to Dinefwr.

But the impatient Abbot thought it only prudent to approach Earl Roger too. God was no respecter of persons, and it seemed there was a pressing need to root out witchcraft and paganism in Ceredigion. To the fury of Cadell, Bleddyn was employed as a reluctant go-between; he enjoyed the hospitality of Aber Teifi as well as that of Dinefwr and Ty Gwyn ar Daf, and he would not willingly offend any of his ports of call. But he did his best, for a man did not insult his own powers by making an indifferent use of them, and Constable Robert FitzStephen responded with enthusiasm on behalf of the Clares.

'Nothing could better subdue the savagery of those parts than such a foundation!' he declared. 'There is indeed, a broken-down old holy place that springs to mind, hard by the great red bog with its great flocks of wildfowl. My grandfather Rhys ap Tewdr settled some monks there once, but the venture failed through sickness and war. And tell my cousin Cadell this, the best security for a new foundation will be a strong Norman hand throughout Ceredigion to keep down my cousin Rhys!'

But Earl Roger was too busy countering King Henry's massive inroads on baronial power to think about monastic foundations. He took five years to answer Robert's plea, five years in which Lord Rhys's own fortunes rose and fell, like the mountain ranges you have to cross before you reach the crown of Cymru.

As for Cadell, Robert's reply so much enraged him that he spent all his time in his visitor's cell writing letters of angry advice to Rhys. He was scarcely seen in public, and the men of Deheubarth began to speak of him, briefly and seldom, with the grieving sadness proper to the dead.

Rhys, however, required no prodding by Cadell, nor by any other man. The winter's quiet of 1159 was broken by hunting forays that took his court along and over the edge of his shortened boundaries. For these careless acts of mere trespass the French took revenge enough to supply provocation to war, and when spring came, Rhys moved his troops with power and speed into a series of well-executed attacks on the French forts that had arisen like fence-posts about his borders. So well did success attend him that the barons were alarmed, and when in June Rhys invested Caer Fyrddin with a large army, he did so with such cunning use of the modern engines of war that that great castle nearly fell to him. The armies of no less than five earls, Cornwall, Roger of Hertford, William of Gloucester, Richard of Pembroke, and Patrick of Salisbury, as well as three princes of Gwynedd, Hywel, Cynan, and a resurrected Cadwaladr, failed to dislodge him by force.

Although he was outnumbered, the strength of his position, and the resource and skill of his defence allowed him to agree to a truce on not intolerable terms; and everybody went home until three years later the war, like an ill-smothered fire, broke out afresh.

2

'It is an age of quarrels!' sighed Bleddyn at Dinefwr one February evening in 1160 when the rains flowed endlessly. The huntsmen sulked indoors round their fires, kicking their dogs, cuffing their children, drinking too much mead, and enduring the spleen of women prone in the dull days to take fancied offences amongst themselves. Queen Gwenllian was grieving for the death in Winchester of her father Madog ap Maredudd, King of Powys, amongst the kin of the wife of his old age, Matilda Verdun the Frenchwoman. Bleddyn, stirred by pity, had arrived from Ty Gwyn ar Daf to offer distraction as well as to escape the monastery food. It was always rather sparse at winter's end, and had begun to disagree with him, whereas he knew that Rhys managed to keep a good table, even in Lent.

'An age of quarrels?' said King Rhys thoughtfully, picking his teeth and gloomily eyeing the running battle between Gruffydd and Rhys, his sons by Queen Gwenllian, and Maelgwn, his eldest but natural son. He was inordinately fond and proud of each, but his discipline was erratic. All was harmony so long as Einion taught them military lore; then their rivalry flowed in proper channels. But Rhys could not conceal his opinions for long. When any son did well, the father rejoiced too openly, and the child's conceit grew loud. When any displeased him, a torrent of irritability fell on the culprit's head; this excess of public praise and blame increased their divisions.

'Perhaps you are right, indeed,' he said. 'There is my quarrel with the French, and the hates that thrive between each of these. Henry is at odds with his overlord Louis, King of France. What other dissensions occur to you?'

Rhys always liked to pick Bleddyn's brains. He knew that the cyfarwydd met strangers of both low degree and high, but then, so did kings. But Bleddyn had friends also in the middle category of men; and Rhys knew less of these. They were below his familiarity and above his condescension. Bleddyn knew people like Jehan of Bordeaux, the sea captain with gold rings in his ears who had taken Cadell across the sea to Acquitaine, and Pieter of Flanders, the merchant who brought rich stuffs to Caer Fyrddin and went home with wool from Ty Gwyn ar Daf. Queen Gwenllian bought satins from him; Rhys loved to see her splendidly arrayed on great occasions.

'Old men, as usual, say that times have never been so bad,' said Bleddyn. 'Take Barba Rossa, this red-bearded Emperor, whom men call great. He tilts at Papal power like his predecessors. He wants all Italy, that he may recreate Rome's ancient empire. Pieter the Fleming calls it trying to grasp quicksilver in his hand, for the new Pope, Alexander III, will repel the Emperor like a corgi defending his backyard. In Germany, the barons live like little kings, conducting private wars, while the towns league together in fear of them and look to Barba Rossa for protection. But in Italy, it is the barons who support the Emperor, and the towns that oppose him, with Pope as ally. Which shall be master, Church or State? It is the same quarrel in Lloegr, where kings have quarrelled with Popes since the Bastard took the crown. Henry bites like a dog on his claim to invest bishops and abbots with their rings and staffs. He is deaf to the Pope's fury and the Archbishop's feeble protests.'

Rhys muttered, 'If only some cleric would arise of a temper equal to Henry's! There's no one ready to endure his unstopped fury.' He spoke like a man who had long been probing the strength and weakness of his enemies, with the baffled lassitude of a peace-time general marking time and storing his strength against his next war. 'What news from Ty Gwyn ar Daf?'

'Young Gerallt FitzWilliam of Maenor Pyrr has spent a month there in the library,' said Bleddyn drily. 'Your cousin Angharad's boy, her youngest. Stuffed full of learning got from the monks of St. Peter's Abbey at Gloucester, brimful of opinions, too. He goes to Paris next year, where there is what scholars call a university, a little world made all for them. He will not be ignored. He directs his flow of polished Latin at every man of eminence who comes his way, not so much currying, as bestowing favour. He is, however, ardent in worship, and is clean and neat in his person,' added Bleddyn, willing to be fair. Rhys was amused, but not much interested in Gerallt, and Bleddyn chuckled.

'Ah, my lord, you're after some military titbit from Dyfed, from which to plan a skirmish with the French to occupy your men!'

But Rhys only grinned quietly into his beard and said nothing; his officers, too, were reticent, and Bleddyn was obliged to stoop to gossip with the men-at-arms. Then he discovered that they all had their eyes on Llanymddyfri castle. Rhys had surrendered this to the barons at the time of the truce, confident that he could win it back when he wanted to cut his next dash. Meanwhile he took a quiet interest in watching the masons and architects of the King of Lloegr strengthen it stoutly in stone. Large sums of treasury gold were going into the work.

'The more the better,' said Lord Rhys. 'I want to see what it looks like when it's finished. Then we can topple it over.'

Bleddyn, summoned by the obligations of his eminence, went on to Powys. It should never be said that Bleddyn Cyfarwydd failed to mourn, with the true and sounding ring of sorrow, the death of Madog ap Maredudd, and as he went, he studied metaphors and tried out phrases on his tongue. Fair play to Madog, Powys had stayed one kingdom under him for all the storms that rocked it. His situation in the North and East of Cymru had forced him to balance his running war with his brother-in-law in Gwynedd by an uneasy alliance with the King of Lloegr. He and Owain took turns in tearing up the border between them; their savage dispute was an open, true, and bitter bond, unlike the mincing care that lay between Madog and Henry.

Bleddyn, travelling incognito, avoided the homes of the uchelwyr as he travelled north, and knocked on the doors of lesser folk, who received him with the kindness which it was the pride of every Cymro to extend to strangers. This allowed him to give his voice a holiday and to listen rather, for silence was the obverse of his craft. Many a dull conversation he endured for the sake of some good thing that might emerge, like a juicy plum from an otherwise indifferent pudding.

'Who will follow Madog?' he asked them. But they could not say.

'Llewellyn is slain, druan!' they said. 'The eldest gone! And the other sons are struggling, Gruffydd, and Owain Fychan, and Owain Brogyntyn, as well as Madog's brother Iorwerth Goch, that redhead, and his nephew Owain Cyfeiliog.'

'And the widow, that French girl?'

'Ach!' they said. 'Matilda Verdun? She feathered her nest, that one. She and her Winchester kin pounced on CroesOswallt on the Border, and fortified it well. Weak in his old age, poor Madog was. They made him sign that lordship off to her and to any sons she might have after his death. Oh, she shed tears in proper plenty at the funeral—all the Meifod people were watching! But she married a new husband, one John FitzAlan, before her handkerchief had time to dry.'

Bleddyn had been rather pleased with the praise of Madog that he had prepared, but when he reached Meifod, the uchelwyr heard him with such patient politeness that he knew he had, after all, arrived too late, and that they were tired of mourning him. Only one thought dwelt in every head. Who would follow Madog?

Disgruntled, he went back to give the news to Rhys, who smiled with satisfaction, for Powys would be out of action for many years to come, and would be no embarrassment to Deheubarth.

'And Llanymddyfri?' asked Bleddyn eagerly.

But Lord Rhys appeared to have lost interest in Llanymddyfri, and was more absorbed by the delight of holding his first baby daughter in his arms. Bleddyn, disappointed again, turned his back on the world, and for the next eighteen months remained incommunicado in a guest cell at Ty Gwyn ar Daf, insensible alike of winter's blast and summer's fire. Now, while the world was quiet, he resolved, he would at last write down the stories that the Mabinogi made. When he had taken them, they were worn and shapeless from rough recounting in more clumsy mouths than his. It had been his pride to tell them each time with more precision; he had refashioned them to his own taste, with singular points of brilliance here and there. Now, they were set, and must be inscribed. He would suffer no man to change them.

When Bleddyn wrote the last word and came out of his cell, it was the summer of another year, but of which one, he was not sure. He stood on the green lawns, blinking. Would his characters, he wondered, stepping from their pages, live in the minds of other men and women, without his voice to give them motion, and the chord of his harp to send the breezes blowing through their hair? The monastery company pressed round him, monks, summer pilgrims grey with dust, chapmen with their bundles, and cautious Flemish traders. Eagerly they welcomed him back to the world, and told him the great news.

'Llanymddyfri has fallen to Lord Rhys!' they cried. 'Like a ripe plum it fell!'

But Cadell was shouting with frustration as well as with excitement.

'It is meaningless to take Llanymddyfri unless he plans a large campaign to follow! Bravado is not enough, however brilliant! Has he mustered his allies in Cymru behind him first? No! Powys is broken, Gwynedd is too shrewd to stir. Alone, Rhys is bound to fail. Tell him to remember the wisdom of our father Gruffydd, and our brothers Anarawd and Maredudd! Tell him to learn caution and modesty, for his present rashness brings to mind a would-be hero anxious to impress the bards!'

Baffled though he was by the diplomatic delivery of such a message, Bleddyn made straight for Ystrad Tywi, rejoicing in summer and sharing his joy with the upland Cymry as he went. But Rhys was hard to find. It was July, and hot, and Bleddyn grew tired. He discovered that the King was spending the great summer roaming with gusto through his scattered lands, enjoying his triumph, collecting his rents, doing justice on the cylch, bracing the zeal and alertness of his people, and even receiving dues from other men's lordships, to the fury of their French owners. Bleddyn, unable to catch him up, made himself comfortable at Caeo. King Henry was still in France; no baron had yet dared to take revenge for Llanymddyfri; the message from Cadell could wait. So he turned his face to the sun, listened to the tyddynwyr of the Caeo cantref murmuring round him like a hive of bees, and slept.

The King came back to Caeo for Michaelmas with the look of a man who had freely and well expended his energy. His humour was good but sober, and after a day's exchange of greetings and kindness with his wife and children, he fell into the first of a series of watchful silences that struck the court strangely, and made the Queen anxious lest he had found a new cariad in Pencader, or be sickening for a fever.

Bleddyn ventured to remark on his abstraction one October afternoon when the King rested from hunting. He laughed, rather shortly.

'Why, I am thirty!' he said. 'Bleddyn, I am in my middle age! Strange thoughts assail me. Who am I? Where did I come from, and where do I go? What is life and why am I here? Must I always go running about for ever after my inheritance? And what good is it to God?'

What human soul could answer cries like these? wondered Bleddyn.

'These are the questions of life's core,' said the cyfarwydd slowly. 'A man's sense of wonder passes from one strangeness to another. A child takes life for granted, and death is the stranger. The years bring him the knowledge that he must die, and when he has learned that lesson, he dwells with surprise on his summons into life at all. At that point he can begin to live in fulness; he can gather into the palm of his hand all that experience has taught him, like a fruit, extract the seeds, and plant and water them and watch them grow.'

Rhys threw another log upon the fire, and watched a shower of sparks.

'Such thoughts are a sinful waste of time, surely,' he said, with some impatience. 'Knowledge is reserved for hereafter.'

Bleddyn said, 'But God sends these thoughts to measure and to shape our human activities, and to serve as their background. Greatness in the universe around us exacts greatness within us. It is the one appropriate response. As for your inheritance, it is the strength and the style of your struggle that God applauds. The reason and the result are, after all, His business.'

Rhys stretched his thick and sturdy frame, and yawned, and laughed, and slapped the cyfarwydd on the back.

'I like you, Bleddyn!' he said. 'You are better to me than many a priest, saving always old Caradoc. Now, you have been hinting at some message from my brother which you have not yet had the courage to deliver. What did he say?'

Reluctantly, Bleddyn delivered the message, verbatim. When Lord Rhys had stopped laughing, he said, 'I wish I had a tongue like his! Listen, Bleddyn, tell him next time you see him that I have to maintain the reputation won by my forebears and my three elder brothers, of whom he was the stoutest warrior of us all. Tell him that all my opportunities are my angels, and I must seize each as I may to show my power, for a lost chance never comes again! When I took Llanymddyfri, I raised the hearts of all my people by that single gesture of contempt towards Henry for his faithless use of me.' He laughed again, but grimly. 'I raised my own as well. Even if it brings on my doom, at least I have forced him to take me seriously, and a man can sometimes make even disaster serve his turn.'

Bleddyn spent the winter with friends outside Caer Fyrddin to nose out news. He liked watching the great river flowing without haste away. He had friends within the gates, too, and he enjoyed strolling on the quay, chatting to the burghers, while behind him the hill winds brought the smells of dung and woodsmoke to mingle with the tidal breeze along Tywi's edge that had travelled over boats and mud, Llan Stephan cockles, and diluted sea. Sometimes he caught a glimpse of Prince Einion ab Anarawd moving quietly in the crowds, his face half obscured by the folds of his cloak.

'Earl Roger is jealous,' the burghers told Bleddyn. 'It is known that the Prince comes and goes in secret to visit a certain lady in whom the Earl is interested.'

The burghers were affluent, and therefore tolerant of all mankind, Cymry included. Lord Henry, their King, had secured their prosperity, and they discussed him freely, and with complacency.

'He struggles now to regain Toulouse, claimed in the name of his wife Queen Eleanor,' they said. 'Already he has overthrown his brother Geoffrey in Anjou, and seized that province in flat disobedience to his father's will. Oh, he is rampant!' they added proudly. 'He takes what pleases him. He orders the barons. He throws out the bad men who plundered the land before his reign began. He sends out travelling justices in eyre. He plucks Peace, screaming, out of turmoil, and thrusts her down upon the land with as rude a gesture as when he makes war!'

And his chancellor, chimed in others, that Becket, was as high as his master, and now he was home from France where he sat on a horse, in full armour, deacon as he was, at the expedition to Toulouse, and even overthrew a knight in single combat! That was the man, they said, spitting, now coming home full pelt, elected Archbishop of Canterbury by Henry's bidding, now that Theobald had gone. Why, he'd have the Church shackled to the King's side in ten minutes, and snap his fingers under the Pope's nose! And then they laughed, good Christians all, for they were far away enough from Rome to fear retribution more from David FitzGerald, the Lady Nest's son, at last heaved on to the episcopal throne at Ty Ddewi by the united efforts of his family, and by Henry's permission, than from Pope Alexander III.

At the end of December, Henry came back to Lloegr, and Bleddyn understood why Becket had returned before him, for authoritative news reached Caer Fyrddin during the Twelve Days of Christmas that a great army was gathering at the gates of Cymru, ready to invade Deheubarth.

Bleddyn travelled north at once to join Lord Rhys, who, said the upland Cymry, was standing in his strong fort of Pencader.

Winter is hard enough to bear without the woes of war to carry too. In every valley Bleddyn found the Cymry burning their houses and driving their strongest cattle up to the hafodtai in the furthest hills, towards the snow of a hard winter. Men were killing their weakest cows and salting meat. Women were ravaging their garden plots and packing gambos high with food, babies, hens, and piles of brethin cartref in between the spades and knives, looms and spindles, swords and bows, crocks of butter, wooden bowls and spoons, cheeses, and arrows newly feathered from the Christmas fowls.

Rumour ran up from the South. The King of Lloegr, a freckle-faced man, had crossed the river Ebbw at Pencarn by the ancient ford; and such a one, the ancient prophets had said, would master Cymru. The King of Lloegr, said the rumour, growing louder, was coming, leading his burnished army over Gwent, across Morgannwg. At the modern crossing-place, over Ebbw, his horse, with a neigh, took a fancy to refuse; Henry, with an oath, went upstream, roundabout, until he found a shallow place to please his horse. He had not heard of the prophecy; he did not know that he had used the ancient ford.

'His horse knew,' said the Cymry.

King Rhys waited calmly at Pencader for King Henry.

'Henry at Caer Fyrddin?' he said. 'I shall not fight him this winter. I have ground my authority into the land, and Henry hasn't. However large an army he brings to crush me, he will have to take it away quickly, for his men are used to fatter lands than this. You saw no panic amongst the Cymry, Bleddyn. They have gone in good order into the hills, as I commanded them. I have undermined Clare authority in Ceredigion, and my kin will rise, but only at a signal from me.' He shrugged impatiently. 'I've provoked him hither. How can I do business with a man who spends so much time across the water? Now we can quarrel face to face.' And when Bleddyn expressed fears for his personal safety, he laughed.

'I have nothing to lose except my skin,' said Lord Rhys. 'If that goes, Einion can take my place. He's Anarawd's boy. He'll treat the people right.'

Bleddyn, speechless, found himself elbowed by the soldiers, and looked at, not for a story, but to be got out of the way. Groaning, he went aside into the woods to pray, and wait, and watch this King of Lloegr pass. He found a shelter from the wind. He was cold, but more sad than cold; there was nothing he could do for Rhys but pray. God answers a good prayer; Bleddyn opened his heart to Him, and in doing so was comforted, and grew warmer.

The King of Lloegr must have travelled half through the night to catch the King of Deheubarth, for when the clamour of his arrival woke up Bleddyn, the wood still swam within the dark grey, grudging gloom that muffles dawn. He tumbled out of his hole, stiff as a hedgehog disturbed in mid-winter, and staggered across to the fort where the two armies confronted each other in attitudes of mutual menace, moving restlessly within their positions like two pots of cawl set aside to simmer. Bleddyn wormed his way forward, elbowing his way pretty sharply to the place in front that was his due, and his neighbours with reluctance gave way for Bleddyn Cyfarwydd in tacit acknowledgement that this was, it seemed, after all a moment for men of words.

He was a large, tall man, this Henry, with wide shoulders, and the short, thick neck of a person easily possessed by his rages. He was in full bellow. King Rhys, held down on his knees, interrupted the flow.

'I cannot parley with a mad bull,' he said scornfully. 'Where's his master? Where's the King of Lloegr gone?'

Shock ran through the French ranks, and the Cymry cheered. The soldiers who held down Rhys lifted their swords to strike, and Bleddyn was jerked off his feet by the Cymry behind him roaring forward to the rescue. But Henry, glaring, held up his hand, and the commotion ceased. Rhys got up from his knees and dusted them.

'Let us talk together like Christians!' he said shortly. 'And consider my list of complaints. I am obliged to submit to you, and I have done so. Now let Cymru observe the justice for which you are famed, and which I claim.'

After a moment of peril, Henry's anger spent itself on a long gale of laughter.

'The mad bull corners the wild wolf at last then!' roared Henry. 'Get you to horse! Justice I shall do indeed, when I rid this country of its troublesome pest! It's in Hereford you shall answer to me for your treasons, Rhys ap Gruffydd!'

The teulu, with passionate high battle cries, sprang to arms, but Rhys in a rage silenced them with buffet and roar.

'Go home to Caeo!' he shouted. 'Disband! Remember my orders!'

Then very roughly a band of French and Saeson clapped him on a horse and took him away. The other Cymry stood frozen by the orders of Rhys, but Bleddyn found a voice to scream at Henry.

'You think to conquer Cymru if you take one king? Time will teach you truth, Henry! Cut one down and six will rise to beat your bones!' Anger stronger than he had ever known pushed him forward until he could grab at Henry's bridle with a furious pull. The King's rage yielded to astonishment.

'Who are you?' he asked, surprised into mildness. Bleddyn was not impressed, for no other tone was customary in the kings who spoke to him.

'He is Bleddyn the story-teller,' said one of the FitzGeralds in Henry's train. 'He is the greatest of them all and has much influence in Cymru.'

Henry stared into Bleddyn's eyes, pitting his will against that of the cyfarwydd.

'Old man,' he said, 'Shall I not totally subdue, this year or next, your poor country, and enrich it with my authority?'

Behind Bleddyn, the bitter men of Rhys's teulu stood poised, but for Einion's control of them, to disobey their own King's orders. Bleddyn spoke for each of them, for their fathers, for their sons.

'Certainly you will harrass and weaken us!' said Bleddyn. 'And partially destroy us! But then again the Cymry, too, will often prevail against you, King of Lloegr! We are greater than you, for we have more kings than you, and though you seized every one, you would still have Cymru to conquer, where every several man in his land is king!'

Henry's fury turned into a snarl, but still the great crowd heard Bleddyn in a hush, for old though he was, his voice was both vibrant and young.

'Never can the Cymric nation be totally subdued through the wrath of man, unless the wrath of God concurs! I know that on the Last Day no other nation or language shall answer for my people!'

The Cymry roared hard enough to burst their lungs as Henry and his army stood glaring. Then he snatched the reins from Bleddyn's grasp, and rode north with a savage thrust of spurs into his horse's flanks. Men scattered as the mass of his soldiers laid about them with the flat of their swords, too ill-humoured even to bother to kill a few Cymry for luck.

Rhys was taken up through the eastern mountains of Ceredigion, a captive through his rightful realm, right across Powys and over Clawdd Offa into silence. All through that bleak winter and spring, the King's chair in Caeo was empty. But the Queen showed a brave face, and governed in the mountains with diligence and a bold hand. Secretly, through Einion, she caused the scattered teulu to be reassembled, to guard the borders.

'Nothing,' she said stubbornly, 'Shall be lost that has been entrusted to my care!'

A few weeks later, old Caradoc the priest, who had been allowed to accompany his King, was seen in Deheubarth wandering in company with a French knight. They were glimpsed between mists, observed on the higher hills, climbing the more rugged paths, seen between one heavy April shower and the next. Some of the uchelwyr winked and chuckled, and the rumour came that Henry had sent this French knight to find out whether Cantref Mawr with Dinefwr, the heart of Deheubarth, was fat enough to be worth keeping, or poor enough to be tossed back to a lord too slippery to be held in the hand.

In July, Rhys returned to Caeo, master once more of Cantref Mawr on payment of homage to Henry once again, and after losing a few games of chess to him; and he turned to praise Caradoc for his wit and fidelity, calling for the choicest food to be set before the beaming priest.

'My dear friend!' cried Rhys, embracing him soundly. 'You have lived on mountain grass for too long, like any goat!' Caradoc had led the French knight such a dance, he declared, through bogways and by rough crags and moors, that Henry was only too glad to abandon the land to its lord.

'It's all a wild and barren place beyond the river strip,' the knight had told Henry, worn out by his adventures. 'It's unfit for civilized men, my lord, meet only for the barbarians who can live there, strong and lean as deer upon the mountain moss and herbs when other nourishment fails!'

For the last few hot weeks of summer, the men of Caeo and the court were filled with happiness as though Rhys were at the peak of power, instead of restored precariously to a diminished realm. Even when they went down to Dinefwr, when dreary November drove them into the halls, a large calm possessed their hearts like a rich soil where strength could strike its roots anew.

3

Spring sent adventure swinging through the blood, but Rhys respected the peace.

'I'll keep faith with Henry if this time he keeps faith with me,' he said. 'But I'll keep my claws sharp.' So he occupied his restless teulu with the military contests of the ancient games. On Dewi Sant's day, all the ladies of the court, the old men, and the children, were present to applaud the bowmen and the lancers and the swordsmen and the wrestlers and the runners of Deheubarth as they performed their feats of skill under Einion's supervision.

He was directing the archery contest, watching the flight of arrows, and carefully recording the results on his large slate. In the distance, each competitor came up to base, kicking off his right shoe to get a good grip on the grass with his foot, shifting his weight to improve his stance, drawing with care, and loosing his arrow. They shot for the farthest, at an angle into the air, and craned their necks to watch where the arrows fell. But Einion was not attending.

'Einion, bachgen!'

He stood there with his head drooping and an arrow stuck in his left side. He tumbled over slowly, and died. The great crowd gave a simultaneous gasp of horror, and the women screamed, 'Murder!'

'Someone marked him from the woods!' roared Rhys, savagely. 'After him, teulu!'

Pandemonium followed, as dogs and men leapt forward. One of Einion's men was missing; they scoured the forest for him to Drysllwyn and beyond, but he got away. Bleddyn Cyfarwydd, his knees trembling, pushed his way through a press of weeping women.

'Do not come to me for reasons!' he said harshly. 'I do not know every casineb of the south! How do I know why it happened? Every public man has enemies!'

The report grew garbled as it ran through Deheubarth. 'Killed in his sleep,' recorded the Llan Badarn monks in their Chronicle.

'Of course!' remarked Bleddyn bitterly. 'He was certainly asleep to danger!'

The traitor, it was later learned, won across the border into Ceredigion, where Earl Roger received him like a brother, with a welcome well prepared beforehand. Then Bleddyn understood.

'Roger was always jealous of Einion!' he said. 'That girl in Caer Fyrddin liked him best.'

A curious message came from Cadell to the King. 'Now tighten the reins, brother. Sharpen your knife. Now make this disaster serve your turn.'

Rhys heard this with a stricken, stony face, and nodded. At the end of March, he rose, and summoned his armies for a full-scale invasion of Ceredigion.

'This is the end of the Clares,' he said sombrely. 'I shall recover my whole inheritance, and this time, keep it.'

So Lord Rhys and the teulu and the whole army of the hills surged over the border, and drove out the Clares in a full revenge for Einion's death. They destroyed the chief castle of Cwmmwd Mabwynion, and the new one at Aber Rheidol, and ravaged far and wide throughout Ceredigion, wherever the French had found a perch until only the town and castle of Aber Teifi remained in the enemy hands of Robert FitzStephen. Rhys organized a determined siege there which was to continue for the rest of the year, but he gave it only half his attention. He spent the summer in Ceredigion, surveying his lands, restoring order, and receiving the congratulations of all the Kings of Cymru, who sent their heralds south to make a military pact with him. They recognized him as second only to Owain Gwynedd himself, for strength of purpose and a single mind, it was clear, had combined to form in him a statesman and an opportunist who stepped from circumstance to circumstance towards his goal.

As soon as his men had repaired the castle walls at Aber Rheidol, Rhys summoned the Queen to join him.

'I have no intention of living a rough camp life a moment longer than I must!' he declared.

Gwenllian came at once. She surveyed with indignation the disorder left by the workmen, rolled up her sleeves, and began to order the Antaron caethion with shrill cries. She vowed that the stench left behind by the French still rose to her nostrils; she had the floors cleaned of blood and fire, well scrubbed, and sweetened by rushes and freshly smelling herbs. She forbade the soldiers to foul the hall with spitting, dogs, and muddy shoes, and grumbling, they obeyed, reluctantly enjoying the comfort that her strictness imposed. They took pleasure in the sight of her at night, with spindle and whorl, with the firelight glancing on her glowing hair, on the folds of her best robes, and on her earrings of twisted gold. She was brisk and beautiful, happy to have Rhys to herself, away from her own children and other women's brats. She held her head high, maintaining the King's majesty and her own; she had brought with her the great golden torque of St. Cynog for Lord Rhys to wear, and sported her own finest silks and jewels to be admired by the crowd of uchelwyr and boneddigion swarming to the new seat of power. Most of them were blood relations.

'It is rare for me to meet any gwr bonheddig,' said Rhys to Gwenllian, grinning broadly, 'Who does not most carefully announce himself to be my seventh cousin on his father's side, or my fifth on his mother's.'

'And each wants a favour,' remarked Gwenllian. 'It is a tribute to your power. Except that rough fellow from Llan Badarn who came yesterday in his hunting garb. He asked for nothing. What is he, a little country squire?'

Rhys laughed.

'Who, Ednowain ap Gweithfoed? He is the Abbot of Llan Badarn, 'merch i, old Bishop Sulien's great-grandnephew! He and his sons and brothers are old friends of mine from the days when we campaigned against Hywel. They run the place like a great family estate, but people say it has changed a lot since he was a boy. The intellectual tradition of Sulien and Rhigyfarch suffered rude interruption when the Clares arrived. Scholarship went underground, and as he says, when you have to take to the hills, the best learning is that which teaches you to survive! But Ednowain's uncle Henry ab Arthen did what he could. He was the chronicler before the foreign monks took over and tried to submerge Ceredigion below the surface of an alien regime. Ednowain himself is not unlettered, and I suppose his people call him Abbot in the hope that he will eventually summon the old days out of darkness. I must return his visit. He's too independent to ask for favours, but I know why he's so anxious to be friendly. There's a kindness he can do me, too, with regard to Ystrad Fflur.'

A year earlier, Robert FitzStephen had at last installed twelve monks from Ty Gwyn ar Daf in a new home in front of the great Gors Goch Glan Teifi in eastern Ceredigion, and shown them the vast expanse of moorland on the mountains behind, where their sheep might graze. Now that Lord Rhys had recovered the gwlad, the new Abbot begged the rightful lord of Ceredigion graciously to confirm the grant of land made by the Clares.

'Grant of land!' repeated Rhys contemptuously. 'What is this site, and how far do these lands extend that Roger allowed them to enter in another man's inheritance? I'll have to look into the matter!'

He rode over one fine June morning up the Ystwyth valley and past Ystrad Meurig castle, once more restored to Constable Iestyn Fychan, who had kept his promise and laid aside his magic powers. Lord Rhys had no desire to see his daughter, the mother of his eldest son, Maelgwn; she was married now, and absorbed in rearing other children. But he paused to see Iestyn, whose opinions he valued, and were, as usual, offered gratuitously.

'Ystrad Fflur?' he grumbled, frowning. 'I'm sorry for those poor young fellows. What possessed Robert to put them where he knew the old monks in your grandfather's time came to grief? Oh, of course, he's an ardent fowler, and thought it would make a useful hunting-lodge for himself. If he had asked me, I would have advised against it. The winter brings that little stream the Fflur up in flood too near their doors, there is no shelter in front of them from the prevailing south-west wind and rain which blow against them right across the Gors. Their vegetable garden is bound to suffer.' His eyes gleamed. 'I know some spells,' he murmured resentfully. 'They work, too, in a bad season, to improve the weather, but your Father Caradoc made me give them up, all but one, otherwise I'd be glad to help them—'

'That will not be necessary,' said Rhys, rising hastily.

'—but simples at least I can offer them,' continued Iestyn imperturbably. 'Old age and the rheumatics will claim them all too soon. Young they may be now, but every year the horny fingers of this harsh upland winter will thrust its pinch of gravel ever deeper between their joints. It would have been far better if they had been tucked into that valley behind Rhyd Fendigaid. It's more sheltered, and it always seems to trap the sun, and it's got the mountain pools behind. I'm quite prepared to be friends with them, my lord, if it's true what I hear, that they are not like yr hen daclau 'na down in Llan Ddewi Brefi, too proud to know their neighbours.'

Rhys inspected the valley on his way to the monks' quarters a few miles away, and saw Iestyn's point. Then he interviewed the young Abbot, Father Dafydd, to whom he took an instant liking. He told Lord Rhys with enthusiasm and considerable pride about their building work and plans.

'We follow the example of St. Bernard our Founder and his companions who fifty years ago went forth from Citeaux into the wild place of Clairvaux!' he said with a glowing face. 'First we raised this rude church, hewing the wood from the trees below the mountains.'

Rhys inspected it, with interest and curiosity. He discovered that the refectory and dormitory, built one above the other, and connected by a ladder stairway, were built on to the church and shared its roof. The dormitory was a mere garret, where each monk lay at night within his wooden coffin.

'I would dread the darkness of so confined a space!' exclaimed Rhys.

'Oh, it's snug enough, especially in winter,' replied the Abbot hardily. 'With the lid slightly open for air, and our thick garments to cover us, and plenty of hay!'

'What are your aims? What do you want to do in Ceredigion?'

'An abbey! An abbey in stone, where we, and those who live around us and who visit us, may worship God in worthy surroundings!' Father Dafydd sighed. 'We are on the main pilgrim route from north to south of Cymru, and pilgrims would flock to our doors. If only it could be in a less exposed position! Meanwhile, we prepare for that major building enterprise, we tend our sheep, still few in numbers, and we seek out respectable men in the neighbourhood to join us as lay brethren. They have been few and far between, but now that your campaign is over, my lord, we hope to find more amongst returning soldiers.

There is much we can offer them—a life of joy in the word and work of God, a chance to learn their letters, opportunities of opening up the wilderness of Cymru, by your permission, we trust—as well as modern skills in the breeding and development of fine sheep flocks, and a better class of wool. In short,' concluded the Abbot, 'we seek to lead them into both this world and the next.'

He hesitated, and looked anxiously at the King.

'I do hope, my lord Rhys, that we shall have your goodwill behind us in this holy place?'

To the Abbot's deep dismay, Lord Rhys replied with a hint of anger. 'You shall have nothing of the kind! You were brought to this site without either my knowledge or consent, and I hereby give you six months' notice. Let no man cast the reproach in my teeth that I let the Cistercians of Ceredigion build their Abbey so unworthily, hard by a swamp! No!' he declared, his broad chest swelling with purpose as he turned squarely towards the bewildered Abbot. 'You shall tear up the charter of Earl Roger! I shall give you new lands, greatly enlarged, and you shall hold them by the pleasure of none but Rhys ap Gruffydd. And you shall build your splendid Abbey in the valley to the north-east where there are encircling hills to guard and give you shelter!'

He rode back to Aber Rheidol with the sound of their loud, delighted cheering ringing in his ears. His own heart was lifted up by a new and hitherto unknown pleasure. Now, as he himself was beginning to rebuild his gwlad of Ceredigion, the Cistercians were building up their own spiritual community and Abbey, in a new centre of culture and worship, just when that of Llan Badarn was declining. The Cymry had come to love the monks of Ty Gwyn ar Daf; boneddigion sent their younger sons to them when their own divisible land threatened to yield portions too small to satisfy a pushing youngster. Some uchelwyr did the same; and it seemed to him that Ystrad Fflur would inherit this goodwill.

'I like the prospect of a great Abbey rising in a savage place, and nurtured by me,' Rhys murmured to himself. 'And how pleased Cadell will be!' He chuckled suddenly. 'This Abbot shall be my friend. He shall be my counterpoise to the Bishop down below in Ty Ddewi, and to all the FitzGeralds and other French that hedge him round about to trouble me!'

As he began to descend from the uplands, the sense of peace and freedom that he had achieved accompanied him into the valley, and began to refine the coarser instincts that had thrust him thus far into his career. Wherever he looked, the tumbled hills sent him the same message of encouragement.

'Here there are holy places too,' he thought, 'in many a valley, many a wrinkle between long mountain folds. I want to make my Ceredigion people feel that God dwells not only in cathedrals, but elsewhere, too, and that He has a care for them here and now, after many a generation of dismay.'

And with that thought came the conviction that he was, at last, taking true possession of his gwlad.

But Rhys could not ignore the older foundations. He paid a courtesy call to Llan Ddewi Brefi, in the hope of weaving a friendship between the neighbouring communities, but without much success; at Llan Ddewi Brefi there was some jealousy, and at Ystrad Fflur some amused disdain. Neither side had much use for the other, in spite of his efforts; it was the usual clash between old traditions and new, and mutual tolerance was the best he could achieve.

It was the same in Llan Badarn, where he found Ednowain and his wife and family busily restoring order to the llan after the ravages of winter and of war. Proudly they showed him the Chronicle, now springing into new life, and the cathedral church where Ednowain and his sons took their regular turns as serving priests at mass, though with their farm boots on.

'I hope to revive the learning of Rhigyfarch in my grandsons, whatever!' said Ednowain defiantly. He was contemptuous of the celibate newcomers at Ystrad Fflur. 'It's all sheep with them!' he said. 'They will have to ride in all weathers after the wandering flocks far beyond earshot of their bells, half way to Rhaiadr and Buellt across the mountains. I'm a cattle man myself,' he said with satisfaction.

'Ah, but they will make money through the wool trade with the Flemings,' said Rhys, hoping to stir a similar interest at Llan Badarn.

'Flemings!' uttered Ednowain, chewing his beef contemptuously. 'There have been enough of those down in Dyfed. If you're not careful, my lord, you'll have them running the monks at Ystrad Fflur as well!'

But he conceded that there was a case for permitting the foundation, since it was an area notorious for pagan superstitions, and they were a decrepit and sickly lot at Llan Ddewi Brefi nowadays. For the King's sake, he would extend a brother's hand if a meeting with the pioneers could not be avoided, but let Lord Rhys draw up the boundaries with care!

Rhys left in a mood of mingled pity and irritation. Ednowain, blindly following the old ways, met the new world opening to Cymru with the obstinate resistance of an old soldier, very different from the King's own open, opportunist spirit, which was apt to judge and test new ways, and borrow from them freely what he thought might suit his people best.

'He won't contribute much to the stir and throb of new life in Deheubarth!' muttered Rhys. 'Any suggestion or rebuke would be useless. He fought so well for me, and he is too influential a landowner to offend!'

Lord Rhys was to have need of Llan Badarn bowmen before many months had passed. All through August, gossip wagged an energetic tongue, telling Henry that Rhys had won back Ceredigion, and telling the Cymry that Becket, now Archbishop of Canterbury, was making trouble for Henry; he had embraced the cause of Rome and turned against his King's aim to use the Church in England as his tool. Never was there such a turn about of loyalties. Henry, raging at Northampton in October, demanded large grants of infantry from his barons to crush Rhys. The news rang through the Border courts, and the echo, through market and fair, tavern and churchyard and tyddyn, reached old King Owain Gwynedd who, bitter at the loss of his grandson Einion, made common cause with Deheubarth. Hitherto he had considered Rhys more daring than sagacious, but the swiftness and power of his advance into Ceredigion, and the skill that had turned his setbacks into jumping boards from which to leap further, now won his admiration. Ceredigion, swift to shrug off unwelcome authority, had lit a forest fire that was roaring far beyond the gwlad. Cymru united, and the mountains were alive with speeding messengers. The ties of blood were tightened, mighty armies assembled, and one mind was achieved. Here was no local rebellion, but a nation up in arms!

Henry, alarmed, used the spring of 1165 to patch up quarrels with enemies behind him, with France and Flanders, summoned feudal troops from Scotland, Normandy, Anjou, Acquitaine, and Poitou, as well as Flemish mercenaries, and sent cartloads of weapons and armour to be stockpiled in Amwythig within the walls of the Severn-looped town; while in the forges of Dinefwr the continuous ring of anvilled iron was heard beneath the winter's cloak of snow, and muttering and excited talk continued throughout the Christmas feast, a groundswell under even Bleddyn's most military tales.

Maelgwn and Maredudd, Rhys's elder boys, had won permission to accompany their father on his next campaign. Bright-eyed and silent, they practised with the teulu in rain and frost in day-long exercises in Ystrad Tywi. At night, in the hall, they sat just long enough to fill their empty bellies before curling up like stones under their deerskins. Even the Queen and her women worked hard through the short days, weaving the warm, earth-coloured cloth and making the clothes in which the soldiers of Deheubarth might spring like fangs upon the French.

As soon as the court had heard the Easter Mass, Rhys and his army marched north-east to join the forces of his uncle, Owain Gwynedd, and the main host of the princes, at Corwen. It proved to be a strange campaign, largely devoted to manœuvre and counter-manœuvre. No mighty victory on either side was won; Dafydd ab Owain Gwynedd did raid Tegeingl, but Henry not only relieved Rhuddlan but also recovered Basingwerk as well. The Cymry were outnumbered; the weather was too good for them, but perfect for Henry's heavy-armoured knights. There had been nothing for it but for the Cymry to husband their more limited strength; they withdrew into difficult terrain where they had the advantage, and allowed Henry to return to Amwythig. He then marched to Croes Oswallt to make a spearhead push into the heart of Cymru, to separate North from South, but the venture ended in a skirmish in the Ceiriog valley between some of his men and a few outriders of Cymru's main force.

'A bad lot they are, those French or Flemish or English or Poitevins, whatever they call themselves, you don't know what you're fighting nowadays,' said Rhys contemptuously to Bleddyn, who had arrived with outworn advice from Cadell, on a pony with too much philosophy for military errands. 'Some of them committed sacrilege in a church, removing its timbers for lighting their fires! Our men of course were eager for immediate punishment, but Owain Gwynedd lifted up his hand. ''Don't interfere!'' he said. ''God will take His own vengeance!'''

Owain was proved a true prophet. The good weather that Henry had wasted on the Tegeingl castles broke with a week of torrential rain in which all Cymru lay awash; and when in a last despairing push he tried to scale the mountains of the Berwyn range, the hard truth about the soil of Cymru at last entered his impassioned understanding. When a heavily armed man and his horse were soaking wet with rain and sweat inside their massive iron and leather garments, and they were struggling against wind and rain on slippery hills retreating into endless mountains, and food was low and nowhere to be had for man or beast in all that desert, what could a violent man do but go home and deliver himself up to other evil?

That was what Henry did. He fell into the longest and most dreadful rage that his barons had yet beheld; and he ordered all the twenty-two Cymry that he had seized as hostages, to be blinded. Then they were callously sent home. One of them was Maredudd ap Rhys of Deheubarth, who had lived only to be a good bowman. A knife turned in Rhys's heart as he took his son to Ty Gwyn ar Daf, to be succoured by the monks.

'I have protected Deheubarth from Henry,' said Rhys bitterly. 'But at what a cost!'

The monks crowded round in pity, but Maredudd pushed them aside with much the same savagery that his captors had used on him, until Cadell lurched forward to grab him.

'Only one hand I've got that works, nephew, only one sound leg!' he growled. 'Pity you won't get from me! I challenge you!' he roared to the astonished boy. 'Yield your manhood to work for God's kingdom here, in ways that you have never dreamed of!'

Stunned, Maredudd suffered his uncle to use him as his crutch, and to be pushed into the refectory to be given immediate heart with wine and food. He was sufficiently calm at the end of a week to send a message to his parents. He would stay at Ty Gwyn ar Daf. His worst pains were over, the summer sunshine helped to heal, and the monks' talk interested him; but he did not wish to be forgotten at Dinefwr. He had heard that his mother was with child again, and he begged that if it were a boy, the child's name should be Maredudd.

The Cymry did not rejoice too loudly throughout that watchful winter. Rhys had been as much concerned to hold the Cymry together and to advance his own influence amongst the princes, as to beat off the French. He had got on well enough with the men of Powys, and had promised the hand of his eldest daughter to Einion Clud.

'Deheubarth certainly remains in my hands, but it was God's victory, not ours,' said Rhys quietly to Cadell, below the steady rumble of Dinefwr's Christmas feast. 'We may reap the fruits only through vigilance and a strong alliance throughout Cymru. There is much fighting still for us to struggle through. Henry strengthened Rhuddlan, Basingwerk, and Prestatyn, and Owain will not rest until he has got them back again. He helped me, so I have promised to help him next year. Meanwhile, there are Aber Teifi and Caer Fyrddin waiting to be won.'

'You will never take Caer Fyrddin,' said Cadell. 'I strengthened it so well that it can withstand all but the most prolonged of sieges.' He paused, savouring the bitterness that gave a relish to his satisfaction. 'But sooner or later you will recover Aber Teifi, Rhys, and then power in the South will be locked in a firm balance. As lord of Ceredigion, Ystrad Tywi, and most of Dyfed, you will be able to strike out north, or south, or east. You can put a ring round Caer Fyrddin, and reduce its strategic importance.'

Rhys leaned back, smiling. He was thinking of Aber Rheidol, where he had first felt within himself the power to gather Cymru in his hand. He and Gwenllian had climbed the ancient earthwork on Pendinas and looked out to sea one bright day when all things stood revealed and all things seemed possible. The little trefydd to the south were clear, Llan Non, Llan Sant Ffraed and Aber Arth and Aber Aeron; he could see almost to Aber Teifi. And to the north, all was clear; there were Tywyn and Aber Mawddach under Eryri; all the land of Meirionnydd leaned over to him, and as for Lleyn on the farther rim of this great bowl, it lay like a field mouse flat on its belly, with its ears laid back and its nose reaching out towards the morsel of Ynys Enlli.

He sighed. Influence was one thing, dominion another. He put his temptations aside, and decided to confine his dreams to Deheubarth, for the time being.

4

In the years that followed, the French drew in their horns, and King Henry, overwhelmed by problems of his own, kept well away from a pugnacious Cymru. In the North, Owain Gwynedd, in two campaigns, won back the strong forts of Tegeingl, partly with the help of Rhys. In the South, Lord Rhys by his own efforts and by craft, at last won Aber Teifi. He tore down enough of the castle to make it useless to the French, and took his cousin Robert FitzStephen captive. He banished the Flemish burghers for a time, though he was good enough to let them leave with half their moveables, because they had shown a wholesome fear of his ferocity and kept quiet. All through the South, wherever he went on cylch, Rhys made all men aware of his firm grasp of power, and Deheubarth, launched into a period of steady peace, began to prosper.

But Rhys was puzzled to know what to do with Robert.

'I can't keep him cooped up for ever,' he complained. 'The bards used to sing of my generosity, but they have been quiet lately. Sometimes I wish I had never taken the fellow prisoner, but how else can I keep him from mischief, short of killing him, which I will not do, for his mother did once give shelter to my father.'

'Do you remember O'Ruarc, whose wife Devorgil was seized by her paramour Diarmaid King of Leinster?' asked Cadell.

'What has that to do with Robert?'

'Much. Listen. Diarmaid was sent packing from Leinster by O'Ruarc's friend the King of Connaught as soon as he gained power as High King of Iwerddon. Diarmaid then turned to Henry. Three years ago, that was.'

'I was too busy then to take notice,' said Rhys. 'Henry's insatiable for kingdoms. Wants an appanage now for young Prince John, I suppose, John Lackland. Can't get the elder boys to divide up any of their own territories in his favour. He's been watching Iwerddon for years.'

'Pope Adrian II sent him a Bull of authority to conquer it,' said Cadell drily. 'He was Henry's old tutor, Nicholas Breakspear. For the enlargement of the Church's borders, the Bull said, as though they weren't Christians already out there. And for the restraint of vice, the correction of morals, and the teaching of virtue.'

'They could do with that, evidently,' said Rhys.

'Henry accepted Diarmaid's homage and fealty, and told him to pick his captains from amongst the more obstreperous French barons,' said Cadell. 'Encouragement for the adulterer was hardly in line with the Papal Bull, but I suppose he thought any crack in the door would do for his barons' swords to get a purchase in. And it was all he could do in view of his quarrel with Becket, though I hear that they're on better terms again. Well, Diarmaid went touting around in the South, offering Irish crowns to any man who would help him to win back his own, and the French are responding to the sound of trouble like monks to a church bell. And they say Strongbow from Castell Gwent, that Clare, is going.'

'Times have changed!' said Rhys with satisfaction. 'A generation ago, these Clares were let loose by their kings into Cymru to satisfy their land hunger. But now that the Brothers Deheubarth have closed Cymru to them—'

'—they are lured into Iwerddon to act as a battering-ram for Henry's more leisurely invasion,' finished Cadell. 'Think well how this will affect us, Rhys. Now listen. Maurice FitzGerald is going too. He has been promised the crown of Wexford.'

Rhys grew thoughtful.

'Robert will not like his half-brother to cut a dash founding a line of Irish kings while he frets in prison,' he said. 'You are right, Cadell. I had better let him go as well.'

Next day the news buzzed through Dinefwr that Robert Fitz-Stephen was to be released in order to pursue his fortunes in Iwerddon; and he had sworn an oath never to take up arms again against his cousin Rhys.

Events in the North also threw into relief the growing strength of Deheubarth. Owain Gwynedd died, and left a power gap in Cymru that only Rhys could fill. Bleddyn brought the news, and the court was filled with wonder. It was strange, said the uchelwyr, to think of the old King gone, so long pre-eminent in Cymru. In Deheubarth, men had so long loved to listen to tales about Owain, sharpen their claws upon his reputation, sneer at his wisdom, and criticize his skill in moving his military pawns about this chessboard they called Cymru, that they were astonished at the sense of loss his absence brought.

'Did he make his peace with the Church?' demanded Rhys. His uncle Owain had been excommunicated for marrying his beloved first cousin Cristin, all against the canon law.

'No,' replied Bleddyn with an understanding look. 'But the monks of Bangor gave him Christian burial nonetheless.' Rhys exchanged smiles with his own first cousin and wife Gwenllian. The Church in the South had deemed it politically imprudent to denounce their own union; but should the blow fall, Rhys felt that he had friends at Ystrad Fflur who would take his part. Then he asked for further details about the crisis in Gwynedd. Bleddyn shook his head sorrowfully.

'Things are worse than they were in Powys after King Madog died,' he said. 'They say that Prince Hywel is slain.'

'Hywel slain!' said Cadell; and he wept, remembering days when they had campaigned together as friends.

'By whom? His brother Dafydd?' Bleddyn nodded.

'Ah, he's the roaring strong one to force his will upon the gwlad!' said Rhys angrily. 'He'll have his knife into all his brothers one by one, or drive them out—Iorwerth Tightnose, Rhodri, Cynan, Maelgwn, and of course, young Madog. Is he all right?' Bleddyn smiled.

'Oh, Prince Madog, he's the sailor of the family, the merchant adventurer—'

'He's a pirate with salt in his blood!' said Rhys. 'I've heard stories about his goings-on in Lundy, with a gang of ruffians driven out of all the other nations!'

'Madog,' said Bleddyn, 'has sailed with a crew as daring or as mad as he, to find a new land that he declares he knows lies westward of Iwerddon. It is true, he has this new needle, called a lodestone, with wonderful properties, as a navigation aid in addition to the sun and stars, but its use has involved Madog in considerable trouble. He has been obliged to build his ship with nails of horn instead of iron, on account of some evil influence exerted by iron on this new device.'

Sadly, Dinefwr prophesied doom for Madog. Clearly, he would never trouble Dafydd more.

One morning in January, 1171, the young Prior of Ystrad Fflur, Seisyll, rode down to Ty Gwyn ar Daf on convent business. He looked forward to meeting Lord Rhys, who always went hunting in Dyfed during the Twelve Days of Christmas, and invariably dropped in to see Cadell. As he journeyed, Seisyll seized the chance to count his blessings and arrange any ideas he could catch on the wing; they advanced and fled with the speed of starlings. He was a war orphan, whether Cymric, French, Flemish, or Saeson, no one knew. Once, he used to ponder his origins, staring into a fire or the bottom of a pool. All that these meditations taught him was, that sparks of fire were struck in his own heart too, and that the particles of pond mud that followed the motions of his stirring hand were like the grains of dust from which the Lord made Adam. Earth was his body, fire his heart and mind, and for his spirit he had the Lord's own breath. Here he was put, with knowledge enough for him, though clouds interrupted the prospect behind and before. Forward his face must turn, into the wilderness, clearing a space about him as he went, and finding, as he travelled, what his task must be.

'I am young, I have my health and strength,' he said aloud. 'I never get tired on the hills, and I have a degree of common sense. Ystrad Fflur very quickly shows a man his best and worst to cherish and chastise!'

And now, he thought with glee, Father Dafydd had made him Prior. Then he sighed. The old Prior, who had but lately died, had been a good friend. They would miss him, though Seisyll had never thought much of his administrative skill.

'I must pray for humility, as a moderating grace,' he murmured. 'Daily, I fear.' He shivered, and drew his cloak closer about him. It had snowed lightly the previous day, but now the sun, like a mitred bishop in a bare cathedral, shone with bravado on a landscape brown and sodden in the thaw.

'I have a way with a sheep-dog,' he declared. 'And I can handle men. But can I manage kings?' Anxiously he reviewed the items on the agenda, which concerned the convent's difficulties.

Illness and accident amongst the monks had held up work on the timber buildings in the more sheltered valley Lord Rhys had bestowed on them; they could not yet afford to build in stone. Then, shepherds were few and ignorant, escaped caethion mostly. And to crown all, Lord Rhys's own armies, roaming to and from the wars with Henry, had scattered the sheep, nor had they been above helping themselves to mutton by way of willy-nilly contribution from the Abbey.

'We could hardly begrudge them satisfaction of their urgent needs,' Father Dafydd had pointed out, when Seisyll grumbled. 'Now, be discreet in your discourse with Lord Rhys, Seisyll. If we are to afford an Abbey built in stone, we must make money. But look at our sheep, still scraggy and only marginally improved after six years' management! It takes time to build up fertility in the neglected ffriddoedd. It is urgent to make arrangements now for proper winter-quarters for them. But in which direction may we expand? Now this is your first big task as Prior, and you will know what to say. God's blessing on you!'

Seisyll stared between his pony's ears, and concentrated on the narrow path. His elation balanced a burden of heavy responsibility.

When he arrived at his old monastery, fresh from the upland silence, Seisyll was bewildered. Here was a laughing, shouting crowd of travellers, the hub of the universe, eating heartily. He watched a group of proud uchelwyr making their way to the top table between rows of rich Flemish merchants and burly French lords. The world hurled by in a rowdier, more swollen stream than he remembered, sending its eddies rushing in to erode simplicity.

'The world must enter, in order to understand our values, Seisyll,' said Father Cynan, divining his thoughts. 'Look! See how geniality arises!'

Conversation was certainly mixed, and general. Men of different races were talking to each other, moved by interest, curiosity, and that ebullient and indiscriminating goodwill that sometimes springs between the most ill-assorted Christians that one can fancy.

'Lord Rhys it is,' added Father Cynan, 'who has brought peace to life with such a roar in the road outside Ty Gwyn ar Daf. You shall meet him tomorrow, Seisyll. He dines here at noon.'

Seisyll brightened. But still he felt a stranger. The lowland air was now too thick for him. Five monks he knew had died. His contemporaries were stouter, for all their frugality. Most of the novices now were Cymry. And a sheep-dog that he himself had helped to train was not there any more. It seemed to him that God had shifted and shaken his old home as a cook by the fire stirred his cawl with a spoon to prevent it sticking to the pot.

Lord Rhys arrived next day with his older sons, a great company, and the gift of a wild boar for the monks' table. Seisyll was placed next to him at dinner.

'Ystrad Fflur? The new Prior? I remember you. Your name is Seisyll. I want to talk to you. Have some wine!' Seisyll was forced to eat and drink more than he was used to do.

'You're a young man,' said Lord Rhys. 'Young men must keep up their strength. No meat? I don't believe in a meagre diet for working men. You should drink mead for your health, I've often told Father Cynan. I mean to send my opinions to Citeaux, for the Rule should be changed for any community living in a winter climate as severe as yours. Now, what is your problem? Winter quarters for sheep? Well, plenty of land all round you, isn't there? Help yourself! I thought you Cistercians were all for taming the wilderness!'

'We are not asking you for cultivated land, my lord,' said Seisyll, rather affronted. 'Our Rule forbids it. We win our own from the wilderness that other men despise. But which is wilderness and which is other people's property? For summer, certainly, there are mountain pastures enough to the east, far from men's dwellings. But winter requires something better on the lower ground if we are to build up healthy flocks. We take what we can above the bog-line, but always with the fear that we trespass upon the gwely of some decimated teulu, and the consequent risk of court action brought by an unsuspected survivor. But it all looks like wilderness to us, even in the more populous parts. I mean—' He hesitated. Discretion was not his strong point, after all.

'Out with it!' said Lord Rhys. Seisyll decided to be blunt.

'The boundaries are all obliterated by the battlefields!' he said. 'The ground is covered by coarse weeds growing rankly between skeletons! Oh, yes, we still find unburied corpses on the undrained land! The surge of power, my lord, first between the French and Cymry, then between Gwynedd and Deheubarth, and lastly between yourself and Lord Henry—well, after all! It has swept in successive tides between South and North until Ceredigion really looks like—'

'An empty cauldron scoured by dirty hands, I suppose,' said Lord Rhys grimly. 'Well, what do you want of your chief scullion?' His voice was tolerant, if cool, and Seisyll in relief plunged knee-deep into detail.

'My lord, will you of your kindness but tell us where we may *not* venture to reclaim, and we guarantee with God's favour, in ten years' time to clear the best valleys of encroaching scrub and double the flocks not only on our own but also on our neighbours' ground. We have started already as traders in wool, through our contacts with the Flemish merchants, and every June we send pack horses laden with fleeces down to Caer Fyrddin. We have to bargain narrowly with Master Pieter of Flanders, but on the whole we get a fair return, and put every penny by for stone for the Abbey.'

Lord Rhys regarded him with approval.

'Well, you know what you want,' he said. 'Yes, the necessary permission shall be written down. The areas where you may *not* venture. I'm afraid, later on, it will have to be, in despite of your Rule, in the reverse form of a grant of those areas where you *may* settle, otherwise legal complications may result. I can think of various pieces—you will not mind if they are scattered in various parts within and beyond Ceredigion. Dreadful rough ground, all of it, well cultivated in the old days before the invasion, but now reverted to the original anialwch. There are some nice flat parcels by the sea, and there is the coastal fishing—the mackerel in summer will make a change on Fridays from Llyn Deifi trout.'

'Coastal fishing and a port, my lord, for ease of transport and to speed our fleeces to their profitable markets, and transport the stone! Commerce will grow—'

Lord Rhys laughed and clapped him on the shoulder. 'Yes, indeed, a new age comes, this young man sees it, and forward we must march in Deheubarth, my white monks and I!' He turned his solid frame right round on the bench, swung a mighty fist, and declared to his brother, 'Cadell! This year I'm going to build up Castell Aber Teifi, and I'm going to spend my summers there! You shall find me an architect, and work with me. There are thrifty merchants in the town, Flemish or French is all one to me so long as they are eager to prosper and to serve our purposes, as are these monks of mine upon the land. I'm tired of being lord of a lean race, brother, and I swear I'll put fat and flesh at last upon the bones of all my people! I tell you I shall harness heaven and earth to till Deheubarth now that peace has come! You watch the crop grow, now, and pray for it, and count the sheaves for me!'

'God prosper your purposes,' said Cadell, a broad smile creasing his haggard face. He raised his sound hand like a bishop, and every monk replied, 'Amen!'

Into the silence that followed, a distant sound thrust itself. A growling rumour arose outside, entered the monastery, and accumulated loudly in the corridors. Three frightened monks came rushing through the refectory doorway, clutching their robes with their left hands, crossing themselves with their right. They fell before the Abbot and Lord Rhys, and panted out, in white puffs of breath against the frosty air, that the Archbishop was dead.

'Murdered!' they gasped. 'By the King of Lloegr's knights—in his own cathedral of Canterbury—at the very altar steps!'

There was an awe-filled pause. Lord Rhys said, 'I don't believe it! There was talk of a reconciliation!'

'The King disowns the deed, but murder was done,' they told him, with long shocked faces. 'The merchant who told us had it from one of the King's own servants.'

While cries and groans rent the air, the fresh countenance of Lord Rhys turned as white as a monk's. His lips moved feebly in search of some adequate oath, but he could not find one.

'What a dreadful deed,' he said at last in a whisper; and then, curiously, 'Poor Henry.' Not another word could he utter. Sickened and trembling, they all hastened to the Abbey church, and prayed.

The thought of Henry recurred often to Lord Rhys during the next two years, much of which he spent at Aber Teifi, ordering the masons working on the castle walls, when he was not up at Ystrad Fflur watching the monks wading into the wilderness, clearing the ground, and establishing their granges. The river town rang with the sound of hammers on stone, and the loud quarrelling voices of Lord Rhys and his brother. Building was a passion with Cadell; in this one sphere he would not part with his majesty, and presumed still to dictate in public to Rhys. Rhys argued back with all the power of his lungs until presently he would fall into a sulky silence from which he would emerge to give orders that made plain he had changed his mind to match his brother's. Any remaining irritation fell upon the head of his pensaer, who worked as a boy years ago with Cadell on Caer Fyrddin castle, and was rather inclined still to be too much under his thumb.

During the peaceful intervals between crises, they had leisure to brood on the significance of the news that sped to them from west and east, from Iwerddon and from Lloegr.

'Strongbow and his knights are in Waterford!' announced Prior Seisyll, fresh from Ty Gwyn ar Daf, the central agency for news, where he had been copying a book required for the Ystrad Fflur Library; Father Dafydd was determined that no one should sneer that scholarship, amongst the monks of the cefn gwlad, was subordinate to sheep.

'Strongbow has married his ally Diarmaid's daughter Eva! Diarmaid is sick, and Strongbow has taken Dublin!'

And then, 'Diarmaid is dead, and Strongbow is crowned king.'

'So, they're all winning crowns over there,' said Cadell. 'I don't think Henry is going to like it, Rhys. Not one of them yet has asked his permission to be king.'

'No,' said Rhys frowning.

'Aren't you delighted? Trouble for Henry, brother!'

'Trouble for me, too, perhaps,' said Rhys with a black look.

'A pirate kingdom on the opposite shore! The sons of Nest and their friends are successful too soon to please me.'

So he listened with the more sympathy when Bleddyn, who had been wandering in Gwent, telling tales, and listening, spoke of Henry's penitence.

'Gone very stiff-necked had Becket,' said Bleddyn. 'Gone beyond reach. A man of marble since Henry thrust him into clerical power.'

'Pride or piety?' said Rhys. 'Both, I suppose. A saint,' he concluded, shaking his head in mistrust. 'To a common man like me, Henry's rages are easier to forgive than such implacability.'

'This murder has told on him,' said Bleddyn. 'He declares himself innocent, yet makes barefoot penance for the rage that gave his men the impulse to commit it. He ages fast, men say. Circumstances range themselves like rocks about him, but Henry, like the high tide of some ungovernable sea, hurls himself on them.'

'Perhaps his fortunes are turning,' said Cadell hopefully, but Rhys was silent.

'The Pope and the King of France lead Christendom in loathing him,' continued Bleddyn. 'The common people fear him. His barons mutter furiously against his encroachments into their feudal power, and his family life is falling into ruins.'

'See how he is punished for his quarrel with the Church!' said Father Dafydd. 'But as Henry's star falls, yours rises, Lord Rhys. Yours is the name that comes naturally to men's lips throughout Cymru. Since Owain Gwynedd died, it is here in the South they find their one strong centre.'

This was pleasant to hear, but he knew it already. The paths to Aber Teifi were wearing out with the cavalcade of embassies that rode hard from every prince in Cymru to win the favour of Lord Rhys, the central spider in a web of diplomatic and marriage alliances.

'What of young Henry, the heir he had crowned King in the Archbishop's absence to ensure an orderly succession?' he asked.

'He thinks he is equal to his father, and complained to his father-in-law the King of France that he is not allowed to rule!'

Rhys grunted, and reached for an apple.

'Typical of these modern youngsters. Can't wait for their sires to die. Maelgwn and his brothers are the same. They can bend their bows a bit further than their fellows, so claim authority at once! Not one of them, Father Dafydd, will learn from me the lesson of unity. They will never be known to a later age, as Anarawd and Cadell, Maredudd and I were, as the Brothers Deheubarth!'

'But you were brought up in adversity,' Father Dafydd pointed out. 'You had to combine against the common foe to win any land at all. Your sons are less fortunate. Their inheritance is won already, and the foe well beaten back. Their struggles therefore must be between themselves.'

When summer came, Henry roused himself, rose above his troubles, and prepared to strike the necessary blow in Iwerddon. It was essential, he reflected, first to make friends with his enemy Rhys in order to control his errant vassals elsewhere. With a great force, he entered Deheubarth, hoping that there he need exchange no blows, and that he could save his soldiers for any campaigns required overseas. He sent heralds to Rhys, requiring his attendance at Caer Fyrddin, and provisions for the army. A note of grudging goodwill sounded through the peremptory message, and he returned the hostage son, Hywel.

'Now's your chance, Rhys!' urged Cadell. 'Here is Henry, bereft of friends, and with an army you can easily summon others to overcome. No one in Lloegr or Cymru will lift a finger to help him if you rise! A couple of pitched battles, a captured English king, and the terms will be yours to dictate, within the walls of Caer Fyrddin!'

'In the old days, when we were weak,' said Rhys slowly, 'You urged me to make peace, when I wanted to fight. I listened to you. Now, when we are strong, you urge me to fight, but now you must listen to me. A lesser man than I might take advantage of Henry's difficulties to stir up yet more trouble for him. I know the best and the worst of him now. I prefer to have him as a strong friend rather than as a weak enemy. He will be more useful to Deheubarth so—to Cymru.'

'Your gallantry is stirred,' said Cadell grudgingly. 'And your vanity!'

Rhys grinned.

'Pity rather,' he said. 'But interest most of all. It is shrewder now to be generous. I prefer to put Henry in my debt. I also want to see my cousins the sons of Nest made to toe the line in Iwerddon.'

'You leap too suddenly to your conclusions,' said Cadell. 'I myself would be slower to believe Henry's professions of goodwill. You know what he is capable of.'

'It's not a bad foundation for a friendship to know another man's worst,' said Rhys. 'And we have been faithful enough enemies. Lloegr and Cymru lie in one bed and neither can dislodge the other, so we may as well stop kicking.'

Lord Rhys had ordered his entire teulu to attend him and his sons at Caer Fyrddin, where he was to greet King Henry. Queen Gwenllian and her daughters were there also, splendidly arrayed. All the members of his court were there, and all his chief officers, his penteulu, his smith, his canghellor, his pencerdd, his bardd teulu, and even his footholder. He was followed by a large and important part of his uchelwyr, each with his separate retinue of fighting men. Behind came a great herd of cattle. The size of the Deheubarth procession was seen rather to outnumber King Henry's army. Lord Rhys brought his people to a halt, while his fine present of cattle was moved forward to be received by Henry's men. King Henry, astonished by this magnificent reception, and more impressed than he would admit, turned a gracious face towards Lord Rhys, and called him 'Friend.'

'Indeed, he needs one,' muttered Cadell.

Henry was explaining that he was on his way to make a formal annexation of the Irish lands. Rhys, in his suavest tones, was offering to facilitate the army's passage through his realm.

'Your realm?' Henry's eyebrows shot up, and the well-known glare lit up his blood-shot eyes.

'Mine indeed,' said Rhys blandly. 'I lash my tail as required.' His uchelwyr grinned, and thought of Einion Clud. Rhys had lately put his foot on this obstreperous son-in-law, and extorted seven of his best men as hostages, as guarantee of future obedience. Henry gave a short laugh.

'Very well, Lord Rhys. You've won your little principality or kingdom or whatever you call it in your Cymric tongue. Keep it.

But as far as I'm concerned, you are Lord of South Wales and my vassal. Now swear fealty,' and he stretched out his hands.

'Power and the proper use of it come from God,' said Rhys solemnly. 'Each of us in this island is indispensable. You are a good king, Henry. I acknowledge this, and your overlordship, and I am your man—' Here he placed his hands within Henry's, and Henry smiled with relief. '—so long as we both shall live.' Henry scowled, but there was that in Rhys's eyes that told him he was in no position to argue, and that he must not quarrel over forms of words with this man as he had done with Becket.

In the hard, measuring look that they exchanged while Rhys was on his knees, each for a moment forgot his pride, and accepted the fact that he was obliged to look for, and lean on, the best of the other. Then they shook hands, and proceeded to enjoy themselves.

In the following spring, King Henry returned in a good hwyl, having extorted submission from the new Irish kings. He made a generous gift to the shrine of Dewi Sant, a remarkable cope, and ten whole silver shillings. To Lord Rhys he was most gracious, and created him his Lord Justiciar of Wales, a post that Rhys accepted with complacency, good humour, and a wink at Cadell. Bleddyn, watching the scene ironically, remembered the encounter at Pencader.

'Hardly a gift of greatness to Lord Rhys,' he observed in Cymric to his neighbour in the carrying voice that he made no effort to lower. 'Merely an acknowledgement of its force in him.'

His neighbour could not help grinning. The French and King Henry were irritated by the sound of this libertarian tongue, so uncouth to them, but thought it better to pretend they had not heard.

IV

The Lord Justiciar

(1171—1189)

1

Satisfied by his understanding with Henry, Lord Rhys with his retinue briskly rode on cylch round Ceredigion throughout the spring and summer. 'Justiciar of Wales?' Men tried the curious phrase upon their tongues, and laughed. It sounded well, but they saw little change in their lord. The justice was much the same, in spite of this new jury system he had introduced, and Lord Rhys, as usual, made merry in the gwestfa at night, after a morning in the saddle and a hard day's work in the courthouse. He seemed very thirsty these days, and clearly, he liked the ladies still. Queen Gwenllian had been left behind at Dinefwr with her little girl Gwenllian, who had the measles. One day, Rhys alighted at the gwestfa which was in charge of the second husband of his sister-in-law, Elen, King Maredudd's widow. Then gossip flared.

It reached Cadell on a summer visit to the monks of Ystrad Fflur, by the mouth of Master Gerallt, nephew of the Bishop of St. David's, and considered his certain successor. The Bishop, old, tired, and indolent, depended much on him, sang his praises, and spread his fame as the most brilliant disputant at the University of Paris, with Adam of Wales a close second. The monks, curious to see Gerallt, crowded round him.

He was young, still under thirty, with mettlesome, intelligent eyes. He was going to Brycheiniog, and had gone out of his way to have a look at Ystrad Fflur. He had no shyness; he assessed his company with a rapid glance, discarded all save Prince Cadell, Father Dafydd, and Prior Seisyll, and plunged at once into his opinions on matters both ecclesiastical and lay, awarding praise and blame with impartial liberality. He was a bad listener; he disliked to be informed, save in answer to his acute and rapid questions; even then he listened with the sneer of one whose understanding had anticipated the replies.

'We hope to build in stone,' they told him hopefully, 'with the architect Lord Rhys had for Aber Teifi. The lead for the roof will come from the many veins of ore that occur within our granges. Prior Seisyll is surveying those in the north. There are two close by, but they are almost worked out. The lead was used to rebuild

Castell Ystrad Meurig, and the workings filled in with loose rubble, for the lay brethren believe that this will turn into ore again one day—but perhaps not soon enough for our purposes. We shall have to depend on Cwm Ystwyth and Cwm Rheidol, where outcrops occur on the steep mountainsides above the swift and flooding streams.'

'I know,' said Gerallt. 'The smelting is done in beehive-shaped kilns, and the ore is mixed and burned with timber cut from the hills. Oh, yes!' he informed them. 'When the Clares were masters in Ceredigion, Ceredigion lead found its way to the roofs of many a new stone castle, church, and house in Lloegr.'

He put his finger tips together judicially.

'Plenty of lead, then. No great expense to you there. But how will you reach it?'

'We have the ancient tracks,' said Father Dafydd, rather amused by this magisterial interest.

'In the middle and south, yes! But without bridges, how can your waggons penetrate with any ease the north, that mountainous and river-torn terrain? You must build bridges, Father, good solid ones, none of these rustic timbers thrown across low summer streams that winter's turbulence will cast aside like autumn rubbish!'

Father Dafydd made no comment. His plan for bridging the gorge of Rheidol was well in hand, though he did not propose to disclose it to this guest, who had no claims to be Visitor. But Brother Cynfyn piped up.

'We use the fords!' he cried. 'We cross Teifi at Rhyd Fendigaid, the ford of the Blessed Ones, that pilgrims have used for centuries. That takes us up to our first hospitium for travellers—Yspytty Ystwyth they call it there. I am going to be in charge of another farther north. Then there's Rhyd-y-Groes not far away, where the Holy Cross stands—'

'Fords!' said Gerallt contemptuously. 'You are men, not cattle. Bridge the rivers! Bridge them!'

To change the subject, Father Dafydd begged for news. 'By you, Master Gerallt, we shall, I know, be well and accurately informed.'

Gerallt, purring, turned to courtly matters, on which he was an authority. Indeed, the world and its ways stirred in the very swing of his skirts. All the eminent were his familiars, and he mimicked them. Bishop David his uncle; King Henry; Lord Rhys himself who was his mother's first cousin; Adam of Wales, now racing Gerallt up the ladder of Church promotion; two or three French lords, and a Cardinal; all these enwogion, instead of beads, they saw him tell, with satisfaction on his fingers. News he brought; the magnificence of King Henry's gift to Ty Ddewi had put to shame its crumbling shrine; people had long been murmuring against its condition; even his uncle the Bishop had been heard to say that something should be done. And scandal Gerallt did not shrink from telling. Lord Rhys was in his cups too often, and the Lady Gwenllian was angry, distressed, and ashamed. And there was an ugly story going round, about Lord Rhys and his niece, the late King Maredudd's daughter.

Prince Cadell, crimson, thumped a furious fist hard on the table.

'Cannot my brother find occupation enough in time of peace?' he roared. 'With so much still to be done in the kingdom? Our niece,' he added quietly, 'is a wild and silly girl who needs a whipping. She has never known a father's stern authority.'

In the shocked silence he left them, and rode south to Aber Teifi, there to lift his brother, the monks hoped, out of his sins.

A month passed before he returned. Father Dafydd said soberly, 'Lord Rhys has been much in our prayers, and so has your niece.'

'She is to have a child,' said Cadell brusquely. 'My brother's. It was the result of a drunken and disgraceful frolic, and Rhys, tired and thirsty after a long day in the courthouse, surrounded by women, could not tell one from another, and the wine flowed too freely, as usual.'

'He is at heart a good man,' said Father Dafydd, with an effort. 'Though sorely beset from time to time by the sins of the flesh. He will rise above them. We pray for him daily and value him still.'

'He has greatness in him,' said Seisyll gently. 'He will yet perform a great work for the Church.' Cadell was comforted.

He was exhausted. He had found Lord Rhys sunk so deep in remorse that the court complained that government was neglected. Cadell, in his savage way, had seized power, forced some degree of discipline upon his brother's jeering sons, and with a strong pull forced the horses of disorder to a stop. He found the reconciliation with Queen Gwenllian difficult to achieve; she would see no one. As for the young niece, Cadell went to visit her; he used his acid tongue on her with moderation, to lift her from despair, though not from shame, which he thought it only proper she retained. He betrothed her to a soldier, Trahaearn Fychan of Brycheiniog, an ally of Lord Rhys, although he also owed allegiance in respect of certain lands, to William de Breos. He was a man of authority whose firmness would rule her turbulence.

'She fears him,' said Cadell. 'That is the right beginning for a foolish girl's marriage to a good man.'

He sighed, and sought diversion. 'Found any more lead mines?' he asked Seisyll.

'Another in Cwm Ystwyth,' replied Seisyll, beaming. 'And while we dig ore from the mountains, we dig it out of men, for it occurs to me that we are all, Lord Cadell, a mine of God's undiscovered treasure, below our cultivated or neglected surface soil! Our part in Creation is to dig out, educate, bring forth by the struggles of the daily second birth, this treasure from ourselves and from each other!'

'Did you dig any treasure out of Gerallt?' asked Cadell. 'His surface soil is well cultivated, it seems.'

'Oh, very,' said Seisyll, his face falling, but Father Dafydd smiled. 'No weeds at all there, nor any thorns save pride, and they lie round him like a tall hedge. He cannot see me on the other side, digging into the same seam that runs under his own ground.'

'Why, didn't you get on with him?' asked Cadell. Father Dafydd laughed aloud, and Seisyll looked at him reproachfully.

'We quarrelled in an impatient moment outside the privies,' he admitted. 'In making conversation as we waited I discovered he was going to visit old Jordan, Archdeacon of Brycheiniog, so I said he would get a good welcome there as the Archdeacon's wife was a kind and hospitable woman, famed for her virtue as well as for her cooking. That started it. Gerallt boiled over, called her a concubine, said he intended to eradicate the malpractice of centuries, old misbehaviour in the Celtic

Church, enlightened clergy, his privileged lot to eradicate, et cetera.'

'And what did you say?' asked Cadell, now grinning broadly.

'I said our clergy had always married, celibacy not their custom, thought it very fitting this should be confined to monks—"Some distinction should be preserved between ourselves and you!" I said. Well, that unloosed all the Church Fathers on my head. All the authorities he quoted—half I never heard of. Typical Schoolman he is,' grumbled Seisyll. 'Argues for the victory of a truth he knows, not for its discovery! Master of Logic he is indeed, not its slave! "Well," I said at last, "I can't rival you in learning or in disputation, but let me tell you this," I said, "if Logic enchants you, Master Gerallt, let me remind you that your uncle the Bishop by example gives approval to the custom you revile, since he is himself a married man!" That stamped on his favourite corn, evidently, and I will not go into details of what followed. We have both done penance since, and apologized to each other.'

Cadell, much cheered, wiped his eyes, and went into vespers chuckling gently to himself. He quite forgot his brother's sin, and for the rest of his stay listened with sympathy to the sound of the unclouded anger of old Archdeacon Jordan, which reverberated across the mountains. Master Gerallt, far from wilting under the tempest he had provoked, suspended him at once from his office, and wrote with a flourish of Latinity to Canterbury, accusing Jordan of such colourful sins that the Archbishop deprived him at once of the archidiaconate.

'How long will it take Gerallt to convince the Archbishop that he himself is the obvious successor?' said Seisyll.

'Feeling in Brycheiniog is running very high against Gerallt,' said Father Dafydd. 'The Archbishop will not dare to nominate him yet.'

Seisyll sniffed. 'A year or two, and I expect we shall have him over there, looking about him for more trouble. He will very positively establish the exact boundaries of his archdeaconry, and then, doubtless, we shall hear of some little disagreements.'

The first few months of 1173 were swept by a relentless east wind. Lord Rhys, much subdued, retired to Ystrad Fflur to chastise himself, and lose weight by a severe Lenten diet of repentance. He was vigorous even in melancholy, filling his heart with prayer in the chapel, and his mind with readings from the Holy Scriptures, though he was not, thought Father Dafydd, much of a reader. Little rain fell; the flocks starved on brown, bitten pastures. The winter fever attacked the monks with energy; the store of oats, shared with the local sick and aged, soon gave out; too much salted fish and a lack of winter greens produced skin troubles and bowel difficulties that no one escaped.

'I deserve it,' said Lord Rhys, but he looked with envy at the wiry infirmarian, who retained a degree of health on very meagre fare.

'How do you keep from ills?' he asked.

'No time to think of my own—got to mend other people's,' said the infirmarian. 'But I too rattle like an ill-greased cart towards my middle age.' And off he went to attend to Brother Cynfyn, who had sprained an ankle while struggling to clear a well-chosen site above Rheidol for his yspytty.

'It was once a Druid site, and their spirits curse us!' exclaimed Cynfyn. The infirmarian scolded him for believing local superstitions and for listening to Iestyn Fychan's garrulous accounts of his career as wizard, and deplored his tendency to hysteria.

'Is Cynfyn really fit to be in charge of an yspytty?' asked Lord Rhys privately of Father Dafydd. 'For a successful venture, so much depends on the temperament of the few men you choose to live together in isolation!' He had, hitherto, been much impressed by the care with which the Abbot mixed the merry with the silent in just proportions, so that in each grange a sober cheerfulness might prevail.

'He is an excellent organizer, in fact, tenacious of detail,' said Father Dafydd. 'True, his health is a constant worry to him when his energy is under-employed, but I suppose every convent of monks has one such member! We have no mirrors here, but in a slack season, Cynfyn will spend minutes at a time over a clear pool, observing the colour of his tongue and the pallor of his cheeks. He feels his own pulse at frequent intervals, imagines a new complaint each week, and can never find a diet to agree with him. I am always quoting to him our Founder Bernard's energetic scorn of hypochondria. All in vain! But Cynfyn thrives on work, and when he's busy, he forgets all else.'

They all thrive on work, thought Lord Rhys, as he took his share of menial tasks. It absorbed them; these brothers were in the full current of God's pulsing purposes. The energy of their feelings, released in prayer and praise, overflowed, so that their superabundant joy entered the heart of every visitor. The neighbouring sick, youngsters eager to learn their letters, courtiers, pilgrims, pedlars, and cheeky boys after kitchen scraps, all received their fill at Ystrad Fflur. Lord Rhys, reduced to humility and patience, found that his preoccupation with his own shame was dissolving into a more constructive mood. He longed to build.

'You worship in a wooden chapel still,' he said. 'When are you going to start on your stone Abbey? Look now, you're beginning to prosper. I'll give you a start, Father Dafydd. We'll order that freestone the pensaer mentioned, from Bath way, down there in Gwlad yr Haf, to cope your portals, arches, windows and pillars. It had better come round by sea to Aber Arth, nice little port for you there, gives you the shortest land journey from the coast to Ystrad Fflur. Sea transport would get your fleeces to the South more quickly, too. And I shall persuade my cousins the sons of my uncle Cadwgan and his wife Gwenllian to let you have certain lands north of Aeron in the cwmmwd of Anhuniog, including Morfa Mawr. They are always ailing, and have no heirs. I dare say they will join your Order soon, and you can turn their plâs into a mynachty. Quite a wilderness, their land is, so it will be quite within the spirit of your Rule to accept it.'

The gratitude and delight of Father Dafydd pleased him, and but for the breach with his wife, Lord Rhys was almost happy. As for the monks, they glowed. In this moment they had yearned for, they assembled in silence their sources of strength. The Father had given them a shelter to praise Him in, a home, food, land, humble and powerful friends, some knowledge and strength, and a small treasure of gold. From the peace of mind the Son had granted them came their zest for living; by the favour of the Holy Ghost they were free to launch out on the tide of His power. More than ever they struggled forward to extend life's edge, creating there the new thing God desired within this now peaceful kingdom.

They thought with affection of the battered, cunning, coarse, courageous man who had established peace, Lord Rhys himself, building firmly on the strong foundations other men had laid. Somehow, his reckless sins faded as they thought of him. They could remember only the best of him, that he was bold and impetuous, shrewd and truculent by turns, that he was loved as well as feared, that he was generous and just to friend and foe, that, in government, he had a free strong mind, rooted in the best traditions of Cymru, and flowering in a judgement swift and sure, unfettered by precedent.

Meanwhile, Queen Gwenllian, pale with bitterness and grief, spent a miserable Lent, nor did Easter bring her comfort, much. 'I will not forgive!' she declared to Cadell, when at last she agreed to receive him. But Caradoc, the aged household priest, entreated her; Bleddyn, who journeyed unweariedly between Dinefwr and Ystrad Fflur, trying to repair the torn fabric of their lives, plied her with humble messages from Lord Rhys; the sufferings of Christ put her at last to shame.

'Until this child is born,' she stated regally then, 'I stay silent.'

Inspired by the slender hope this hint afforded him, Rhys immersed himself meanwhile in the Abbey's building plans, and interviews with the pensaer. Spring pushed forward slowly; by May, a shower or two had modified the country's shabby look, the cold winds dropped, and a wave of heat oppressed the Bog and lay like a hand on the hills; smoke rose without a ripple, straight as a woollen thread hung between spindle and whorl. On Ascension Thursday, as the monks emerged at dawn from Matins, the storm broke. The sky cracked, thunder pealed, a whirlwind blinded them with their own blown garments. They staggered into the chapter house, and collapsed, trembling, on the benches. Across the valley, they heard the wrench and groan of uptorn trees. Lord Rhys sat with them, listening with tears streaming down his cheeks, as a penitent to the final loud reproach.

The tempest raged over Cymru as the pent-up rains roared down. The hard, dried Bog sucked in the water, and became a lake with an island in the middle. Teifi burst its banks and flooded the monks out to a depth of six inches, and retired, leaving floors and walls covered with mud and green slime. The smell was nasty and lingered for weeks after they had finished cleaning up. On the third day, they awoke to a blessed silence. Thin gleams of sunshine lit up the devastation, which they regarded, feeling like Noah after the Flood.

Across the valley, trees had broken down in swathes like grass beneath a giant's feet. All the ways were strewn with broken trees and branches; the river flowed over the surface of the land, foaming, a sullen brown. The monks stopped for no more than a Pater Noster before going out in search of the victims of the storm. Lord Rhys himself led them; a man reborn in the need for instant action, he gathered an army of strong men, and roamed the hills until all souls were accounted for. The bodies of two shepherds were carried home lamenting; their stricken sheep and lambs were left where they lay, to be buried later.

'It is a judgement on me,' said Rhys heavily, that night.

'No,' said Father Dafydd. 'You look for it in the wrong place. His judgement is always appropriate. It is on your family that the blow fell, and on your prestige.'

'If I may say so, Lord Rhys,' said Seisyll, emboldened by a day spent in manual labour beside this muscular monarch, 'you lack logic. Now if I were a heretic, I should answer you—'

'No!' said Lord Rhys, appalled. 'How?'

'That it is as unjust for God to allow all to suffer for the sin of one as it was for Him to allow the One to suffer for the sins of all.'

'You are no heretic, I hope,' said Father Dafydd. 'But if you were, perhaps you would tell me how to answer your own outburst? You and your logic!'

'You could say,' said Seisyll, eagerly, 'that God seldom respects our demand that His punishment be confined to the individual sinner. In His eyes, each soul is but part of the whole people; each people but part of the whole world; even one generation of mankind is but one part of the universal whole that sweeps from past to future. God's concern is, the just development of the whole, and what one person does, or does not do, affects all, and of course, vice versa. It is a shorter-sighted heresy than most that does not allow for the existence in God's mind of profounder considerations than our narrow wits can grasp—though sometimes leaping imagination may dimly begin to comprehend His grand design!'

'You are on dangerous ground,' said Father Dafydd coldly. 'And I find your theology as amateur as your logic. A good thing the younger brethren are not at hand to hear you erect a heresy in order to knock it down. You know you are not competent in the higher learning.'

Seisyll grasped Humility by the tail as it galloped past, and submitted.

'No,' he agreed. 'But I cannot help, sometimes, giving in to wonder.'

'Neither can I, Seisyll,' said Lord Rhys, soberly.

Weeks of work followed to make good the damage everywhere. Rain fell throughout June, but the smell of wet grass was their comfort, and in July a high, hot sun dried out a splendid crop of hay. But it was a bad year for fruit; in their orchards and woodlands a plague of insects settled on every bush and tree, devouring most of the leaves, and causing the rest to wither early.

But Lord Rhys did not wait for their erratic harvests. After hearing that his niece had given birth to a son, Meurig, at the height of the great storm, he lost no time in riding south to a formal reconciliation with his wife. Urged by Caradoc, she received him with honour and dignity in the crowded and expectant hall. They then sat at supper, eyeing each other with hostility and hope, exchanging few and commonplace remarks. The harpist's soft music irritated Gwenllian; so did the curiosity of the court; hysteria rose, and she could stand the strain no more.

'I have a headache,' she said, feigned indisposition, and retired.

Lord Rhys stared at his wine, too dismayed to finish it. Bleddyn, unasked, began his most enthralling story. Presently, under cover of the applause, Rhys stole up to his wife's chamber, knocked, and after delay, was admitted.

All night the gossips kept watch on her window, and noted that the light burned into the small hours. For long the voices rose and fell; the emotion, though not the words, drifted down to the eager listeners. They were able to report next day, with satisfaction, that at least the cold politeness had melted, and that Lord Rhys and his Queen were on comfortable quarrelling terms once more. The news was received with thankfulness throughout Deheubarth; the people knew that when Gwenllian shouted, she loved, and her many partisans felt that she had given back their lord to their devotion.

2

It was clear to Father Dafydd, when he visited Lord Rhys at Michaelmas, that the scandal of the past year had been lived through and largely left behind. Their lord's recovered cheerfulness was reflected in the contented note of the court's steady roar; he had reformed his life, and entered with energy into the dignity of middle age.

The hall bustled like a market place. All sorts of people struggled to preen themselves in the light of Lord Rhys's comprehensive stare and stuff themselves at his generous table. Not only the teulu, uchelwyr from all over Cymru, and a FitzMartin son-in-law from St. Dogmael's were present, but men of middle rank also. There were Flemings from Dyfed as well as French merchant burghers from Aber Teifi, solid men with keen business faces, aping their betters, and presuming to adorn their robes with fur.

Rhys noted Father Dafydd's appreciative look.

'It is the Lady Gwenllian's doing,' he said. 'Order and seemly entertainment must be the aim. When Bleddyn comes to us at Christmas, he will enrich our imaginations so well that the antics of the Lord of Misrule will lose their attractions.'

He scowled at his fool John Spang, who had offended Queen Gwenllian, and sat with his elbows on the table, eating a leg of chicken in a sour silence. He lacked occupation.

'Hywel Sais brought him back from Lloegr,' said Lord Rhys. 'He's a funny fellow. That reminds me—' He went to speak to this son, so many years a stranger to his kin. Father Dafydd, tired after a long journey to and from Citeaux for the annual Cistercian conference, wondered idly what they were discussing. Plans for a new suit of armour in the style at Henry's court? Hywel was apt, these days, to have his brains picked on sundry matters; by his sisters, on ladies' current fashions and hair styles in Lloegr; by his father and brothers, on military matters and politics. Lord Rhys encouraged this; it helped to reabsorb Hywel into some degree of familiarity with his brothers; change was in the air, and Hywel had come home at the right moment. Lord Rhys was determined to improve not only himself, but also his family, his court and his kingdom; all must march alertly with lifted chins and sharp minds into Europe's new age.

Father Dafydd was surprised to learn from Prince Cadell that Hywel was on the point of going back to Henry.

'He will be a useful ambassador,' said Cadell. 'The young king, the heir, is at war with the old one, his father, so Rhys, to show friendship, sends his own son to serve Henry in France. Henry is fond of Hywel, and Rhys is not slow, by this loyal gesture, to boast his own parental power. Men will mark the difference, he knows, and say, Lord Rhys knows better than Henry how to hold his sons, though I fear,' sighed Cadell, 'that the inference is not well founded. The sons lack scope for authority, and divide the court too often into brawls. You see us, Father, at a good moment. How is it with you?'

'There is a little matter in Penweddig,' said Father Dafydd, sighing also. 'Ednowain of Llan Badarn—'

'Ednowain?' said Lord Rhys, returning. 'Is he giving you trouble?'

'It's a question of ownership,' said Father Dafydd. 'He complains we encroach.'

'Sometimes I wish he were Lord of Cantref y Gwaelod!' groaned Lord Rhys. 'But don't tell him I said so. He resents the one or two legal innovations I've borrowed from Henry's system. Well! I'm going to make good my promises of last spring!' he said more cheerfully. 'And Prince Cadell wishes to join your Order, up at Ystrad Fflur.' They both smiled with pleasure at Father Dafydd's delight. 'And he will help you over that border problem. Now, tell me all about Citeaux!'

Father Dafydd gave a weary chuckle.

'Oh, politics arise within our Order too!' he said. 'There are always problems between Cistercian houses to discuss, local divergences from our common Rule, heart searchings, explanations, and disagreements! All these have to come up on the conference agenda. The number of points for decision increase to a remarkable degree annually, and the conference is becoming an instrument so unwieldy that instant decisions cannot be arrived at, and must be entrusted to a small committee of superiors, after all the rest of us have journeyed home.'

'There must be hundreds of Cistercian houses now,' remarked Cadell, 'multiplying with speed throughout Christendom!'

'Yes, praise God! But the task of their direction is huge. As we cannot totally withdraw from the mechanics of life, we have to try to put them in their proper place, but alas! even for monks, such matters loom too large,' complained Father Dafydd. 'The thought of them intrudes upon our thoughts of God. My own one comfort is, that the more perfectly I order Ystrad Fflur's affairs, the more I liberate more holy men than me to make more perfect prayers.'

The arrival of Prince Cadell at Ystrad Fflur was timely. In Cymru, when you start building anything more permanent than a hafodty, all the neighbours come to watch if not to lend a hand. When you start building in stone, all the world passes remarks. It was fortunate that the monks of Ystrad Fflur had been obliged to wait a few years; the interval allowed them to lay the foundations for goodwill strong enough to stand the strain of the envy of their ecclesiastical neighbours. So, when it became known that Prince Cadell had donned the white robe of a Cistercian monk, Ystrad Fflur rose in men's esteem, even amongst the clâswyr of Llan Ddewi Brefi and Llan Badarn Fawr, for all their indignation that he had ignored their prior claims to his notice.

'What could they expect?' demanded Seisyll. 'They are closed corporations, confined to members of their own families!'

'Celibacy has its advantages,' remarked Cadell. 'It gives you more independence of choice when there are no heirs of the body for whom you have to make provision.' Indeed, he thought, every intelligent and ambitious youngster who lacked influence turned his hopes towards Ystrad Fflur; unfortunately, this compounded the existing resentment.

'When first we came, Ednowain sent us a curt message of welcome, rather like the bark of a guardian corgi, pointing out the boundaries of his own estates,' said Father Dafydd. 'Come with us, Brother Cadell, to help us to make peace with him.'

So they rode over to Llan Badarn, to an icy welcome which thawed at the sight of Cadell, thin and yellow in his new white robe. He took the trouble to speak kindly to Ednowain, recalling his valuable feats of arms on behalf of Lord Rhys.

'You commanded a regiment of brothers and cousins, fierce monks from the hills. You were some of the best soldiers I know. I remember well,' said Cadell.

Ednowain, mollified, did business with a better grace with Father Dafydd. By reference to the written arrangement with Lord Rhys, a reasonable understanding as to boundaries was, after some argument, arrived at; the slight dissatisfaction that remained on each side was evidence of the justice of the settlement.

'Fair play, you are a fellow Abbot,' said Ednowain at last. 'Though you are in the modern style, I suppose you mean well in your way. Now, let's understand each other once for all. You carry on as you like on your side of the boundary, and don't you interfere with me. Then I won't interfere with you.'

'I promise that,' said Father Dafydd, shaking hands, and turning the conversation to farming methods. He pushed his opinions, gently, on culling and breeding, provision of over-wintering fodder, early bite, storm shelter, and other aspects of sheep management that together tended gradually to raise the standards of his flocks and the value of their fleeces. He lost no opportunity to make a free gift of his knowledge to his neighbours. Whether or not they used it was up to them.

Then they considered the world around them.

'Trouble up north again!' said Ednowain. 'Dynion y gogledd yn ymladd! Dafydd ab Owain kicked out his brother Maelgwn to Iwerddon, but they say he came back and was caught. Dafydd has grabbed the whole of Môn, and with that granary behind him, he'll be able to round up the other brothers one by one, you'll see, in their forts about Eryri. Rhodri? He's dead. Yes, there are one or two small nephews of no importance. Yes, Dafydd has sat down again in triumph on his father's throne, and crammed the crown down harder on his brow.'

'—and the brawls, or little wars, between King Henry and his sons—'

'For shame to them!' said Ednowain. 'And the Queen, Eleanor, poor woman, clapped into prison. Why? She's too old for Henry now, that's why!'

'It is said she supported her sons' demands for more liberty to govern their separate lands,' said Father Dafydd.

'Go on, she had something done to Walter Clifford's poor girl Rosamond, that Henry took such a fancy to!' said Ednowain. 'The Queen was driven to it by jealousy. Why, she even sent messages to her first husband the King of France to beg him to help her sons against their father! Such a family! Yet he's a strong king, Henry, and can crush barons, and give good government.'

'They are all unhappy,' said Father Dafydd. 'It would be a kindness to pray for him.'

'I suppose it would,' said Ednowain. 'I'll do that. He's not a bad fellow, in the core, and at a distance.'

Relations improved also in the Llan Ddewi Brefi direction. Fortunately, the winter of 1174 brought heavy illness to the clâswyr and their families, so that when the Ystrad Fflur infirmarian journeyed there unasked to succour them, the clâswyr lacked the energy to resent his kindness, and accepted it with simple gratitude. He won them over completely when he praised their children's intelligence. As for his potions and balsams, unguents and inhalants, infusions, bleedings, and purgings, quite in the Salerno style, and very different from their own indigenous remedies, these stirred up so much interest that convalescence set in rapidly.

'I think we have taken root,' said Father Dafydd, when the infirmarian returned with a grateful load of cheese. 'We have been fitted in, looked at sourly, warned off, endured, profited by, and taken at last for friends. Now we can lay that foundation stone at last!'

They were already taking delivery of the freestone from Gwlad yr Haf; where the hills and valleys between Aber Arth and Ystrad Fflur were too steep for the laden carts, a relay of monks, lay brothers, neighbours, and tenants, carried stone-filled hods on their bent shoulders from one man to another backwards and forwards across their hundred-yard stints. Even Father Dafydd, a scholar ill-fitted to hard labour, insisted on taking his turn, and developed a heavy chest cold in consequence. His monks blamed him for taking unnecessary risks with his health.

'Never let it be said,' he wheezed, undaunted, 'that the Abbot did not help to carry the stones of his own Abbey!'

The infirmarian grunted in exasperation, laid the Abbot face down upon a pallet, and relieved his feelings by vigorously rubbing some balsam of spice and herbs into his back in order to draw off the bad blood with its evil humours from the lungs; Father Dafydd nevertheless suffered on and off for the rest of the winter and spring. Prince Cadell too was ailing; they exchanged grim glances, each wondering how long the other would last; but both survived to see the cornerstone laid, in the presence of Lord Rhys himself, the Abbot of Ty Gwyn ar Daf, Ednowain, a representative from Llan Ddewi Brefi, and all the uchelwyr of the cantref.

His brother's weak appearance struck Lord Rhys with anguish.

'Looks like a skeleton!' he growled to his wife, when she asked after Prince Cadell. Then he thumped angrily on the table and called for a good tune. He could think better to music. If Cadell died—. A death required a birth, he thought, rebelliously. Life must go on, be created anew! But a birth required a marriage. He took comfort in planning another match. Gruffydd was a promising lad. There had been feelers lately from old William de Breos, lord of Radnor and Buellt; he had a granddaughter aged seven.

He glanced about his new hall in Aber Teifi, and his unseeing gaze came to rest on the new roof timbers.

'Very handsome they are,' said Bleddyn, who had been watching him. 'How well it sounds in your new hall, the music! All the laughter, roar and talk from our throng below resounds very well against those massive beams. Indeed, Lord Rhys—' He hesitated artistically until Lord Rhys snapped 'What?' and gave him his whole attention.

'Pity,' said Bleddyn, 'you don't have a festival here to celebrate the completion of the castle hall, with music and poetry, some kind of contest, open to all comers.'

'Prizes!' exlaimed Lord Rhys. 'Free hospitality! Announce it throughout Cymru by my heralds in each gwlad—of course! My dear Bleddyn, why didn't I think of it before? My new Abbey a-building, my sons coming up to manhood, more marriages to be made—By all means let us hold a great celebration! Gwenllian, you hear me? You agree?'

Queen Gwenllian, banishing a shudder of horror at the thought of the cost and housekeeping involved, took the required leap in the dark.

'Of course!' she said with spirit. 'But why confine it to Cymru? Let them come from every part of this island!' As well be hung for a sheep as a lamb! If he was bent on it, nothing but the best would do, for her as well as for him! They put their heads together with much enjoyment, and began to plan.

'I'll go and tell Cadell!' said Lord Rhys.

But by the time he reached Ystrad Fflur, Cadell was dead, and Rhys was only just in time for the burial. They laid him beyond the eastern wall, in a corner near the future altar, with his face to the mountains and the rising sun.

'He died to the sound of masons ringing their chisels on the stone,' said Father Dafydd. 'We feared it disturbed him, but he said No, it counterpointed the harps of heaven very well.'

Lord Rhys stood in silence, swallowing his hiraeth.

'I have no links left with the old days now,' he said at last. 'My sister Nest died the other day. There is Gwladus, to be sure, but her second husband Seisyll ap Dyfnwal and her sons naturally claim all her attention. And there's some trouble about his lands, I hear. They lie partly within the lordship of the Earl of Hereford, ruler of Brycheiniog and Upper Gwent. There's some quarrel going on between them.'

'Boundary trouble, no doubt,' said Father Dafydd with sympathy. 'What is the Earl's name now? Miles of Gloucester who married the heiress Sibyl had five sons and two daughters.'

'Henry at the moment,' said Lord Rhys. 'But they're dying off one after the other, or being killed, and men talk of a curse. There are sisters, and the elder one, Bertha, is the wife of old William de Breos of Sussex, your neighbour over the mountains. It's their son William's little girl who is to be betrothed to my boy Gruffydd at King Henry's next court at Oxford in June.'

Privately, he wondered if his brother-in-law's quarrel was going to upset the arrangement; but no. Old William de Breos pushed through the crowd of barons at Oxford, beaming; a little girl in blue silk was grabbed in one broad hand, and the arm of young William de Breos, her father, held firmly in the other.

'Here we are, Lord Rhys! Where's your son? Let's make the match with King Henry's approval!'

But Gruffydd was in the stables, inspecting horses, and kept them waiting. Old William laughed.

'Doesn't care for little girls! All for horses, swordplay, the chase! A splendid fellow! But in a few years, Lord Rhys, eh, William?'

'Oh, more than a few years, I think,' said young William sulkily. 'She is very young and small.' Old William grinned at him, winked at Lord Rhys, and pushed his son rather savagely in the small of the back.

'Fond father,' he remarked. 'Can't bear to lose her. Congratulate Lord Rhys!' he hissed. 'Justiciar of Wales! Lord of the South! Excellent prospects! Trouble I've taken to bring this about! Say something!'

'We are very honoured by the alliance,' young William murmured, reluctantly repeating the speech he had been obliged to learn. 'We trust that many years of peace and prosperity will ensue. Admiration for your achievements, Lord Rhys, famed throughout the Borders—' He mumbled towards his inarticulate close. Lord Rhys, suavely smiling, suitably replied. He liked old William, and Bertha was all right, but he could not imagine where this son of theirs came out of. Between them, clearly, there would be no goodwill beyond the forms.

Gruffydd was eventually dragged from the stables, and made to utter a sentence of obligation for the prospect of his charming bride, but since by that time Matilda herself had gone astray, hostile and hungry, her seniors, laughing off their irritation, were obliged to get down to business without her. She did find refreshment, but unfortunately stained her bodice with spilled wine, so did not care to return, preferring to peep at Gruffydd from a corner. She noted that he was much bigger than her brothers and had golden hair, and her indignation began to subside. Afterwards she, like Gruffydd, was well scolded in private for this defection, so both went home sulking, with a hearty distaste for betrothals. Lord Rhys and old William, however, returned from Henry's court in good spirits, each certain that he'd had the best of the bargain.

'That puts matters on an even keel between us,' said Lord Rhys to his wife. 'Young William is an awkward customer, but his father holds the whip hand, and I think he's good for several more years yet.'

Queen Gwenllian grunted. In her opinion the marriage was too far off to be certain, and she had more pressing immediate cares, preparing for the Great Eisteddfod at Christmas, 1176.

'Oh, eighteen months should give us ample time!' said Lord Rhys. But as he enlarged his ideas each time he discussed them, she doubted this.

The rosy glow in which he returned to Deheubarth was dissipated by news from Gwent. The quarrel between Seisyll ap Dyfnwal and Earl Henry of Hereford, Lady Bertha's much younger brother, erupted into violence, and in an encounter between the two men, Henry was slain.

'A fair fight it was!' cried the pedlars who thronged the doors of Dinefwr. 'But the French call it murder, and have sworn revenge!' Young William de Breos especially, they added, who was fast friends with his uncles. After a burst of fury against his brother-in-law, Rhys calculated the risk to his son's prospective marriage.

'Old William wants the match and will control his son,' he reflected. 'Bertha has but the one young brother left, Mahel, to take the Earldom of Hereford, and there are no other heirs. Old William will not weep if he too falls. The lands will revert to Bertha and her sister, and he will grab as much as King Henry will let him keep.'

Lord Rhys prophesied truly. Four months later, a quarrel erupted amongst the French themselves. Mahel turned his ire not against the Cymry whose violence had brought him power, but against Walter Clifford, whose pirate castle of Bronllys threatened him. There was an attack, commotion, and fire. In the midst of the uproar, soldiers hurled stones from the keep on top of the foe below. Mahel, hit on the head, died instantly.

Father Dafydd, visiting Lord Rhys at Aber Teifi, found him in a black hwyl.

'Henry has taken his chance of splitting up too large a concentration of baronial power, but old William de Breos has doubled his lands in one stroke! He's been granted the two Cymric lordships that Hereford controlled, Brycheiniog and Upper Gwent! Radnor and Buellt are already in his clutch!'

Father Dafydd nodded. It was certainly a threat to Deheubarth.

'It is a moment for your noted prudence,' he remarked. 'The more dangerous a man is as an opponent, the more valuable he is as a friend. Can you not hasten that marriage? No, I dare say she is still too young.'

With regal ease Lord Rhys put aside the problem he could not for the moment dominate, and his face cleared.

'Now, what's this I hear about my cousin Gerallt, the new Archdeacon of Brycheiniog?'

'He went up to reform the clergy of Elfael,' said Father Dafydd with a grin. 'Seven members of one family shared the incumbency. They did not care for Gerallt's modern idea that every independent llan should submit to a higher ecclesiastical authority, so they greeted him with a hail of clerical arrows. He emitted a roar so savage that the ambushing clergy quailed, and when he got off his horse, hitched up his skirts, and marched forward like a lion alone, none dared assail him, especially as the cry went round that he enjoyed the protection of his kinsman, Prince Cadwallon of Elfael. He had no trouble with them after that.'

'He takes after Rhys ap Tewdr,' said Lord Rhys, satisfied. 'And then?'

'Then he marched up to the church of Ceri, which was a bone between bishoprics. He got there in time to celebrate one mass, thus taking possession for the diocese of St. David's, just before his old university friend, Bishop Adam of St. Asaph, arrived. There was a battle of prayers, bells, and arguments, clerical curses, interdicts, and mutual threats of excommunication. Uncanonical and void, retorted Gerallt, as coming from a bishop not his own! In the end, the bells won. He had the bellrope in his large hands, and there is nothing like a bell well rung, is there, to establish the power of a bishop and his archdeacon? Adam and his men rode away in haste, pelted by stones and the curses of the men of Ceri.'

'Gerallt is like us. He gives none of his rights away. I'd put my money on him every time,' remarked Rhys. 'Pity he's not the bishop instead of that uncle of his. Gives away Church lands right and left for the asking, does David FitzGerald, every time one of his daughters gets married to some local French lord. His brothers and uncle, too, have benefited. But he's done it once too often. The chapter of canons has protested and demanded an examination of the register of Church lands. And now, a further scandal! The Bishop has made off not only with the register, but with the official seal as well! I think he's going to pieces. The canons say they will prosecute him at King Henry's next council.'

'He has upset Ednowain of Llan Badarn also. He came rushing up to Ystrad Fflur in a great way the other day,' said Father Dafydd. 'He heard a rumour that David FitzGerald was going to sign his llan back to the French monks who were swarming there before you, Lord Rhys, turned them out. Ednowain swears that any party of Bishop's men or French monks who come to Llan Badarn will find him armed and horsed and as ready now to do battle as in the old days. He says that properly speaking, Llan Badarn is the seat of an ancient bishopric, and he is the bishop, by rights!'

'I dare say,' said Lord Rhys, with a weary grin. 'He's told me that tale on many a winter evening when he had leisure to refresh his mind amongst old grumbles. But what made him come to you?'

'He did us the honour to ask us to take over the Chronicle,' said Father Dafydd. 'Their chronicler, Ifan 'Sgrifennwr, has died. He was their best scholar, but not much use on the farm, said Ednowain. If they have to turn Llan Badarn into an armed camp there won't be much time for writing, he says, and he knows we are all good writers in Ystrad Fflur.'

'That was magnanimous of him indeed, and a tribute to the good relations your wisdom and diplomacy have established between you,' said Lord Rhys, much pleased. 'So you are to be guardians of the Chronicle! What do you think of it?'

'It is a mighty tome,' said the Abbot. 'Its earliest pages appear to record events now clouded by the mists of antiquity. How many of the early entries are genuinely contemporary I would hesitate to declare. Much, I fancy, must be attributed to the enthusiasm of a more recent historian. Some of the handwriting, for instance, chronicles a period in remarkable excess of man's normal span. Nevertheless, for the past three hundred years and more, the clâs at Llan Badarn, even the French interlopers, chwarae teg iddi nhw, have borne faithful witness to events in Cymru and Lloegr as they saw them. It is no light inheritance we have received.'

The harvest that year was abundant, and hearing that old William de Breos was ailing, Lord Rhys hastened to buttress their shaky relationship with a gift of figs from the old Roman gardens of the Ceredigion coast, some of Queen Gwenllian's wine and honey cordial, and a string of fine black cattle on the hoof. He chose for his ambassador his cousin Gerallt, in whose archidiaconate the de Breoses resided. Gerallt, who was never loth to bask in the beams of great men's eyes, and loved to multiply the links between French and Cymry, accepted at once. Old William, with the taste of honeyed wine on his tongue and the flatteries of Gerallt ringing in his ears, eyed the cattle greedily and sent a fair message back to Lord Rhys, who thought his trouble well repaid. Unfortunately, old William grew worse, and on Advent Sunday, died. His grasping but reconciling hands were gone.

Young William raised his thin head.

'I am lord of Radnor and Buellt and of Brycheiniog and Upper Gwent as well,' he murmured to himself. 'But these are blood-stained lands. The shade of my uncle Henry goes unavenged on the Cymry, and Seisyll ap Dyfnwal lives free.'

But he gave no sign of his thoughts. His look was peaceful and pious and he attended many masses, greeting the children who stared at him as he emerged from church, and patting their heads.

The snow on the meadows round Abergavenny lay undisturbed save by young people shouting in their winter games. Young William, the new lord, kept Christmas with his wife, Maude de St. Valery, his sons and his daughter, making merry with his kin, and giving a banquet for King Henry's great servant, Ranulf de la Poer, the Sheriff of Hereford. Before the year died, he sent his summons to Seisyll and his son, and to many leading men of Gwent, to be entertained at his castle and to hear a royal ordinance on the bearing of arms. They came in good faith and in a mood of Christmas peace, trusting that under the new lord, affairs would be justly ordered. When they entered Abergavenny castle, loosened their swords, and took their seats at the long tables, and drank their wine, William de Breos rose, and read the royal ordinance.

'You will therefore submit to lay aside all arms henceforward,' he declared. Cries of 'No!' burst out on every side; then William struck his own sword on the flagstones. A line of soldiers advanced in silence from the shadows behind the guests, and in silence slew them. The guests, groaning and bleeding, were left to die, while William's army rode out into the territory of Seisyll. They laid it waste, burned his hall, and took away the Lady Gwladus, after killing her younger son, the seven-year-old Cadwaladr, as he clung to his mother's arms.

3

There was a great silence in the land. Some calamities go beyond lamentation; the courts of Cymru were numb, slowly comprehending a depth of infamy hitherto unplumbed. Bleddyn, on his way to his son in Meirionnydd after Christmas at Dinefwr, broke the news to Father Dafydd. It passed, in trembling tones, from the monks to the lay brethren, and from these to the tenants, until at last, between Aber Arth and Ystrad Fflur, each member of the human chain laid aside his load of stone, and wept. Anger followed.

'The desire for revenge will keep the Cymry warm this winter, however cold it is,' said Bleddyn in a quavering high voice as he rode away north.

'What will Lord Rhys do now?' wondered Seisyll, turning to Father Dafydd, in whose eyes a hard look made its rare appearance.

'What can he do, unless he goes to war?' he said. 'It is the Cymry of Deheubarth that he rules. He has no authority over a

French baron who happens to be the lord of his brother-in-law. William de Breos had the usual rights of jurisdiction over his vassals.' He spoke with a bitterness never heard from him before. 'He exercised them.'

Then he bade Seisyll prepare to ride with him at once to Dinefwr.

'At this time, all who love the King must go to him. Rhys is our Brenin, crowned by God and by the trust of men.'

As swiftly as men and horses could, in the hard low months of winter, travel over rugged ground, they went south.

They were not the only travellers. Dinefwr was thick with vassals filled with rage, sorrow, and a thirst for revenge. These uchelwyr received no welcome from Lord Rhys, who would see no one. When he was not out riding, exorcising his anguish and fury, he spent hours with Caradoc in his chapel, at prayer. It was his sons who greeted the visitors, and with them plunged into ardent discussion of what their father ought to do. The air in the hall was foul with the breaths of too many angry men. The monks stood in their midst, ignored, their ears ringing.

The entrance of Queen Gwenllian imposed a brief, impatient silence. She was not a great beauty, but she moved with the grace and splendour of a queen, and she had a direct and formidable glance. It was not many weeks since she had given birth to her youngest daughter, an ailing child of whose life they had once despaired. Little Gwenllian had clamoured to be godmother to her baby sister, and in his sadness, Lord Rhys allowed this. The baby began to thrive.

'Now we shall have two daughters with the same name,' the Queen had said in a resigned voice.

'Fawr and Fach!' said Lord Rhys with a sigh and a laugh. This was the child of their reconciliation, and he was so relieved by her tardy progress that he did not care by what name she was called.

Now the Queen welcomed Father Dafydd and Seisyll, with a hostile glance at the rest of the company, and took them up the stone stairs to her private chamber.

'I must apologize for the sons of Lord Rhys,' she said. 'They are too busy lapping up advice from every hothead in Deheubarth to care for the comfort of our more valued guests!' Anger had stained her cheeks with scarlet, and brought the light of battle to her eyes. 'I pray for peace!' she said, nevertheless. 'I beg you, my Lord Abbot, advise my husband well.'

But when Lord Rhys entered, haggard, with red-rimmed eyes, it was clear he needed no advice. He embraced his visitors in a silence that they feared to break by any condolence.

'You will be glad to know,' he said, 'that my sister suffers no more. I have had masses sung for her and for Seisyll and for my nephews and for all the other victims.' He drew a heavy breath, gazed at his wife as though he derived strength from the very sight of her, and poured out wine for them all.

'Thank you for coming,' he said. 'I longed to be able to talk to Cadell, and you were his friends. I have prayed to God to tell me what to do. I long to make war upon de Breos. I long to plunge a dagger into his black heart. I long to act according to my old rash, impulsive reputation. But I will not.'

They drank in silence.

'I intend to disappoint de Breos,' he continued. 'It was all aimed at me, that infamous revenge, as a provocation to war. He came fresh to the saddle, and listened to his uncle, Philip de Breos, who was not so wise as old William, and to Ranulf Poer, who told him to try a tilt against Deheubarth. They all desire to see my kingdom crumble into digestible portions. They are jealous of my power and also of my friendship with Henry, and this I will not have destroyed, though it is true that I have had to endure the hasty blinding of a son by his command, and must now endure to lose other kindred by his baron's more calculating hand.' He exchanged a look with his wife. 'No, I will not make war, although my sons can talk in loud voices of nothing but vengeance, and shame, and pride,' he said. 'But the shame lies with de Breos, the pride with me, and vengeance is for God to choose. It is too terrible a crime for any but the King of Kings to punish.'

He smiled grimly over the wine.

'Of course, He will certainly appoint His natural instruments to do this at the proper time,' he said. 'Already the silence accumulating in the hills begins to frighten de Breos. I hear he is a stranger to sleep.'

The time of Lord Rhys's mourning ended in a clearing burst of rage. Each visitor to the hall had brought his dog with him; the place was full of dogs, and Queen Gwenllian complained of the dirt and smells. She complained with such vigour, and set the caethion to work clearing and cleaning the hall with such energy that Lord Rhys lost his temper, and roared, 'Dogs! Too many dogs, are there? I'll get rid of the dogs!' and gave angry orders for every dog to be hanged.

'Every dog I see shall hang!' he declared, and hanged the dogs were. They proved to be mostly his own, for all the uchelwyr had discreetly withdrawn from Dinefwr. Nevertheless, and despite the general and horrified disapproval, and his own subsequent sorrow, the proceeding gave him great satisfaction, for every dog was hung in the name of William de Breos. But it was a long time before the kennels recovered their former glory.

One fine May morning, Prior Seisyll was riding over Mynydd Bach. He had been visiting the grange at Morfa Mawr. The sun was shining in his face, curlews were calling overhead, and he was happy. He had found all well with the brothers, winter losses of cattle had been low, and the crop of lambs heavy. The fleece harvest in the summer after next should fetch a record count of gold, and Seisyll lost himself in calculations of the probable cost of the new Abbey, for with a mason's daily wage as high as fourpence, and even a labourer's at a penny, he had to watch accounts with more than common care.

After crossing the banks of Sarn Helen, he got off his pony at the edge of the Bog, and paused, as every creature must, to stare at the wilderness that defied the monks, those vast and sweeping acres below a hushed sky. They pretended to tame it here and there, nibbling round the edges and reclaiming a half or quarter acre to a pastoral use, and even contrived to sling a short cut on planks across the narrowest part for their barrow loads of stone. But still it lay there unperturbed, living its primeval life, idle, sluggish, and agriculturally unproductive.

'Perhaps,' murmured Seisyll, 'it pleases God to keep this independent tract fit for birds, not mankind, to remind us in the heart of our domains, that the earth, and all that therein is, belongs to Him.'

The sound of the bell of Ystrad Fflur came tolling out to him, then stopped. It began again, and stopped. It was a mourning bell. Some great man must be dead. As he listened, the day passed into afternoon, and Seisyll, alarmed, hurried across the short cut. Not until he reached Ystrad Fflur, breathless with haste and fervent prayer, did he discover that the bell had been ringing because the Bishop was dead.

Ednowain of Llan Badarn with Dafydd of Ystrad Fflur and Seisyll travelled south together on their way to the funeral.

'It is not that I mourn the man,' said Ednowain flatly, 'but I must show respect to his office. Llan Badarn must show its face on great occasions within the gwlad, especially now, in view of the old association between the two cathedral churches.'

Father Dafydd sighed.

'My reason is no better than yours,' he said. 'Ystrad Fflur is still young, and must make itself known. But we must pray for the Bishop, who was certainly our brother.'

'To think that only last January,' said Ednowain, 'they say his furious canons cornered him, cringing, outside the very door of King Henry's council chamber! They say he promised his all to make amends, if they would but withdraw their threat of prosecution. At last they relented, after forcing him to disgorge the key of his personal chest. I wonder what's inside?'

'Who will be Bishop?' said Seisyll.

It was a strangely perfunctory funeral. The canons hurried through the service, eager to open the chest. Flushed with their January victory, they had already made another push in March, when the Bishop lay dying. To King Henry's displeasure, and Richard of Canterbury's wrath, they had then declared the bishopric of Dewi Sant to be the metropolitan throughout Cymru, subject to Rome alone.

'I expect Gerallt was behind that move,' Seisyll had said at the time. 'Scraping up every ancient right he could lay his hands on to upgrade the office that he hopes to hold. He would like to be able to sign himself Giraldus Cambrensis.'

'Oh, I don't know,' Father Dafydd had replied. 'The Frenchman, Bishop Bernard, pushed by the canons, made the same claim years ago. There was nothing new in the announcement. They know that Gerallt shares their views, and it was simply their way of indicating that they mean to make him Bishop and Archbishop.'

Gerallt loomed large at the funeral, though it was observed that he left the company of the canons at the earliest chance, to plunge into earnest talk with Lord Rhys. Ednowain and Seisyll nudged each other.

'He has been backwards and forwards for months between King Henry and Lord Rhys, briskly canvassing!' said Ednowain.

'Lord Rhys smiles, but he says little,' said Father Dafydd. 'I understand he is not going to interfere in this election. But both of them enjoy Gerallt's company, so I suppose it's a settled thing, and he has worked hard enough for it, I must say. And it is time they had a zealous bishop in this diocese.'

'They will not find another Sulien in a hurry!' said Ednowain.

He contrived to be present when the chest was opened, on the plea of cousinship with certain canons.

'Two hundred marks!' he said in amazement for the twentieth time, on the journey home. 'Meddyliwch! Two hundred marks put by for a rainy day!'

'What did Gerallt say?' asked Seisyll.

'His eyes and mouth formed three round O's. Then recovering, he observed that at least his uncle had impoverished the bishopric more sparingly and modestly than the other bishops did!'

For all their expectations, the canons defeated their own ends very largely by putting Gerallt top on a short list of four candidates, without even waiting for Henry's congé d'élire. This was enough, to those who knew the King's cantankerous hwyl, to damn Gerallt's chances at the outset. King Henry was not the man to have his bishops thrust upon him, and August brought the news of Gerallt's failure. Henry rejected him, and thrust upon the canons Peter Lee, the Prior of Wenlock, as their new Bishop. Gerallt's critics at Ystrad Fflur were surprised at the pang of disappointment that assailed them, Seisyll especially. William de Breos was pleased at the failure of Lord Rhys's kinsman, but his mother, the widowed Lady Bertha, who had come to live in Brycheiniog, grieved openly. Lord Rhys said nothing, inscrutably, but was known to be disappointed. As for Gerallt, he retired to his duties in his archdeaconry, and was heard to exorcise his anger on the bells. Presently he announced that he was going back to Paris, to make a further study of the canon law, and theology.

'He has to arm himself with knowledge against his next battle,' said Seisyll, with more sympathy than he would have thought possible a month ago.

Lord Rhys, his presence decked with iron dignity, had received a kind welcome from Henry at his January council. William de Breos was there also, but no one greeted him; indeed, he was advised to go home. William began to understand that his crime had antagonized not only the Cymry, but the French as well. He sat in his hall, the prey of remorse and resentment, while his wife upbraided him, and his mother Bertha brooded angrily on her son's shame, and the expectation that the Lord Justiciar would immediately cancel his own son's marriage plans.

But Lord Rhys did not give himself that trouble, being absorbed in the more important and immediate matter of the Great Eisteddfod; so William de Breos was left suspended in uncertainty in addition to his other emotions.

It was with anxiety that Rhys and Gwenllian watched the weather that summer, for the success of their plans depended entirely upon a bountiful harvest. Heaven smiled, however, and sent rain at the right time, of the right amount, and followed with a sun so strong that Deheubarth reaped crops of record size and exceptional quality. Throughout the summer and autumn, the carpenters were busy making chairs, benches, and trestle tables to accommodate a thousand men. Contributions to the Aber Teifi feast came in from all the uchelwyr; Ystrad Fflur sent down two dozen sheep; not a hunter returned from the chase without parting with a portion of his bag to be salted away for winter stews; and Prince Maelgwn ap Rhys came into his own, to the annoyance of Queen Gwenllian, for he was a better marksman than her own sons except poor Maredudd Ddall, and he would never shoot again; and she was forced to depend upon Maelgwn's skill. In grim silence she accepted his offerings, maintaining the opinion that she might not utter, that a bastard is forced to be more successful than other men need be.

Maelgwn bestrode two families at once, with the persistence of a reckless rider determined to tame an ill-matched pair of horses. He was thrown every time, on one side or the other. He was short and burly like his father; by twenty-three he had swollen with importance and begun to lift his chin. When his manners offended too many in his father's court, he cantered sulking to his mother in Ystrad Meurig, where she lived in minor majesty as the castellan's wife, a handsome, dark, and lively woman, the mother of many other sons, with much authority gathered in her grasp. When they, in turn, had had enough of him, he had recourse to Hywel Sais, whom he found congenial to his situation; he galloped about the countryside with half-a-dozen cronies, young like him, and showed all his large white teeth in sudden flashes when people hailed him, 'Maelgwn! Tywysog! Pob hwyl i ti, bachgen!' Prince and boy, they saw him with pleasure plant his feet upon his own ground, for he was one of them, and kin to many thereabouts.

Prince Maelgwn and his friends went up in early December to Ystrad Fflur to go wildfowling on the Bog. With their falcons, they took a great number of birds, swans, and geese, and ducks of many kinds. They returned to the Abbot with faces red and swollen by the wind; their eyes were bright with staring at the sky. Small and large and heavy feathered bodies hung and swung all round their horses, and some they took round to the Abbey kitchen, well satisfied with their own generosity.

'You'll be glad of some extra,' said Maelgwn, banging a swan down heartily on the kitchen table, 'to feed the travellers going to and from the Aber Teifi feast. They'll be coming in droves. We shall have enough to feed the whole of Cymru, and as many as care to come from Lloegr and Alban and maybe from Iwerddon too, if any man dares to cross the sea in this weather. Venison, mutton, beef, pork, hare, various birds, sewin, trout, eels, carp, soups, pies, puddings, fruit preserves, custards, cakes, mead, wines, honey, cheese, apples—my father must have his apples—and figs. You wouldn't believe the fuss that's going on down there. The Lady Gwenllian isn't fit to speak to.'

Father Dafydd and Seisyll wanted news.

'Have you seen the new Bishop yet?'

Maelgwn scowled.

'No fear,' he said. 'He knew my father wanted Gerallt. He's keeping out of our way. My father sent him a formal message of welcome, and an invitation to the Feast, but he hasn't answered yet. The canons don't like him, and he's having his revenge on them for voting for Gerallt. Let the clergy do the least thing out of place, and he's down on them like a dragon, fining them a cow or an ox or a couple of sheep or a load of hay. There was one poor fellow who begged to be forgiven, to avert the fine, but Peter Lee doubled it on the spot. And the more he begged and grew frantic, the more this Bishop laughed and fined him even more, and said he'd teach his clergy to obey.'

By a common impulse the monks all crossed themselves.

'One thing I will say for him,' said Maelgwn. 'He is going to reconstruct the cathedral, he says. Apparently his anger was great when he saw its condition, and this has made him even more vindictive. Well, he has David FitzGerald's chest of gold to start with, and if he goes on taxing people like this, he will soon be able to afford to build, and now that my father has made peace in the land, and made it possible for a steady stream of pilgrims to go down to Ty Ddewi, the money will come pouring in to the shrine.'

Many more travellers than was usual for mid-December knocked on the door of Ystrad Fflur for shelter during the week before Christmas, and they were all going one way, like the birds in winter, to the South. Most were from Gwynedd and Powys, though many Saeson arrived as well, and even a minstrel or two from Alban. Several musicians came from the Marcher courts, very willing to enjoy free hospitality, and perhaps win a prize.

The whole convent of monks longed to visit Aber Teifi too, but it was not convenient. Father Dafydd must attend, though he was not well; the weather was damp, there were more colds about than usual, and Seisyll himself for once fell victim, and had to submit to the ministrations of Brother Cynfyn. Their infirmarian was away in Ty Gwyn ar Daf, making a copy of some new manuscript that had itself been copied from copies all the way up through Italy and France from monastery to monastery from the original hand of a Salerno physician. Cynfyn could not help wondering how many errors might creep in from hand to hand, and would the prescription therefore at the end prove safe?

'Our own infirmarian is a very careful fellow,' he conceded. 'But he has to take other men's writings on trust. I know well the dangers! After writing through a long cold day, especially if it be a fast day, the mind will wander, the numb hand shake, and the eye jump over words or lines, or else, which is worse, quite mistake the sense, so that you are tempted to correct what you think must be an error either in the original, or in the copy that has reached your hands. Thus heresies may very well ensue.'

The ills of winter, however, kept clear of the court of Aber Teifi, where no one had the time or inclination to be indisposed. Queen Gwenllian, resplendent in blue and gold, looked about her with great satisfaction towards the end of the first night of the Great Eisteddfod. Her eyes had been everywhere, her clapped hands and gestures had sent the servants scurrying in every part of the hall to attend to the wants of each guest, and now, between mouthfuls, she had time to inspect at leisure the uchelwyr who had been briefly presented to her.

She took particular note of Ednyfed Fychan from Gwynedd. He was the friend and counsellor of young Llewellyn, her own sister Marared's boy by her poor husband Iorwerth Tightnose, who was destroyed by his own brother Dafydd.

'Ednyfed wants to marry Gwenllian Fawr!' said Lord Rhys. His wife glared.

'He has the impudence? A nobody whose only boast is that he is my nephew's friend?'

'Impudence is in his favour. Where would I be now without it? He is not a nobody. He comes of a respectable family and has generations of considerable landowners behind him. Look at that great head! Sagacious, alert and steady, I can trust my girl to him.'

'Why don't you make a push for Llewellyn himself?'

'No,' said Rhys softly. 'For years we have had these alliances between the princes of North and South. It's time to plant my power in the ranks of lesser men, and I am well satisfied with his pedigree. If Llewellyn ever wins his crown of Gwynedd, Ednyfed will be the rock on which he builds his fort. So, I've promised him a daughter of mine if he can make his master king.'

For his part, Ednyfed was impressed by the splendour of Lord Rhys's court and the fertility of his lands. He had taken a particular fancy to the small but rich coastal plain that extended southwards from Llan Rhystyd for four miles. Now he looked about him at the Cymry and French and Saeson, eating and drinking their fill in a mood of good fellowship. He sat amongst sons-in-law of Lord Rhys, nephews from the South, princes from Powys, a few French barons, and numerous clergy. The new Bishop was there for a short time, a tall, pale man who said little, smiled once or twice with reluctance at John Spang's antics, and pecked at his food. He heard a poem or two, and went.

'I have business elsewhere,' he said loftily. He left the impression that he had timed his visit long enough to pay the required compliment to the King's Justiciar, and short enough to show his indifference to the Prince of Deheubarth. But Lord Rhys was too well satisfied with the success of his feast to take offence. He exchanged amused glances with his chief guests; they, enjoying a respite from their own divisions, found much entertainment in watching the poetic and musical rivalries of lesser men, and laying bets on the winners. The poetry prize was won by a bard from Meirionnydd, who sat afterwards at the head of a table in a splendid new chair, laying down the law on the finer points of cynghannedd and appraising kindly the efforts of his fellows. The prize for music went to some unknown youngster from Deheubarth, who afterwards melted modestly into the shadows at the rear of the hall, to be thumped on the back by his friends. Not one man there was displeased with his long midwinter trip. They were indeed being well entertained.

'He does us proud,' muttered a man from Gwent. 'Nothing too good for his guests. Every attention, plenty of food and drink, comfortable couches, a well-run hall—a good housekeeper is Queen Gwenllian—and the finest clothes to be seen on every side, the fairest women, and the best of good company!'

On the last day, a messenger arrived from William de Breos, bearing, to the general surprise, a gift of costly velvet for the King's Justiciar of Wales.

'As such, I accept it from one of Henry's barons,' said Lord Rhys coldly, and quelled the muttering in the hall with a freezing stare.

'Look at Lord Rhys's lips curling!' whispered Seisyll to Father Dafydd and Ednowain. 'What does the messenger say?'

'Oh, it's some smooth message!' said Ednowain. 'De Breos has bitten his nails to the quick in remorse long ago. He understands that he has made a mistake as well as committed a crime, and is trying to win back lost ground. There's a gift for young Prince Gruffydd too. His eyes flash with anger, but the father nods, and the son dares not reject it.'

'I thought that betrothal would lapse after the killings,' said Seisyll. 'Young the little girl is yet, of course, and things may improve. What is her name?'

'Matilda,' said Father Dafydd.

'Ma-llt-a,' said Seisyll.

'All this truck with the French,' grumbled Ednowain. 'He overdoes it. Upsetting our ways! Borrowing from theirs!'

Lord Rhys heard him. Ednowain, bold and loud, spoke up with his usual independence, though he had indeed dined well.

'I'm not afraid to tell you to your face, my lord, I don't approve of all your modern innovations! Undermining the traditions of Cymru!'

Lord Rhys stood up, his eyes still bright from the encounter with the messenger of William de Breos. He met Ednowain's challenge now with zest, and turned it, like all else that crossed his path, to his advantage.

'Listen!' he said, and silence fell, thick as a soft cake waiting for a knife. 'I value a good thing from whatever source it comes, ours or theirs, for what is good is God's. As for the traditions of Cymru, I'm as proud of them as you are, Ednowain, more so, perhaps! But we must not live to prop them up if they cannot stand unaided, nor must we let them confine our energies.'

Hearing him speak, a little crowd surged into the back of the already brimming hall, and his voice deepened to a carrying boom.

'We are an active and expanding people in an age of change!' he declared, and the court applauded. 'A growing youth in a pair of breeches too tight for him will not run very far without splitting them, will he?'

When the roar of laughter subsided, he said, with emphasis, 'A tradition is a wonderful thing to inherit. It enriches us, but it is not something to observe with uncritical respect. It is a tool you have been given. Its worth to you depends on whether or not you can find a use for it under new conditions, when better tools may come to hand. If not, it is just a decoration like these ancient swords that make a pretty pattern on my wall. You do not use them, but you remember and respect them, because they brought success to the struggles of your ancestors to whom you owe your life and inheritance. And of course, they may come in handy again some day.'

The listeners were exhilarated, and fell into private arguments, for and against. For many, his words pulled up something deep from their minds, some truth that leapt to answer. They saw one of the sons standing by, with the younger man's half-smile of scorn of and pride in his elder. What was he saying now?

'We are not so dead that new traditions cannot still arise!' declared Lord Rhys. 'For all we know, today we start another, by my feast! Of course things change! For worse and for better, and you have to choose between them, decide and dare, for the man who resists all change resists life, though he may have a value as a whetstone to provide a cutting edge for other men's wits! New aspects creep into all old things, and even Bleddyn has to give a new twist to his tales from time to time.'

He was silent, pursuing another thought, then he added firmly, 'I prefer power to the name of king. I have a certain skill in navigating the shoals of politics, and as the wind changes, I am prompt to alter course as I can between the sandbanks, though I never change my destination, and tradition is my second mate, not my first.'

Then he thanked his guests, the competitors, the judges, his cooks, his servants, his wife and sons, and the people of Aber Teifi. His audience broke into prolonged and steady cheering and applause, and the feast came to a formal close, though celebrations in the town continued into early morning, for Lord Rhys sent every man away with his compliments and consolation prizes of value, as well as surplus hams and cheeses. They went forth ready cheerfully to face bad weather; they were armed with stories, boasts, rumours, and news enough to last the winter through. Men talked round their fires about the Great Eisteddfod all through Lent; the greatness, wisdom, and magnanimity of Lord Rhys were very firmly fixed in people's minds; his fame redounded throughout the gwledydd, over Clawdd Offa, and into flat Lloegr beyond.

4

Nothing succeeds like success, and at Henry's Oxford Council in May, Rhys found that his great Eisteddfod was beginning to pay for itself. It had won him friends amongst the Border barons, for the French were always taken by display. Henry, all out to please the princes of Cymru, allowed Dafydd of Gwynedd an English bride with the lordship of Ellesmere, and Rhys was quietly made welcome to the land between Dyfi and Mawddach that he claimed, if he could grasp it.

'Still ashamed of the treachery of William de Breos they are, I dare say,' said Father Dafydd, when Lord Rhys went up to Ystrad Fflur to see how the Abbey was getting on. He answered the Abbot's unspoken question.

'A marriage between Gruffydd and the daughter is out of the question so long as the killings are unavenged,' he said shortly, then turned to his eldest daughter's state, widowed and heart-broken by the recent death of Einion Clud.

'She refuses to consider another husband,' said Rhys. 'What can I do with her? She will quarrel at home with her mother, and a widow alone is every man's prey.'

'She should work,' said Father Dafydd. 'Grief is a form of energy, to be used positively. Let her live with other ladies in like plight, in a nunnery.'

'Ah, we passed one of those at Godstow near Oxford,' said Lord Rhys. 'That little girl from Llanymddyfri that Henry was so fond of, Walter Clifford's daughter, poor Rosamond, she was brought up there. Poor child, she was no recommendation for a convent education, but nuns are helpless against kings, and Henry can charm when he has a mind to. Yes, we will establish one here in Deheubarth, and they shall rear Gwenllian Fawr as well, with the daughters of the uchelwyr. She is forever getting into mischief with John Spang, and needs stricter supervision than her mother has the time to give. The nuns shall keep them all well out of the way of licentious rulers like Henry and Lord Rhys.'

Then he inspected the ten foot high Abbey walls. 'What are the holes for?'

'We do that every four foot rise on purpose. The pensaer told us to put them a few yards apart. We put poles into them to support the planks on which we stand as we build higher.'

'Won't it make the Abbey very cold?'

'We shall stuff the lower holes with plaster, and leave the upper ones open, for ventilation, covered within by tapestry, of course. These holes will be required again for future repairs to walls or roof.' Father Dafydd frowned. 'We are in a difficulty with regard to the internal jambs of the great east window. We dare not proceed without the pensaer's expert supervision, but he is away advising the Bishop about the new cathedral to be built at Ty Ddewi. When we get him, he gives us, fair play, of his best, but messages are apt to come rushing up from Ty Ddewi, requiring his instant presence to discuss some inspiration of which the Bishop is newly seized. So we do without him until, at the next impasse, we stick again, and little messages pursue the pensaer in the opposite direction, summoning him hither.'

'Cadell would have known how to manage him for you,' said Lord Rhys, sighing. 'I should like to see my Abbey finished before the Bishop's cathedral. I had better summon the pensaer for my own purposes. That will winkle him out of the Bishop's clutch, and show which of us is master. He shall advise me about this castle I propose to build at Rhaiadr Gwy. I want to let the smoke from its fires drift down south-east to tickle the nose of William de Breos, to let him know it's there. Just a plain fort without frills, as I want to keep costs down. It will be enough to keep the pensaer at work for the summer up this way. You shall have him two days a week, Father Dafydd. Bwrwch chwithau ymlaen, fy mhechgyn i, a phob hwyl i chwi!' With which encouragement he left them, and turned his horse's head towards Aber Teifi.

But he did not long stay there. Lord Rhys was restless, and Queen Gwenllian sighed, knowing her husband's thoughts had turned once more to war. At least it would keep him busy and away from sin, she supposed; but she regretted the inevitable inroads on her stores of food.

The sons of Cynan, who lorded it in Meirionnydd now that poor Prince Hywel was dead, had not attended Henry's court at Oxford. Dafydd, their unlawful king, with his eyes on Ellesmere and an English bride, had not demurred when Henry granted Lord Rhys's demand, on the pretext of some antiquarian claim, to push his boundaries further north. But when the sons of Cynan heard the news, fury rode through their land.

'It will go hard with Lord Rhys if he tries to put his purpose into practice!' men said, even in Deheubarth. 'It goes against Nature. Meirionnydd was not meant to be ruled by the South. Bad luck will come of the venture!' And a difficult and dreadful year in fact followed.

'He has too many sons to provide for, not enough lands to divide, I suppose,' said the men of Deheubarth, bitterly, watching their own sons marching away north to cross the Dyfi on a season of aggression that broke the peace coarsely, filled the valley with smoke, and spilled blood on the fields with little to show for all the reckless efforts made to penetrate the narrow ways round the coast and up the high and shadowed cwms.

But Lord Rhys persisted.

'With the North divided, now's my chance,' he thought. 'Get the matter settled before young Llewellyn and Ednyfed Fychan come into the saddle, then they'll have to accept the status quo. Ednyfed, with his eyes on Gwenllian Fawr, won't let his master lay a finger against me.'

But he made no headway.

'What can Lord Rhys expect?' said the guests in the common dining-room at Ystrad Fflur. 'His forces fight for greed only, whereas in Meirionnydd the army of the sons of Cynan is swollen by every brave man fighting for his hearth. Why, every woman is ready to rise with her carving-knife grasped in her hand!'

The army of Deheubarth was composed of young and inexperienced men, seasoned with a few more battered warriors. The young men were ripe for adventure; they had heard that war was glorious. The old men did not want to leave their peaceful fields that prospered under their care, the ageing wives that they had come to love more dearly, and their springing sons. War disarranged their designs. Lord Rhys and Prince Gruffydd led their men on many valiant excursions into the North, but when the fury of the people drove them back time and again to Tomen Las and the old French fort of Castell Gwallter with sorry losses, and heavy rains washed all their hopes away, at last Lord Rhys took off his helmet. He looked around him with hot and disappointed eyes, and let the rain stream down upon his burning forehead. He heaved a deep sigh, like a man from whom a fever ebbs. He looked up at the smooth blue walls of Meirionnydd.

'God does not wish it, then,' he said, made peace, and repented.

Thwarted in the North, he retired to Dynefwr in pouring rain, and cast about in the South for something virtuous to do. He became tired of passing judgement on the endless list of legal cases that had accumulated in his absence, tired of Queen Gwenllian's nagging tongue, and the continual rain that was spoiling the harvest. Having kicked the toes of his shoes into holes, he whipped the caethion out of the way, sat down, and pondered. Then he sent for Father Dafydd, and demanded counsel.

'I want wider horizons!' he announced, pacing with energy up and down the hall. 'But I have to be content with my present boundaries. I must encourage, where I am, the rising prosperity of peace. But peace brings leisure, and leisure breeds mischief. Something positive is required to plant the Word of God up and down the land. My people are starved of spiritual riches, as I am, save in Ystrad Fflur. But whom shall I send to them, where turn for messengers? To this Bishop?'

He expressed, in vivid terms, his opinion of Peter Lee, and Father Dafydd raised a hand in deprecation.

'True, he has quarrelled—'

'He has quarrelled with everyone! He has suspended and excommunicated his canons and all the archdeacons save Gerallt, and gone back to Wenlock, where he came from, into retreat! He says the people of Ty Ddewi have driven him away, and I don't blame them, for he cares about nothing but to build his cathedral, and to collect his episcopal dues. But I find this chaos in the Church intolerable!'

'He has quarrelled, as you say, with all save Master Gerallt,' said Father Dafydd. 'He was absent, of course, but returns soon. That will leave him, perhaps, the rôle of mediator.'

Lord Rhys considered.

'Yes,' he said, 'that will show my influence at work in its proper place, behind the scenes, for he is my cousin's son. I have no wish to intervene personally. But even with this quarrel patched, the tyddynwyr of Deheubarth will still be as sheep without a shepherd!'

Then Father Dafydd mentioned the pastoral work of the brothers of Prémonstré, and their close association with the Cistercians, and Lord Rhys, like the good opportunist he was, seized on this at once.

'Why can't I have some of them up here?' he demanded. 'We'll find some central place in Deheubarth for another abbey! I shall have four abbeys then, and one cathedral, as well as all the clâs foundations with their llans. And a nunnery too!'

Gwladus, the widow of Einion Clud, was already preparing with delight for her new life as Prioress. A young woman, tired of crowded courts, she looked forward to living in the country silence. Eager and ignorant of the religious life, she plunged nevertheless with faith into its strange world, certain of one thing only, that if she could govern Einion Clud's ramshackle household, she could govern anything. For the rest she looked to Father Dafydd.

'I will advise you myself, my daughter, on the spiritual side,' he had told her. 'I will help you to choose fitting and experienced companions, and Seisyll shall help you to administer your lands.'

So she found herself established at last as guardian of a sheltered estate provided by her father, near the ancient llan whose foundation was traditionally ascribed to Llyr. It had a southerly aspect on the valley floor, with a mountain behind it where the nuns' flocks might roam in summer. She was very happy; she had the right disposition for the Cistercian life. She was adventurous and able, prompt in business, offered plain goodwill to all she met, and enjoyed work. Contemplation was a discipline new to her, but Father Dafydd found that she brought to it an honest, serious, and determined mind, and a loving spirit, very humble in approach. As for Seisyll, he confessed with gratitude that her friendship brought him joy.

Unfortunately, one of the first duties of the new Prioress was to attend a mass for the soul of her brother-in-law, Lord Cadwallon ap Madog of Maeliennydd, murdered by Roger

Mortimer. The nuns, silent and aghast, hastened to their prayers. Lord Rhys and King Henry, what would they do now? Fear seized them, for there would be war!

King Henry, however, stamped his foot like a Cymro when he heard the news. His honour was shamed, for Cadwallon had been returning from the king's own court when the murder occurred, protected, as he thought, by a guarantee of safe conduct. Cadwallon was betrayed, and the Lord Rhys ap Gruffydd mightily offended. Henry punished the murderers. 'I know my friends, and my enemies!' said Henry; and he caught the chief culprits. Some he put to death, Roger he imprisoned; and those who eluded his claws were forced to lurk as outlaws in the Border forests.

As for Lord Rhys, he watched events grimly, arranged his troops in full array mustered about his borders and kept them there, alerted, waiting, until he was satisfied that Henry had taken every step necessary to express to Rhys his sorrow as well as his anger. Troops passed up and down Deheubarth, on their way to and from their duties. Hot, short-tempered, and exhausted, rudely interrupted from garnering their own harvests, they made inroads upon that of Ystrad Fflur, by the great amount of food and drink that their numbers obliged the monks to set before them.

Meanwhile, Lord Rhys had been dropping hints in another direction, and presently Gerallt ended his studious retirement in Paris in a renewed blaze of importance. He was not loth to do so. He had kept a close watch on the affairs of the diocese, and when he heard that Bishop Peter, without consulting the discarded canons, had gone to Rome to attend the Third Lateran Council summoned by Pope Alexander III at the end of the weary Papal Schism, he went home, very willing to show his indispensability to the Bishopric he had been refused.

He turned up at Dinefwr on a cold day in March. Lord Rhys was in residence, and Father Dafydd and Seisyll happened to be present; and they eyed him with curiosity.

'The sun was shining as I came over the mountains,' said Gerallt, rubbing his hands and blowing on them. 'I saw a buzzard flying north. It will be fine for Easter.' His eye caught that of Seisyll, and they exchanged curt nods. Then, compelled by a common impulse to bury the past, they approached each other and said, they were pleased to see each other well. They spoke of swans and blackbird songs, which had been more prompt in changing that year. Seisyll found him knowledgeable about birds, which it was Gerallt's delight to watch and wonder at when on his travels throughout his great archdeaconry. As he forgot himself in adoration of this aspect of Creation, he became quite agreeable to Seisyll.

'Well now, how do matters stand?' asked Lord Rhys bluntly.

'You may have heard,' began Gerallt deliberately, 'that the canons, full of complaints of the Bishop's treatment of them, sent a commission to Rome, to try to catch the Pope's ear first. They raised once more, but without success, the old question of the metropolitan status of St. David's.' He looked round, complacently. 'I am on a mission of reconciliation. Archbishop Richard appointed me as the Bishop's commissary. I shall investigate with an impartial mind, since I was absent during these troubles.' After refreshment, with a bland, judicial smile, he left.

Seisyll was surprised to learn that he had any truck at all with the Archbishop of Canterbury; in spite of the episode of Archdeacon Jordan, he thought that Gerallt was one of the zealots who would not accept his overriding authority. But after Easter, when he heard the rest of the story, he was even more astonished. Gerallt reappeared, beside himself with rage.

He had been to Ty Ddewi. He had pacified the canons. He had, with difficulty, persuaded them to make a reluctant submission to their Bishop. He had been to Wenlock, to see the Bishop, recently returned from Rome, to persuade him to relent.

'Do you think he would listen, that intransigent man? He sneered and made threats to me, Gerallt! I resigned my commission at once, went over his head, straight to the Archbishop, and demanded the instant reversal of the Bishop's sentence on the canons!'

He was heard in silence. Sympathy restored his calm, and he rode away with feelings more under his control.

'Now what will happen?' asked Lord Rhys, exasperated.

'Oh, there will be a grand synod at St. David's,' said Father Dafydd. 'The Archbishop, if he is wise, will oblige Peter Lee to restore much of the property he wrested from the cathedral chapter. And there will be a formal reconciliation between the Bishop and the Archdeacon of Brycheiniog.'

'I fear Gerallt has compromised his position with regard to the metropolitan claims,' said Seisyll. 'He can never resist being important. How injudicious he is, after all, and how impulsive!'

'But how human,' said Father Dafydd. 'I think he was really sorry for the canons.'

Events fell out as the Abbot foretold. Gerallt, as Bishop's deputy, restored the diocese to a degree of order, and pursued his self-appointed task of reconciling the Cymry with the French.

'But this,' he pointed out significantly to his friend Lady Bertha de Breos, 'is difficult in view of past events.'

She quite understood this reference to the killings.

'A further approach by your son to Lord Rhys might perhaps make for better feeling,' he said. 'I fear that my influence alone may be insufficient to avert trouble from the men of Gwent.'

He was, of course, in a position to know, she thought. She took his words as a warning of imminent disaster, and hastened to tell her son. William de Breos, who had long been living in dread of retribution from the Cymry, became even more nervous.

'Another fortress,' he mumbled. 'I'll get Ranulf Poer to help. Dingestow, that's the best place—'

'Another fortress!' stormed his mother. 'Use your wits, my son, and thank Heaven that Lord Rhys has never formally withdrawn from that betrothal! Approach him with a candid acknowledgement that your grief led you into sin, make a token compensation and make your peace with the Cymry of the South! Until that marriage is made, you will live in terror of their revenge, and in the contempt of all the other French! He is a man of much more power than you know! Why, all the Cymry owing nominal service to you look to him in their hearts as their lord!'

'I tried,' he said sulkily. 'I sent an emissary to that great feast he held five years or so ago. Shabby treatment he got, and a curt answer. Maude was very angry, so we left it at that.'

'Maude? Are you, a de Breos, ruled by your wife? Why doesn't she look after her daughter? Your wife is always out riding abroad with muddy skirts to oversee your castles—have you no other lieutenant you can trust? That child Matilda looks like a common soldier's brat! And she could be Queen of Deheubarth if you chose!'

Seething, he called for his horse, and galloped off in search of Ranulf Poer. Another fortress, yes, at Dingestow!

When she was quite sure that they had both gone, Matilda herself emerged from her hiding-place behind a tapestry. It was true her mother had little time for her; she was reared by servants, and had to make her own way in the world. She was thirteen now. Life drew her forward and rebuffed, mocking her ignorance as she attacked it with alternate confidence and fear. In the stolid faces of the men and women of the castle of Abergavenny, she found no guidance. All they wanted were, their creature comforts, and as much gold and power as they could come by. All they feared were, her father, sometimes the anger of priests, and always the evil eye, and the Cymry quiet in their mountains. At night, the very castle walls seemed to listen, awaiting a five-years'-old vengeance as yet untaken.

'Queen of Deheubarth!' she thought. The words rang like bells. 'A common soldier's brat!' That stung. Matilda called for her maid, called for hot water, tore off her dirty smock, washed herself, donned her best robe, brushed and braided her hair like a lady, and thought about her one glimpse of the stranger called Gruffydd until her mind's eye recalled him to her in every feature, compact and clear.

'You're a fine grown girl, Lady Matilda,' said the maid with a saucy look. 'And pretty enough, for all you're a bit thin. When will you be married, I wonder?' She laughed when Matilda shook her, panting, 'Have you heard any rumours, Alys?'

'No,' said Alys, 'but old Gwen, the wisewoman in the kitchen, saw your fate in the cauldron on Saturday night. She knows.' She added, with a sudden rapt, mysterious look, 'He is a Cymro.'

Matilda was terrified, but there was delight in her terror. If Gwen's vision were true, she would penetrate the mountains whose foothills screened them. Her thin strain of Cymric blood stirred; she longed to go riding to their crests to gaze, to ride, and be free! She knew that wonders lay beyond; old Gwen had said so. Gwen's mother had been a Cymraes, and told her the tales that furnished Matilda's huge, too vacant fancy, between the roundels that the jongleurs sang, the old adventures of King Arthur's knights, the tales of our Lord and His disciples, and the travels of the kings of the Crusades.

'How can this be, a Cymro?' cried Matilda. 'Blood lies between us!' But she believed it. It could be none but Gruffydd ap Rhys, but blood must be wiped out by blood; all the tales said so, and Matilda waited with taut nerves, for what must come.

It was on one night in June that she awoke at last to the sound she had so long been listening for with dread, the blood-curdling yells of dying men. Her father was still absent in Dingestow, with Ranulf Poer, building another castle in haste during favourable weather, but he had left his wife and daughter well guarded by what he thought a strong defence. With their women, they had just time and strength enough to fly into their refuge, the uppermost small chamber of the keep. Lady Maude was the last to bundle them in, breathless and resolute, and bolt the door. Someone burst into hysterical wailing, but was slapped into silence. High above an intemperate hurly-burly in the courtyard, they trembled and listened, clasping each other tightly. Missiles of burning, scalding pitch, swept across the air outside, and sent a dreadful smell into the small room; Matilda sat choking and feeling sick. Most of the women were on their knees, gasping out fragmented prayers. Lady Maude sat like a stone.

'The keep is inviolable,' she told them in a hard clear voice. 'My husband has provisioned us well. In the chamber below we have ample stores of food. We have water also. This keep is built over a well that has never yet run dry.'

They shivered, and waited, sleepless. When morning light came, to reveal the charred timbers of the castle smoking in silence, the Cymry with their violent contempt had gone. Matilda saw torn heaps of rubble that had been walls. Bodies lay strewn on the stairs and in the moat, half floating, and the women wailed, and ran, and were silent, tenderly lifting each head to receive in their own hearts pangs like the arrows that had brought death in the night.

Matilda went back to the shell that was once her chamber. Her tapestries, her robes and rugs and furs, finery slowly collected against a nebulous marriage day, lay in ashes. But she felt nothing but relief.

'At least I'm alive,' she thought, 'and it's over.'

Three nights later, her father returned in the dark, haggard, in a battered suit of armour, on foot, and wounded, with the sorry remnant of his men. Dingestow, he said, half-built, had fallen; Ranulf Poer was dead. Matilda pitied her father, but could not weep for Ranulf Poer; she had always blamed his evil influence for the killings; and in her heart, she thought the vengeance was but just.

The news leapt through Cymru and Lloegr like a flame through a dry hay-rick. After nearly seven years of waiting, the kinsmen of Seisyll ap Dyfnwal, and the men of Gwent, had struck without mercy, and the Cymry rejoiced.

'Pity they didn't get William de Breos, but at least they crushed that Ranulf Poer,' men said.

Both Lord Rhys and Henry thought it their duty to fall into a major rage, and the King of Lloegr was said to be threatening an expedition against the Gwent Cymry. Father Dafydd, who had been ailing all the winter, pointed out that each was in a difficult position.

'Lord Rhys's honour as King's Justiciar has been offended,' he said faintly from his sick-bed. 'The peace he guaranteed was broken. He must now show public anger towards the culprits, however satisfied his private thoughts may be. Henry's royal authority has been insulted by the killing of his own Sheriff of Hereford. But his natural rage is overshadowed by shame when he remembers William de Breos's intolerable treachery.'

In Abergavenny, dismay and grief were followed by domestic spring disorder and frantic rebuilding. Life from William de Breos's other estates came flowing into his court. One day, amid the dust let fall by the plasterers at work high overhead with their lime and gravel, Matilda and her mother were summoned to her father's presence. He said, 'Matilda, you must go to stay with your grandmother, to be arrayed richly, as becomes a de Breos. Tell her to bring you to the King's next Court of the Marches, and to meet me there. You will have three months. That will be plenty of time.'

Lady Bertha was brisk and strong, with a voice that commanded obedience. She assessed her granddaughter with one swift glance.

'Of course,' she said. 'Clothes, and for a marriage too, I fancy. But can you order a household, child? Can you heal wounds? Do you know the herbs and simples to cure the winter sickness and the agues of spring? Do you know how to rear children in health and cook meals for hungry men? Can you weave and make garments to clothe them? If you can do none of these things yourself, you will be helpless in your servants' hands, and can never impose your will upon them. Three months! Why not the last six years? But your father always has been both obstinate and rash, and your mother careless. Come!'

Lady Bertha taught Matilda many things that her mother had never had time to impart. She was eager to learn, and though she received little praise, she knew that she pleased her grandmother. When the moment came to go to Court, Lady Bertha embraced her and gave her a heavy jewel on a chain that Matilda promised she would wear always.

'It will delight your children when you lift them on your lap,' said Lady Bertha smiling. 'Grasping and twisting this object in their greedy fingers, they will forget to cry.'

While Matilda learned the arts of housewifery, the Cymry kept their knives sharp, and waited. But Henry did not carry out his threat of invasion. During the three months preceding his next Court of the Marches, various sweating messengers, including Archdeacon Gerallt, galloped between Lord Rhys and Henry, William de Breos and Henry. No public announcement was made, but it became clear that that efforts were at last being made on all sides to bury old animosities. The Abbot of Ystrad Fflur was summoned to wait on Lord Rhys, to bear him company to Henry's court. But his sickness was worse, and it was Seisyll, newly returned from a visitation to Ystrad Fflur's first daughter monastery at Caerleon, who had to travel through the night to reach Dinefwr just in time to join Lord Rhys's company before they began their journey at dawn. He had gathered a small, but substantial band of sons and uchelwyr and the Abbot of Ty Gwyn ar Daf, and Gerallt, Archdeacon. Everyone was splendidly arrayed, especially Prince Gruffydd, but not a man bore arms, other than swords of ceremony.

Seisyll looked enquiringly at the Abbot of Ty Gwyn ar Daf, who smiled, and said, 'We go as witnesses. We go to support Lord Rhys, as his counsellors and friends.'

It was a hard swift journey without much mercy for either men or horses, and the splendid garments were sadly rumpled by the time the party reached King Henry's court. Lord Rhys, with Prince Gruffydd, marched straight to the throne. Scorning half-measures, he made a full and humble apology as Justiciar of South Wales for the killing of a King's Sheriff.

'It is what I myself would require from any who offended my own authority,' he declared bluntly, turning from one side of frowning barons to the other. Then he stared straight at Henry with his chin out.

'I am here also in another capacity,' he said. 'I demand mercy for the avengers of Seisyll ap Dyfnwal, Gwladus his wife who was my sister, and their sons, and their companions, whose odious and treacherous murder by William de Breos and others went unpunished by any prince for six long years. Neither by you, my lord Henry, nor by me, was punishment administered for that dreadful crime. For six years, the shades of the dead have wandered, crying to their own people, who listened, and now have answered, and at last, these shades rest.'

Many, scalded by his words, crossed themselves, and Henry, remembering another crime that had seared his own heart, bent his head. No man wished to defend William de Breos, who had fouled French honour. At last Henry spoke. He did not apologise for William. He had set aside his rage, and was in his brisk and best and business mood.

'On one condition,' said Henry, in the hoarse loud voice of the man who must impose his will. 'I will forgive my enemies, if you will forgive yours, Lord Rhys ap Gruffydd.'

He turned to Prince Gruffydd.

'Gruffydd ap Rhys, what happened to the bride your father promised you? She was to be a de Breos, but I forget her name.'

'Mallt—Matilda,' muttered Gruffydd.

'You shall wed her before you go home again,' said Henry. 'Plenty of bishops here. Are you content?'

Gruffydd looked at his father, who looked impassively at Henry.

'If my father and Your Grace agree, I am content,' he said.

'Well answered,' said Henry. 'Now, Rhys?'

The barons waited anxiously. The peace of the Marches depended on the reply. Rhys bent his head slowly.

'I seek peace,' he answered, and added reluctantly, 'I agree.'

Henry turned to William de Breos, who stood tensely waiting.

'I know your mind, Lord William. Fetch your daughter. Where's the Archbishop? I'll see this marriage made today.'

William de Breos mustered his dignity, tried to meet his master's eye, failed, bowed, and murmured, 'As Your Grace pleases,' and went, amid satisfied sounds from the barons, who looked as though they thought this feud was coming to a very fitting end.

The Abbott of Ty Gwyn ar Daf nudged Seisyll.

'Did I not tell you we came to be witnesses?' he whispered.

Matilda, with her grandmother and mother, was sitting in an anteroom. They had been left forgotten for hours, until Lady Maude, storming at last into some remote kitchen, returned with a subdued scullion bearing food and wine, but Matilda could not touch it. In that stuffy place she felt like death, and her grandmother had to pinch her and hold a bottle of some strong sharp liquid underneath her nose until she had choked and coughed her way back into a more acute discomfort. Each of them was ignorant of what the day might bring, and as the leaden minutes passed, the sense of doom increased.

It was at six o'clock in the evening that Matilda was summoned to the castle chapel to be married at once to Prince Gruffydd ap Rhys. She stumbled, blinking, out of the darkness, into the chapel's lesser gloom. It was crowded with people. Which was her bridegroom? She stood alone near the altar. The place was warm and the air foul, made tolerable only by the bunch of herbs that her grandmother pushed into her hot clutch, with an urgent whisper not to faint again on any account, and by the smell of new timber from the roof. A man stepped to her side. Matilda darted one quick look at the scowl he gave her, and looked away. Was this unwilling stranger Gruffydd? Her heart sank.

They were married with many prayers, in the presence of the King of Lloegr and his court, and of the Lord Rhys and his retinue. The Lady Matilda de Breos became Princess Mallt, wife of Prince Gruffydd ap Rhys of Deheubarth. The spectators saw a pale young girl with a frightened face, and a bridegroom, burly like his father, frowning fiercely at the altar. After that one swift glance of mutual distrust, they ignored each other.

At the feast that followed, Seisyll, yawning, watched Gerallt, like a contented bee, buzzing agreeably from baron to baron, from King to Archbishop to Abbot, greeting his many friends, taking to himself and his influence much credit for the match, and helping to make the party go, for it lacked continuum. William de Breos drank a ceremonial cup of wine with Lord Rhys and tried to make conversation; but Lord Rhys, grave and aloof, barely spoke. As for the young couple, they looked tired to death. Gruffydd, after asking if she preferred red wine to white, relapsed into silence. Various people claimed their right to kiss the bride; the King was one of these, but she was too dazed to take much note of him; her cheeks and mouth felt coarse and scratched by bristles.

It was a long banquet, and the forced mirth soon became real. The women, gay and excited, took Matilda to a bedchamber hung with splendid tapestries, undressed her and put on the fine embroidered nightgown that was her grandmother's gift. She was in bed when the door burst open and all the merry throng came roaring in, carrying the bridegroom on their shoulders. He too was in his nightgown, looking less excited than cross. They stared at Matilda, shrinking under the bedclothes, burst into renewed laughter, and shouted things that made her hide her burning face. They would not go until Gruffydd, with a determined smile, climbed into bed beside her and kissed her under her right ear. Then they went, bawling good wishes, banging the door behind them.

Gruffydd gave a long sigh, looked at Matilda sideways, climbed out of bed, and bolted the door. Then he came back and stood looking at her without much expression, but more kindly than before.

'It's about seventy miles from my father's court of Dinefwr to this place,' he said in a round Cymric voice that chewed up consonants and vowels as though they were roast mutton. 'We travelled all day to get here in time. And last night I had scarcely any sleep. My tailor kept on waking me to fit my new clothes, and as it is they're too tight. I'll come to your bed at a moment not of other men's choosing, but of my own, if you don't mind—and of yours, of course. So if you could spare me a carthen—would you be warm enough without it?'

Matilda stared at him in silence from a white face. He helped himself to a bed quilt, smiled kindly enough, and kissed her hand.

'Good night, Mallt,' he said, rolled up the quilt on the floor at the foot of the bed, and slept at once.

Matilda went quite limp. Everything inside her, the sore place in her heart, the hours of waiting and fear, the strange years ahead, thoughts of her parents, grandmother, brothers, Gwen, Alys, the cats and dogs at home, overcame her like a drowning wave. She cried under the bedclothes as quietly as she could, and when she was quite worn out, she stopped, and yawned.

Then she sniffed. Mallt! Was he always going to call her that? Half moan, half whistle, as though he were calling a bitch to heel!

5

On the whole, Lord Rhys was satisfied with his French daughter-in-law. Fourteen, but she looked younger; not strong enough to please him, but then clearly she had been cooped up and neglected. Butter and eggs and kindness would fatten her up and bring a twinkle to those eyes, which were large and fine; he liked them. Sharp and quiet she was, watching her step, and still frightened, he could see, of Gruffydd, who was, after all, ten years older. But sense and dignity informed her movements; her back was straight enough; and she made no complaint, thought Lord Rhys approvingly, on the weary ride home from Dinefwr.

Mallt first saw her new home on a sunny afternoon in May. It crouched like a shaggy wolf, snarling on its rock above Tywi, winding below. Her heart beat madly. What did this castle hold for her? She clenched her teeth and prayed that she might at least stand upright when she dismounted. But three days' unaccustomed riding had so stiffened the inner muscles of her thighs that when Gruffydd lifted her off the horse to the ground, she had to cling to his arms to keep from falling. Lord Rhys laughed with pleasure.

'Well done, Lady Mallt fach!' he shouted for the benefit of the smiling men and women assembled to greet them outside the great entrance. 'You cling to your husband always, and never let him go!'

Scarlet, Mallt tried to join in the laughter, though she felt like bursting into tears. Amid loud cheering, Gruffydd led her to the large calm lady in the gateway.

'Mother, I bring to you my wife, your daughter Mallt,' he said formally. A hard blue stare surveyed her. Queen Gwenllian said, 'Croeso Arglwyddes,' and her voice was dry like that of a lord who, watching a stranger approach, passed the time of day with him while deciding whether or not to let down the drawbridge.

Mallt did her best with her manners. She was dizzy, and curtseyed with difficulty. She overbalanced, and rolled to the ground. A tear began to fall in spite of her determination.

'Brenhines—' she began in a whisper. She did not know what to say to this statue. She did not mean to flatter, but a queen of this old race the Lady Gwenllian certainly was, whatever King Henry maintained. And who was Matilda de Breos to diminish the honours due to one whose dignities she meant one day to inherit?

Then Queen Gwenllian was lifting her up, and embracing her, and her arms and voice were kind.

'Dere di, cariad,' she said. 'Wyt ti wedi blino. Rhaid i ti galw fi Mam, nid Frenhines.'

The drawbridge was down, and a mother indeed she always was to Mallt.

In the long summer, Mallt grew, and grew happy. Life in the Border castles had been nervous and boisterous and rough, watching for trouble. Here in Ystrad Tywi in the sunshine there was security, with no need to watch. She never knew tranquillity before; her heart was lifted as by a great and steady hand, and her thoughts unfolded, unafraid. Gruffydd took trouble to please his bride, because it was his duty; she submitted to him, because it was hers. But they had become such firm friends by the end of the summer, that duty had turned into delight, and the political marriage that they had entered into, he with reluctance, and she with apprehension, had become their common source of strength, joy and purpose. Lord Rhys and Queen Gwenllian regarded them with pleasure.

'Gruffydd has been lucky!' he said. His wife beamed.

'Mallt is going to have a baby,' she said. Lord Rhys bounded to his feet, waved his arms, slapped his thigh, and cheered.

'Bendigedig!' he roared, and the whole court came running to him, elated, and full of congratulations and rumour. But Maelgwn was jealous, and made up malicious songs about the couple that made his cronies laugh immoderately. Lord Rhys heard him, and delivered a clout that sent him rolling.

'Cau dy geg, cythrael di-werth!' Maelgwn shut his bleeding mouth, slowly, but the resulting rage that simmered inside him was directed not against his father, whom he loved, but against Gruffydd.

Oblivious of others, Gruffydd and Mallt sauntered by the river, under the trees, and marvelled that any two people could be as happy as they. In the winter, the Cymry came down from the hills and forests, and went to live indoors, snug, fat and cheerful in the cold weather of the lean season, fed on the stored plenty of a summer when no wars came to crush their harvests. There was time for ceremonies, and a heart for songs, and an appetite for stories. Mallt listened eagerly all over again to Culhwch and Olwen, Taliesin, Geraint and Enid, and Peredur the son of Evrawc.

'You know them?' said Lord Rhys, astonished.

'They are my favourites!' said Mallt. 'This was the company old Gwen would summon from the chimney shadows. She had us all at her feet, the scullions, the soldiers' children, my brothers, and me.' People smiled at her with pleasure, and Maelgwn's eyes glittered in the firelight.

'You're getting round them,' said Gruffydd softly. 'Maelgwn doesn't like it.'

But if Maelgwn resented her, the two Gwenllians hailed her as a gift, for Mallt knew other stories that they had never heard.

Time after time they begged her for the Song of Roland, or better still, Aucassin and Nicolette.

'They will never leave you now, the Gwenllians,' said Gruffydd. 'They will be after you all day long for stories!'

Fawr was the same age as Mallt. She was gay, and big, and beautiful, and yellow-haired, like her mother. Fach was six, red-haired, white and tiny, and always wailing.

'She looks so fragile!' said Mallt with pity.

'It was never thought the little one would live,' admitted Gruffydd, and Mallt trembled to think of Death, so eager to snatch Gwenllian Fach.

'Don't worry, that one isn't going to die, she's too spiteful,' said Gruffydd vigorously. 'She crawls about under the tables at banquets, pinching people. We have to whip her. Mind you keep her in her place, Mallt. As for Fawr, I told my father the other day that it was time she was married and had her own baby—mooning about the hall, dreaming of this and that, giggling with John Spang and every soldier who catches her eye—what behaviour is that for a princess of Deheubarth? But he told me to mind my own business, that she should have her husband when Gwynedd was fit to receive her—did I want her to land up north in the middle of strife, and have to be locked up like Rhodri's wife, my sister, in a broken-down fort for safety? Fawr is promised to Ednyfed Fychan, but druan a hi, she'll have a long wait. My father is waiting for Llewellyn to overthrow Dafydd first, but how long can he keep Ednyfed on the string?'

Gruffydd's first son was born in early June. The rejoicing in the hall below was uproarious and unrestrained, and Mallt, listening with greed to this her proper tribute of praise, could not bear to miss the slightest bellow. The birth of her son confirmed her importance. At the baptism, the uchelwyr and their wives paid as much court to her as they did to Queen Gwenllian, if not more, by reason of her youth and their curiosity. Archdeacon Gerallt, who performed the ceremony, was most condescending. Three-quarters French, he was happy to see another French Cymro come into the world, and a second cousin's child at that. He was pleased to display a familiarity with Mallt's family tree, and eager to entertain her with ramifications of his own.

'A good thing we didn't ask Peter Lee to christen Rhys,' said Gruffydd afterwards. 'Babies can't endure him, and all his christenings end in uproar. Gerallt is almost as good as a bishop, you know. King Henry offered him Llandaff only the other day, but he wouldn't take it. St David's or nothing, he said. What's more, he claims it should be an archbishopric. He's got a big pull with the canons, and I hear Henry refused his election there lest he develop into another Thomas Becket.'

Gerallt stayed only one night at Dinefwr. He was going to visit his brother at Maenor Pyrr before crossing to Iwerddon to stay with his half-uncle Robert FitzStephen, and others of his mother's kin who had found dominion there.

'He will find a few changes at Maenor Pyrr since his brother inherited!' said Lord Rhys at dinner after Gerallt had gone. 'And he will feel the draught now that his mother my cousin Angharad is dead. She and the Lady Nest, his grandmother, were always in his backgound to provide support and sympathy.'

'What will he do next?' asked Gruffydd curiously.

'Make a name for himself somehow beyond Cymru that he may be the more important inside it when he comes back, I suppose,' said Lord Rhys with his mouth full.

He was not pleased by this abrupt departure. Gerallt might have waited to witness his formal gifts to Ystrad Fflur next week! Rhys would have given much for so fluent a gossip to be present at Llan Sant Ffraed by Rhaiadr Gwy, to take to Henry a glowing report of his cousin the King of Deheubarth's might and generosity and of his huge endowments to the noble Abbey rising steadily amid the Ceredigion mountains. Still, with all that crowd expected, word was bound at last to pass through to Lloegr and its king. If only the weather would hold!

But it broke. Thin clouds piled up like poultry feathers on a kitchen floor. The cavalcade of Deheubarth, under sodden sheepskins, rode over the mountains through steady rain. The ladies, wet through and grumbling, took their time to get dry, steaming before a blazing fire in the castle hall, before emerging into the churchyard where Lord Rhys stood in front of a huge throng of monks and uchelwyr, lay brethren and tenants. He was reading from a great parchment. His hair, his gold crown, and his best embroidered robe were wet. Raindrops like tears streamed down his face, so that the envious might have said that it was with sorrow, not with pride and joy that he confirmed his massive gifts to the Cistercians.

'—Health and Peace,' he cried. 'Be it known to all of you that I, Rhys, Proprietary Prince of South Cymru, have begun to build the venerable Abbey entitled Ystrad Fflur, when built have loved and cherished it—'

One by one the ladies moved slowly through the armed and cowled ranks to reach Lord Rhys and his sons.

'My three sons also, namely, Gruffydd, Rhys and Maredudd—'

His great voice was drowned by the roar that greeted his grandson in the arms of Mallt. Lord Rhys began to read the seemingly interminable list of lands granted to the Abbey. The sun crawled out between clouds; clothes dried on their wearers and steamed in sudden summer heat. Men looked at Lord Rhys, and at his ladies, and at each other, pleased with the improving weather, the formalities that flattered every man's importance, and the prospect of a good meal at Lord Rhys's expense.

'Nanneirth in its boundaries, that is to say from Nant y Fleiddiast to the Gwy, from the Gwy to the Hedernol, from the Hedernol to its source, from thence across to Blaen Ystwyth—'

Lord Rhys's grandson raised objections, and the crowd smiled.

'—between Buarth Caron and Dinas y Drittwyr, from thence along the course of that river as far as the grange which is called Castell Flemish—'

The baby complained again, and Gruffydd took his son from Mallt into his own arms.

'—whatsoever is contained within all the afore described bounds, in plain, in wood, in waters, meadows, pastures, cultivated and uncultivated ground, I Rhys and aforesaid sons and my whole posterity—'

Gruffydd lifted the young Rhys high, while Lord Rhys waited with a bland smile for another roar of applause to die away.

'—do give in fee by perpetual rights to the monks of Ystrad Fflur and their successors.'

This was the end, then. The baby, whose temper was souring, struggled in his father's arms.

'—and these are the names of the more eminent places within

these bounds,' said Lord Rhys ominously, with a quelling look at his grandson. Expertly, Queen Gwenllian removed him.

'—Rhyd Fendigaid, Dôl Fawr, Llwyn Gog, Tref y Gwyddel, Ffynnon Oer—'

Concentration began to disintegrate. The crowd watched Gruffydd, erect and military, and Rhys Gryg, who was struggling with a cold. Young Maredudd was not tall enough yet to reach the vision of any but the first few rows. None of the natural sons had been invited. Pity Maelgwn druan was not there, muttered the Ceredigion uchelwyr; had his grandfather Iestyn Fychan been alive, he would have fought for his inclusion! But there, they supposed that this was, after all, a day for Queen Gwenllian's sons. The crowd began to be restless. Lord Rhys, having exhausted his gifts of land, appeared to be giving away the sea itself.

'—as far as the mouth of the Arth to Aber Meylir, and the weirs and all the fishery on the shore and in the sea, from the mouth of the Arth to the mouth of the Aeron, we offer to the said monastery for ever.'

Lord Rhys cleared his throat, and smiled at his subjects.

'Also from my own proper fish-pond one day and one night in every week,' he concluded graciously, and then he began calling loudly for the witnesses and the pens and the ink, and it was over.

But the day left its mark. Maelgwn gave no immediate sign of resentment at his omission; he stored his grievance. But to Mallt, looking back in later years between the clashing swords and rearing limbs of warriors in the foreground, the Cymric arrow nailing Norman thigh to horse, the beleaguered cataracts of fury pouring on the enemy below, it seemed that the first signs of trouble dated back to that great assembly at Rhaiadr Gwy. They pushed into the peaceful years like the first moles of spring scratching up into a fertile field. The young sons of Lord Rhys, as each came of age, went tilting at trouble, fired by Bleddyn's tales, and Maelgwn's rebellious example. These errant knights, eager more for fame than riches, reaped curses, rather, from friends and foes alike, and the full weight of their father's wrath, from which they fled into the courtyard, to repair their damaged self-esteem by boasting to their companions of the feats they had nearly pulled off.

In the dark months, Dinefwr was dull, for Gwenllian Fawr was ailing with the winter sickness, Bleddyn was ageing and had retired north, John Spang had toothache, and Gerallt on his return from Iwerddon, had stayed in Cymru long enough simply to castigate his clergy and collect outstanding dues, before he made straight for King Henry with a report on the condition of Iwerddon. He entertained the King so well that he was persuaded to prolong his stay in Lloegr to act as court chaplain as he wrote down by day the accounts of Irish life with which he enlivened the winter nights.

Even spring's return brought further gloom to Lord Rhys, despite the joy with which he welcomed the birth of Mallt's second son. Father Dafydd died, to be succeeded by Seisyll; and then a fresh disaster struck when Queen Gwenllian fell ill. When he rode round the realm on cylch, the Queen was his chief companion. He enjoyed the comfort and dignity that her presence brought, and her private counsel too. For her part, she was determined to ensure his well-being and his correct behaviour. In winter, they always travelled across the banks and plains of milder Dyfed; in spring and summer they ranged throughout the mountains and valleys of Ceredigion, and in autumn, they went visiting in Ystrad Tywi. Together they endured the discomforts of uncertain weather, coarse wayside fare and rough beds, until at last, stiffened by pains in the joints that made riding or even travelling by litter, an agony for her, Queen Gwenllian was obliged, to her anger, to stay behind. Lord Rhys was greatly disconcerted, and there was a distressed discussion, in which his wife, for once, made all the decisions.

'I'll go in search of health to Llan Llyr, to stay with my daughters,' she said. The two Gwenllians were there with Gwladus; Fawr was convalescing, and Fach was having her mind improved. 'Mallt, you must go on cylch in my place, to look after my husband and my sons. I shall take your children, and a strong and healthy wet nurse for the baby.'

Mallt was reluctant to part with her children, but gratified by this promotion. She submitted. The Queen's instructions were simple, but emphatic.

'If he gets wet, make him change his clothes at once,' she said. 'See that he gets enough to eat on the road in addition to all those apples, but don't let him stuff too much when you reach the gwestfa, especially the first night when the maer always tries to put a banquet before Lord Rhys to win his favour. Make sure that the beds are clean and dry, that the floor is well swept and strewn with dry rushes—if you think they are damp, have them swept out at once and tell the caethion to put down rugs—and see that there are no holes in the roof. As a rule, they are very careful to have everything in good order if they think we are coming, but I remember one place where we had to shift our couch three times in the same night to avoid the drips overhead, though I grant you it was an exceptionally wild night with a strong gale from the south-west and torrents of rain. Ceredigion that was. You will find,' she added, '—that there will always be plenty of hot water for washing in the bath-houses, for they take a pride in keeping up good fires.'

She looked with disapproval at Mallt's dirty gown, marked by her children's sticky hands and kicking feet.

'Take your best clothes and jewellery. Lord Rhys likes us to make a splash. It gives the people something to look at and be proud of, and something to talk about in the long winter evenings, and I know they are all curious to see what Prince Gruffydd's wife is like. Bleddyn has been singing your praises wherever he goes. Poor Bleddyn! I wonder, is he still alive?'

Mallt remembered her first progress through Ystrad Tywi for the white-hot rage in which Lord Rhys set out. It was a fine morning; they were cheerful and ready, awaiting his pleasure, when he burst out of the hall, swearing, hurled himself on his horse and rode away hard from Dinefwr.

'What's the matter?'

'Maelgwn wants a lordship in Ceredigion—or else Cadwaladr demands a castle in Dyfed!'

He went unsatisfied, whichever son it was. Lord Rhys, warned by King Henry's example, would not give a square inch of land to any son, nor give him any office he himself could not directly oversee.

'Why should I, when I'm in my prime?' he bellowed. He was fifty-four already, but no one dared to ask, who should come after? Of course, thought Mallt, Lord Rhys meant her husband to inherit all his dignities; though he never said so. No doubt he meant also one day to allot a subordinate lordship to each of his other sons; but he would not say; and he rode away roaring. Gruffydd and Mallt and the whole teulu, close on a hundred strong, did not catch him up until they drew rein, panting, outside the gates of the clâs at Llan Deilo.

They feared he would scorch the canons with the smouldering embers of his wrath, but Lord Rhys had expended that upon his poor flogged horse, and he entered the building with no more than a savage glare that silenced welcome, and gave a cutting edge to his announcement. The canons heard with dismay that their mother church of Llan Deilo Fawr, with many of her subordinate chapelries, was to be yoked to the jurisdiction of Lord Rhys's new foundation at Tal-y-llychau, a few miles away on the road to Caeo, where he had settled a body of young and energetic Praemonstratensian clergy, in order to satisfy the spiritual needs of the Ystrad Tywi people. These, who lived remote from Ty Ddewi, Llan Badarn Fawr, and Ystrad Fflur alike, had long been neglected by the complacent and elderly local clâs.

Mallt listened with dread, for Lord Rhys was in the mood to speak a few blunt words.

'Look at the people in Ystrad Tywi!' he said. 'Which of you takes the trouble to bring to them the living messages of Holy Scripture? Do you cultivate this wilderness? Do you seek to christen and marry and bury them without a thought of milking them with a multiplicity of costly masses?'

They looked at him like thunder-stricken sheep, and he flung a final pebble.

'And when did you ever offer me a sermon worth the hearing?'

That really did draw sparks from their eyes, and Gruffydd nudged his father, who took the hint and changed his tone.

'Understand me, I'm a sinner, too,' he said. 'I am a rude blunt man like my subjects, and I pity them and me that we starve here on the edge of plenty when we might be feeding on the Word of God. Come!' he said, and suddenly his eyes and face glowed, he was another man, and even his hair seemed to grow brighter. The canons, angry and bewildered though they were, could not withstand his force. 'I bring you adventure and the stir of new life into the staleness of your middle years. You and the canons of Tal-y-llychau together will work to bring the love of Christ Our Lord, like a plough, into every cwmmwd, every little tref. You will dig like good gardeners, you will fertilize and plant and water the good seed in the hearts of my people, and shelter the growth within the garden of Holy Church. Men will flock to your altars for their trust in your leadership into eternal life, and they will remember each of you by name, like Teilo, like the saints, in years to come, and the generations now in God's shadow, when they come to light, will call you blessed.'

There was little the canons could say in reply; Lord Rhys had seized their anger, shaken it, and restored it to them as a whip for zeal and a pastoral staff for love, all through the valley. A few querulous murmurs did arise, concerning such minor matters as legal possession, tribute of cattle, hereditary claims, boundaries; but these arose like the ghosts and clanking chains of their own dispirited ceremonies and withered hearts, and they sounded so irrelevant that they died away as they looked at each other like men subjected to the pangs of rebirth.

'I do not flatter myself that the effect will last,' remarked Lord Rhys, as they pushed on to Myddfai. 'There will doubtless be ructions, appeals to the Bishop, and all the rest of it, but it's worth the risk, for they were getting very slack. I look to the clergy to trounce me, as a rule, but the laity has a duty to stir them up in turn sometimes.'

In the journeys that followed, Mallt saw Lord Rhys get through all his business with admirable despatch and economy of time and temper. He contrived to make every encounter serve his purposes, and in the evenings, when the toils of court work were over, he exploited the geniality diffused by meat and wine to explore men's hearts and parade his own views. Daily she saw him with impatient gestures question every witness, deftly separate false from true, pounce on the salient facts, and weave these into a rough but solid basis for the settlement of wrongs.

But they lived that year of brisk journeys against an anxious background. In Holy Week, when Lord Rhys paused at St. Dogmael's on the way down to Ty Ddewi, a horseman wet with sweat arrived from Llan Llyr. He gasped out that Gwenllian Fawr was very ill; the Queen begged her husband to go with all haste to Ty Ddewi to pray for her recovery. Lord Rhys, terrified, was all for rushing back to Llan Llyr, but Gruffydd opposed him, with success.

'We are slightly nearer to Ty Ddewi than to Llan Llyr,' he pointed out. 'If we go to Llan Llyr, she may have time to die before we get there. If we go to Ty Ddewi, an immediate mass may save her.'

It was not a ride so much as a headlong flight from death to life. Lord Rhys invaded the half-built sanctuary of Ty Ddewi, turned a ravaged glare to Heaven and roared out his desperate demand that his daughter be restored to her parents. Mallt, angry as well as frightened, touched Lord Rhys's arm, not gently.

'Be quiet!' she said. 'This is not the way. Don't think of yourself, think of Fawr. You cannot take God by storm!'

He stopped his fierce prayer with a sigh, and with his mouth half open, like a lost child turned his eyes of misery on her. He reached for her hand and kept it in his own, all through the mass, and in the silence in which he heard it, she believed God's mercy came. Afterwards, he patted her head.

'Da merch i, Mallt fach,' he said.

On Easter Monday, a messenger brought happy news. Gwenllian Fawr was saved. The doctors, inspired by so many prayers, had worked like angels around her bed. In his gratitude, Lord Rhys was ready to impoverish his entire realm to beautify the cathedral, Bishop Peter Lee notwithstanding; the gratified canons also extorted a promise that when he died, Lord Rhys should be buried, not at Ystrad Fflur, where his brother Prince Cadell, lay, and where his own affections clung, but at Ty Ddewi. Cornered within his own generosity, fearing a relapse for Gewnllian Fawr, and very much against the grain, he agreed, and they showed him the favoured position, near the altar, and not very far from Dewi's tomb, that they had reserved for his own.

'Well, what could I do?' he growled later, when Queen Gwenllian reproached him for his weakness. 'It was the chief reward they wanted. They know that as many will come to see my tomb and bring their gifts to the cathedral, as come to venerate Dewi's bones. That promise was worth more to them than anything else I was prepared to give.'

The more he thought about it, the angrier he became with the canons for their temerity, and he shook his fist.

'I'll outlive you all!' he shouted. 'I'll make you wait longer than you like for my funeral!'

But when he saw Gwenllian Fawr, languid but alive, his curses died away, and thankfulness made him quite silent.

The rest of their journeys that summer proceeded under thin rains, and they moved sullenly into autumn under clouded skies. The weather, and her responsibilities, took their toll of Mallt's nerves.

'What is the matter with us all?' she demanded one day, in a burst of irritability and despair. 'The world is grey, the very wind is hushed, every face is dull with discontent, and even the dogs look anxious!'

'I don't know,' said Gruffydd, taking her hand. 'Only it seems we have all been young for a long time, and now, suddenly, everyone is getting old too quickly. My brothers march into manhood with uneven strides, my sister battles for her health, and both my parents struggle against old age. But you, Mallt, are rising into the beauty, strength and power, that made my mother once the hinge of all Deheubarth.'

So he flattered Mallt at least into health and contentment. But she was to think vaguely later that perhaps that dull time was one of those pauses in life in which the significance of things past begin to be understood, and hearts are fortified against events to come—just as there must be rests in music, to give shape to the air.

6

But if Lord Rhys and his wife were passing their prime, neither would admit it. They defied the encroachments of age. Gwenllian, racked with pains, exacted obedience with more force than was wise; her own sons escaped her, but the care of her younger daughters and her grandchildren satisfied her need to rule.

'It gives Mallt the freedom to flaunt herself about Deheubarth!' said Maelgwn in his cups one night.

Gruffydd retorted with a colourful description of the low company his brother kept; and Aber Teifi's canopy of oak rafters began to reverberate with another of the noisy public quarrels that threatened to shatter the realm as though it were a fragile vase.

It awoke Lord Rhys, and then the thunder came. For some time an increasing thirst had shown that his vigorous journeys in all weathers were beginning to tire him. He emerged now from lethargy, and insulted each of his sons in his weakest point. Maelgwn was a little man who tried by roaring to show himself a lion; Rhys Gryg, by gestures of authority, aimed to show his importance afar to men to whom his croak would never reach; Cadwaladr was an ambitious fool; Hywel Sais had little eyes that moved from side to side to watch where his advantage lay; Gruffydd lacked his brothers' spirit to rebel—

Wild, Mallt rose and stamped her foot.

'Such ingratitude to such a loyal son as this I never thought to hear from you, my lord!' she panted. But Lord Rhys merely turned to Gruffydd and jeered.

'You even leave it to your wife to defend you!' he said.

Gruffydd, shaken by this blow from the hand that fed him, was too stunned to reply, and Mallt thought her tears of rage and disappointment would never stop. Later it was Gruffydd himself who once again gave comfort.

'He cannot see his greatness yet in any of us,' he said. 'Perhaps he doesn't want to. When we are quiet, he spurs us to action by a burst of scorn, and when we resort to violence, he fears for his authority, and cracks us down. There will be a sequel to this brawl. But hold your tongue, Mallt. My father values you.'

Gruffydd was right. Maelgwn and Cadwaladr went sulking into Dyfed, picked a quarrel with some Flemings and French near Tenby, and in the fight with knives that followed, Cadwaladr was killed.

The news was broken to Lord Rhys in private, and the court did not see him for many days; even Queen Gwenllian, who was not Cadwaladr's mother, grieved. Presently a message from Ty Gwyn ar Daf brought news of the burial that Lord Rhys had been too stricken to attend, and another piece of news. Then he emerged.

'Henry has lost a son,' said Lord Rhys, in the ghost of his usual voice. 'Geoffrey his name was. In some tournament or other. These youngsters! Poor Henry.'

He was quietly employed for the rest of the evening, dictating to the monk a letter for the King of Lloegr, finding solace for his own grief in offering comfort to another. Then he felt himself disposed for conversation, and began to question the monk for further news of Henry. As there was nothing fresh to relate, they reverted to old stories of the king's domestic discords. Like two dogs, they dug up bones of gossip buried long ago, and chewed them all over again with renewed relish.

Maelgwn, burning to revenge his brother's death, did not burden his father's court at Christmas. He waited in Dyfed with his men, and it was not until after Epiphany that news reached Dinefwr of Tenby's destruction by burning, by Maelgwn. His father heard the news with unalloyed satisfaction, and in Ceredigion, his kindred were delighted, and paid the bards to sing his praise.

Mallt said angrily, 'To have a son revenged is good, but for another to be the instrument without his father's knowledge or permission is surely an insult to Lord Rhys!'

'Maelgwn and my father understand each other,' said Gruffydd, in the grudging tone he used when speaking well of his half-brother. 'You cannot expect any breach of the peace to be undertaken in Deheubarth between Cymro and Fleming with the knowledge of the King of Lloegr's Justiciar. That would be an act of war by my father against Henry, for which Henry could punish him. Now, if the Flemish complain, my father can justly plead ignorance, and lay the blame on the hot blood of youth.'

Maelgwn reappeared at Dinefwr at Easter, smiling at the loud roar that acclaimed him; he eyed his father boldly as he went forward with a swagger to the expected formal public reproach. To the court's but slight surprise, none was given; but neither was any welcome offered. For a moment the slightest of smiles was exchanged between father and son, before each turned away from the other. It might have been a salute between equals, and Mallt was speechless with jealousy. Why had Lord Rhys never looked like that at Gruffydd?

On the day that Gerallt returned from another visit to Iwerddon, full of his travels with Prince John, news came that Jerusalem had fallen to the Saracens, those godless fiends delivered on to the Holy City by a hissing desert wind, like a judgement on the sins of men. Gerallt, feverishly impatient, was all for rushing his cousin to Lloegr at once to discover King Henry's purposes, and could not understand Lord Rhys's more laconic reaction.

'There will certainly be a Crusade!' cried Gerallt eagerly. 'You will not wish to be in the rear of such a movement, my lord!'

'I will declare my position at the proper time,' replied Lord Rhys, with a smouldering glance which imposed the silence in which he preferred to receive this new idea. But the more he thought of the possibility of a new Crusade, the more he welcomed it. The death of one son, the wildness of others, the ill-health of a daughter, and his wife's ailments, all inclined him to feel that he ought to make some effort to help to deliver the Holy City. He thought about it more and more, and his heart warmed. When he was invited to visit the palace of the Bishop of Hereford to welcome the Archbishop, who proposed to tour Cymru to preach the Crusade, he accepted with grace.

'Gruffydd, you shall attend me, and Mallt as well,' he declared. She was a good girl, a good wife to his son. Homesick she must be, now and then, though her parents had never troubled much about her. 'You shall have a chance to show off your husband and children to your kindred! What is the good of being established in pride if you cannot assemble the audience you wish to impress? We shall meet your grandmother at Brycheiniog and your father at Hereford. You must make yourself as fine as you can, and,' he added, pinching her cheek with a kindly hand, 'you shall have a new gold necklace.'

Mallt was overjoyed, and Queen Gwenllian, already inspecting Lord Rhys's best robes, running a practised hand over the worn fur, nodded approvingly.

'You deserve it, indeed,' she said.

But Gwenllian Fach was very jealous.

'It won't be King Henry's court you'll be going to!' she taunted.

'I should hope not!' said her mother, shocked. 'That rough place? All those quarrels with his sons! He has no family life to speak of any more! Even his wife Eleanor stooped to scheme with her first husband the King of France to afflict her second, and is in prison for her pains! A court, my child, is nothing without its queen!'

They went up into Brycheiniog in a mood of pomp and joy. Lord Rhys, on a proudly pacing horse, turned his possessive head from side to side to observe other men's lands; two or three sons besides Gruffydd attended him, and the great trotting romp of his teulu gave the alarm of his approach and thundered up the rear. Mallt, wearing her splendid necklace, tingled with joy and excitement, though she wished Gwenllian Fawr were riding at her side. She could not forget the great eyes staring at her when she saw Mallt try the necklace on.

'You must wear it whenever you like, Fawr!' Mallt had said, in pity for the girl's white face; but Fawr shook her head.

'In summer I wear flowers,' she said, 'and in winter I am ill, and need no decoration.'

Her listlessness frightened Mallt, who tried to rouse her by teasing her about Ednyfed Fychan, who had recently been sending her impassioned odes, and rings, and wooden spoons, wonderfully carved. But Fawr was scornful.

'He is only in love with my father's power,' she said. 'He hires a bard to write the odes. John Spang's wit means more to me. The rings never fit, and the spoons are carved by servants. If he wants me, let him come himself!'

Mallt stared at her, and Fach, thirteen and marriageable, who thought she knew everything, tossed her red hair.

'How stupid you are!' she said, 'Why waste time worrying about how he treats you? I'd make him worry instead!' Her green eyes sparkled through long sandy eyelashes. 'I'd flaunt the handsomest man in the teulu as my cariad—or John Spang if you like, since he's always been hanging about you—and I'd force my father to come to quick terms with Ednyfed lest I ran away into a match of my own fancy's making!'

But Gwenllian Fawr was exhausted.

'You can have him,' she said.

Fach caught her breath.

'You mean that?' she asked, and when Fawr nodded, she stood still, her strong gaze focused on the invisible mountains of the North, dreaming. But her dream was clear, creative, and full of purpose. 'Very well,' she said. 'He's ambitious, Ednyfed, isn't he?' she murmured. 'So am I.'

And what would come of that episode? wondered Mallt as she went down to Brycheiniog with Gruffydd, in Lord Rhys's enormous train. But Mallt forgot the Gwenllians in the face of the immediate need to impress her grandmother. The critical eyes of Lady Bertha indeed saw little to blame and much to admire as the great pageant approached, and paused for the night, and passed by. But as they sat with her at supper, Lord Rhys unfolded all his power to charm, and Mallt saw with surprise her rigid grandmother, in her seventies, smile at him like a young girl. She had scarcely time for more than a kind embrace and an approving word for her granddaughter and her children, so anxious was she for conversation with Lord Rhys. Mallt was silent with indignation. She had never expected to have her dignity diminished by her father-in-law's urbanity.

It was the same in Hereford, in Bishop William's palace, which overflowed with barons and prelates who had little time for Mallt and her children. Even her father's grave pleasure in greeting them was smothered by his haste to speak to the King's Justiciar of Wales. Lord William de Breos, like all the world, had some favour to ask. Lord Ranulf de Glanville was Lord Rhys's equal in eminence; Archbishop Baldwin was nominally the central figure of the banquet; but it was Lord Rhys who commanded all men's eyes.

It was, indeed, a most successful occasion. Good humour rose to a peak; mutual goodwill became firmly rooted until at last, even Mallt derived satisfaction from the spectacle of fresh buds opening on Lord Rhys's mighty staff of power. Besides, Gerallt was in restless attendance on the Archbishop, and his witty pleasantries made Mallt forget her own dignity and laugh aloud. This transformed her; the barons beamed; the bishops craned their necks to see; and Gerallt, like a master of ceremonies with a friendly hand possessed of one of hers, drew her forward to a more deserving place, where she might the better be admired. Gerallt indeed, with his successful fighter's smile that always turned down at the corners, was the evening's good angel, walking and moving and talking and bending down to whisper and flatter and laugh and turn with a swing of the wings that were there on his shoulders but could not be seen.

So secure an understanding appeared to fill the hall that Gerallt, in a pleasant hush, approached his cousin and dared to tease him publicly.

'Congratulations, Rhys!' he said. 'On either side, old enemies are now your friends! Both of them Clares, whose inheritance you now possess!'

His laughter fell gaily into silence of a quality that must have told him that he had at last judged ill. Mallt heard her husband hiss and mutter, 'Fool!' One or two hands amongst the barons automatically stole to their sides, and waited. But Lord Rhys took his time to finish the usual apple that ended his meal. He considered Gerallt with a disparaging stare, then bowed to his neighbours on either side, Bishop William, and Walter FitzRobert of Clare.

'Ah, yes,' he said tranquilly. 'We were indeed deprived of—our inheritance—' he leaned on the words, '—for a time by the Clares, but we mustn't grumble. Since it was our fate to be losers in those days, we had at least the satisfaction of being dispossessed by men of good family who were far from being ragamuffins.' He reached for another apple.

The Bishop mustered the courtesy to bow to Rhys, scowl at Gerallt, and say, 'And we Clares affirm that since we had to lose those lands, it pleases us to see so noble and upright a prince as Rhys ap Gruffydd in charge of them. Your health, my Lord! Now, what about the Archbishop's route to the South? We need your advice.'

The company stirred, and muttered an appeased growl. Gruffydd gave a short, impatient sigh.

'Why do they flatter him?' whispered Mallt. 'What are they trying to get out of your father?'

'Troops!' he whispered back. 'The promise of bowmen to help King Henry to fight King Philip of France!'

Lord Rhys, however, was not dissatisfied with this conference at Hereford, and a few months later, he made it his business as ruler of the South and prince pre-eminent of Cymru, to be present at the opening of the Archbishop's campaign, at the church of Radnor on Ash Wednesday of 1188. Lent had arrived with a scatter of snow in the mountains, and the church was full of red-faced Cymry puffing white breaths in all directions as they looked about them to greet their friends.

'I pity the Archbishop his task in this weather, of travelling to persuade men to leave their firesides in such a climate, and to journey, frozen, to such a distant land,' said Lord Rhys loudly, and the Cymry nudged each other. As a Christian he was bound to encourage the Crusade, but clearly he hoped it would not drain off too many of his best men.

A rush of cold air came into the church on the slowly swaying robes of the Archbishop and his attendants, Archdeacon Gerallt, Archdeacon Alexander of Bangor, and Father Seisyll from Ystrad Fflur who beamed on all the neighbours he could see as the procession moved forward. Bishop Peter was there, with his pinched face. Gerallt looked harrassed; the domestic details of the tour were in his care. As for the Archbishop, every man's gaze was fixed on his noble countenance. His voice, clear and tender as a bell, rang in their hearts as they listened eagerly to Alexander's translation of his eloquent challenge to all gallant Christian warriors to redeem their sins by going forth with kings upon a new Crusade to deliver Jerusalem from the outrage of the infidel.

'Take the cross of the Crusade!'

The final great cry filled Radnor church, as the Archbishop raised ecstatic arms high above his head. Gerallt moved forward with deliberation, and laid himself prone on the floor at the Archbishop's feet. A great stir began in the congregation, as slowly, one man after another cut loose the ties of home and kindred and prepared to move forward to kneel at the altar, pale, determined, and eager. There was a stir in the front row also. Gruffydd had started forward; then Gruffydd and his father whispered energetically; then Maelgwn jumped up.

Gruffydd said savagely, 'It is more proper for me to volunteer than for Maelgwn!'

Straining forward from Lord Rhys's restraining hands, they turned the matter into a race for prestige; both could not be allowed to go; they faced each other, hating.

'No,' said Lord Rhys, but there was a wild gleam in his own eye. 'It will have to be Maelgwn. You are needed in Deheubarth. He is a very valiant fighter. Let him go!'

Maelgwn grinned triumphantly as he knelt at the altar, with a glance all round him as he did so. For him, the Crusade was inspired more by politics than by religion, but his instinct for bravado was unfailing. Gruffydd grunted. Honours were even, and at least Deheubarth was rid of the fellow for a time.

But the Archbishop was approaching Lord Rhys.

'And you, my Lord, the most valiant of us all?' he begged, smiling. Lord Rhys smiled back, with longing, and would have moved forward, but that Gruffydd, with a look of horror, clutched him back, and in his turn hissed 'No!'

Lord Rhys, with a half-laugh, waved his hands, coughed, and said, 'I will consider when I reach my home, my lord Archbishop,' and the congregation, with a sympathetic cheer, clapped him on the back with jealous affection as they emerged, shivering and breathing deeply of the icy air, into the grey, still afternoon.

But when he reached home, other matters awaited him. Lord Rhys had never seen such scowling faces as those of the Ty Ddewi canons whom he found waiting for him in the great hall of Aber Teifi.

'I could not get rid of them,' declared Queen Gwenllian, when Lord Rhys, with a groan, asked her why she had not sent them packing.

'Well, what is it, reverend sirs?' he asked them drily. 'I am not often honoured by a visit from you.'

They did not waste their words. 'This Archbishop who comes into Cymru, he means to celebrate mass in our cathedral?'

'That is the arrangement,' said Lord Rhys patiently. 'In all the four cathedrals of Cymru, to be exact.'

Then their eyes flashed, and their voices rose and the sparks flew. Over their dead bodies, they exclaimed. Did Lord Rhys not understand that this was a clever way of establishing Canterbury's supremacy over the ancient Church of Cymru, and especially of demolishing the undoubted claim of Ty Ddewi to the primacy of Cymru? Could Lord Rhys not see that by yielding to the flattery of these people that the Church of Cymru was betrayed?

At that he fell into a memorable rage that hushed the whole hall and made the court tremble, as well as blush to hear the canons' shameful origins, and shudder at their miserable destiny.

'And is that all your concern?' he ended scathingly. 'Do you, little men, think first about yourselves? Did Christ Our Founder make His Church for your own importance? Is it nothing to you that His Holy City is defiled by infidels? And you babble to me of supremacy!'

'Besides,' he added with a sudden sage, judicial calm, 'why do you turn to me? You have your Bishop to advise you!' And his lips curled up in most emphatic scorn.

The leading canon did not budge.

'Your highness knows well enough that our Bishop is the creature of Canterbury, we are grievously disappointed by the attitude of Archdeacon Gerallt, and we come to you because we know you are the shield of Cymru, and if you wished, you could still stop this visit.'

'Well, I'm certainly not going to interfere in Church matters,' said Rhys, somewhat mollified. 'Besides, I think you're making too much fuss about it. The Archbishop comes to Cymru as the Papal Legate, and I take it you acknowledge the Pope's supremacy, or does your independence know no bounds? Clever men indeed could turn the encounter to their own advantage. Now go, and let me hear of no more nonsense. And when the Archbishop comes, give him, as Cymry, a hearty welcome for his own sake, for he is a worthy man of much goodwill. As for Gerallt, be very sure he knows what he's about, and your primacy is next to his heart.'

The canons took his advice, and when some weeks later Archbishop Baldwin dined at St. Dogmael's Abbey, he was sincere in his praise for the canons of Ty Ddewi, and even Gerallt, in a grudging voice, was heard to speak well of the Bishop's hospitality. The Archbishop's celebration of the mass had proceeded without incident, and Bishop Peter was satisfied.

The company pitied the Archbishop that he was not undertaking this arduous pilgrimage during high summer, but he made light of the perils of spring, and though his face bore the marks of exhaustion, he could not forbear to boast of his long and painful walk from Central Cymru all the way down to the South, and thence westward along the coast, through sandhills, and through fords. All were satisfied with the journey; the only unhappy episode had been the killing of a poor young Cymro outside Ty Gwyn ar Daf, just as he was hastening towards the Archbishop to take the cross.

'Ah,' said the Archbishop heavily. 'It was a soldier of St. Clears who committed this great sin. I could not absolve him until he had taken the Cross in the place of his victim.'

Lord Rhys heard with some concern that although the crusading sermons were delivered in Latin and French, with brief translations, even people who understood neither of these tongues were so much affected by them that they flocked in great numbers to take the Cross; and it was with trepidation that he sat down next day in St. Mary's Church at Aber Teifi to listen to Gerallt. He did not mind losing a few score Flemings from Dyfed, but it was another matter to see the men of Aber Teifi answering the call; and indeed the impression on the congregation of Gerallt's fire and force was more profound than Lord Rhys cared to see, for a stream of active-looking men went forward to receive their crosses.

John Spang turned in his sarcastic way to look at his master, and said, 'Well, dyna ch'i, Rhys! I'm sure you're delighted with your cousin Gerallt for sending off a hundred of your men to the Crusade! What a pity his sermon wasn't in Cymraeg! Then they would all have gone!'

Lord Rhys had the grace to shrug, and to chuckle with the rest of the assembly.

'I am proud of their gallantry!' he declared. 'Although I dare say that, like that poor fellow at Ty Gwyn ar Daf, half of them are only running off from trouble!'

Then he escorted the Archbishop on his way north through Ceredigion as far as Dyfi, where the party was to be handed over to the care of the sons of Cynan, in the diocese of Bangor. He felt, as he watched his guest depart, that further damage, whatever, could hardly now be done, and that Deheubarth had done very well by the Crusade. Gruffydd, who had accompanied his father, returned with a heavy cold, for the clouds in the mountains opened, and they all got drenched. Lord Rhys, who was instantly rubbed with goosegrease by the infirmarian on arrival at Ystrad Fflur, escaped a chill, but the Archbishop, who refused all treatment save a little urgent chiropody, developed a cough that never afterwards left him; indeed the tribulations of this journey made their mark on him, and no doubt hastened his death outside Acre, three short years later.

'They preached themselves hoarse at Llan Bedr,' said Gruffydd to his wife between sneezes. 'We looked in on the clâs at Llan Ddewi Brefi, and then were glad to rest at Ystrad Fflur. But the Archbishop and Gerallt were scandalized when we called at Llan Badarn Fawr and found that old lay Abbot Ednowain still going strong, with his married sons acting as officiating priests in turn. I've often hinted to my father that he should do something about Ednowain, but he's one of his own old soldiers and a friend, so I suppose he will just leave things as they are. Then we met my half-brother Cynwrig loping barefoot across country with his hunting pack, looking like the backwoodsman that he is, with hardly any clothes on into the bargain. He was very gracious to the Archbishop in that condescending way of his. I can't think why the Archbishop was so impressed.'

The party returned with news that plunged the court into sorrow. The sons of Cynan, whom they had met with considerable ceremony, had announced the death of Bleddyn Cyfarwydd.

'Bleddyn gone?' said Queen Gwenllian in tears. 'Ah, he was the best cyfarwydd of them all!'

'None of these young ones springing now will ever equal him!' said Lord Rhys with emotion. 'None but he will be remembered by an age to come!' He remained quiet with grief at the loss of yet another old friend. Then he lifted his head and fixed his thoughts with gratitude on the comfort of having work to do. The Abbey of Ystrad Fflur was still only three-quarters built, and he longed to see it finished, for it promised to be very fine indeed.

'It will be a long time,' said the pensaer, 'before the new cathedral at Ty Ddewi can rival it. But that will be a creation on so huge a scale that several bishops will be enthroned and buried under canvas canopies before the roof is finally laid in position—bog oak, the hardest wood known, fit to last a thousand years.'

Lord Rhys listened without comment. He was consumed with curiosity, but he would not give the Bishop the satisfaction of seeing the patron of Ystrad Fflur poking about round the foundations of the cathedral, eyeing the great mounds of purple stone quarried from the cliffs of the adjacent bay of Caerfai, questioning the builders, and making rough guesses of the costs involved, dearly though he would have liked to do all these things. Instead he spent much of the summer at Ystrad Fflur, pushing the monks to yet greater efforts, and even rolling up his sleeves to do some of the masonry himself.

Gruffydd, who knew that some complicated legal cases awaited his father's judgement in Ystrad Tywi, was concerned by this preoccupation. When he protested, 'Oh you can go,' said Lord Rhys. 'You know the law by now.'

But Gruffydd was more vexed than flattered.

'It's all very well,' he said. 'I can settle their disputes, but it's their king's justice that these people want, not mine. You risk the loss of their goodwill by a prolonged absence. People are grumbling already about the time you spend in Ceredigion!'

But Lord Rhys turned back to his plastering without a word, leaving Gruffydd furious and uneasy. Only one thing gave him comfort, apart from Mallt's companionship; it was a quiet summer free from quarrels, in Maelgwn's absence.

'He'll be back, though,' said Gruffydd gloomily to Mallt. 'He'll find something to displease him, make some excuse to come home—not that I really blame him. A lot of fine talk and hard bargaining went into this Crusade, with Prince Richard seizing a chance to cut a fine figure at all costs. Apart from Richard, the leadership is not inspiring. Barba Rossa is too old, well over sixty, and King Philip of France—can you see France and Lloegr working in harmony together? He's a fox, is Philip. He'll encourage Richard to heroic ventures that will keep him away from his French Duchy for a very long time.'

V

The Lion Rampant

(1189—1197)

1

One hot day in July of 1189, Mallt, with her third child, a girl, was sitting with Queen Gwenllian in her great chamber in Aber Teifi castle, trying to entertain Gwenllian Fawr with the baby's antics. Fawr, listless and thin, lay on a couch, and the Queen, too stiff and painful to do much herself for her daughter, was giving a wealth of instructions to two able-bodied women from Caeo. The room was full of fretful complaints and the baby's demands, and Mallt longed with sudden passion for solitude and freedom. It had been a tiresome spring, and the court, taking its tone from Lord Rhys, who had been frequently out of temper, was in an irritable mood. In the absence of Maelgwn, Hywel Sais had paired off with Owain, a younger brother; they had begun to be troublesome, to parade their importance and to annoy the French, now in Dyfed, now down below in Cydwely, by a series of light-hearted taunting raids of a rather childish nature, seizing sheep and cattle, pushing down walls, and setting fire to doors and roofs. When complaints were made to Lord Rhys, it was Gruffydd who suffered the torrent of his public rage, for failing to control his brothers. More and more, Lord Rhys left things to Gruffydd, while he went on his own restless journeys, to the new community at Tal-y-llychau, to Ystrad Fflur, and to the priory at Aber Teifi, in which he had recently begun to take an interest.

Mallt, rocking her baby, stared with envy at the green trees on the other side of the river. She longed to go riding down to the open sea. Her dream grew vivid as the thunder of distant hoof-beats broke on the air, softly, then more loudly. Fach darted up and ran to the window.

'A messenger!' She clattered down the steps, heedless of her mother's command to remain. She knew all the messengers. Fach was always the first to speed their dismounting and worm out their news from them while they were breathless and had not the strength to resist her importunities. She was back in two minutes with a white face and huge eyes.

'Henry is dead!' she said. 'He was fighting his sons!' Her voice quivered, and Queen Gwenllian crossed herself, and groaned in dismay and apprehension.

'There will be great changes now!' she said. She was no longer young, to strengthen and restrain her lord. He would be stirred up to use too much energy, more than an old man had to spare.

But in the hall, Lord Rhys showed no emotion. He asked the messenger for details of place and time, making searching enquiries as to the whereabouts of Prince Richard, Prince John, and the various Lords of the Council. Then, with a gift of gold, he dismissed the man to a good meal. With a wooden look on his face, and in his very bright sharp eyes in which no tears were forming, he waved away his counsellors and sat back in his chair. He looked much older, and for a few moments he was very still. Then he reached for an apple from the bowl beside him, and for the rest of the day, while he sat there, chewing, with his eyes fixed upon some point or person no one else could see, no doubt he arrived, coldly, at various decisions.

Then everything happened at once.

Three days later, Gruffydd left Mallt without warning, in the early hours. He embraced her, sprang out of bed, dressed, and obliged her to buckle on his armour. War! She was outraged.

'We make war suddenly!' he said, kissed away her protests, and went gaily, like a boy off to raid an orchard. The courtyard below rang with the clatter of men and horses. When daylight came, she went, still dazed, to Queen Gwenllian.

'But this is peace-time! Lord Rhys is King's Justiciar!' protested Mallt. 'He will not break the King's peace that he has sworn to keep!'

'There is no crowned king in Lloegr,' replied Queen Gwenllian steadily. 'Lord Rhys is now no man's servant, for Richard was not crowned and sworn to in his father's lifetime. Had Lord Rhys sworn to him, the situation would be different. As it is, my husband has no liege lord that he must obey. My husband is King of Deheubarth, and there are cantrefydd of his inheritance that he has yet to recover.'

'But it is like treachery,' muttered Mallt without thinking.

'Treachery!' said Queen Gwenllian, with a raised voice and flashing eyes. 'Who are you, a de Breos, to talk of treachery?'

Her words were like stabs in Mallt's heart. It was the first time the Queen had made the slightest reference to the killings.

'My husband owes no consideration to a man who fought against his own father, who was my husband's friend and lord. Let Richard hold Cymru if he can.' She turned her scornful eyes away at last. Presently she spoke more kindly to her son's wife.

'Mallt fach, you have yet a lot to learn,' she said. 'Politics are hard on a woman, and indeed they are harder on you than on most. Tell me, what are you, French or Cymraes?'

'I am what Gruffydd and my children are,' she replied, wondering when her heart would burst. 'I belong to Cymru.'

Queen Gwenllian embraced her, and Mallt's heart grew less heavy. Nevertheless, for two days she shook with fear and could scarcely touch food. Then she roused herself, and crept down to the Priory church, where she prayed herself into a state of exhaustion and calm; she gave gifts for masses for her husband's safety, and the sympathy of the Prior, who knew the secret divisions of her heart, gave her comfort.

'Fix your mind and heart on God, Who made us and loves us and died for us and rose again and holds us in His hands,' he told her. 'He will give you strength to endure both sadness and joy. Do not think of yourself, nor of your husband, nor your children, nor your parents. All goodness is contained in God.'

She knew that he knew that what he said was true, and though she did not understand why, or how, she accepted his words, and tried to obey. As she tried to fix her thoughts on the sufferings of Christ, and on His mercies, and on the sorrows of His Mother too, it seemed to her that God, with a large gesture, planted something whole, and strong, and sure, in her heart, something of His permanence, something of the calm at the heart of His radiating power.

After ten days Gruffydd returned, hard on the heels of a message that Lord Rhys with all available sons had swept like a storm through Rhos and Penfro. They had taken Castell Talacharn as well as Llan Stephan, and now Cydwely castle was in their hands, whence Lord Rhys could invade Carnwyllion, and then Gwyr.

'Come on, Mallt!' he said. 'I've come to fetch you and the children. We are going to keep watch on Dinefwr and the Ystrad Tywi castles. Make haste!'

With a sore heart, Mallt embraced the Gwenllians. Fawr said, 'Do not forget me, Mallt,' then Fach seized her in an ardent clutch and said in a stifled voice, 'Father has arranged my marriage to Ednyfed at Easter! Fawr doesn't want him, so I'm having him!'

Mallt was astonished in the midst of sadness, and Gruffydd, who had a poor opinion of the match, grunted.

'Ednyfed! How he throws his weight about! Anyone would think he was a king, but he doesn't even come from kings!'

Gwenllian Fach gave her brother a look of authority.

'But kings will come from him one day, by me,' she said.

So they parted, and while Lord Rhys besieged Caer Fyrddin, and Queen Gwenllian and her daughters retired to Llan Llyr, Gruffydd watched the North and East. Mallt, at Dinefwr, spring-cleaned. The porter rounded up the caethion from their huts below the hill, and while the men hewed wood and drew water, their women, with coarse high voices, tackled the hall with brooms and pails, making war on spiders who had spent the winter spinning undisturbed in the rafters and behind the tapestries. These, with the carthenni, well beaten, were still spread out upon the rocks and grass when Gruffydd returned from Llanymddyfri bringing an unexpected guest. It was Gerallt, distraught, exhausted, and travel-stained.

'Richard has sent him over from Normandy to try to pacify my father,' said Gruffydd shortly. 'He's coming to Lloegr himself next month to be crowned, so the crisis approaches. And John is going to marry my cousin Hawys of Gloucester, the Glamorgan heiress, whose inheritance is too good for a landless man to miss, so he'll be another to reckon with.'

Then Lord Rhys arrived, in a stern and satisfied military mood. He paid scant heed to Gerallt's expostulations.

'I am my own free man once more, my cousin,' he said heartily. 'I'm certainly not going to curb my pretensions in favour of a man who took an army against his own father.'

'But consider, Rhys, the danger you run! The King means to lead an army against you in the South, and Richard is no mean warrior.'

'Neither am I,' said Lord Rhys. 'Strength is the only thing the new King of Lloegr will respect in me, so I must increase it while I have the chance.'

'Maelgwn has a rebellious spirit too,' added Gerallt, frowning. 'He makes much trouble amongst the Crusaders. Many complaints are also laid against your other sons, and the King desires you to keep them under better control.'

Lord Rhys choked upon a surge of rage.

'Go and tell him the pot is as black as the kettle!' he roared. 'I'll have no dealings with any disobedient son, whether mine, or Henry's!'

When King Richard came to Lloegr, he did not, after all, march into Cymru to challenge Lord Rhys. His mother advised him against it. Queen Eleanor, released from prison, returned quietly to a position of influence, and used it shrewdly to advise her sons. Her first concern was to get Richard crowned and acknowledged, and her second, since he would go on this Crusade, was to get him married. John could make himself useful in Cymru, she declared, and deal with this rising.

John did indeed proceed to Worcester with an army, and was amiable enough to the princes of Cymru who met him there and made their submission. Lord Rhys went too, urged by Gerallt and by Gruffydd, but having got there, proved intractable.

'I've never seen my father so obstinate,' said Gruffydd afterwards to Mallt. 'The best Prince John could win was to get him to promise to abandon the siege of Caer Fyrddin, and he only agreed because he had finally proved the hopelessness of trying to tear down the fortifications of my Uncle Cadell. But when John begged him to go with him to London to meet the King, there was trouble. "Oh dear no," said my father. "What was good enough for Henry is good enough for Richard. His father always travelled across Lloegr to meet me and to hear my counsel." So we came home. We shall have a splendid chance for more campaigning, though, as Richard is going overseas soon, and John, having made one gesture, is now too busy ingratiating himself with people who matter in Lloegr to bother much with Cymru. He's satisfied that my father isn't going to carry war into Glamorgan—that was his chief concern.'

Autumn was dreary for Mallt. Her sons were in Caeo, learning the traditions of Deheubarth. Gruffydd, brusque and short-tempered, was often absent, galloping up and down Ystrad Tywi, summoning fresh armies as it were from the very ground with his stamping foot, to serve Lord Rhys. Men were eager to elbow out the French, to surge, like a swollen stream, wherever weakness yielded to their weight. They were not in a mood to brood on their own divisions, but where ancient feuds persisted, Gruffydd, in the courthouses, in the gwestfeydd, dealt justice rough enough to silence them.

Her evenings were therefore long and lonely, and entertainment poor, for all the best bards and cyfarwyddwyr had gone to Aber Teifi to Lord Rhys. When Mallt had finished mending the tapestries and household linen, and was tired of spinning and weaving, she commandeered a great length of cloth on which to embroider the exploits of the House of Deheubarth. She remembered how Matilda had contrived to quieten her nerves while she waited for King William to complete his conquest of Lloegr.

One wet night in November she was stitching away at the linen when the porter opened the gates to admit Maelgwn.

'Maelgwn?'

Alarmed, she rose to her feet. Gruffydd was at Drysllwyn. She would have to receive him alone, but for the usual visiting uchelwyr hanging on in hopes of a supper, waiting to catch Gruffydd on his return with the odd appeal or request that it was now so much more convenient to submit to him than to Lord Rhys at Aber Teifi.

'Where is my father?' he wanted to know. 'What are you doing here?' And he began to call for wine and food as though he were Lord of Dinefwr. His eyes were hotter and more reckless than ever.

'Why aren't you on the Crusade?' retorted Mallt, and turned to the staring servants. 'Serve the Prince what he requires!' she ordered, for she was mistress here.

'Crusade!' he said with scorn. 'That cut-throat rabble? Half of them are only out for the loot and land they can get by the way, and the rest, including Richard, think of nothing but their own glory! Good luck to Saladin, I say, a noble man and gallant in his ways, and much more pleasing to God than many a Christian!'

There was uproar, knives were drawn, and Maelgwn jeered. This did not improve matters, and Mallt had to stamp her feet and yell for order and get a few blows in herself, hurling in the midst of turmoil and blasphemy, before she could quell them. She could have done without the offensive admiration that he turned on her.

'I like your spirit, Mallt!' he said. 'Ah, my father picked the wrong son for you! It's a gallant husband you deserved to win!' He dared to seize her waist, and threw her carelessly away with a laugh when she hit him.

'Don't worry!' he said. 'I've no ambition to make you a widow. I've got a wife of my own in Ceredigion, worth two of any Frenchwoman, and I've got a couple of sons as well.'

'Why did you come here?' she panted.

'Why not? This is my father's court of Dinefwr! I come back to a kind welcome, indeed, and to rumours of battle on every side! Why shouldn't I come home to guard my interests in a time of tumult?'

'What is that roaring outside?'

'Only my teulu,' he said, with the pale light of menace in his eyes. 'They are relieving the guard.'

'By whose orders? It is my husband, not you, who is Lord Rhys's lieutenant in Ystrad Tywi!'

'There are going to be changes,' said Maelgwn, walking down the hall slowly, insulting various uchelwyr whom he knew to be Gruffydd's friends. Mallt came out of a daze of fright and anger to grasp the fact that these poor gentlemen were lying gagged and bound. All her servants had disappeared, and the sides of the hall were lined with strange faces.

Mallt ran to her chamber, where her women had already taken refuge. Nobody stopped her. Laughter followed her up the stone steps. She was filled with shame as well as fury. Lord Rhys's best castle to fall so easily to the brazen fellow! She had failed Gruffydd! Mallt was in despair. Presently she noticed that her women had stopped moaning, and were listening intently. She listened also. Behind the roaring in the hall below was thunder of hoof-beats on the Tywi banks. Gruffydd was back! Mallt prayed, and thought of that other night when she was young, at Abergavenny, when the Cymry fell upon the French like the dragon himself. Her fear then was nothing to her terror now. Now, they would fall upon each other.

It was a short if sharp engagement, which ended when Maelgwn's men discovered that their furious assailant was Lord Rhys himself, with Gruffydd and Rhys Gryg and his own great teulu. Maelgwn, maddened by rage and thwarted ambition, was the last to stop fighting; he disappeared under the weight of a dozen men, who bound him and left him on the floor.

'Into the dungeon with you!' roared Lord Rhys, purple-faced. 'Stay there and rot!'

But when Gruffydd brought this news to Mallt, she erupted.

'I will not know a moment's peace while that creature is at Dinefwr, though it be in the stoutest dungeon! If you love me, Gruffydd, send him to my father, far away from Deheubarth! He will guard him very well for you! What consideration do you owe to Maelgwn? Is he even of your blood? He bears no resemblance to your father!' It was her private opinion, as well as that of Queen Gwenllian, that half these children whose paternity Lord Rhys so carelessly acknowledged, were none of his begetting. In the morning, after dining and wining too deeply when he was out on cylch, in his younger days, his recollection of the events of the night before was sometimes dim; but pride would not let him disavow any child brought to his notice; besides, daughters were useful for alliances, and sons for war.

'Maelgwn is Lord Rhys's son all right,' said Gruffydd reluctantly. 'Old men say he's the spit of my great-grandfather, Rhys ap Tewdr.'

But he took the hint, and without further delay he sent off Maelgwn under heavy guard to William de Breos, to Mallt's great relief. His going was scarcely noticed by Lord Rhys, whose face was stern and heavy, like that of another man, whose thoughts were elsewhere. When Gwenllian Fawr was mentioned, his face crumpled, and he banged his fist on the table.

'She's dying!' he shouted in a strangled voice, and drank deeply until his pain was dulled. He spent his days with his smith and his uchelwyr, inspecting his arms and his horses and the troops that Gruffydd had trained; but he went through these actions mechanically. Every time he spoke, he shouted. Mallt grew cold, and old, grieving.

It was a strange Christmas. The men went away down the valley before the Twelve Days were ended, to take St. Clears. Lord Rhys planned to give this to Hywel Sais. Rather than part with lands he held already, he preferred to provide for his sons by dispossessing other men from places that he claimed were his by right of ancient heritage.

Mallt watched them go, and one cold morning in the New Year, she rode off quietly with her child and the nurse and two grooms towards Llan Llyr, to see Gwenllian Fawr. As soon as they left Ystrad Tywi behind, and climbed towards Ceredigion between low hills, Mallt's spirits rose, and by midday, when a cold wind sent the clouds racing from the sky, she was almost happy. Winter's castle lay behind them, ahead was spring, between snows, and perhaps Lord Rhys was wrong, perhaps Fawr would improve as the days grew longer. The country, that morning, was all hers, because she loved it, the hardness of its rocks, the strength of its oaks, the tenderness of its earth, the surprise of every swelling hill, and its tingling air. She rode alone, ahead of her companions. She had never needed, nor enjoyed, solitude so much.

Long after nightfall, she knocked on the great oak door of Llan Llyr, and waited, shivering. It opened, slowly, and Gwladus, with tear-stained face, peered at her. She put her arms round Mallt's neck, and drew her within.

'Wyt ti wedi dod, Mallt fach!' she whispered, and kissed her cold face. Mallt could hear the nuns chanting sadly in the distance.

'How is Fawr?' she whispered back, and Gwladus, weeping afresh, replied, 'Mae hi wedi myn'd, Mallt fach, mae hi wedi myn'd.'

She had gone back to God in peace while Mallt rode on her way with joy.

They buried her in the llan, near the graves of older nuns. A message was sent to Lord Rhys, who received the news in stony silence. He refused to go to Llan Llyr, but when his short campaign was successfully ended, with St. Clears safely in Hywel's hands, he summoned Queen Gwenllian back to Dinefwr. They embraced each other with dry eyes and seared faces, and sat down in a remote silence that no one dared disturb, save that the bardd teulu, further down the hall, was trying over on his harp a tune that he was in the middle of composing, an undertone of gossip came up from the company nearest the door, and two or three dogs chose this of all moments to pick a quarrel.

With the return of its Queen, life at Dinefwr became serene again. She said that Mallt had looked after the castle very well, but that serious inroads had been made at Christmas into the wine supplies.

'It's all very well for Lord Rhys to revel in his reputation for generosity, but it is I who has to do the managing,' she said. 'It will not do to put the best wine out for all the common company.'

When spring advanced and grief abated, life sent its messenger from the North in the shape of Ednyfed, who came at last to claim a bride. He was tall, alert, sagacious. He and Gwenllian Fach pleased each other. One look between them was enough, one tart exchange of discourtesies.

'Gwenllian!' said her mother. 'Respect this gentleman!' And she began to apologize to Ednyfed. But Lord Rhys, laughing for the first time since Fawr had died, stopped her.

'Save your breath, indeed!' he said.

It was a quiet but cheerful wedding, and Lord Rhys's wedding gift of an estate at Llan Rhystyd was most acceptable to both bride and groom. The court made merry, and felt all the better for it after their weeks of mourning, even though Fach did decide at the last moment to burst into tears as she hurled her arms round her parents' necks. Ednyfed picked her up and put her on his horse, jumped up behind her, and rode away. The last thing they saw was her handkerchief, waving wildly, before a bush of hawthorn hid them from view. An old memory stirred in Lord Rhys as Queen Gwenllian turned to her husband and asked, for the hundredth time, 'Who does she take after, tell me?'

He answered, as usual, rather drily, 'My poor sister Gwladus.'

As much to escape the unnatural silence left in Fach's wake, as to attend to lands recently recovered, Lord Rhys was often absent on cylch that summer, within the hills and plains and coastal sands of Cydwely and beyond, into Carnwyllion, where the land's edge was fortified by great sand dunes, crowned by coarse grasses, tossing like a woman's hair. There, from the top of the dunes, he looked across an unfamiliar, sluggish sea, where the current of a tidal estuary sank below the levels of the cockle-pitted sands; over the water on the horizon lay the outline of the fertile land of Gwyr, far and pale in the heat. Lord Rhys, running dry sand through his fingers, turned to Gruffydd.

'You know, if we took the castell of Aber Tawe, we would have all that cwmmwd,' he said.

But before he was ready to develop that idea, his aggression was diverted elsewhere. November brought his daughter Angharad, the wife of William FitzMartin of St. Dogmael's, weeping to her parents' court, together with her three little girls, and complaining bitterly of her husband's character and habits. They were both pig-headed, and had bickered for years. At first, Mallt had scant sympathy for this sister-in-law.

'I marvel at the folly of women who try to rule their lords by the power of their loud voices!' she told Gruffydd. Then it occurred to her that Angharad lacked the influence over her husband that the mother of sons would naturally wield; that was, thought Mallt, with a complacent glance at young Rhys and Owain, at bottom the whole trouble, and she looked at her more kindly.

Angharad was greeted with kindness and a proper degree of indignation. Lord Rhys found it expedient to let his anger with his son-in-law William thunder abroad, and though Queen Gwenllian, who had suffered often within her own marriage, urged her daughter to consider the wisdom of a reconciliation, Angharad, nervous and distraught, would not hear of it, and even talked wildly of retiring for ever to Llan Llyr.

Lord Rhys kept his indignation with William FitzMartin simmering over Christmas and well into the New Year. The fellow was proving unreliable as an ally at this juncture, inclined to jib at Lord Rhys's legitimate efforts to make good his undoubted hereditary claims, and this quarrel with Angharad provided a splendid pretext for directing his next campaign, at a moment when it suited him, into North-West Dyfed. Let William watch out since he would not toe the line.

Angharad, to the court's surprise, viewed her father's intentions with less satisfaction than alarm. She went so far as to expostulate.

'You are surely not going to make war upon my husband?'

'Have no fear, merch i, I'll teach that French dog a lesson for ill-treating a daughter of Lord Rhys,' he replied with relish, and would hear her no further. She went running to her mother, all her indignation given a new direction; but when she learned that Lord Rhys, having taken William's chief castle of Nanhyfer, had actually handed it over to Gruffydd, her rage was uncontrolled. She called her own father a traitor, a breaker of oaths, forgetting William's faithlessness to herself. With her children she left with a suddenness equalling that of her arrival, and sped hot-foot to rouse, encourage, and console her defeated husband, and throw all her energies not into a reconciliation with William, for by now she had forgotten the cause of the quarrel, but into rebuilding their joint fortunes; so that what her mother's advice had failed to achieve, was instantly provoked by her father's temerity.

2

Lord Rhys's action at Nanhyfer did not go unremarked, and Archdeacon Gerallt had some cutting things to say about it in his new book, 'The Itinerary through Wales.' Father Peter, the new Abbot of Ty Gwyn ar Daf, brought a copy with him which his monks had made, when he visited Aber Teifi on his way to make his annual Visitation to Ystrad Fflur. He was a man who contrived, in the oil of his flattery, to mix a drop of ridicule; his effusions towards Lord Rhys, whom he considered a declining force, could not be trusted, as Lord Rhys could see. 'Yr hen ddyn gemllid 'na' he called him. To Gruffydd, as to the rising power of Deheubarth, the Abbot was less effusive, and therefore more polite, and Gruffydd was unfortunately pleased.

But Lord Rhys was not so easily to be made ridiculous. He countered the Abbot's heavy flattery by praising the blunt sincerity of Seisyll, and he dismissed Gerallt with a scornful laugh.

'It is hard to ride two horses at once!' he remarked. 'As a Frenchman, Gerallt does not care to see my power increase; but as a Cymro, he would despise me for failing to snatch my slightest opportunity. He is in the pay of the Queen Mother, the Regent, and he must pitch his tune to suit her ear. As for William FitzMartin—' He snapped his fingers, and spat.

But Lord Rhys remembered these pricks; his wife observed the anger that he sought to hide, when he intercepted little smiles at his expense between much younger men. His hands trembled, and in the set of his great head, she saw a tremor, which did not leave him. She herself was ailing, grieving for the loss of Gwenllian Fawr, and the absence of Fach, and she relaxed her hold over him as she began to slide into the languor that follows increasing pain. He would look at her, and fidget, go out of his hall, roaring for his horse, and go about Teifiside, riding until exhaustion obliged him to kick open the door of the first tyddyn he came to, and cause the frightened inhabitants to attend to his wants, his thirst, his hunger, his weariness, and again his thirst. Many times Gruffydd and the teulu had to spend a night and a day scouring the countryside until at last they found him, dirty and haggard, unaware of the bedstraws sticking out of his still golden hair. Then they persuaded him to come home.

It was a disjointed summer that no one could enjoy. The bards, failing to pierce the future, and therefore being uncertain whom to praise, were in a baffled mood, and sang indifferent songs; and when the sun's face was darkened one fine afternoon in May, alarm and fear confused them. It was, men whispered, the portent of a great man's passing; and they watched Lord Rhys from the corners of their eyes, and he knew it, and sneered at them. He lived; other men it was that died.

'Archbishop Baldwin has gone!' announced Abbot Peter, arriving hot-foot with news from Ty Gwyn ar Daf. 'They're dying like flies outside Acre. Ranulf Glanville is dead, too. The army is on bad ground there, in a most unhealthy situation. Let us hope matters will improve now that King Richard has reached them. I suppose you have heard he is married at last? Queen Eleanor finally found a bride to please him. A Lady Berengaria from a little province near Acquitaine called Navarre.'

'Never heard of it ,' said Lord Rhys shortly. He was grieving over Baldwin's loss, Baldwin, who had walked with him, with steady strides, from south to north of Ceredigion. 'It's all one to me whom he marries.'

Queen Gwenllian nudged him; she did not trust this Abbot. Lord Rhys glared at her, but when the Abbot proffered further gossip about the way Prince John was acting the king throughout all his lands—'a good third of the kingdom all told'—and about the unrest that the Chancellor William Longchamp had been sent to quell—'he had to seize Wigmore and a couple of other Border castles, and has sent Roger Mortimer into exile'—he heard him intently, in silence, and did not even grunt, though he said after the Abbot had gone that it was a pity Prince John had not been obliged to take the Cross.

But it was the news from Elfael that struck Lord Rhys with force and roused his real rage. Einion ab Einion Clud died suddenly by the hand of his brother Gwallter, and William de Breos, seeing his chance, marched in at once to seize Elfael under Gwallter's nose, thus joining his Radnor lands to Brycheiniog, consolidating and rounding off his territories north to south. He had coveted Elfael for a long time, and lost no time in building two castles, with the help of his wife and his constable Payn, one in Lower Elfael, and one in Upper, on the banks of Colwyn.

At dinner, Lord Rhys tore at his meat roughly, and darted many malignant glances at Mallt, and would not speak to her. She had become so much his daughter that this silence made her suffer; but she was Matilda de Breos, and she would not let him see the tears that gathered, fall. She understood his rage; he had valued the alliance with Elfael that had kept her father's power in check, and desired to be revenged. Her pleasure in her father's enlargement was entirely dimmed; she wished that he were powerful somewhere far away; and she trembled in dread of the day when Deheubarth should march in strength against de Breos.

But while Lord Rhys struggled to summon the energy required for major action, an event occurred that thrust aside for him for many months all further thought of war.

Queen Gwenllian fell heavily against a stone step one day, and could not rise. Amid shouts and commotion, she was carried by strong men into her chamber.

'She's had a stroke!' they said fearfully. 'We need a wisewoman!'

Gruffydd came running, and Lord Rhys, panting, and pale with dismay. Queen Gwenllian herself had always been their wisewoman. They all looked at Mallt, who mustered her sagacity and lifted her chin into authority. She must be the wisewoman now. She arranged the Queen comfortably, and sent for the physicians of Myddfai. It was easier to look after her than to cope with Lord Rhys, who hung about trembling, and roaring contradictory orders that were not obeyed, for no one was listening.

Mallt seized Gruffydd by the arm.

'Find occupation for your father!' she hissed. 'Have masses sung for your mother's recovery! Give alms to the needy! Govern Deheubarth! Or if you must, make war! But get him out of this chamber!' But Lord Rhys refused to budge.

Slowly, Queen Gwenllian recovered, but her right arm and leg were limp and motionless; her speech was thick and slow. Lord Rhys sat with her for hours every day, avid for a word. One day, she managed to lift her good hand to his shaggy head and say,'Scissors!' He burst into delighted tears. On his next visit, he was neatly trimmed and groomed, and his appearance won a smile from her. This encouraged him; he brightened, and seized feverishly upon every small sign of her improvement. Over her bed, he held long conferences with her physician Rhiwallon, a grave young man with wisdom in his glance.

As he spoke, and questioned, he did not let his wife's arm go. It was her bad arm, and absently he pinched and kneaded, as a housewife kneads dough, the plumpness he had always loved. Her shoulder heaved slightly, and he started.

'Go on!' said Rhiwallon. 'There is life in your hands, Lord Rhys. There are some who have that power. You are passing it into the dead limb. Continue for a little while, but do not hurt her with your great strength, and do not make her tired.'

With a rapt face, mouth slightly open, he worked over the arm with energy, but gently. Then he applied the same movements to the right side of her body, instinctively digging and searching for life with his fingers down to her hip, her thigh and leg, tracing the course of the muscles, pressing and moving her toes, squeezing her foot in his broad palm. Then, when she sighed, and stirred again, he rose in silence, and went.

His wife's illness changed Lord Rhys. He became withdrawn and sullen, as though all his force and thought had been drained into the ends of his fingers. He continued daily his ministrations to Queen Gwenllian, and gradually her limbs began to respond to his devoted touch. He would allow no one else to handle her in this way until at last, seeing his exhaustion, and having learned from watching him, Mallt persuaded him to let her help; but he would not give up. He was convinced that he alone, by sharing his strength, could keep his wife alive.

'The sons she gave me, and the daughters, and she herself, cariad annwyl,' he muttered. 'God shames me by the goodness He has always shown to me.'

His preoccupation caused him to neglect the government of his lands. He stopped going out on cylch. Gruffydd in Ceredigion, Rhys Gryg in Ystrad Tywi, and Hywel in Dyfed, acted for him. People grumbled at his absence; old men who loved him argued with their sons, who began to sneer at Lord Rhys, now clearly, they said, in his dotage. In the hall, men looked at him, and at each other. But he noticed things like this no more. He was like a flame within a horn lantern, seen but unreachable, plunged in a profound contemplation that separated him from his sons, and rendered the attention he gave to his suitors joyless and perfunctory, so that men who had taken the trouble to travel all the way to Aber Teifi to get justice from Lord Rhys himself, went away grumbling, and sometimes hostile. He never mentioned Maelgwn, but Mallt thought, Perhaps he misses him. She longed with such passion for something to rouse Lord Rhys, that she felt she could even bear to endure Maelgwn's return.

But nothing could penetrate Lord Rhys's abstraction until spring brought Father Seisyll, on his way back from a conference at Citeaux. Hope lit in Lord Rhys's stare, and he produced a real smile for this old friend.

'Come, sit by me, and eat and drink your fill!' he said. 'Then tell me how it is with you, and what goes on abroad. I'll pick your brains, Seisyll.'

'Acre has fallen,' announced Seisyll, munching. 'King Richard brought a vigorous and business-like approach to the effective management of the siege. The King of France did not feel well, and went home. The Crusaders quarrelled about who should be King of Jerusalem. Richard beat off the Saracens at Arsuf, but the enemy were mighty soldiers, and twelve miles from the Holy City was the nearest he could approach to it.'

'He's heard about John by this time, I dare say. He'll come home now,' Lord Rhys said. He stroked his nose gently, making plans again at last, and he listened with attention to what Seisyll had to tell him of this new development all over the West whereby many lords were commuting for money rents the labour services owed by serfs allowed to occupy vast tracts of waste lands, which were then gradually brought into profitable cultivation.

'In this way,' Seisyll pointed out, 'they are increasing the value of their properties, and at the same time filling their treasuries with gold and silver with which alone they can acquire the silks and spices and other luxuries of the East, for these Venetian traders demand spot cash for their goods.' Lord Rhys was very interested.

Next morning, when a message came to say that William de Breos had been made Sheriff of Herefordshire, the old blaze flared in Lord Rhys's eyes. His visits to his wife, who was certainly better, grew shorter from this time forward, as his plans matured.

After Easter, Lord Rhys sent off Gruffydd into Dyfed with a roving commission 'to see what he might come by'. He did not precisely direct him against the lands of the Bishop, but as these were less well defended than those areas within the French clutch, clearly Llawhaden offered the most tempting target. This was where the Bishop lived when he was not in progress in Lloegr, sampling the hospitality of one monastery after another, in search of carvers, or masons, or manuscripts; Gerallt had accused him of travelling in order to economize on other people's backs, although he admitted that the object of the

Bishop's parsimony was indeed to save up money in order to pay for the new cathedral.

'Saving up!' spluttered Lord Rhys. 'Most of the building money has been found already by extortion from his own clergy!'

The court rejoiced therefore when word came that Gruffydd had thrust himself and his troops into Llawhaden castle and recovered an area where Deheubarth's power rose to a pitch that alarmed the French. On the whole, Lord Rhys was content to direct his new acquisitions in Dyfed from a distance, and apart from one visit to Llawhaden and Nanhyfer to inspect the dispositions made for him by Gruffydd and by Hywel Sais, he spent most of his time in conference with his smith and his armourer, so it was clear that further plots were hatching.

One May morning, the waiting-women came running in to Mallt in consternation.

'Oh, Lady, Prince Maelgwn has returned!' they said.

Mallt was petrified.

'Does Lord Rhys know?'

The women looked at each other.

'Lord Rhys himself arranged it!' they said.

Mallt, brimming with indignation, sat silent as their flowing tongues ran on. It was by a mixture of persuasion, bribes, and guile, that Lord Rhys, in Gruffydd's absence, had recovered his eldest son. Gruffydd was wild when the court moved to Dinefwr in July to find that Maelgwn was high in his father's favour once again, and that he was to lead the Ceredigion force within Lord Rhys's army at the siege of Aber Tawe castle. It was the nearest that Gruffydd ever got to rebellion. But Lord Rhys was rough with him.

'I am not answerable to you!' he said to Gruffydd. 'I have need of all my sons, working as one. Anarawd and Cadell, Maredudd and I, we worked as a team. Why can't you do the same? See you to the Ystrad Tywi recruits.' And he angered Gruffydd by treating Maelgwn with all his old kindness. Mallt avoided him; Maelgwn, from a distance, jeered, and put about the tale that he had escaped by a stratagem, by his wit and skill. Lord Rhys, overhearing, laughed, and did not contradict him.

But the siege of Aber Tawe castle was an ill-conducted enterprise. All through that hot summer the Deheubarth army vainly deployed their latest instruments of siege, while the well-provisioned defenders looked out smugly, having heard the sounds of altercation in the camps outside; they applauded Lord William de Breos for having let Maelgwn loose on purpose to be an embarrassment to Lord Rhys. In the hot weather disagreements grew loud; and when the best men turned from the land quarrels to cool their tempers in the sea, the treacherous currents that swept the Bay carried them off.

A hush fell on the whole army.

'This is a sign of God's displeasure,' said Lord Rhys, and in spite of Gruffydd's protests, he ordered the siege to be abandoned. The army returned to Dinefwr in mid-September, trudging crossly out of a heat mist at the far end of the valley, each man laying the blame for the failure of the siege on someone else.

The next visit of Father Seisyll from Ystrad Fflur brought news that 'Poor Gruffydd ap Cadwgan has gone!' Lord Rhys received the announcement with a silent gesture of sorrow, and as men will, he began to calculate the age this elderly cousin must have been.

'I am sixty myself!' he stated, with a challenging stare round his company, daring belief. But in spite of the polite murmur of incredulity that he lapped up with satisfaction, it was becoming less impossible to believe. The death of Fawr, the siege of Swansea, the loss of some of his best men, his wife's illness, and the strain of shouting at his quarrelling sons, had taken it out of him. The choler mounted with ease into his head when anger claimed him; the cords of his neck stood out like tree branches; he brushed aside and crushed the views of younger men; he had leisure for nothing but to listen for, and rout, the approach of an enemy that no one else could see.

But Father Seisyll had picked up two startling though contradictory rumours on the road; and at last Lord Rhys listened with full alertness.

'A packman told me what he heard this morning in Caer Fyrddin,' he said, and a hush fell on the hall. 'Some say King Richard is dead; others, that he is a prisoner in Vienna, in the hands of his enemy Leopold Duke of Austria, whom he offended somehow, not so very long ago. They say, that Richard sailed from the Holy Land, leaving the Bishop of Salisbury, Hubert Walter, to bring his troops home. Richard's ship was blown off course by stormy autumn winds—he should have known better than to leave his journey so late in the season! The gales drove him to Corfu, where the pirates took pity on him, and, for a consideration, lent him a craft. But that was shipwrecked near Ragusa, and Richard, washed ashore, saw that he must bluff his way home overland.'

'Whatever made him go near Vienna?' demanded Lord Rhys, exasperated. 'What a first-class blunderer! Now Leopold and the King of France will be rubbing their hands, and making the most of his disaster. No, he's not dead if they have laid their hands on him! He's more valuable to Leopold alive! You and I are going to pay dear to bring him home and prop him up on the throne of Lloegr again! Anything rather than have John creep into power!'

The country rang with conflicting rumours. All John's henchmen in Glamorgan swore that Richard was dead; but the Cymry, with disbelieving jeers, considered that Lord Rhys, the crabbed old man, was a shrewder judge of how the matters lay. It was said, that John was so eager to step into his brother's shoes, that he had even done homage to Philip for the family's French dominions.

'More fool he!' said Lord Rhys, lifting his head up from an interview with his treasurer, a hard-headed assessment of resources, ways and means.

'What King is worth a hundred thousand pounds?' said Lord Rhys, when he heard the fantastic terms of ransom for Richard's person, proved at last to be alive. 'I'll make a voluntary, token, gift, but a quarter of my income and moveable property I refuse to give! I'm sworn to no man!'

The Cistercians could not afford to be so independent; not only were they obliged to part with a fourth part of their wool, but, like all the cathedrals and abbeys and churches throughout the land, they had to sacrifice much gold and silver, chalices and church furnishings, to win back Richard. There was no end to the grumbles and the stories. The King of Lloegr's adventures were at least a boon to the teulu, at a loss for entertainment in the nights of a long winter when sickness was more rife than usual. The name of Richard sounded like an incantation through the hall; the latest twist to his epic was that he was discovered by the faithful searching of his devoted troubadour Blondel, by singing Richard's own song below the prison walls, and hearing his master chanting a verse in reply. This pleased everybody; it was like one of the romances. But Lord Rhys had heard enough of Richard. He was tired of Dinefwr too. He wanted to consolidate his gains in Dyfed.

'Come on, let's go to Aber Teifi,' he said, when Lent began. 'Plenty of fish in the sea and the river there.'

It was high time; even salted meat got tainted after many months, however strong the spices which they used to disguise the fact. The court rose with relief, and regretted only that Queen Gwenllian, druan, would be absent, in Llan Llyr. Courts were too noisy for her now, she said; she would get better in a quiet place, and brokenly she instructed Mallt on how to govern the kitchens at Aber Teifi. But Mallt, with her husband, was sent into Ceredigion on cylch, after taking Queen Gwenllian to Llan Llyr.

'You rattle the reins for me a bit up there,' said Lord Rhys to Gruffydd, and turned his eyes towards Dyfed.

'What about Maelgwn?' said Gruffydd. Maelgwn had gone jaunting off into Dyfed already, without leave, in alliance with Hywel Sais. 'What about Nanhyfer?'

'You do as I tell you,' said his father testily. 'I'll see to that!' Gruffydd left with lowered brow, and Mallt had to bear the burden of his spleen.

'My father thinks he's a man of forty!' he said. 'He thinks his strength can cope with anything! That couple will run rings round my father, and who will suffer most? I shall! You have no idea of the struggle I had to win Llawhaden! And though my father takes the credit for gaining Nanhyfer, it was I who did the donkey-work! Well, we shall see how he gets on alone in Dyfed, with those two let loose down there. Wouldn't you think he had learned, after Aber Tawe? He will live to rue the day he got Maelgwn out of your father's clutch.'

'Never mind,' said Mallt. 'Think of the chance you will have now of establishing your power in Ceredigion. Maelgwn seems to think he owns it.'

Gruffyd's anger cleared, and his face grew bright.

'Da merch i, Mallt!' he said. He hugged her, and laughed. 'He thinks he's going to twitch my tail in Dyfed! Well, I'll twitch his in Ceredigion!'

So they went into every cantref, every cwmmwd, every gwestfa. During these exhaustive progresses, Gruffydd grew in stature. In his judgements, he, like his father, drew sagacity from some ancestral well. Wisdom is one thing, thought Mallt; he could win respect in Ceredigion, but could he win their love? Maelgwn was one of them; his mother had been a Ceredigion girl. Maelgwn was their rally boy; why, he had only to grin round in triumph at his teulu to set them crowing with glee. But Maelgwn and his cronies were elsewhere; Gruffydd, by a mixture of authority, show of force, and mercy, began to gain strength. He was his father's deputy, wedi'r cwbl, men said; a steady man he was, never went roaring about like some of his brothers, terrifying the cattle of honest men. Slowly, he made his impact on the well-defended heart of Ceredigion; week by week, valley by valley, tref by tref, he got to know, not only the uchelwyr, but the boneddigion as well, and in the end, he won them, not so much by speech, as by silence. He listened, considered, understood, and made friends.

Mallt sat beside him and smiled. She smiled at the old men, but never at the young ones, so she gained their women. She took trouble to admire their children, wild and watchful as the ponies on the hills. She told them stories she had heard from Bleddyn and old Gwen; it was not, perhaps, a seemly occupation for a princess of Deheubarth, but in a small place, where the entertainment was necessarily poor, high in Penweddig where the mountains loomed, crushed in a hall too small for comfort, idly in pity she began to fill the silences of awe that checked their mirth in Gruffydd's presence, as a damp cloth stifles flames.

She made friends also in Llan Badarn, where Rheidol ran past on its gravel floor. The low hills on the other side swelled and twisted in the arrested motion of a stormy sea. In foul weather she could hear the ocean groaning in the south-west wind, and large, grey-bellied clouds came sailing up the sky. Ednowain's daughters, matrons of middle age, showed her kindness, and she began to discern the variety of the Cymry ruled by Lord Rhys; each separate valley was its own peculiar world. It was difficult to remember that Aber Teifi was unfamiliar to her hosts, that Llan Ddewi Brefi must scarcely be named, as a rival llan, and that for them, the people of Cwmdeuddwr were no better than Pumlumon wolves. She found her friends true, but rigid, and their voices sharp; their geniality, frosted by experience and caution, took its time to thaw.

'They are very well-informed,' said Gruffydd. 'How do they hear these rumours before I do? A man told me last month that Saladin was dead. I laughed, and called it wishful thinking; now today comes this message from Ystrad Fflur to say, the news has just come through from the South, to say that Saladin is dead!'

Mallt shivered. 'They have seers,' she murmured, but Gruffydd was scornful.

'More likely to be intelligent guess-work!' he said. 'Yet, what can these know of the East? Richard must be angry with himself if this news is true. If he had waited a few months longer, he could thrust himself now into the Holy City. But there, rulers cannot let their kingdoms crumble behind their backs, and must come home to prop their power up.'

News from Dyfed did not reach them until they arrived at Ystrad Fflur at the end of harvest.

'Wiston castle is delivered to Lord Rhys,' announced Seisyll. 'His son Hywel Sais showed great valour, and they have Philip FitzWizo and his family in safe custody, and shown them mercy.'

'Where is Maelgwn?' demanded Gruffydd. There was silence. It seemed that Maelgwn too had distinguished himself; he was hand in glove with Hywel. Gruffydd's genial humour curdled as all his old suspicions returned.

'Ah!' he said to Mallt. 'He thinks that Ceredigion will be his when my father dies. He wants to extend his power into Dyfed as far as he can push, twisting my father, pretending friendship with that Sais—Mallt! I've been too soft in Ceredigion! Rattle the reins, my father said. Yes, and rattle my sword as well!'

That was the end of comfort and happiness for Mallt that summer. Her husband sent her promptly down to Gwladus at Llan Llyr as though she were a piece of heavy luggage to be stowed in a cupboard. The next thing she heard was, he had turned out the custodian of Ystrad Meurig castle, who was married to Maelgwn's mother, and deprived him of his office for various imaginary crimes. Mallt wrung her hands.

'Maelgwn will kill my husband!' she cried. 'Those brothers will not be satisfied until one or the other is out of the way!'

Her arrival at Llan Llyr at least brought joy to Queen Gwenllian, who was very weak, and dwelling in the past.

'Gwenllian Fawr!' she whispered gladly. Lord Rhys came to see her less and less often, for her stony looks unmanned him.

'Where is my husband?' she would ask him to his face. 'Why doesn't Lord Rhys come to see me?' It was not until Lord Rhys, sobbing, clasped her bodily to him with well-remembered love, that she knew him.

'Rhys, Rhys!' she said, and smiled at him before her comprehension went, and she lay back exhausted.

Though he might not often dare to disturb her, and himself, he would not move far from her. So Hywel and Maelgwn had it all their own way down in Dyfed; they were indeed embarrassed by their own success, and had to destroy one or two of the forts, including Llawhaden, for they had insufficient troops to hold them all. Mallt's anger rose when she heard about Llawhaden; that had been Gruffydd's prize, and when the news came that the Flemish, in a sudden spurt, had beaten them off for a time, she was quite pleased.

Only the happy letter from Gwenllian Fach, announcing the safe arrival of her son, gave pleasure to their anxious hearts. Lord Rhys smiled, though for him it was no new pleasure; he had many grandchildren. But messengers had a value in themselves, apart from their messages. He carried the man off for a good meal, and a long drink, and further gossip from the North. He remembered that he had another grandson there; Rhodri's wife, his daughter, was dead some years ago in childbirth, but young Gruffydd lived. When he was satisfied that Gwenllian Fach flourished—'Mae'n digon o fenyw, hon'na,' he muttered to himself, nodding—he asked after Rhodri's son. Rhodri had perished struggling with the sons of Cynan, said the messenger, but the boy was well fostered.

Lord Rhys shifted his great weight on the bench, sighed, and said nothing. Grandchildren had to make their own way; sons were hard enough to satisfy; for a daughter's offspring, all that he could spare were pangs, and prayers, and good advice. If he could latch on to Ednyfed's fortunes, to Llewellyn's—

'Llewellyn's the coming man,' said the messenger confidentially. 'Fine fellow of twenty, now, full of himself and his rights. His mother Marared and her Powys kin watched over him after poor Iorwerth Drwyndynn went. Itching to get his uncle Dafydd out of the way he is now, collecting his friends and his strength under Ednyfed.' Lord Rhys listened idly, as the man chatted. Time must be passed, while his wife lay dying.

Queen Gwenllian lingered until late December. Gwladus and Mallt nursed her between them. Occasionally a son would come to look at her and kneel weeping for a blessing that she could not give. Angharad came, but grief made her a poor nurse, and she could not understand why her sisters' eyes were dry. She was at last reconciled to her father, for her mother's sake. Gruffydd came often, riding through the rain, and scorning to change his wet clothes. His haggard looks boded ill for the future, and when Mallt looked from him to Lord Rhys, she was tempted once more to despair. But there was no time, and her daughter was screaming in the next chamber, wanting a story.

The burial had to be at Ty Ddewi, because that was where Lord Rhys himself was going to lie. It was a quiet occasion; the crowds were subdued, and there were no long eulogies, since she herself had long ago forbidden them. Gerallt arranged everything, and stayed talking to Lord Rhys all that bleak week at Aber Teifi, until his voice was hoarse and had to be lubricated with an elderberry cordial. His good heart gave all its strength to rouse another man from sorrow's torpor. And he made Rhys listen and forget himself as he heard the story of Gerallt's friend, old Wecheleu, the ignorant poor anchorite of Locheis in Elfael, how by a miracle he had learned to speak Latin, though not grammatically in cases, after eating a loaf left on his altar.

'And he can reprove so well,' said Gerallt, wiping his eyes at the memory. 'I asked him to pray for me, that I should know and understand the Scriptures for my soul's health, and what did the good old man do but grasp my hand earnestly and say, "Ach, Gerallt, don't say Know, say Keep! Vain it is to Know," he told me, "unless you Keep!" And he has healing powers, too, that those grasping Cistercians of Abbey Cwm Hir try to stop him using, for they grudge the loss of gifts they could be extorting from patients at their own infirmary. When he asked for my advice I told him that his power came from God, so let him use it, but to beware of spiritual pride! He should be in the calendar of saints, old Wechelau—' Gerallt ran on through his stories, claiming the unfailing attention of all his hearers; curiosity always elbowed them whenever Gerallt came to stay. Now, when he had gained the whole interest of Lord Rhys, he turned the conversation round to affairs of state, and broke the news that Hubert Walter, some months back from the Crusade, and already elevated to the Archbishopric of Canterbury, was now to be Justiciar of Lloegr as well, with full powers of the Church and State clutched firmly in the one hand.

'And Ranulf Glanville trained him,' added Gerallt, with meaning in his tones.

'And Ranulf knew it was well to be watchful of Cymru, and hold it down if he could,' said Lord Rhys. 'So we had better watch out, I suppose that you would say.'

'Well, common prudence, Cousin,' said Gerallt carefully. 'Display of your well-known wisdom in your policies, moderation in Dyfed, in particular towards the Bishop—'

Lord Rhys ignored, loftily, the reference to the Bishop.

'The Queen Mother instructs you, no doubt,' he said. 'She's afraid I may be beguiled to side with John in this quarrel he's busily promoting. She need not trouble. We've done pretty well in Dyfed the past couple of years. I've got two of my boys down there now, rounding matters off. We shan't attempt to take Penfro, of course. We haven't the necessary sea power to undertake its successful siege, for well I know the strength of it and the enormous stores they hold within its granaries.'

'Caer Fyrddin,' began Gerallt tentatively, and Lord Rhys smiled.

'It has its uses in the hands of the crown of Lloegr,' he said drily. 'The Ystrad Tywi men are always badgering me to take Caer Fyrddin. Its possession is a matter of prestige with the younger ones. But they don't understand how strong my brother Cadell made it. Besides, we profit by the coastal trade the presence of a strong French garrison brings.'

'Funny thing,' he remarked presently, crunching into a fresh apple. 'Hubert Walter in his present position—just such a one, I dare say, as Henry desired Thomas Becket to be.'

3

Lord Rhys was wrong about his sons. They had not remained in Dyfed. On Christmas morning, as the court returned from hearing Mass at St. Mary's, a panting servant brought the procession to a halt. He gasped out some message. Lord Rhys was rather hard of hearing.

'Speak up!' he demanded, cupping his ear irritably.

Maelgwn, shouted several voices at him at once, stuttering with anger, Maelgwn, the vile one, had come on Christmas Eve, had come with catapults to Ystrad Meurig castle, and destroyed it, raging about as it pleased him.

Lord Rhys trembled, and said nothing. His teulu looked at him aghast, and in consternation at Gruffydd, who snarled with sudden rage, then checked himself.

'I don't believe he has destroyed it!' he said. 'He wants it for himself. He knew my back was turned, took advantage of my absence and my sorrow, and battered his way inside! But I'll drive him out! I'll stamp on him!' He moved forward urgently, propelling his father by the elbow. But Lord Rhys shook him off with one easy swing of the arm, and Gruffydd staggered to the side. Lord Rhys stood immoveable, until silence was absolute.

'Get my horse and armour,' he said, in a thick, difficult voice. 'Arm yourselves, teulu. No, wait. Dydd Nadolig yw hon, wedi'r cwbl. At dawn, make ready to march.' Then he walked on slowly. Once, he stopped to look round him with a hostile glare. He drew his sword, and used it as a third foot, all the way back to the hall.

When it becomes generally known that a great man is failing, all the world begins to take advantage of his weakness. Maelgwn by his cruel triumph got his blow in first of all. Gruffydd was not allowed to accompany his father on the expedition to recover Ystrad Meurig.

'You watch Aber Teifi!' Lord Rhys told him, and away he went, demonstrating his fatherly scorn for Maelgwn by the smallness of his retinue, and trusting in the splendour of his mere authority to crush this son. But Maelgwn was older now, and harder; he was determined to force at last his father's hand, and wrest from him the mastery of part of Ceredigion.

In Aber Teifi, matters were never more confused. The hall was unruly; more people than was proper pushed in to shout their claims. The burghers were dissatisfied with the clamour in the town that discomfited their trade, and every man with a grievance chose to parade it now.

Abbot Peter of Ty Gwyn ar Daf smacked his lips with unseemly gusto over more mutton than Mallt thought was fitting.

'King Richard is out of prison!' he said with relish. 'Soon he will be home again to rule his kingdom!' He turned to Gruffydd, whom this news plunged into thought. 'I was talking to the Abbot of Tal-y-llychau the other day, poor fellow, such a pity.' He munched. 'A beautiful mutton, my lord.'

'What is wrong with the Abbot of Tal-y-llychau?' asked Gruffydd impatiently.

'Why, he is very earnest in his desire to be a Cistercian. He has this wish to change his Order. Others of the brethren too, I'm told. Such a pity good Lord Rhys saw fit to bring in Praemonstratensians. And they themselves, they see the virtues of our superior Rule!'

'My father chose a preaching Order on purpose,' said Gruffydd curtly. 'The people needed pastoral care.'

The Abbot shrugged his shoulders. 'Between ourselves, that is neither here nor there,' he said, condescending but eager. 'Are not our Cistercian Abbey churches and minor chapels open to all who pass by? Do we not succour all the sick and needy within the radius of at least a dozen or even twenty miles? It is to the White Brethren that men turn in their distress, and never, my lord Gruffydd, have we been known to fail them.' This was true, yet men of middle estate had often been heard to complain of the monks' inclination, especially under this Abbot, to pounce upon acres by way of extorted reward.

The Abbot leaned forward persuasively.

'Now, if you were to allow an amalgamation, or transfer, the lands granted to them could if truth were told be better administered by us than they are at present by them, and the brethren themselves would be well satisfied, I am assured, and the people of those parts could not but benefit.'

Mallt nudged Gruffydd warningly, willing him to say No straightaway. But she knew that he was wary of this insinuating man, who had influence amongst the uchelwyr of Ystrad Tywi and Dyfed, and she was not surprised when by an impatient pinch on her thigh he bade her mind her own business.

'It shall be thought of,' said Gruffydd in a guarded voice. 'My father is away on business.' The Abbot suppressed a smile. Everybody knew what the business was, hammer and tongs, father and son, deplorable.

'Ah yes, your father!' he remarked with eyebrows raised, as though he had forgotten Lord Rhys. 'How is he now? His most melancholy bereavement will add to the burdens of age. He is fortunate indeed that in you, my lord Prince Gruffydd, he has a most wise adviser, a sage deputy, who can safely be trusted to make decisions on his own responsibility—'

Here Gruffydd found him no longer endurable. He rose to his feet.

'My father is his own adviser,' he said bluntly, and went out muttering, 'How is he faring now? That's what I want to know! What do I care what these Abbots do?'

Most unfortunately, these last words reached the Abbot's ears, and he construed them into a kind of permission. Mallt remarked to Gruffydd afterwards that a ruler cannot guard his tongue too well, as Henry had discovered, to his cost.

Two days later, an agitated message from Father Seisyll dealt a coarse shock to Aber Teifi. Lord Rhys, far from having humbled Maelgwn, was Maelgwn's prisoner, and had been moved to Nanhyfer's dungeon, and William FitzMartin, camping at Trefdraeth, was chortling with glee.

Mallt clung to a table, for the world was falling. Gruffydd, in the shouting distance, was raving out orders to the teulu; men ran about on every side to seize their lances and their bows and quivers in the yard, each with a look of outrage on his face.

'Half strength I leave with you, Mallt!' roared Gruffydd. 'Don't leave the castle! Guard the food store and let the garrison eat but sparingly! Be shrewd and suspicious of strangers and admit no person to the tref or castle other than merchants, clerks, and waggoners known to the watch!'

'Where are you going ?' she asked stupidly.

'Nanhyfer, where else?' And with a brusque embrace he hurled off, driven by ungoverned anger, like a dry leaf giving sport to a capricious wind.

Once before she had been left alone; then, she had fallen prey to Maelgwn. She shivered; even with a great fire, the hall was cold in winter without a merry throng to keep it warm. The servants looked at her anxiously, and brought her wine to cheer her heart. Fear began to recede. She sent for Hengyfraith the constable. He was a sturdy man, with a twinkle behind his authority that rallied her spirits better than the wine had done. They discussed rations, troops, weapons.

'Pob peth yn iawn!' he uttered in his loud, peremptory voice. 'Maelgwn would need more than a catapult to take this Castell Aber Teifi that Prince Cadell had a hand in building, and as for the townsmen, every man's hand is against him! They look to Lord Rhys to defend their lives and their property, and they invoke his name as often as they do the saints'!'

That night, Mallt had a strange and vivid dream. Lord Rhys was alone, and small, in a dark place, and he spoke to her.

'I am alive,' he said in a tiny voice far away. 'And for the moment I am crushed, or I seem to be.' He was battered and unshaven and unkingly to see, and in her dream she wept, and was indignant when he told her irascibly to stop snivelling.

'I've had my ups and downs before. I'll bounce back, I can promise you!' he said. He grew larger as he spoke; he reached his proper size again; he grew so huge that all she could see was the light of triumph in his eyes. She awoke to find that the tapestries had been drawn back, and that the sun's unclouded winter strength was dazzling her.

He was back at Aber Teifi before the end of January. He arrived in a raging temper, venting it all on his rescuers, Gruffydd and the teulu, and declaring that he had been freed from one set of jailers only to fall into the hands of another; that it was no business of anybody's to interfere in any quarrel he chose to conduct with his sons, that even before Gruffydd and the teulu had made a tardy appearance on the scene, he had already tricked Maelgwn, who had delivered him into Hywel's custody.

'A day after the fair you were, my boy,' Lord Rhys was shouting, as they clattered furiously to a stop in the stable yard. People could hear him from across the river. 'Fox and goose I played with that pair!' he boasted. 'Soft and sly is Hywel when I get round him on my own, after all, ready to free the old father, ready to quail when I roar!'

'You had to bribe him,' said Gruffydd sullenly. 'You had to give him Nanhyfer, that I, not he, helped you to win.' But Lord Rhys turned his blaze on him.

'Who made you my judge?' he stormed. 'By what right are you critic of my dispositions? I know my sons, their strength and weakness! You'll never be Prince of Deheubarth, Gruffydd! None of you will, worse luck! Not one of you yet can master me! Maelgwn has the fire and strength, but not the head. Hywel has the head, but I can't trust him. You're faithful enough, but where's your push and power to plan? Oh, that my three best sons were all rolled into one!'

He dismounted, bellowing, and tottered into the castle, red and glaring. No one dared to speak as he grabbed wine and gulped it down. The hall began to fill with the teulu, and the leading burghers, though it was not thought safe to approach with their welcome until he had eaten. He ate, indeed, with relish and obvious hunger. But the burghers had to retire with their loyal relief unspoken. The only creatures whose heartfelt welcome gave him joy were his dogs; the rest of the world it was, that night, might hang.

'But what happened?' Mallt asked, when at last Gruffydd was fit to be spoken to. 'Why did they take him to Nanhyfer?'

He scowled.

'Hywel wanted to keep the FitzWizos in custody somewhere as far from Dyfed as possible,' he said. 'Maelgwn had Nanhyfer in his clutch just then, but Hywel said that was too near, so Maelgwn suggested seizing Ystrad Meurig from me, and dumping them there. They did so, in my absence after my mother died, after pushing down the outer rampart with that catapult they found at Wiston. Maelgwn, having pounced on it with glee, could not resist trying it out. When my father turned up, he was so furious to see the damage they had done, that he could scarcely speak for rage. Maelgwn and Hywel, seeing the smallness of his retinue, seized their chance to argue with him and push their claims to independent power. When he refused these, they dared to lay hands on him and threaten to keep him shut up until he should give in. There was no room at Ystrad Meurig with FitzWizos filling every nook and cranny, so Hywel locked him up at Nanhyfer. Well, my father has never been one to pamper his dignity when he knows he has to cut his losses, and he did not hesitate to strike a bargain with Hywel. Hywel betrayed Maelgwn by setting my father free in exchange for the lordship of Nanhyfer, which Maelgwn thought he had secured for himself. But he hasn't,' said Gruffydd, with a tired gleam of satisfaction.

'And Maelgwn will get the lordship of Ystrad Meurig, that's clear,' said Mallt bitterly. 'He too will get round your father one of these fine days. Anyway, I suppose it was time they had castles of their own to live in with their families. They were becoming quite impossible at court. And Ystrad Meurig doesn't mean that Maelgwn gets the whole of Ceredigion; the people of Aber Teifi would never endure him, nor would the rest of the gwlad, after the way he treated Lord Rhys. It seems to me, Gruffydd, that in spite of what your father said to you, you're the one who comes out of it best, after all, you're the son he has to turn to in the end, so be comforted.'

'Cariad Mallt!' muttered Gruffydd, and they clung together.

Even at the cost of scandal, imprisonment, and brawl, the court was quietly agreed that the new arrangement was a healthy one. Two sons, at least, were established as they ought to be, and by driving a sharp wedge between them, Lord Rhys had turned the pair from cronies into rivals for his favour; Maelgwn's fury against Hywel was unbounded, Hywel took care to avoid him, and their father it was who had the last laugh after all. As for scandal, well, Lord Rhys rose above his people's grins with his usual majesty; had not gossip always buzzed in polyphonic chorus behind him? Good and bad, his life had ever been an open book for the men and women of Deheubarth to scan for their entertainment in the dark evenings.

But Lord Rhys, raised above grief by his recent adventure, was about to sink again into its torpor, when a further exasperation most fortunately roused him, in the shape of Master Gerallt's book, his Description of Wales. There was something to approve, and something to quarrel with, on every page. Many a time the volume, handsomely bound for his benefit, was hurled on the rushes, before curiosity conquered him, and rewarded him next time with passages of praise.

'Very fortunate indeed we are,' he exclaimed drily when he had read every word, 'that we have another Judge than Gerallt to approve us and condemn!'

Father Seisyll also, travelling uncomfortably through the rain, provided solace. It was hard to concentrate on your own sorrow when your sympathy was demanded for someone else's woes.

'Foot-rot, that's the trouble, Lord Rhys,' he said, sighing. 'It's all this rain, puddled pastures everywhere, huge morasses in the mountains, and the Bog is just a lake with an island in the middle. We've off-wintered as many sheep as we can in the lower granges, Morfa Bychan, you know, and Tir-y-Mynach above Elerch there, and Morfa Mawr, but we've had a hard time culling the poor beasts. Building work has been impossible. We had hoped to get up to roof level on the presbytery, but God stays us. The winter sickness has begun to strike in Llan Ddewi Brefi, and our infirmarian has been dosing us all in the hopes of warding off an epidemic and increasing our vigour, and he begged me to ask you to drink this cordial daily. It is a recipe I acquired at Citeaux this summer, said to be most efficacious.'

As an offering to grief, it rather lacked style, but Lord Rhys, invited to survive and stir about, brightened. He sniffed it, winked at Seisyll, and took a stiff dose there and then, to the Abbot's horror, who protested that a spoonful only, twice daily after meals, was ample.

'Twt-twt,' said Lord Rhys. 'You can never have too much of a good thing. Not bad at all; it's almost as nasty as one of poor

Gwenllian's. I'm much obliged, Seisyll. Sure to do me good.' he sighed, and looked glum again. 'I've come to it at last,' he said. 'An old man physicking himself in the corner, while his family grumbles. But I've a long way to go yet!' he said strongly. 'And things will be done in my way, in my own time, as always! They think I'm past it, Seisyll, but I'll show them! Sixty- two! That's not much more than middle-aged, is it? Why I know old men in Ceredigion who have lived to be eighty and more!'

There and then he came out of the dumps, and dedicated himself to many more years of mischief and wisdom yet. A very old sparkle came back into his eyes, and he obliged the court to listen to one of his youthful adventures. Every turn of the tale was familiar, but nobody minded; men nudged each other, and drew nearer.

'Lord Rhys is in the hwyl tonight,' they said, and listened with pleasure to the voice that resounded through Aber Teifi's hall, once more round and resonant, imperious and true.

In the dull days, he became so short of entertainment that he began to notice Gruffydd's little girl. She ran so free with the brats of the soldiers and of the burghers that her garments, covered with common dirt, became indistinguishable from theirs, and when she was interrupted in her play, even her features, noble though they were, put on the same scowl that marks all children as equal in the sight of God. But in a clean frock, and with her face washed, and with sweetmeats tempting her, she amused Lord Rhys, for she reminded him of Gwenllian Fach, and alas! she began to be pert. She was the first granddaughter with whom Lord Rhys had much acquaintance; he spoiled her unconscionably; it was a new entertainment for him to enjoy the pleasure of a child's society without its pains, for of course, as soon as she became a nuisance he turned her over to Mallt with a rebuke for failing to teach her good manners.

In March, he was roused to momentary vigilance when news raced through the South that King Richard was home again.

'Home!' snorted Lord Rhys. 'His domicile is Acquitaine!'

Richard came into his kingdom, watching his people with defiant, suspicious eyes, putting on the king again, putting on his crown a second time in Westminster Abbey, lest any man should dare to suppose that his humiliation by the Emperor and the Duke of Austria had diminished his royalty. Now, said men, he will undertake to curb Lord Rhys.

'Not he!' said Lord Rhys. 'He'll pick up his money bags, slap down John, and disappear into a dust-cloud for another term of years!'

And so he did, nor did his subjects miss him much, being well governed under Hubert Walter's firm, authoritative hand.

Well then, men said, watch out, Lord Rhys will launch out into a fresh campaign. The French were alert for news from Aber Teifi; Hubert Walter crouched; and William de Breos tensed his muscles. But Lord Rhys was not in the mood; summer was poor; his gains already were considerable; it took fine weather nowadays to tempt him into the discomforts and ardour of war; the loss of his wife had affected him more than people understood, and he preferred to speed the building of his Abbey. Let it be finished soon, while he yet lived! But he stayed too long at the table, ate too much, an inclination to lumbago reduced his enthusiasm for the chase, and provided him with an excuse to lay the cares of the cylch in Ceredigion yet again on Gruffydd's shoulders. With careless disregard for the lessons of the past, he allowed Hywel to lord it throughout most of Dyfed, and Rhys Gryg he employed on messages to the men of Ystrad Tywi.

'At your age,' said Lord Rhys, 'my brother Maredudd and I were running the whole kingdom for your uncle Cadell when he went to Rome. Time for you to learn government, so that you can be a help to Gruffydd some day.'

Mallt, governing the hall with growing discontent, doubted the wisdom of dispersing so many sons about the realm, each with his retinue, but who was she to advise Lord Rhys? She dreaded the future.

4

A year passed. In the last week of February, the chills of winter crept away, and a heavy storm of rain pelted down on Aber Teifi, removing the odours of the last stale rubbish dump, as through the town the piled up débris was swept away by gales into the runnels churning up the ground between the houses. The town breathed and brightened, spring came full and strong, like an invader, swelling the sap-filled buds to bursting, inspiring with its balmy breath the thoughts of men to love and war. Children were springing into youths and maids; Mallt's women grew gay in their best coloured dresses, and giggled foolishly like girls in corners when handsome strangers came to court. Old women spinning spun their webs of gossip too, and choice bits echoing round the walls were served up with wit by John Spang to entertain Lord Rhys. But Mallt could not smile. I have never liked jesters, she thought sullenly. They make more mischief than their worth in passing laughter pardons. Still, she supposed that their life was difficult, and after all, John Spang's consummate glee had never been the same since Heaven claimed Gwenllian Fawr. Like his master, he aged; and every time his worst puns raised a derisive peal, his lean and harrassed countenance would beg Mallt's eyes for mercy. It was hard, after all, to refuse, and reluctantly her lips would begin to curve upwards.

But so fine a spring must certainly announce a restless year, and she remained on edge, expecting evil of all kinds. It came, and in a curious way, Mallt herself was a contributory cause. After Easter, Gwladus, with her coif awry, came down in a flurry from Llan Llyr, with bad news from Powys.

'Cadwallon's murderer is back from exile!' cried Gwladus. 'Roger Mortimer! Why did Richard free him? He began to enlarge himself as soon as his King's back was turned, until William Longchamp had the sense to banish him! Why has he been forgiven now? Trouble he must make, that man, and since Hubert Walter is too strong to let him stir it up east of the Clawdd, what does he do? Why, he turns west, of course, attacks Maeliennyd, and rebuilds Castell Cwm Aran! Hubert Walter does not care how far men ravage in Cymru. In his best days, my father would be quick to answer such a threat against his power, but now, he will not stir!' She was staring with belligerence at Mallt, as though it were her fault.

'Why doesn't Gruffydd take the lead?' demanded Gwladus. 'He is old enough! But he lacks the gift to take prompt action. Why don't you urge him, Mallt, to carve his own path? Or are you still too French to cross your father's policies, and do you watch them from the corners of your eyes?'

At first, Mallt was too astonished at this far from nun-like speech to blaze back. Then cold fury lifted her above her normal calm.

'I am faithful to my husband's policies as well as to his person!' she shouted, for all the world to hear. 'And to those of Lord Rhys! I have two sons by Gruffydd, whose interests I intend to guard against all comers, French or Cymry, even against my father himself, though Heaven forbid that he should ever interfere within Deheubarth! As for Gruffydd, he is wiser than I am, and certainly than you, and I would never presume to master his decisions. And if you think that Mortimer, who desires to rival my father's power, is acting now in league with him, you were never more mistaken!'

'You're wrong there, two of a kind they are, all French together,' returned Gwladus sulkily. 'But I apologize, Mallt. I do not really think you other than devoted to Gruffydd and your sons and to my father too. I wanted to provoke you, for I find your prudent calm exasperating in times of strife.'

'What must I be to please you? A spitfire to rouse all the sons of Lord Rhys? You and your blunt speech! It's a luxury you can afford! I am a Cymric princess made, not born, and I cannot let my tongue wag so free!'

For all Mallt's hurt, that quarrel cleared the air. Her friendship with Gwladus was strong enough to stand an honest clash, and she was glad that someone had been bold enough to speak a thought that must have been lurking everywhere. Gwladus had wanted Mallt to declare herself; the outburst gave them both relief; their words would echo beyond Aber Teifi, if the court gossips, straining their ears at the keyhole, could be relied upon, and Mallt hoped that they would reach her father. They did, but the effect was other than she would have wished.

Pursing his obstinate thin lips, William de Breos caused his scribe to reach for his quill and his inkhorn and write two letters, one to Hubert Walter, and one to that sensible shrewd fellow, the Abbot of Ty Gwyn ar Daf, in whom, it appeared, the Dyfed French had found a friend. He had never cared for the Deheubarth marriage for his daughter, and now, to have her turn

Cymraes, and spit at him, right across Cymru! Lord Rhys was weak, and he, the Sheriff of Hereford, was strong.

'I'll bring them both to heel,' he muttered, signing his letters with a flourish of thin fingers.

Back in Aber Teifi, second thoughts told Mallt that Gwladus's instincts had been sound, after all, and she turned to Gruffydd.

'But Mortimer's push is a signal that further trouble will be a-brewing, if Lord Rhys does not stamp his foot this moment at his enemies!' she said beseechingly. But Gruffydd merely laughed.

'Deheubarth is secure enough from outside attack,' he assured her. 'But it's Ystrad Tywi that worries me. What is Rhys Gryg doing there all this time?'

But the omens multiplied, and loomed. On Whit Sunday, news came from Hywel in Dyfed of an attack on Wiston by the Flemish supporters of the FitzWizos. The other French, too, began to lash their tails; there was some influence at work; Hubert Walter and de Breos were clearly behind the surge, urging each enterprise against the Lord of Deheubarth, now that he was beginning to yield, as people said, to the ills and comforts of old age. Even William FitzMartin discovered the courage to dare to raise another castle to replace his own lost seat at Nanhyfer. At Trefdraeth, on the coast nearby, he assembled his scattered resources, and with nervous haste threw up a fort, and within the blurred outlines of a rough, sea-sounding land, claimed to be lord.

'Lord of the fishes, then,' was all Lord Rhys would say, between mouthfuls, when he heard the news at dinner. 'Hywel can spare him a few. Don't want Angharad to starve.'

But quarrels grew loud between Hywel and William, and when Mallt at last begged Lord Rhys to interfere, 'Let them fight it out, indeed,' said Lord Rhys, his eyes bright on the venison. 'It's all in the family.'

Then Maelgwn had the impudence to descend from Ystrad Meurig on Aber Teifi, roughly but spendidly arrayed, holding his short body like the king he thought he ought to be, approaching his father with the suavity, aplomb, and twinkle that Lord Rhys relished, for all that each had imprisoned the other.

Mallt's thoughts were bitter when she heard him speak the words she had longed to hear her husband say.

'Come, my father!' he said confidently. 'Come with me! It is time to go on a new campaign! Let's push your borders forward against the French! Let's try a fall with them in Dyfed. With William if you like, or suppose we black the Bishop's eye?'

But all he got were chuckles and a wary head shake. 'How high is the Abbey now?' was all Lord Rhys said. His lumbago was better, but it had kept him back this spring, and he dreaded to hear that the roof had been put up before he paid his now regular summer visit to Ystrad Fflur.

'Oh, no danger, they're nowhere near the roof yet,' said Maelgwn. He was disappointed; he went down into Dyfed in his loafing way; he missed his crony Hywel, no doubt, and thought it might be worth his while to bury the hatchet.

'Now for trouble!' said Mallt. 'Where he goes, all the hounds of darkness follow!'

Gruffydd grasped his sword. 'At least I can make ready, even though I may not stir,' he said, and began, by judicious measures, to take in the slack of discipline within the teulu. News and noise came up from Dyfed meanwhile; mouths opened, eyes grew wide, and men grinned and nudged each other on the paths the merchants and the pedlars used, and hoarse mead-laden voices told the latest tale of Maelgwn, now fast friends again with his brother. They were forever irritating French and Flemish alike, as though to invite a fresh offensive so as to force their father to a new campaign. Peace was at once too easy and too hard for them; they longed for war.

They got more than they bargained for. A flame of gossip licked across the summer hills; William de Breos was moving in strength across the South into Dyfed.

Mallt understood at last exactly how Angharad felt when her father had tried to crush her husband. Anger at her father's presumption, fury at Lord Rhys's senile complacency that invited this, and love for both, tore her to pieces. Sententious messages reached her from de Breos, by the officious hand of the Abbot of Ty Gwyn ar Daf, urging her to use her influence, as a daughter's duty, for a peaceful submission by Lord Rhys to his authority, for which he had a royal warrant. Mallt would not answer. Savagely, she clung to Gruffydd, and made her choice.

'Since I can betray neither, I'll abandon both! These old men's quarrellings are not to meddle with my right to live! We must turn our faces forward, Gruffydd, and our backs on them! Our day is now, and our sons' is coming all too soon!'

'Da merch i!' was all he said, but his face lit up with love and triumph. That was the night that they created life once more; they made the fourth child they had both so long desired.

Next morning Gruffydd went south with a small army. Lord Rhys proved unable to direct affairs; his tongue seemed to fill his mouth, and when he uttered sounds, no one could understand a word he said. He sat all morning, expending an energy not observed in him for many months, trying to articulate, his right fist occasionally pounding the table. When he failed, he fell into a brooding silence.

News of his seizure sped through Deheubarth. Mallt sent for Rhiwallon, in Cantref Bychan, but Rhiwallon could not come; he was attending Rhys Gryg, who was not well.

'Rhys Gryg?' she said, storming. 'Since when has he been more mighty than his father?'

Lord Rhys watched her as she looked at him, and she thought, this illness is going to separate his false friends from his true. He made no further effort to speak. Mallt cared for him, assisted by his servants. They rested him, they cut down his food; Mallt administered herbal infusions, instead of heating wine. He submitted. What more could they do?

'The speech will come back,' said Hengyfraith. 'My old father was the same.'

Mallt grew tired, watching, ordering, planning, and working longer hours than agreed with her. She rejoiced when found she was with child once more, and she told Lord Rhys. His eyes gleamed, his distorted mouth twisted, and with his left arm he embraced her. Much cheered, she left him, and though her heart still ached when she thought of her own father, somehow confidence, like a healthy tree, took root in her mind. As for Lord Rhys, he sank into an almost unnatural calm, as the weeks passed; he never tried to speak, but day by day as he lost weight, his eyes became alert and bright.

Quite suddenly, life's revolutions began to speed up, as though some great grindstone had been fitted with a set of these new gears, while outside the old mill-wheel made its ancient, steady turns. A panting message by one of Gruffydd's men announced that de Breos, with a great company, had cut through their insufficient force to seize St. Clears, and with it some of Hywel's best men.

'But where was Hywel Sais?' demanded the court. 'Where was Maelgwn?'

Maelgwn was teasing the Bishop. Hywel, distracted by too many strong points all requiring attention at once, was torn between castles. Only Gruffydd had been near enough to attempt resistance; but he failed.

Then Lord Rhys, for the first time, lifted up a hand, and spoke, and they understood his speech, slurred and difficult though it was.

'Fetch my sons,' he said, and they came at once, Gruffydd, Maelgwn, and Hywel, a disconcerted, angry chorus, driven at last to asking their father what they ought to do, and urging each a different policy, each demanding instant action in a different place.

'No,' said Lord Rhys. Maelgwn and Hywel glared at Mallt, but their father ignored them, and paid her the compliment of unfolding his ideas with some deliberation in her presence.

'You cannot all be generals,' he said, 'And until you can learn to submit to one amongst you, you must suffer me still to be your lord. I have not been well, and perhaps not wise, you have not been clever, the season is too late and poor for action now, and for this winter we must keep to a policy of defence along a strong line from Nanhyfer, along the Preselau, to Dryslwyn. Any place we hold below that line must take the risk of enemy attack, but further north than that, no Frenchman comes.'

His gaze transfixed each grumbling son at last into silence and submission, and they settled down to an autumn of watchful calm, a cloak to cover secret preparations for the spring.

Lord Rhys, whose stony silences became a habit, would not discuss his purposes; his first care was to exercise his body, to shed unnecessary fat, to restore his health. Privately, he took up arms long laid aside, and spent an hour each day with sword and lance, recovering a warrior's strength and skill. But in the hall his movements were as indolent as they had been before, so that his reputation for lethargy was undisturbed.

But instead of calm, calamities befell them, one by one. First came the Bishop, bold in the knowledge that de Breos was near at hand, with courage at last plucked up to travel to Aber Teifi to make complaint.

Glancing at a hand-picked clutch of canons behind him for support, 'My cattle!' he cried. 'My dwelling and my lands! Recompense I require, Rhys ap Gruffydd! Your evil sons have roared through Dyfed, laying waste like brutes that trample in the corn! Restitution! Or else the penalties of Heaven, as well as earth, will follow, O miserable man!' He flourished a list of depredations, and folded his arms.

In silence Lord Rhys had heard him. In a slow, courteous voice he replied,

'O vulture of the Church,' he said, 'O pest of Menevia, scourge of clergy, lord of Gehenna—'

The teulu laughed, the Bishop crimsoned, the canons paled; Lord Rhys, fluent in his recovered power of speech, sank his voice to a purr as coloured epithets occurred to him. Mallt sat, frozen and appalled. Gruffydd was chuckling, Maelgwn was laughing his head off, her women made the sign of the Cross and fled. She stayed until a dig in the ribs from Gruffydd, and a jerk of the head, hinted her away. A scene unsuitable for ladies, it was clear, was about to follow. Aghast, she left them, knelt in her chamber, and prayed. Cries of horror from the canons floated up the stairs, and gales of mirth from the teulu. A tumult began; the deputation was being thrown out amid loud imprecations. Wild shouts of fright and savage yells maddened the episcopal horse and the canonical ponies; Mallt heard them clattering on the yard below as their riders somehow contrived to mount them under a hail of kicks and blows; then they galloped off. Down in the hall, the mirth went on all night, and she never saw Gruffydd. Indeed, she bolted her door.

Next morning, she remained with the cooks in the kitchen, making jelly from great piles of mountain ash berries that Father Seisyll had sent down from Ystrad Fflur. It was a task that demanded concentration, and by the time the linen bags full of red honeyed liquid had been set to drip steadily into the cauldrons, they had all achieved a degree of composure.

The hall was no place to visit, with so many sluggards sleeping late in corners. But at noon Mallt appeared there, with an army of caethion behind her, and with her broom she sent every laggard flying. The floor was foul; even the caethion grumbled as they swept and scrubbed and strewed fresh rushes. Then she stayed quietly in the women's quarters, keeping her daughter firmly by her side. What was going on in the hall?

'Prince Gruffydd and Prince Maelgwn speak much together in low tones,' reported her women, taking turns to listen and to peep behind the wooden screen. 'They speak to Lord Rhys. They are laughing together.' Such unnatural friendship seemed to Mallt sinister and doom-laden. With a shudder, she retired to her chamber, and listened to the evening noises increase. There was glee in the roar. Gruffydd never came near her. During the night, horses and riders came and went, and in the small hours, a tumult of armies thundered all about the castle walls. Mallt and her daughter, with the untroubled child in her womb, lay clasped together in her bed, sensing the quivering beat of one another's hearts. As the mother's body warmed and steadied her, the daughter slept. Exhausted, at last Mallt also gave the reins to slumber. But she dreamed of her father and of the Bishop, and she heard a great cry rise all round her, of 'De Breos! De Breos!'

She awoke to silence, early, to find Gruffydd beside her. Thankfully she clutched him to embrace and scold. He looked at her ruefully, and sat on the side of the bed.

'You will scold me yet more,' he said, 'and shrink from me, when I tell you that your husband is excommunicated, together with all his brothers who took part in last night's adventures, and my father too.'

She crossed herself. It had come.

At last, 'What have you done?' she said. To her amazement, he smiled, and then began to chuckle.

'We were going to punish the Bishop,' he began. 'We went down in the night through the woods, Maelgwn and Hywel and I and a few others. Nice dry night it was, with the fallen leaves rustling, kicked up, and falling again, and the whole wood smelling of winter. We followed to the priest's house where Peter broke his journey, and seized him as he lay in bed, and dragged him screaming in his shirt and drawers, barefoot, back through the woods to my father, to finish the conversation we began the night before, which was disrupted by the canons' intervention.'

She shivered. 'What did you do to the Bishop?' she asked. 'He is cruel, but he is the Bishop.'

'He didn't sound like a bishop,' replied Gruffydd. 'He was swearing in several languages as we dragged him through the brambles, rousing the echoes as we passed, and we were pursued by a company of your father's men. We knew yesterday that they could not be far away from the Bishop, or he wouldn't have had the nerve to come over. But I must say we never dreamed they were quite so close. We shoved him into the gatehouse while we turned to deal with them—did you hear us?—but we were outnumbered, and they forced their way inside to free him. Then off they galloped, with the words of excommunication ringing in our ears.'

'Have you reflected how bitter a thing it is to be banished from Our Lord's table?' asked Mallt in dismay, crossing herself.

His eyes flashed.

'Father Seisyll will admit us!' he said. 'He owes no allegiance to any bishop, and he will take no heed of this. Peter Lee has long required humbling. Every man and woman in Deheubarth knows it. Do you know how many clergy wives and families are forced by his grinding heel to become pensioners of my father's charity, generously and freely granted? No, nor do I. I have long lost count of the pleas that I have heard at every courtroom on the cylch. No, Mallt! Someone had to punish him, and teach him where the power of Deheubarth lies.'

'You were very wicked,' said Mallt, but Gruffydd, answering her relenting eyes, chuckled again and said, 'Da merch i! Ha! Long may the Bishop's thorns and corns confound his feet!'

This event, like Lord Rhys's illness, sieved off his foes. The two Cistercian Abbots divided, and came down heavily, one on either side of the fence. Father Seisyll, bursting with indignation, sent an instant invitation to Lord Rhys, his family, and entire court, to hear the Christmas Mass, and partake of the Sacrament. But Father Peter of Ty Gwyn ar Daf found it convenient to profess shock at Deheubarth's disgrace.

'It puts me into a horrible position!' he complained. 'Where may I turn for the protection of the secular arm? I cannot look to an excommunicant! Ah! But here are still some sons not within the ban. Prince Rhys Gryg in Ystrad Tywi—'

Secretly, as Lord Rhys learned later, to his most vivid rage, Father Peter sent a flattering message to Rhys Gryg, much to Rhys Gryg's satisfaction. Father Peter believed in striking while the iron was hot, and turning other people's misfortunes to his own good, so he came out into the open with the blandly importunate demand that the Abbey and dependencies of Tal-y-llychau be forthwith absorbed into the Abbey of Ty Gwyn ar Daf. The matter, he announced, had already received favourable consideration under Lord Rhys's roof. Rhys Gryg, anxious to please so influential a man, and revolving in his mind a bold stroke on his own account, raised no objection, and at once Father Peter sent lay brethren of a muscular kind to Tal-y-llychau by night, to seize the Abbot, drive out the other monks, and round up the choicer cattle for Father Peter's own pleasure.

But the excommunication also divided the cautious from the bold amongst Lord Rhys's subjects; and those who were discontented already in Ystrad Tywi by reason of his marked preference for Aber Teifi, made religion a cloak for their rebellious tendencies. It also gave William de Breos, who was well-known for his pious care to observe all the ceremonies of the Church, a chance to strengthen his hold south and westward of Caer Fyrddin. Gruffydd, with his eyes on Mallt, urged his father to parley.

'Let's come to terms with Lord William,' he said. 'Some arrangement should be possible—he is Mallt's father, after all.'

He quailed under Lord Rhys's glance.

'I? I to beg for peace?' said Lord Rhys, in a tone dangerously quiet. 'Is that what Mallt wants? I, Lord of Deheubarth, I to treat with William de Breos? I deal with kings,' he said. He turned to Mallt.

'You may speak,' he said coldly, and leaned back in his chair.

She gripped the table as she stood.

'My father will enlarge his power as and wherever he can,' she said. 'He builds a little empire for his sons. And I'm his true daughter,' she added. 'I claim for my own sons as many lands as can be won for them, and kept. I will not have their inheritance snatched away in favour of my brothers' sons.'

Lord Rhys nodded, and no more was said. But Gruffydd was unhappy.

'Aber Teifi's too close to Dyfed,' he muttered to his wife later. 'I want you away, out of reach of your father.'

'Why, do you think he can sway me?' she asked angrily. 'I am my mother's daughter too, and she is valiant, though she never spared much love to me. I refuse to give ground before the enemy has even approached Ceredigion!'

'I know you're stout-hearted, cariad,' he said. 'But your presence here will tempt him to advance. If you remained here, and if the castle fell to him, what hostages you'd be, you and the child you carry! Why, half Deheubarth wouldn't be enough to ransome you!'

That struck her, and she gave in. 'But I won't go to Llan Llyr!' For her present condition, she felt that Gwladus had too blunt a tongue, nor was there any midwife there of any standing.

Gruffydd consulted his father. Lord Rhys surveyed him with a ravaged glare.

'Your wife! What's wrong with Llan Llyr that it doesn't please her? Has she fallen out with Gwladus? Send her anywhere you will. Do anything you like. Don't worry me.' He gave Gruffydd one glance of suspicion and dislike before clapping his hands for a monk who was hovering close by, with parchment, quill, and inkhorn. As Gruffydd went, much puzzled, 'Go!' added Lord Rhys. 'I'll find another son to serve me.' He sat down white and shaking, and Gruffydd ran back to him.

'What has happened?' he demanded. 'Who has provoked the wrath you vent on me?'

'Are you so ill-informed? Always the last to know the latest news? Rhys Gryg, your friend and brother, did he not confide his plans in you? He and Maredudd, the little cocks strutting to and fro in the valleys—' Lord Rhys began to splutter, and Gruffydd to be alarmed.

He turned to the monk. 'Tell me!' he ordered.

'Your brothers have turned the hearts and heads of the young men of Cantref Mawr and Cantref Bychan to follow their leadership,' came the answer. 'They have taken Dinefwr and

Llanymddyfri. This excommunication gives a reason or excuse.'

'Dinefwr!' cried Gruffydd, scarlet. His rage became as strong as his father's. 'I'll get it back for you!' he declared. 'I'll take the teulu—'

But Lord Rhys was not listening. 'Mi twylla i'r ddau o nhw,' he muttered.

Gruffydd sat down. 'Trick them?' he said alertly. He bent his head towards his father's own revengeful stoop. 'How?' Lord Rhys began to talk in low tones. Mallt, who was eavesdropping, could no longer hear, but she had heard enough, and grew hot with fury. When she thought of Rhys Gryg's little wife tittering at the table where Queen Gwenllian once presided, in the place which now belonged to Gruffydd's wife by right, such a surge of hatred swept her through that she scarcely had the strength to reach a chair. And what of the safety of her sons, in the heart of Cantref Mawr?

She battered Gruffydd with demands to know what was going on.

'A safe messenger has been sent off to the captain of my father's strong fort of Pencader, with strict orders to go over to Rhys Gryg!' said Gruffydd with a fierce grin.

Mallt stared at her husband. 'But the captain is Hengyfraith's brother. His loyalty to Lord Rhys is a byword. Rhys Gryg will never believe it!'

'Oh, Rhys Gryg is vain enough to swallow anything. He has been working on the men of Cantref Mawr for a long time, and he thinks he has won them all. It was my father's own fault! He hustles me about in Ceredigion and in Dyfed, and I cannot be in three places at once. What chance had I to counteract Rhys Gryg's influence in Ystrad Twyi?' Then he looked at her with more attention. 'Oh, you're thinking about the boys,' he said, with a calm she found unendurable. 'They'll be all right. Geraint's grandsons know where to hide them if there's trouble, but it won't come.'

He left her, little comforted, a prey to fears she had to learn alone to overcome, by making plans for a future that other wars might rise to spoil. She did her duty by Aber Teifi, though she herself might be away by winter's end. They salted pigs until her sides ached and her hands were pickled. They spun wool and wove cloth enough to clothe an army; moss-dyed it was, though her fearful fancy stained it all with blood.

'Well done, ch'i,' said Lord Rhys, with much satisfaction, as he paid a visit of encouragement to the weaving-room. He had come to ask Mallt to show him her store of cheeses. 'In time of war,' he pronounced, 'there is no food more important to the fighting-man. Easily carried in a shoulder bag or pocket, with the odd half-eaten piece tucked into the bottom of the quiver or the belt-pouch, it will carry an archer through the day across rough country where no supplies are found to snatch at.'

He rubbed his hands and nodded at the shelves piled high with skimmed milk cheeses, above a stone floor where crocks of butter were drawn up in battle ranks. The dried mutton, the sides of cig moch, the salted fish, the oats and honey and preserves, were enough to last the garrison well through the winter and spring and early summer.

'Victory begins with a good harvest the year before, and hard work in the kitchen by the women,' said Lord Rhys. 'Well done, Mallt. Gwenllian would indeed be pleased.' He kissed her very kindly, and went off, armed with a cheese and a bag of apples, to cope with Rhys Gryg.

Little blood was spilled in the encounter. Rhys Gryg and the stripling Maredudd, preening themselves in the admiration of the youngsters of Ystrad Tywi, rode confidently with their troops to Pencader, and a flattering reception from Hengyfraith's brother. When they stood within the gates, 'I submit to you,' he repeated, looking at them less sweetly than he did at first, 'at Lord Rhys's orders. And at Lord Rhys's orders I retain you here until he comes.'

At that point the scuffle started; Rhys Gryg lost his two front teeth, and Maredudd's nose suffered. As for their companions, they were ambushed and taken with a neat precision by Lord Rhys and Gruffydd, with the teulu, by a well-timed pincer movement. When it was over, Lord Rhys with a swagger moved amongst the battered band. They watched him with fear and with respect for the sly efficiency of his pounce. The eyes of each man fell before the contemptuous glare that raked him, measured, and reduced his size. Covertly, they observed with amazement the military trimness of his carriage, in an old man that rumour said was breaking up, and that most of them had never seen. They did not know that Lord Rhys regarded this occasion as a splendid chance to review, astonish, and impress the youngest reserves of his power.

At last, 'Go home!' he said. 'And learn the old tricks well before you stumble in the new. I'll give you the chance to take the measure of your present lord before you trip over your toy generals. You are almost old enough, I think, for real campaigns. Go home, and if I hear no further ill from Cantref Mawr and Cantref Bychan, you may yet serve me.'

Rhys Gryg and Maredudd were bundled off to Ystrad Meurig, to cool their heels and consider, with the assistance of Father Seisyll, the virtues of obedience. Their followers, faced by Lord Rhys's broad, disdainful back, looked at each other, and went home, driven to the subdued conclusion that they were not yet important enough for him to punish. Their fathers received them with thankfulness and loud abuse. For the rest of the winter, the sons indulged the fathers by providing an attentive audience whenever their sires were moved to remember the days when it was their pride to follow Lord Rhys. The young ones thought they might, after all, pick up a wrinkle or two from the old boys.

5

The autumn storms of rain and gales had died away by mid-December. The earth dried out under bright cold skies. At night all the stars of heaven twinkled richly like Christmas baubles strewn by a packman on a velvet cloth, tempting Mallt's women with his trivial toys of glass, winning the coins that rattled sparsely in the grinning teulu's money-bags. As the cold deepened, Mallt's cares increased. Raw frost defied the feeble noon-day sun; ice in the ways and by-ways brought many a portly burgher low, and a larger crop of sprains and broken bones than usual were brought to her to be healed. Wounds she had learned early to dress, but bones, she found, required a special trick in setting. She learned it from Lord Rhys. The armies of the kings of Cymru produced their own rough surgeons; in Deheubarth, Lord Rhys himself was the one who best knew by instinct and experience the tender place where he must press heavily and hard; Iestyn Fychan had taught him. Mallt and her patients each endured the moment's agony of screams for the faith they all had in her power to heal. Gruffydd and most of the sons of Lord Rhys shrank from this office; only Cynwrig, the huntsman, silent and calm, watched, and presently learned to do the same.

'He prefers to practise first on human beings,' said Gruffydd. 'Before he dares attempt to heal his injured horse or dog.'

Then the Christmas cooking reared its head. It was always a nightmare to Mallt, for someone might always be heard to draw an unjust comparison with the well-nigh impossible standard set by Queen Gwenllian at the Great Eisteddfod of Christmas, 1176, which she thought it extravagant even to try to emulate. And the thought of her father creeping up along the coast troubled her. All these matters, and her increasing weight for far too many hours upon her feet, dragged down the muscles below the corners of her mouth, furrowed her forehead, and gave her eyes a concentrated glare that Gruffydd thought it wiser not to meet.

Not until the last three days before the feast did the annual unearthly joy of the Christ-Child's birth steal across the fields into Aber Teifi's windows and begin to lift the burden in her heart. Then she was calm; around her, mirth rose, but it was not loud enough to spoil her bliss; and though in the distance smiths were still hammering new red-hot swords, and fletchers with precision set the points on arrows, and bards found fresh subjects while they sharpened knives, yet the purpose that possessed them all struck her as true; it matched her own; and in the New Year, travelling north amongst her own Cymry, she turned her back on the troubles of the South. All her three children were with her; she had claimed them all at last within her care, and she forgot the agonies of the journey in watching their wonder and glee as they rode up into a gwlad that was strange to them.

At Aber Rheidol, their elderly escorts liberated younger men for service with Lord Rhys. Mallt rested, and took her time to reach Llan Badarn. Ednowain's daughters, warned of her coming, came to greet her, smiling; their pleasure split the rind of dry phrases that covered their warmth, and soon they were exclaiming at her children's size and beauty. Snug and dry Mallt and her family lay that night in their wooden houses, though a gale had risen, and all through the hours of darkness when Mallt stirred she heard the wind, like water falling, roaring on the valley floor.

When the news came that her father was nearing Nanhyfer, Mallt longed to ride back to Aber Teifi to defend its walls. But her place was here, guarding her family, and being guarded by the three matrons, Bronwen, Olwen, and Ceridwen, their husbands, and sons and brothers, the priests and farmers of the llan. She was alert for news. Not many travellers came up from the South in winter, but when a wave of warm air brought an early stir of spring in mid-February, she thought, Now my father will make his assault on Aber Teifi. And Lord Rhys will surprise him by the valour of his defence, and they will kill each other!

But no.

'Father Seisyll is here!' cried Bronwen, rushing in to Mallt's room one morning without ceremony. 'There is news from Caer Fyrddin!'

Caer Fyrddin? Winter's dazzle in the morning stands no higher than a man, and Mallt, standing in the doorway, was blinded by the glaring lances of the sun, slung underarm. She moved forward, fumbling in the light. At last she saw Father Seisyll in the yard, dismounting from his pony.

'Caer Fyrddin?' she said, forgetting to greet him. 'But my father was besieging Nanhyfer!'

'Ah!' exclaimed Seisyll, lifting his robes up with both hands, and picking his way through the muddy yard to meet her. His face was dirty and looked very tired.

'Duw a bo gyda chwi, arglwyddes! Of your father I know nothing. He is still beating against Nanhyfer, I suppose. But Lord Rhys, and your husband, and many other sons, and the teulu, they have made a sudden push to Caer Fyrddin! They have cut him off to the south-west, your father. And the town is burning in deliberate contempt of Lloegr's royal power. Woe to the king and burghers who oppose Lord Rhys! The town is a ruin, many men are killed or driven off, their families fly westward to de Breos, and Lord Rhys like a beacon turns to Ystrad Tywi!'

'And the castle?'

'The castle stands, of course, untaken. Who could succeed where King Cadell fortified?'

It was all Mallt could do, in the following days, to master her sons, who struggled to follow Lord Rhys; there was only one grandfather that they deigned to recognize. Young Rhys indeed eluded her grasp, and reached Yspytty Cynfyn before he was caught. Father Seisyll promptly impounded him at Ystrad Fflur.

'Lord Rhys promised me!' spluttered the boy. 'That I should accompany him on his next campaign!'

'When you are of age, next year!' said Father Seisyll cheerfully.

'Next year?' blazed young Rhys. 'By next year my grandfather will have crushed all his enemies, and how will I have helped him?'

'We must not waste your energies, nor your goodwill,' said Seisyll, forbearing to argue. He sent a reassuring message to Mallt, and initiated Rhys into the secrets of dressing stone. Presently his mother received a letter from him, full of self-satisfaction and pride.

'I am building an Abbey,' Rhys declared. 'I complete my Latin, and am far advanced into a course of Music, Rhetoric, Logic, Mathematics, and Astronomy.' The Llan Badarn ladies, to whom she showed this letter, were reluctantly impressed, but clearly thought that so much learning was not quite fitting for a prince. Mallt thought so too; let a prince keep learned men about him, like casks of wine matured, for handy reference; for himself, wisdom in the hearts of men, and in warfare, and in his own laws, these were best.

'When his call to arms at last arrives, all else will be forgotten,' she said resignedly. 'Meanwhile, he is in safe keeping, and his wits sharpen.'

Lent passed, and Easter came. Where was Gruffydd? Mallt's heart was full of wordless prayer. The priests of Llan Badarn prayed, casting compassionate looks at her; but the service stopped abruptly when a horseman clattered shouting into the churchyard. As she listened, the first pangs of labour assailed her.

'Lord Rhys!' was all she could think of when a respite came. 'All the hosts of the South! Gone up Ystrad Tywi through the mountains of Buellt and on into Elfael, into my father's lands!' She was torn between impatient desire for the birth, which tarried, and for further news, and that was slower still. Before further pelting messengers announced that Lord Rhys had seized and burned the great fort of Castell Colwyn, whence de Breos had dominated Upper Elfael, Mallt's second daughter had been born. Another girl! Mallt's pleasure was tinged with disappointment. She would not pass into history, nor her sister, either, but at least she served as a grace-note to Lord Rhys's triumph.

By the time Mallt was on her feet again, rewarded by the baby's vigour, they knew that the army of Lord Rhys had crashed on to the heights above Radnor, de Breos's own stronghold, and overwhelmed the defending forces of his neighbours, Roger Mortimer of Wigmore, and Hugh de Say of Richard's castle. Forty French knights were killed, and numberless men.

One evening as the sisters sat spinning and weaving, and Mallt rocked her child in the cradle, Bronwen spoke.

'Your father is at Aber Teifi's gate,' she said, with the dreamy deliberation of a seer. 'And the Lord Rhys is attacking Castell Paen, but this time your mother is not there defending it.' In silent awe they heard her, and believed, nor did they dare to ask her how she knew. Perhaps, thought Mallt, in the pattern of shuttle and warp and woof, or the speed of her spindle, her visions came.

Next morning a packman arrived from Ystrad Fflur. As soon as he opened his mouth, he confirmed Bronwen's vision.

'I thought of going to Aber Teifi, but it's not worth my while,' he said. 'Gwilym Brws is busy burning it. And Powys is rent by alarms, now that Lord Rhys and his engines of siege have forced Castell Paen to surrender. I'll go north and spend my summer on the Dyfi shore.'

Lightly he spoke, for his own small business, like a dandelion growing, would always find a crack between two rocks where it might flourish in the shelter of their firm collision. He took their coins with speed, wolfed down a meal large enough for two strong men, and drank his fill of cwrw. Mallt watched him with indignant envy. He was free, of all but his appetites. She was pent within circumstances, the sport of war. Aber Teifi burning? Her kitchens? Her stores? She rebelled, and declared her own war.

'I've had enough!' said Mallt. 'Come!' She packed her bags, collected her protesting children, made a present of her best apparel to Bronwen, Olwen, and Ceridwen, caused the gambo to be laden with her effects, and sought a spirited horse for herself.

'But where are you going?' asked her friends, aghast.

'Home!' said Mallt, firmly. She hardly knew where that was, now, but at least she would turn her horse's head in the right direction, south. It was summer; they could always sleep under the gambo. Perhaps she had more in common with the packman than she had supposed.

A horse, two ponies, two armed men, and a couple of donkeys for the gambo that carried her goods, children, and nurse, were all her train on setting out, but she gripped her horse firmly between her knees, and passed through the trefydd with her back erect and her chin in position. Her passage by was noted; it caused some stir.

'Mallt Brws, druan!' she heard them mutter, 'Yn myn'd 'nôl i'r De!' Someone gave a sympathetic cheer; they went forward to greet her, and offered refreshment, which she disdained to refuse, being amongst her husband's people and her own. Their welcome made bright for Mallt a day of small clouds that travelled above her to meet her and pass. Her armed men smartened up their pace. Dogs and small boys were not the only hangers-on; the older youths as well began to follow her, the ones too young some months ago to be skimmed off for Lord Rhys's army. Their mothers wept and thundered in vain; she did not turn her head to bid them stay, nor go; they followed, as though in obedience to a natural law. By the time she reached Aeron, they were nearly two hundred strong, and the news that came up from the South, of the stench and ashes of Aber Teifi, was balanced by the rumour that rolled down from the North, that Mallt Brws herself had declared war, and was coming at the head of a great army, swelling daily, to drive out her father.

'Mallt! Mallt!' Their cries crowned her, in moments more royal than she ever knew before, nor since.

She found Aber Teifi half burnt out, half alive, but the castle relatively intact apart from some damage to the outer walls. It was not until a remnant of distraught burghers, camping in huddled shacks, told her that her father's army had retired in fear of being trapped between her own and that of Lord Rhys, that a trembling through her heart and all her limbs betrayed to Mallt the measure of her relief and disappointment at having missed him. She thought, he must be quite old by now.

Peace talks were in progress, Hengyfraith told her. He feared there was little left of the harvest in the plains to be salvaged, but he blessed Lord Rhys's care to send up his cattle to the hafodtai well before launching out on his campaign. De Breos had brought an army too large to live off the country, and had exhausted his supplies.

'Have you anything left of my stores?' demanded Mallt, and marched straight to her own kingdom. Little enough remained, but they would manage somehow. They had won. Lord Rhys would be back any day now, and Gruffydd.

'The hall is in a shocking state,' she said. 'Let all the caethion you can lay your hands on in the morning clear it out, and meanwhile, my army must be fed.'

Lord Rhys came back through the mountains, making a bee-line for Ystrad Fflur, that he might give thanks in his own Abbey. He would have liked to linger through early September in progress through Penweddig up to Dyfi's shore, pacing the borders, accepting a harvest of apples and cheeses, reaping his people's goodwill, and dispensing justice as the need arose; instead, he made a great march into Dyfed under a hot sun; the teulu were bravely polished and arrayed, making sound enough to cast the heart of all the French between their teeth; and there it was that he made free with the harvests of persons whose loyalty had been tempered with imprudence.

Mallt sent a kind message to her parents, dutifully announcing her fourth child's birth, and boasting of her eldest son, not yet officially of age, but so forward that Lord Rhys had recently received him into his teulu in a ceremony whose magnificence she was at pains to stress. The recent war she ignored entirely. She knew that the contents of her letter would be repeated from castle to castle from south to north along the March. After that, she kept silence. For a victor, she thought, one short, loud crow was necessary and sufficient.

Lord Rhys remained in Aber Teifi no longer than was needful to reassemble the burghers for a hortatory speech and conference which organized the reconstruction of the borough and of the damaged castle walls. He surveyed with compassion their haggard, battered, and depleted ranks.

'Everything that I have inside this castle I give to you!' he said; and for the rest of the week, in a more or less ordered chaos, the teulu was employed in doling out the hidden, subterranean stores of food, wine, leather, clothing, timber, and iron. The contents of the storeroom vanished in the twinkling of a burgher's eye; but Mallt had saved some bread and honey for Lord Rhys's breakfast. She was not quick enough to seize a roll of cloth; and before she could pronounce a word, the burghers' wives sped by exclaiming, with their arms filled with the contents of her own garderobe, and calling down kind blessings on her head as well as on that of Lord Rhys. She was thankful that prudence had counselled her to wear all her jewellery, and that she had left her best furs and some of the family's heavy winter clothing at Dinefwr, whither the court was going to ride on the following day.

A heavy hand seized her round the waist.

'Mallt fach, wyt ti'n edrych yn sobr iawn!' Lord Rhys was laughing, aglow with delight in his own generosity. 'You don't like parting with your nice clothes, and Gruffydd's best shirts! But you're alive, my dear! You're young and strong! You can strip yourself naked and still be rich!' He stamped off chuckling, and 'Rich!' she heard him cry in the distance, 'Rich!' Rich in freedom, she supposed he meant, she thought sourly; rich in freedom from possessions. Rich or not, when a chill wind of late October blew the next morning, she regretted, with bitterness, the loss of her favourite cloak. She should be thankful, she supposed, that her baby's wraps had been left untouched. She had been sitting on them. She did not speak much to Lord Rhys on that journey to Dinefwr, nor was she in the mood to appreciate the burghers' cheers. It was all she could do to bare her teeth at them.

One reason for the peace that made music through Dinefwr's hall that autumn lay in the absence of Maelgwn. Mallt did not care to ask the reason, lest her curiosity should summon him from the shadows to which he rightly belonged. But gossip soon told her.

'Wyddwch ch'i beth?' said her women, rolling out oat cakes. 'Helping Gwenwynwyn of Powys he is, to defend his castle of Trallwng against Hubert Walter.'

'Making important friends he is in Powys,' muttered the teulu. 'Trust him to go on cutting a dash after we've all come home.'

'Thick as thieves they were when we were besieging Castell Colwyn,' grumbled Gruffydd.

'Huh! Trallwng has fallen!' said the visiting uchelwyr to Lord Rhys. 'Dug a passage underground did Hubert Walter, cunning fox, sent his sappers to undermine the fort!'

'Where's Maelgwn now?' said Gruffydd, gleaming.

But Hubert Walter, with an eye to Lord Rhys and his resurrected power, was moderate in victory, and had spared the defenders. All were allowed to disperse in freedom, with their armour and weapons; only one poor fellow was slain, by accident, said Hubert Walter's men.

'Gwenwynwyn will not let matters rest at that,' said Lord Rhys, sitting on the edge of his throne, with his head poked forward, and his big hands clutching the carved lion-heads on the arm-rests. He looked ready to leap up and away to any part of Cymru; but his eyes, though bright, were quiet. Indeed, the position in Powys was reversed before the year's end, and this time it was Gwenwynwyn's turn to show magnanimity, allowing Hubert Walter's men to emerge scatheless, with raiment and armour intact. Reluctantly, Mallt prepared to welcome Maelgwn; it was too much to hope for a Christmas unsullied by his victorious swagger; he came.

'Oh-ho, Maelgwn!' said Lord Rhys, wrapping his great arms about him in a fierce mutual hug, from which they emerged with flushed faces, bright with an affection that no quarrel could destroy, surveying each other on the same level. As for Mallt, she curtsied, and she kept her distance, suffering an ironic bow.

It was a Christmas season of open weather, bright clear days, and crowds. From every part of Deheubarth men came in droves, to congratulate Lord Rhys, to present their sons to him, to proclaim their loyalty afresh, to mention small favours they desired, and to feast their eyes on him, and wonder, as at a man reborn in strength and power. From Deheubarth and from every court in Cymru they came; from the Marcher lords came goodwill embassies, and from William de Breos, wine. There was a stir of surprise.

Lord Rhys looked at Mallt, and smiled. The court looked askance at the messenger. Gruffydd nudged her forbiddingly, but she rose.

'May I drink with you, Lord Rhys?' she asked.

'If you will,' he said consideringly. 'What is your toast, Arglwyddes Mallt?'

'It is to life and Lord Rhys,' she said. 'To friends and enemies, love and justice, truth and joy.'

By an ancient, common impulse, each poured a few drops on the ground before they drank deeply, in spite of restraining hands and cries on every side that urged them to forbear, to let the dogs lap the wine before they touched it. Lord Rhys drank, and paused, smiling.

'Treachery has died,' he said, and smacked his lips. Mallt drank, trusting God and her father. As they drank, looking into each other's eyes, the court grew pale and breathless. As they put their goblets down, a low and troubled murmur swelled into a rumbling acclaim. In the morning, 'A very pretty wine your father sent me, chwarae teg iddo,' Lord Rhys remarked. 'I rested well.'

But the Christmas sense of well-being that filled the court did not last in the days and weeks that followed. Mallt knew how it would be, with all those crowds, those eager, sweating courtiers. Sniffles and rheums and coughs erupted and multiplied all through Lent, and one by one the strongest were laid low. More deaths than usual occurred. The weakest, aghast at their own immunity, struggled with success against this influence, this intangible plague from the East.

'Always from the East it comes, like wisdom, and folly,' said Lord Rhys, spluttering between sneezes, wheezing, and wiping his brow. He had entered his hall, staggering slightly, but intending to eat his fill. But he looked at the Easter lamb, and groaned, and pushed it aside.

'Apples, please,' he muttered. But he failed at the second bite. The sons grew alarmed, for his face was the colour of clay. He went to bed, and stayed there for three days, too weak to toss about. Gruffydd attended him, covering him with more carthenni, for he was shivering violently, and complaining of the cold. Rhiwallon came, and some other wise men and women of Ystrad Tywi. They sent for the infirmarian of Ystrad Fflur, and dosed and rubbed him with every medicament known to them. By evening of the third day, he seemed to rally, but then he grew confused, talking to absent friends.

'Experience in my hand,' he gasped, interrupting the last rites. 'Plant it, you said—where? How? Such a lot, such a tangle, Bleddyn!' He stirred, restlessly. 'Henry,' he muttered. 'Cadell. Gwenllian.' He was quiet, then his voice grew strong. 'Never mind, Seisyll, leave it now—grow where it likes.' A broad smile lifted him from some muddle. 'Nawrte, Gruffydd,' he said distinctly, and paused, while they waited, trembling and expectant. They had to wait so long that they grew frightened.

'He is resting,' said Mallt hoarsely.

But Gruffydd, with a face like a candle, had laid his left ear to his father's chest.

'No,' he whispered.

It might have been a period of confusion, but for Gruffydd. First he prayed beside his father's body. Then he picked up the gold circle that Lord Rhys had plucked impatiently off his brow and tossed into a corner. Gruffydd's face was ravaged. He gathered together his brothers, Maelgwn, Rhys Gryg, Hywel Sais, Maredudd, Cynwrig, the only ones at hand, and laid down the law in conference with them. As he did so, he held the crown in his hands. Too shocked to demur, and perhaps too ill, for Maelgwn and Rhys Gryg were but newly risen from their sick-beds, they agreed to all his arrangements.

'We must end our quarrel with the Bishop,' he said bluntly. They gasped. They had forgotten the Bishop. 'Rhys Gryg must be our ambassador,' he went on. 'He was not included in the ban.' Rhys Gryg nodded, but Maelgwn groaned.

'It goes against the grain,' he said in a strangled voice; Mallt had never felt so much in charity with him for the consent that this reluctance implied, and Gruffydd felt the same.

'It does indeed,' he said. 'But Lord Rhys must be buried in Ty Ddewi, as was arranged, and I think he had it in his heart to be reconciled with the Bishop. After all, he drank the wine of de Breos. I do not think he would have refused humble pie from Peter Lee.'

So they waited. It was the worst of punishments. It took days for the messenger to reach the Bishop, days for him to consult with Canterbury, a week for the reply. Fortunately, the weather froze, unseasonably, and there was time indeed to weep. It was three weeks before the great new oak door of Ty Ddewi swung open to admit the coffin. But the Bishop moved forward with outstretched hands to bar the way.

'The sinners must be whipped,' he said tonelessly. A shudder went through the cortège as the two eldest canons advanced with knotted penitential cords, and whipped the corpse. The sons, too, submitted. Then the procession moved forward, into the cathedral, out of the rain. But the body of Lord Rhys lay bare to the elements under the unfinished portion of the roof.

After the funeral, Gruffydd and Mallt spent some time in comforting Father Seisyll, who was disappointed, as well as deeply grieved.

'But we were going to bury him at Ystrad Fflur!' he complained. 'We had a choice position all prepared within the sanctuary of his tomb! I know they tricked him down at Ty Ddewi into making some sort of promise extorted from him at a time of great distress, but I never considered it binding, and I told him so. I had prepared his funeral address, for we never know when God's summons will come, and I wanted to do him justice. I did not wish to be taken unawares. I have it by heart.' He cleared his throat and looked eagerly at Gruffydd. 'Would you like to hear it?' They had by now heard many eulogies of Lord Rhys, as well as the funeral tributes, but they had not the heart to do other that beg him to allow them the honour of hearing it. He breathed deeply, and began, in declamatory tones.

Much of it was in the usual vein. Lord Rhys was the Shield of the South, the father of his people, a Samson for strength, a second Achilles for the might of his breastbone, a Solomon for wisdom, the terror of his enemies. There was a lot more, beautifully worded; the exaggerations were inflated by so much love that they stood sturdily erect, like facts. Then he lifted his head, and as they looked and listened, Father Seisyll seemed to rise on wings, to grow larger, to see further, to brush aside present troubles and to survey the centuries past and to come.

'Great-hearted friend! I miss your rough embrace, your prompt, surprising goodness that thrust aside your many sins and brought you, ardent still in age, to seek God in simplicity, and to find Him there. When, I wonder, will He raise up such another for Cymru? Perhaps in the North we shall have to look for him, who knows? Now in Deheubarth a tumult will arise between you, the sons of Rhys, but in Gwynedd peace is arming itself with strength and Llewellyn will presently be firmly lord. It is natural and proper that conflict should follow every finished reign, for how else may true authority be found? But must blood always spill across the path to its discovery? Power comes and flows as God decrees, and struggles to emerge, within and between the kingdoms. Now one, now another, stretches to a new, established greatness that all Cymru comes at last to share. In Lloegr too, the mastery has passed in struggle between the races; Briton and Roman, Jute and Angle and Dane, Saxon and now French, each has seized its turn, and many more will follow in as many thousand years. As in this island, so in the greater world, from time to time a mighty man or nation rises, and gives a special greatness God requires of them, before subsiding into more unfruitful times, like some transplanted tree of Heaven that roots on earth with disquiet, takes its time to put out leaves, and blooms but rarely. But the scent and the seeds of its flowers abide with us still.'

He faltered in his flight; he dropped to earth like a spent arrow. He sighed shakily, and wiped his eyes.

'He had the common touch!' said Seisyll in his ordinary voice. 'Many people have it who are not great men, but you cannot be great without it. Ah, llew oedd e', 'ych ch'i'n gw'bod,' he said simply. 'A lion he was, Lord Rhys.'

BIBLIOGRAPHY

Sir John Edward Lloyd, *A History of Wales from the Earliest Times to the Edwardian Conquest.* Longmans, 1911.

Sir J. E. Lloyd, *The Story of Ceredigion.* University of Wales Press, 1939.

Sir J. E. Lloyd, *A History of Carmarthenshire.* Printed by William Lewis, Cardiff for the London Carmarthenshire Society, 1935.

Wales Through the Ages, vol. 1, *Earliest Times to 1485.* Ed. A. J. Roderick. Christopher Davies, 1959.

E. J. Newell, *A History of the Welsh Church to the Dissolution of the Manasteries.* Elliott Stock, London, 1895.

Glanmor Williams, *The Welsh Church from the Conquest to the Reformation.* University of Wales Press, 1976.

Richard Deacon, *Madoc and the Discovery of America. Some new light on an old controversy.* Frederick Muller, London, 1967.

William Rees, *An Historical Atlas of Wales from Early to Modern Times.* Faber, 1966.

C. H. Talbot, *Medicine in Mediaeval England.* Oldbourne History of Science Library, 1967.

Stephen W. Williams, *The Cistercian Abbey of Strata Florida.* Whiting and Co, 1889.

Dictionary of Welsh Biography to 1940. Article on Rhys ap Gruffydd by "T.J.P."

Giraldus Cambrensis, *Itinerary through Wales*; and *Description of Wales.* Everyman Library, 1935.

Brut y Tywysogion, or The Chronicle of the Princes. Peniarth MS. 20 version, translated by Thomas Jones. University of Wales Press, 1952.

Brut y Tywysogion. Red book of Hergest version, translated by Thomas Jones. University of Wales Press, 1955.

GLOSSARY

a - and
aber - river mouth
Aberdaugleddau - Milford Haven
Aber Tawe - Swansea
Alban - Scotland
Amwythig - Shrewsbury
ap - son of
arglwydd - lord
arglwyddes - lady
aur - gold

bach (fach) - little, dear
bachgen - boy
bendigedig - blessed, excellent
blino (wedi) - tired
boneddiges - gentlewoman
boneddigion - gentlemen
brenin - king
brenhines - queen
Brut y Tywysogion - Chronicle of the Princes
Brycheiniog - Brecon
Buellt - Builth
bwrwch - push!
bychan (fychan) - little, minor

caer - fort
Caer Fyrddin - Merlin's Fort (Carmarthen)
Caer Grawnt - Cambridge
caethion - serfs
canghellor - chancellor
cant - hundred
cantref/ydd - hundred towns (districts of)
Cantref y Gwaelod - the bottom hundred drowned below Cardigan Bay
cariad - sweetheart
carthen, carthenni - blanket(s)
casineb - hatred
castell - castle
Castell Paen - Painscastle
cau - shut!
cau dy geg! - shut your mouth!
cawdel - muddle
cawl - soup
cefn - back
cefn glwad - countryside
ceg - mouth
cerdd - song, ballad
chwarae - game, play
chwarae teg iddo/ i chwi (ch'i)/ iddi nhw - fair play to him/ you/ them
chwi (ch'i) - you
chwithau - yourselves
clas - cloister, body of canons attached to a mother church
claswyr - monks, members of a clas
Clawdd Offa - Offa's Dyke
coed - wood
croes - cross
croeso - welcome
Croes Oswallt - Oswald's Cross, Oswestry
cryg (gryg) - hoarse
cwbl - all
cwm - top of valley
cwmmwd/au - commote(s)
cwrw - beer
Cydwely - Kidwelly
cyfarwydd/wyr - story-teller(s)
cylch - circle, judicial circuit
Cymraeg - Welsh
Cymraes - Welshwoman
Cymro - Welshman
Cymru - Wales
Cymry - The Welsh
cynghannedd - special rules of Welsh poetry
cythrael - rascal

da - good
da merch i! - good girl!
ddall (dall) - blind
de - south
Deheubarth - the South Part (of Wales)
dere! - come thou!
digon - enough

di-werth - worthless
dod - come
dôl - meadow
druan a ch'i/ a hi/ ag ef - poor you! poor thing!
drwyn (trwyn) - nose
Drwyndynn - Tightnose
Duw - God
Duw a bo gyda chwi - God be with you
dydd - day
Dyfi - Dovey
dyna ch'i! - there you are!
dyn - man
dynion - men

edrych - look
eistedd - sit
eisteddfod - contest of music and poetry
enw - name
enwogion - important men

fach (bach) - little, dear
fawr (mawr) - big, great
fenyw (menyw) - woman
ferch (merch) - daughter, girl
ffriddoedd - sheep walks
ffynnon - well
fi - I, me
fy - my
fy mhechgyn i - my boys
fychan, bychan - little, minor

galw - call
gambo - a two-wheeled dray
gemllid - jeering
gog (cog) - cuckoo
gogledd - north
Gors Goch Glan Teifi - Tregaron Bog
gryg (cryg) - hoarse
gwaelod - bottom
gwely - bed, inherited land
gwestfa/feydd - guest house(s)
gwlad, gwledydd - country, countries
Gwlad yr Haf - Somerset
gwr - man, husband
gwr bonheddig - gentleman
Gwyddel - Irish
gwyn - white
Gwyr - Gower

haf - summer
hafodty - summer farm dwelling
hen - old
hiraeth - longing, home-sickness
hon 'na - that one
hwyl - mood

Iâl - Yale
iawn - right
Iwerddon - Ireland

llan - church enclosure
Llan Fihangel Geneu'r Glyn - Llandre
Llanymddyfri - Llandovery
llew - lion
Lloegr - England
Llwchwr - Loughor
llwyn - grove, bush
Llydaw - Brittany

Maenor Pyrr - Manorbier
maer - mayor
maerdref - mayoral district
maes - open field
mawr (fawr) - big, great
meddyliwch! - think! imagine!
Meirionnydd - Merioneth
menyw (fenyw) - woman
Môn - Anglesey
Morgannwg - Glamorgan
mynach - monk
mynachty - monks' house
myned, myn'd (wedi) - go, gone
mynydd - mountain
Myrddin - Merlin

Nadolig - Christmas
Nanhyfer - Nevern
nawrte - now then!
nid - not

oer - cold

pen - head
pencerdd - chief musician
Penfro - Pembroke
pensaer - architect
penteulu - head of family or of men-at-arms
peth - thing
phob (pob) hwyl - best of luck
plâs - mansion
pob - every
pont - bridge
Pumlumon - Plynlimon

rhaid - must
rhingyll - sergeant
rhyd - ford
Rhydychen - Oxford

saer - carpenter
Saeson - Saxons, Englishmen
Sais - Englishman
'sgrifennwr (ysgrifennwr) - writer, scribe
Sweyn's Ey - Swansea

Talacharn - Laugharne
teg - fair
teulu - family or troop of men-at-arms
ti - thou
tomen las - green mound
tref - town or settlement
Trefdraeth - Newport
twyllo - to trick
tŷ - house
Tŷ Ddewi - St. David's Cathedral
Tŷ Gwyn ar Daf - Whitland
tyddynwr/wyr - peasant(s)
tywysog/ion - prince(s)

uchel - high
uchelwyr - noblemen

wedi - after
wedi'r cwbl - after all
wyddwch ch'i beth - do you know what?
wyt ti'n edrych yn sobr iawn! - you look very sober!

'ych ch'i'n gw'bod - you know
ychen - oxen
ymladd - fight
ymlaen - forward
Ynys Enlli - Bardsey Island
yr hen daclau 'na - those old fellows
ystrad - vale
Ystrad Tywi - Vale of Towy